LYNSAY SANDS

RELUCTANT VAMPIRE

AN ARGENEAU NOVEL

AVON

An Imprint of HarperCollinsPublishers

AVON BOOKS
An Imprint of HarperCollins*Publishers*
10 East 53rd Street
New York, New York 10022–5299

Copyright © 2011 by Lynsay Sands
Excerpt from "The Gift" copyright © 2011 by Lynsay Sands
ISBN 978-0-06-189459-6
www.avonbooks.com

First Avon Books mass market printing: June 2011

Avon Trademark Reg. U.S. Pat. Off. and in Other Countries, Marca Registrada, Hecho en U.S.A.
HarperCollins® is a registered trademark of HarperCollins Publishers.

Printed in the U.S.A.

10 9 8 7 6 5 4 3 2 1

By Lynsay Sands

THE RELUCTANT VAMPIRE
HUNGRY FOR YOU
BORN TO BITE
THE RENEGADE HUNTER
THE IMMORTAL HUNTER
THE ROGUE HUNTER
VAMPIRE, INTERRUPTED
VAMPIRES ARE FOREVER
THE ACCIDENTAL VAMPIRE
BITE ME IF YOU CAN
A BITE TO REMEMBER
A QUICK BITE
TALL, DARK & HUNGRY
SINGLE WHITE VAMPIRE
LOVE BITES

THE HEIRESS
THE COUNTESS
THE HELLION AND THE HIGHLANDER
TAMING THE HIGHLAND BRIDE
DEVIL OF THE HIGHLANDS

the RELUCTANT VAMPIRE

One

Drina hardly noticed the rhythmic tap of her heels as she descended the stairs from the plane. Her attention was shifting from the winter-dead trees surrounding the private airstrip to the man leaning against the back of a small golf cart on the edge of the tarmac.

With dark hair and skin and a black leather coat, he could have been mistaken for a shadow if it weren't for his glowing gold-black eyes. They peered at her, steady and cold from between his black wool hat and scarf, and he remained utterly motionless until she stepped down onto the paved runway. Only then did he move, straightening and walking forward to meet her.

Despite the cold, Drina forced a smile. A greeting was trembling on her lips, but died there when he took the small bag she carried and turned wordlessly away. The abrupt action brought her up short,

and she watched blankly as the man walked away
with her luggage. When he slid behind the wheel
of the small, open cart and dropped her bag on the
front passenger seat, she managed to shake herself
out of her surprise and move forward, but couldn't
resist muttering, "Hello, you must be Drina Argenis. Such a pleasure to meet you. Please, allow me
to take your luggage for you. And here, please take
a seat so I can get you to the enforcer house and out
of this cold."

With their hearing, she knew the man must have
heard her sarcastic mimicry of what she would have
liked him to say, but he didn't react by deed or word.
He merely started the engine on the cart and waited.

Drina grimaced. It seemed obvious from where
he'd set her suitcase that she was expected to sit on
the back bench seat. Not welcome in the front, apparently, she thought with disgust as she settled on
the cold, stiff seat. She then grabbed the supporting
bar to keep from sliding off as the cart immediately
jerked into motion. The icy metal under her fingers made her think, not for the first time, that she
should have researched North American winters
more fully before making this journey. It was a bit
late for that, however. But she would definitely need
to take a shopping trip or two as soon as she could
if she didn't wish to end up a Popsicle while here.

With nothing else to look at, Drina watched the
small plane that had brought her here turn on the
landing strip and start away. The moment its wheels
lifted off, the lights on the field suddenly blinked
out and darkness crowded in. For one moment, she

couldn't see a thing, but then her eyes adjusted and she took in the knee-deep snow and skeletal trees lining the path and wondered how long she would be on this contraption and out in the cold.

The woods weren't as deep as they'd seemed from the plane. It only took a matter of moments before they left the woods behind to follow a small path along the side of an open snow-covered yard holding what looked like a long garage and a house. It was the garage her driver steered them toward. The tires crunched on the hard-packed snow as they came to a halt beside a small door. The man who hadn't greeted her, then grabbed her bag and slid out from behind the steering wheel. He moved toward the door to the garage without a word.

Eyebrows rising, along with her temper, Drina followed him inside and up a short hall. She spotted an office and a hallway leading to cells on her left, but he led her to a door on the right and straight into a garage, where several vehicles sat waiting.

Drina cast a quick glance over the few vehicles inside. They were all the same, SUVs, she thought they were called. She followed Mr. Tall-Dark-and-Mute to the back passenger door of the first vehicle. When he opened it, and then simply waited, she eyed him narrowly. It seemed obvious he was going to be her escort to Port Henry, but she'd be damned if he was going to stick her in the backseat like some unwanted guest for the duration of what her uncle had said would be a two-hour journey.

Smiling sweetly, she ducked under his arm and moved past him to the front door instead. Drina pulled it open and quickly slid inside, then turned to eye him challengingly.

His response was to heave a long-suffering sigh, toss her bag on the floor at her feet, and slam the door closed.

"Great," Drina muttered, as he walked around the vehicle to the driver's side. But she supposed she shouldn't be surprised at the man's attitude. He worked for her uncle, after all, the most taciturn man she'd ever met. On this side of the ocean at least. She added that last thought as Mr. Tall-Dark-and-Miserable slid behind the steering wheel and started the engine.

Drina watched him press a button that set the garage door in front of them rolling up, but waited until he'd shifted into gear before asking, "Are we heading straight to—"

She paused as he suddenly slid a letter from an inside pocket of his fur-lined coat and handed it to her.

"Oh here, I was to give you this," Drina mimicked dryly as she accepted the envelope.

Tall-Dark-and-Rude raised an eyebrow but otherwise didn't react.

Drina shook her head and opened the letter. It was from Uncle Lucian, explaining that her escort was Anders and he would be delivering her directly to Port Henry. She guessed that meant Lucian hadn't trusted Anders to pass on this information himself. Perhaps he really was mute, she thought, and glanced curiously to the man as she slipped the letter into her pocket. The nanos should have prevented it . . . unless, of course, it wasn't a physical problem but a genetic one. Still, she'd never heard of a mute immortal.

"Do you speak at all?" she asked finally.

He turned an arched eyebrow in her direction as he steered the vehicle up the driveway beside the house, and shrugged. "Why bother? You were doing well enough on your own."

So . . . rude, not mute, Drina thought, and scowled. "Obviously, all those tales Aunt Marguerite told me about charming Canadian men were something of an exaggeration."

That had him hitting the brakes and jerking around to peer at her with wide eyes. They were really quite beautiful eyes, she noted absently as he barked, "Marguerite?"

"Dear God, it speaks again," she muttered dryly. "Be still my beating heart. I don't know if I'll survive the excitement."

Scowling at her sarcasm, he eased his foot off the brakes to cruise forward along the driveway until they reached a manned gate. Two men came out of a small building beside the gates and waved in greeting. They then immediately set about manually opening the inner gate. Once Anders had steered the SUV through and paused at a second gate, the men closed the first one. They then disappeared inside the small building again. A bare moment later, the second gate swung open on its own, and he urged their vehicle out onto a dark, country road.

"Did Marguerite specify any particular male in

Canada?" Anders asked abruptly, as Drina turned from watching the gate close behind them.

She raised an eyebrow, noting the tension now apparent in the man. "Now you want to speak, do you?" she asked with amusement, and taunted, "Afraid it was you?"

He glanced at her sharply, his own eyes narrowed. "Was it?"

Drina snorted and tugged on her seat belt. Doing it up, she muttered, "Like I'd tell you if it was."

"Wouldn't you?"

She glanced over to see that he was now frowning.

"Hell no," she assured him. "What self-respecting girl would want to be stuck with a doorstop for a mate for the rest of her life?"

"A doorstop?" he squawked.

"Yes, doorstop. As in big, silent, and good only for holding wood." She smiled sweetly, and added, "At least I'm pretty sure about the wood part. Nanos do make sure immortal males function in all areas."

Drina watched with satisfaction as Anders's mouth dropped open. She then shifted in her seat to a more comfortable position and closed her eyes. "I think I'll take a nap. I never sleep well on planes. Enjoy the drive."

Despite her closed eyes, she was aware that he kept glancing her way. Drina ignored it and managed not to grin. The man needed some shaking up, and she had no doubt this would do it. Over the centuries, she'd become good at judging the age of other immortals, and was pretty sure she was centuries older than Anders. He wouldn't be able to read her, which would leave him wondering . . . and drive him nuts, she was sure. But it served him right. It didn't take much effort to be courteous, and courtesy was necessary in a civilized society. It was a lesson the man should learn before he got too old to learn anything anymore.

Harper considered his cards briefly, then pulled out a six of spades and laid it on the discard pile. He glanced toward Tiny, not terribly surprised to find the man not looking at his own cards but peering distractedly toward the stairs.

"Tiny," he prompted. "Your turn."

"Oh." The mortal turned back to his cards, started to pull one out of his hand as if to discard it, and Harper shot his own hand out to stop him.

When Tiny glanced at him with surprise, he pointed out dryly, "You have to pick up first."

"Oh, right." He shook his head and set back the card he'd been about to discard, and reached for one from the deck.

Harper sat back with a little shake of the head, thinking, *Lord save me from new life mates.* The thought made him grimace since that's all he seemed to be surrounded with lately: Victor and Elvi, DJ and Mabel, Allesandro and Leonora, Edward and Dawn and now Tiny and Mirabeau. The first four couples had been together for a year and a half now, and were just starting to re-gather some of their wits about them. They were still new enough to be trying at times, but at least they could actually hold on to a thought or two longer than a second.

Tiny and Mirabeau were brand-spanking-new, however, and couldn't think of much else but each other . . . and how to find a moment alone to get naked. And they couldn't control their thoughts either, so that it was like constantly having a radio playing in his ear, life-mate porn, twenty-four/seven.

Harper supposed the fact that he hadn't packed up his bags and moved on a year and a half ago when his own life mate had died, was probably a sign that he was a masochist. Because really, there was no worse torture for someone who had just lost their long-awaited and prayed-for life mate than to have to stand by and witness the joy and just plain horniness of other new life mates. But he had nowhere to go. Oh, he had an apartment in the city and businesses he could pretend to be interested in, but why bother when he'd set them up years ago to ensure he needn't be there to oversee them, and could travel, merely checking in once in a while. He also had family in Germany he could visit, but they weren't close, each of them having created their own lives centuries ago and barely keeping up with each other.

Actually, Harper thought, Elvi, Victor, Mabel, and DJ were the closest thing to family he now had. When Jenny had died, the two couples had surrounded and embraced him and pulled him into their little family. They had cushioned and coddled him during the first shock of her loss, and slowly nursed him back to the land of the living, and he was grateful for it. So much so, in fact, that he was glad for this opportunity to repay some of their kindness by looking after things while they went on their honeymoons. He just wished that looking after things didn't include a pair of new life mates to torture him with.

Tiny finally discarded, and Harper picked up another card, but then paused and glanced toward the window as the crunch of tires on new snow caught his ear.

"What is it?" Tiny asked, his voice tense.

"A vehicle just pulled into the driveway," Harper murmured, then glanced to Tiny and raised an eyebrow. "Your replacements, I'm guessing."

Tiny was immediately out of his seat and moving into the kitchen to peer out the back window. When he then moved to the pantry to collect his coat from the closet there, Harper stood and followed. The arrival of the replacement hunters was something he'd looked forward to. He suspected Tiny and Mirabeau would now retreat to their bedroom and not be seen much. It meant he could avoid the worst of their obsessive thoughts about each other . . . which would be a blessing.

Tiny apparently saw him coming and grabbed Harper's coat as well. The man handed it to him as he came back into the kitchen, and both pulled them on as they headed for the door to the deck. Tiny had pulled his boots on while in the pantry and headed straight out the door, but Harper had to pause to kick off his slippers and tug on the boots by the back door. It only took a moment, but by the time he did and stepped outside, Tiny was already out of sight.

Harper grimaced as the bitter wind slapped his face. He followed the big mortal's footprints in the snow, trailing them across the deck and down the steps to the short sidewalk that ran along the side of the garage to the driveway. With his eyes on the ground, he didn't see the person approaching until he was nearly on top of them. Pausing abruptly when a pair of running shoes came into view in front of his boots, he jerked his head up with surprise and found himself blinking at a petite woman in a coat far too light for Canadian winters.

His gaze slid from her hatless head, to the suitcase she carried, and then beyond her to the two men by the SUV.

"Hi."

Harper glanced back to the woman. She was smiling tentatively at him and holding out one ungloved hand in greeting.

"Alexandrina Argenis," she announced when he merely stared at her hand. "But everyone calls me Drina."

Removing one hand from his pocket, he shook hers, noting that it was warm and soft despite the cold, then he cleared his throat and said, "Harpernus Stoyan." He retrieved his hand and shoved it back into the safety of his pocket as he stepped to the side for her to get by. "Go on inside. It's warm in there. There's blood in the fridge."

Nodding, she moved past him, and Harper watched her go, waiting until she disappeared around the corner before continuing on to the SUV now parked in the driveway. Tiny and another man, this one dressed more befitting a Canadian winter, with hat and gloves and even a scarf, were still at the back of the truck. As he approached, the new man pulled a cooler from inside and handed it to Tiny.

Rather than turn away and head back to the house though, Tiny said, "Throw your suitcase on top and I'll take it in as well."

Harper smiled faintly to himself. Tiny was a big guy, a small mountain really, and very strong . . . for a mortal. He was also used to being the muscle among his own people and forgot that he was now dealing with immortals who outclassed him horribly in that area.

But the new arrival merely set a suitcase on top of the cooler and turned back to the SUV without comment. Tiny immediately slid past Harper to head for the house, leaving him to step up beside the newcomer and peer curiously into the back of the SUV. There were two more coolers left inside. The fellow was unplugging them and winding up the cords.

"Harper."

He glanced to the man with surprise at the terse greeting, eyebrows rising as he recognized the eyes that turned to him. "Nice to see you, Anders," Harper greeted in return as he reached in to retrieve one of the coolers. "It's been a while."

Anders's answer was a grunt as he claimed the second cooler and straightened from the vehicle. He paused to close the back of the SUV, hit the button to lock the doors, and then nodded for Harper to lead the way.

Harper turned away but found himself grinning and couldn't resist saying, "Chatty as ever, I see."

When the man basically told him to bugger off in Russian, Harper burst out laughing. The sound of his own laughter was somewhat startling, but it felt good, he decided, as he led the way across the deck. Maybe it was a sign that he was finally coming out of the depression that had struck him when Jenny had died.

The thought made him sigh to himself as he shifted the cooler to open the door to the house. He'd been sunk pretty deep in self-pity and gloom for the last year and a half, and while he supposed it was only to be expected when one lost a life mate, it would be a relief to feel more himself again. He was not a naturally gloomy guy but had found little to laugh or even smile about since Jenny's death.

"Here." Tiny was in front of him, reaching for Harper's cooler the minute he stepped into the house. He gave it up and watched the man carry it into the dining room, where he unraveled the cord and plugged it in. The one Tiny himself had carried in was already plugged into a socket in the corner of the kitchen, Harper noted, and supposed the man was spreading them throughout the house to be sure they didn't overload a breaker. The coolers were basically portable refrigerators and probably used a lot of juice.

Feeling the cold at his back, Harper realized he was blocking Anders from entering and quickly stepped aside for him to pass. He then pulled the screen door closed and shut and locked the inner door. By the time he turned back, Tiny had returned and was taking the last cooler from Anders. Harper's gaze slid over the dining room in search of Alexandrina-Argenis-everyone-calls-me-Drina and found her standing beside the dining-room table, shrugging out of her coat.

"If this is all blood, you brought a lot of it," Tiny commented with a frown as he turned to carry the last cooler away, this time heading for the living room.

"Lucian sent it for your turn," Anders responded, bending to undo and remove his boots.

"My God, he speaks again," Drina muttered with feigned shock. "And a whole sentence too."

"Sometimes you'll even get a paragraph out of him," Harper responded, but his gaze was now on Tiny. The man had paused in the doorway of the living room and turned back, a startled expression on his face. Apparently it hadn't occurred to him that now that he and Mirabeau had acknowledged they were life mates, the next step was the turn.

"A whole paragraph?" Drina asked with dry amusement, drawing Harper's attention again.

"A short one, but a paragraph just the same," he murmured, glancing her way. He then paused to take her in. She was petite, as he'd noticed outside, which was a polite way of saying short. But she was curvy too, rounded in all the right places. She was also most definitely Spanish, with olive skin, deep-set eyes, the large brow bone, and straight, almost prominent nose. But it all worked to make an attractive face, he decided.

"Right, of course, the turn," Tiny muttered, drawing his attention once more, and Harper shifted his attention back to find the other man looking resolute. As he watched, Tiny straightened his shoulders and continued into the living room.

Harper frowned and had to bite back the urge to tell Tiny that perhaps he should wait on turning, but he knew it was just a knee-jerk reaction to his own experience. It was rare for a mortal to die during the turn, and in all likelihood, Tiny would probably be fine. However, Jenny had died, and so that was the first thing he thought of and the worry that now plagued him.

Sighing, he bent to remove his boots. He set them beside the radiator, and straightened to remove his coat. Laying it over his arm, he then took Anders's as he finished removing it and crossed the room to collect Drina's as well before ducking into the small pantry in the back corner of the kitchen. It held the entry to the garage but was also where the closet was.

"Handy."

Harper glanced around to see that Drina stood in the doorway to the kitchen, eyes sliding around the small room. Her gaze slid back to him as he reached for hangers, and she moved to join him as he hung up her coat.

"Let me help. You don't have to wait on us." She took the second hanger he'd just retrieved and Anders's coat, leaving him to deal with only his own.

Harper murmured a "thanks," but had to fight the urge to assure her it was fine and send her from the room. The tiny space suddenly seemed smaller with her in it, a good portion of the air seeming to have slipped out with her entrance, leaving an unbearably hot vacuum behind that had him feeling flushed and oxygen starved. Which was just odd, he decided. He had never been claustrophobic before this. Still, Harper was relieved when they were done with the task, and he could usher her back into the much larger kitchen.

"So where is this Stephanie we're supposed to guard?" Drina asked, sliding onto one of the stools that ran along the L-shaped counter separating the kitchen from the dining area.

"Sleeping," Harper answered, moving past her to the dining-room table to gather the cards from his game with Tiny.

"Stephanie's still used to mortal hours," Tiny explained, returning to the kitchen then. "So we thought it'd be better if one of us was up with her during the day and the other up at night to keep an eye on things while she slept. I got night duty."

"They're concerned about the lack of security here," Harper explained, sliding the cards into their box and moving to set them on the counter.

Drina frowned and glanced to Tiny. "But isn't that backward? You're mortal, aren't you? Shouldn't you be up during the day and this Mirabeau up at night?"

Tiny smiled wryly. "That would have been easier all around, but it's only been this one day. Besides, while I can hang out with her during the day or night and keep an eye on her, someone has to sleep in her room, which had to be Mirabeau." When

Drina raised an eyebrow, he explained, "We didn't think it was a good idea to leave her alone in her room all night. There's no fence here, no alarm . . . It could be hours before we realized she was gone if she was taken or—"

"Or what?" Drina asked when Tiny hesitated. It was pure politeness on her part, Harper knew. The woman could have read him easily enough to find out what he was reluctant to say but was asking instead out of respect.

Tiny was silent as he removed his own coat, but finally admitted, "There's some concern that Stephanie might try to run away and get to her family."

"Really?" Drina asked, her eyes narrowing.

Tiny nodded. "Apparently, Lucian caught the thought in her head a time or two. He thinks she only wants to see them, not necessarily approach them, but—" He shrugged. "Anyway, as far as she's concerned, none of us know that, and someone has to be with her twenty-four/seven because of Leonius."

"So we are not only watching for attack from outside, but a prison break as well," Drina murmured. "And because of this, Mirabeau has been sleeping in Stephanie's room with her?"

Tiny shrugged. "This was the first night. We only got here the day before yesterday, and Elvi, Victor, DJ, and Mabel were here then to help keep an eye on things. But they left at four this morning, so . . ." He grimaced. "When Stephanie went to bed, Mirabeau did as well."

Drina heaved a sigh, smiled wryly, and said, "Well,

I guess that will be my gig from now on. I'll have a bag of blood, and then go up and relieve Mirabeau."

Harper had to smile at Tiny's expression. The man looked torn between shouting hallelujah, and protesting it wasn't necessary tonight and she could take over that duty tomorrow. Duty versus desire, he supposed. Tiny and Mirabeau had brought Stephanie here from New York, sneaking her from the church where several couples were being wed in one large ceremony, including Victor and Elvi. They had left via a secret exit in the church, and traveled some distance through a series of sewer tunnels before reaching the surface. They'd then driven to Port Henry, where Victor and Elvi had been waiting to welcome the girl.

While Tiny and Mirabeau were officially off duty now that Drina and Anders had arrived, Lucian had insisted they stay to get over the worst of their new-life-mate symptoms. Harper suspected they would feel a responsibility to help out while they were here. They would probably even feel they should, to pay back for staying here at the bed-and-breakfast for the next couple of weeks.

"Drina's right," Anders announced, saving Tiny the struggle. "It's better someone less distracted than Mirabeau be in Stephanie's room with her. Besides, it's our worry now. You two are off duty."

Tiny blew out a small breath and nodded, but then added, "We'll help out while we're here, though."

"Hopefully, it won't be necessary, but we appreciate that," Drina said, when Anders just shrugged. She then slid off her stool and glanced from Anders to Harper in question. "Which blood do I use? From the coolers or the fridge?"

"Either one," Anders said with a shrug. "More is coming in a couple of days."

Harper moved to the refrigerator to retrieve a bag for her, pulled out three more, and turned to hand them out.

"Thank you," Drina murmured, accepting the bag Harper offered. She popped it to her fangs, then suddenly stiffened and turned to glance over her shoulder. Following her gaze, Harper saw that Teddy was entering the dining room from the foyer.

"I thought I heard voices," the man said on a yawn, running one hand through his thick, gray hair.

"Sorry if we woke you, Teddy," Harper said, and gestured to the newcomers. "The backup Lucian promised has arrived." He turned and explained to Drina and Anders, "Teddy Brunswick is the police chief here in Port Henry. He's also a friend, and he offered to stay and help keep an eye out until you guys arrived." He glanced back to the man, and said, "Teddy, this is Alexandrina Argenis. She prefers Drina."

Teddy nodded in greeting to Drina, and then glanced to Anders as Harper finished, "And her partner is Anders."

"Hmm." Teddy raised his eyebrows. "Anders a first name or last?"

"Neither," Anders said, and ended any further possibility to question him by popping his bag of blood to his mouth.

Teddy scowled but merely moved into the small

back room with its coat closet. He returned a moment later with a coat in one hand and a pair of boots in the other.

"Now that the cavalry have arrived, I guess I'll go home and crawl into my own bed," he announced, settling on a dining-room chair to don his boots.

"Thank you for staying, Teddy," Tiny murmured. "I made a fresh pot of coffee shortly before Drina and Anders arrived. Do you want a cup for the road?"

"That'd be nice," Teddy said appreciatively, finishing with one boot and pulling on the other. Tiny immediately moved to the cupboard and retrieved a travel mug. By the time Teddy had finished with his second boot, Tiny had poured the coffee and added the fixings. He waited as Teddy donned his coat and did it up, and then handed him the mug.

"Thank you," Teddy murmured, accepting it. "I'll clean the mug and return it tomorrow when I come to check on things."

"Sounds good," Tiny said with a nod, as he walked the man to the door and saw him out.

"Well," Drina said, pulling the now-empty bag from her fangs and moving around the counter to throw it out. "I guess it's time for me to go to bed."

Harper smiled faintly at her grimace as she said it. It was only a little after one. Going to bed now was like a mortal going to bed at four in the afternoon. It was doubtful she'd be able to sleep for quite a while. In fact, he suspected she probably wouldn't be able to drift off until just before dawn, and then she'd have to get up with Stephanie in the morning.

She was in for a rough time until she adjusted to her new hours, he thought with sympathy.

"It's the room in the front right corner as you come off the stairs," Tiny said helpfully. "I'm not sure which of the twin beds Mirabeau chose, though."

"I'll figure it out," Drina assured him as she picked up her suitcase. "Good night, boys."

"Good night," Harper murmured, along with the others. He watched until she'd left the room, and they could hear her mounting the stairs. He then frowned slightly and glanced up toward the lights, wondering why the room seemed a little darker all of a sudden.

Two

Drina paused before the bedroom door Tiny had directed her to and eased the door open. The moment she did, someone sat up in the near bed. Mirabeau, she guessed, and backed up as the woman got up and moved to join her in the hall.

"Our replacement?" Mirabeau whispered as she slid the door silently closed. She wore joggers and a sleeveless T-shirt: comfortable enough to sleep in but ready for action if necessary.

"Drina Argenis," Drina said with a nod, offering her hand.

"Mirabeau La Roche." They shook hands, and then Mirabeau asked, "Lucian said Anders was coming with you?"

"Yes, he's downstairs with the others," Drina said. "I came up to relieve you. I'll sleep in Stephanie's room from now on."

"I can't say I'm sorry to give up that job. I haven't slept a wink," Mirabeau admitted dryly.

"I don't think I will either. At least not tonight," Drina admitted on a sigh. She hadn't slept at night since . . . well, actually she didn't recall ever sleeping at night. Shrugging, she added, "Although tomorrow night may be a different story. By then I may be exhausted enough that I do actually sleep."

"Let's hope," Mirabeau said, glancing toward the stairs.

"Go on," Drina said with amusement as she picked up her suitcase. "Tiny is no doubt getting antsy waiting for you."

Mirabeau nodded and turned away. "Good night."

"Good night," Drina murmured, and eased the bedroom door open to slip inside. The room wasn't completely dark, the curtains were heavy, but a faint glow from the streetlights outside was still slipping around the edges. Between that and her eyesight, Drina could see almost as well as if it were daylight. She set down her suitcase beside the bed, briefly considered changing her clothes, but then decided the sweater and jeans she wore would do. She didn't want to wake Stephanie, and wasn't likely to sleep anyway, she thought as she eased to sit on the side of the bed.

"Aren't you going to change your clothes?"

Drina turned sharply and glanced over her shoulder as the young girl in the next bed shifted onto her side facing her and raised her arm to rest her head on her hand.

"You can turn on the light if you like. I'm not asleep anymore."

Drina hesitated, but then supposed if they were going to be roommates, she should at least introduce herself to the girl. Standing, she moved around the bed to sit on the side facing Stephanie as the girl reached over to turn on the lamp on the bedside table. Habit, Drina supposed. As an immortal, Stephanie should have been able to see as well as Drina did.

The sudden light was briefly blinding, but after blinking several times, Drina found herself peering at a petite blonde. She'd been told the girl was fifteen, but Stephanie looked younger. She had a lovely face, but a child's body, still somewhat gangly and flat-chested.

"Hi." Stephanie shifted to sit cross-legged on her own bed. "You're Alexandrina Argenis, but prefer to be called Drina."

"And you're Stephanie McGill," she said calmly, supposing that Lucian must have told Mirabeau and Tiny who was coming, and they'd passed it on to the girl.

"They didn't tell me," Stephanie said with a smile.

Drina blinked. "Excuse me?"

"You just thought that Tiny and Beau told me who was coming, but they didn't. I read your mind."

Drina sat back slightly, her eyes narrowing. The girl certainly sounded as if she'd just read her mind, but it wasn't possible. Drina was old, older than her uncle Victor, and Stephanie was a new turn. The teenager couldn't possibly read her.

"Maybe it's because you've met your life mate," Stephanie suggested with a shrug. "That usually makes you guys readable, doesn't it?"

"Er . . ." Drina instinctively shook her head in denial.

"Marguerite suggested you to Lucian because she thinks Harper is your life mate."

"Crap." Drina sagged where she sat. The kid really was reading her. That was the only explanation since Marguerite had said Lucian hadn't wanted to know who it was so long as it wasn't Anders. She and Marguerite were the only two in the world who knew.

"Plus me," Stephanie said with amusement.

"Plus you," Drina agreed on a sigh. Apparently just meeting the man had been enough to start affecting her. Great.

"It was smart you've played it cool and didn't just blurt out that he might be your life mate. Harper's going to be a hard nut to crack," Stephanie said suddenly. "He'll fight this life-mate business."

"Why do you say that?" Drina asked warily.

"Because it isn't grief that's making him so miserable over Jenny. It's guilt. He thinks if he'd never met and tried to turn her, she'd still be alive. It's eating him up. He doesn't think he deserves to be happy. He thinks he needs to suffer for her dying. He'll fight it and avoid you for the next couple of centuries until he feels he's suffered enough if he finds out you're life mates . . . unless you creep up on him."

Drina stared at her blankly, amazed to hear such wisdom from someone so young.

Stephanie suddenly grinned and admitted, "I'm not Yoda or something. I'm just repeating what Marguerite said to you."

"She did say that, but I wasn't thinking it," Drina said with a frown.

"Yeah, you are. It's nagging at the back of your mind and probably has been since she said it. That and the thought that it just figured you'd finally encounter your life mate, and instead of it being easy like you'd expect finding an immortal life mate should be, it's going to be even more delicate than it would be were he mortal." She grimaced. "I know the feeling."

"Do you?" Drina asked quietly.

"Oh, yeah. Nothing lives up to your expectations," she muttered, then grimaced and said, "Like, before . . . when I was human, I used to fantasize what it would be like to be, you know, different. Special. I even once or twice fantasized about what it would be like to be a vampire. I thought it would be so cool. Strong, smart . . . no one would pick on you, no one could make you do anything you didn't want and all that bull." She sighed and shook her head. "It isn't like that at all. Sure, I'm stronger, and the kids at school couldn't pick on me, but I'm not in school, am I? And there seem to be even more problems than when I was human."

"You're still human, Steffie," Drina said quietly, feeling for the kid. Marguerite had told her all about the girl as part of her effort to convince her to accept the assignment. She knew that last summer Stephanie had been a happy, healthy mortal with her whole life ahead of her . . . until she and her older sister, Dani, had been taken from a grocery-store parking lot in cottage country by a group of no-fangers. The girl had been terrorized and turned against her will, and now her whole life had changed. While Lucian and his men had rescued her, she was now Eden-tate, immortal but without fangs, and she could not return to her previous life. Like Dorothy caught up in a tornado and dropped in Oz, Stephanie had lost her family and friends and been dropped in the middle of an entirely different life not of her choosing. She'd had a rough shake and didn't deserve what had happened to her. And Drina wasn't at all surprised this wasn't what the girl had envisioned when she'd imagined the impossible fantasy of being a vampire.

Realizing that the girl was staring at her oddly, she asked uncertainly, "What?"

"My brothers and sisters always call me Steffie."

"Oh, sorry," Drina muttered. Her brother's name was Stephano and she always called him Steff. She supposed she'd just automatically turned it feminine.

"Your brother's name is Stephano?" the girl asked with interest. Stifling a yawn, she lay back in the bed. "You'll have to tell me about him, but tomorrow. I'm really tired now. Sometimes, this reading-thoughts business is exhausting. Good night."

"Good night," Drina murmured, as the girl rolled onto her side away from her and settled into her bed. She then hesitated a moment, considering whether she should take the time to change now or just turn off the light so the girl could get to sleep.

"Go ahead. The light doesn't bother me," Stephanie mumbled. "Besides, while I know you don't think you'll sleep, you'll stand a better chance of doing so if you're more comfortable."

Drina shook her head and stood to grab her suitcase and toss it on the bed. She wasn't used to having someone reading her mind. She was old enough most people couldn't. And she definitely didn't like it. She would have to guard her thoughts more carefully, she supposed, and then stopped thinking altogether and just concentrated on quickly changing into a pair of white joggers and an equally white tank top.

"Good night," Stephanie mumbled, as Drina closed her suitcase and set it back on the floor.

"Good night," she whispered back and crawled into bed, then turned out the light and lay down. Even as she did, Drina knew she was about to spend a very long night fretting over what to do about Harpernus Stoyan. She'd heard of reluctant mortal life mates, but this was really one for the record books. Only she could wind up with a reluctant vampire life mate.

Harper didn't think he'd been asleep long when he was suddenly awake again. Frowning, he peered toward the window, noting the sliver of bright sunlight trying to creep around the edges of the blackout blinds. He listened for what might have disturbed him, but silence curled around him like a blanket. He was actually dozing off again when a muffled peel of laughter brought his eyes open once more.

Frowning, he sat up and listened more intently, but the house was silent, without even the sounds of creaking stairs or floorboards reaching his ears. No one was moving around inside the house, he decided, but then another laugh reached his ears, and he turned toward the window, where he was sure the sound had come from. Harper peered at the blinds for a moment and then slid out of bed and padded across the floor to the window, which looked out over the garage and driveway at the back of the house.

Sunlight streamed in the moment he tugged one of the slats down, and Harper blinked against it, squinting until his eyes adjusted. He then scanned what he could see of the driveway and backyard. It was a moment before he found the source of the sounds he'd heard, and then Drina came into view on the sidewalk beside the garage. She was slip-sliding her way toward the driveway, her running shoes giving her no traction on the icy concrete. Her clumsy efforts elicited another peel of amusement from somewhere out of sight.

Stephanie, Harper decided, sure it was the girl even though he couldn't yet see her. Turning his gaze back to Drina, he frowned as he took in her winter wear. She wore jeans, which were fine, but the running shoes were completely unsuitable, and her coat was far too lightweight for this weather. She also had no gloves or hat on, which suggested to him that she hadn't been prepared for a Canadian winter when she'd set out on her journey from Spain.

She'd probably thought she would just attend

the weddings in New York, spending most of her time in the hotel, the church, or cars and wouldn't need heavier gear, he thought, and then winced as a snowball suddenly shot from somewhere off to the side and slammed into the back of Drina's head. The hit took her completely by surprise and made her jerk. In the next moment, her feet went out from beneath her and she was on her behind on the icy concrete. She was also cursing a blue streak in Spanish that he could hear even over Stephanie's uproarious laughter.

Concern rushing through him, Harper let the blind slat slip back into place and hurried out of the room, pausing just long enough to pull on a pair of jeans as he went. Once downstairs, he almost rushed outside bare-chested and in just the jeans, but the chill that hit him when he opened the kitchen door, and the sight of the snow-laced screen door, made him rethink that and hurry to the closet in the pantry. Still, he was quick about pulling on boots and a coat, and didn't bother doing up either before rushing back through the kitchen and out onto the deck.

The walkway was empty, and there was no sign of either female as he crossed the deck. For one moment, Harper could almost have believed he'd imagined the whole thing he'd seen from his window, but then he spotted where the snow had been disturbed by Drina's fall, as well as the footprints leading around to the driveway. He followed them quickly around the garage, and stopped abruptly. Stephanie was in the front passenger seat of the SUV, bent over and peering at something under the driver's side, but it was Drina's derriere waving around in the open driver's door as she fiddled with something under the dashboard that brought him to a halt.

The woman's butt was snow-covered and bobbing about like an apple on a river's surface as she worked at whatever she was doing. It was an interesting sight, he decided, and then gave his head a shake and continued forward, becoming aware of their conversation as he approached.

"Are you sure you know what you're doing?" Stephanie was asking, half-amused and half-worried. "I could always just creep in and find the keys."

"I have done this before," Drina assured her from under the dashboard, her voice sounding annoyed. "I *can* do this. It is just that your cars seem to be wired differently than ours in Europe."

Stephanie snorted at the claim. "I hardly think they wire them differently. How long ago did you last do this?"

"Twenty years or so," Drina admitted in a mutter, and then cursed in Spanish, and added determinedly, "I *can* do this. We *will* go shopping."

"Is there something I can help you ladies with?" Harper asked, pausing behind Drina's bobbing derriere and just resisting the urge to brush the snow from it. Really, her butt must be cold, encased in snow like that.

Stephanie glanced to him wide-eyed, but Drina stiffened, her bobbing stopping altogether. She stayed frozen for a moment, jerked her head upward, cursed as it slammed into the steering wheel, and muttered under her breath as she backed out of the vehicle. Of course, he was right behind her and didn't move out of the way quickly enough. Her rear end rammed into his groin, and she trod on his feet.

Gasping an apology, Drina immediately stumbled forward again to get off him, lost her footing, and started to go down. In his effort to save her from the fall, Harper managed to get his own feet tangled up with hers and found himself crashing to the icy pavement with her.

"Are you all right?"

Harper opened his eyes at that concerned query and turned his head to see that Drina had pushed herself to her hands and knees beside him and was eyeing him worriedly. Her coat was open despite the cold, revealing a low-cut silk shirt that gaped slightly thanks to her position. It left him an extraordinary view of full, round breasts encased in a lacy white bra that looked rather fetching against her olive skin.

Blinking, he tore his gaze from the delectable sight and glanced past her to Stephanie, who was nearly killing herself laughing in the SUV, and then he sighed and said dryly, "I'll live."

"Hmm." Drina's eyes drifted down to his bare chest, where his coat had fallen open, and he saw one of her eyebrows rise, but then she scrambled to her feet and offered him a hand.

"Sorry," she muttered as she helped him up. "You startled me."

"My fault," he assured her, taking a moment to brush himself down. He then straightened and glanced to the open door of the SUV. "What were you doing?"

"Er . . ." Drina flushed guiltily and turned back to the vehicle. "I need boots and a heavier coat, and Stephanie needs a few things too, so we were just going to head out shopping."

"Hmm." His lips twitched, and then he said, "So you were going to hot-wire the SUV?"

Drina clucked with irritation at being caught, and then said with exasperation, "Anders has the keys, and I didn't want to disturb him to get them."

"Ah." Harper glanced from her embarrassed and defiant face to the vehicle and back, and then he asked, "Do you have a license to drive here? Or even a Spanish driver's license?"

"Bah!" Drina waved the question away. "We don't need them. If a police officer tries to pull us over, we just control them."

"Ah, yes." Harper nodded. He'd expected as much and explained apologetically, "But you can't do that in Port Henry. You can anywhere else, even London, but not here."

"What?" She glanced to him with surprise.

"Lucian promised Teddy that his people would follow the laws while in Port Henry, and none of us would use mind control on Teddy or his deputy," Harper explained.

Drina narrowed her eyes, and pointed out dryly, "Which isn't promising he won't himself."

"No," Harper admitted with a grin. "But Teddy didn't catch that at the time."

"Hmm," she said with irritation, and then glanced

to Stephanie's worried face and grimaced. "Don't worry. We'll still go. We'll just call a taxi."

Stephanie looked dubious. "Do you think they even have taxis here? I mean, it's a pretty small town."

Drina turned to him in question. "Do they?"

"Actually, I don't think they do. Or at least if they do, I haven't heard of one," Harper admitted, and when Drina's shoulders began to sag with what appeared to be defeat, he found himself saying, "I can take you in my car."

She appeared as surprised as he was by his offer. Truly, Harper had no idea where that had come from. He'd just blurted it without really even thinking first.

"Don't you sleep during the day?" Drina asked with a frown. "Speaking of which, what are you even doing up?"

Harper just shook his head and turned away to start back up the drive, saying, "I'll just throw on a shirt and grab my keys and wallet and be right back."

"My laughing woke him up, but he didn't want to make us feel bad by saying so," Stephanie announced.

Drina turned to glance at the young girl in the SUV. Seeing that Stephanie's attention was on Harper as he hurried across the deck toward the kitchen door, Drina quickly swiped up a handful of snow off the SUV's roof and worked it into a ball as she asked, "Which laughing woke him? Your laughing when I was slip-sliding around on the sidewalk? Or your laughing when you hit me with the snowball, and I went down like a ton of bricks?"

Stephanie turned an unrepentant grin her way. "It was funny," she began, and then her eyes suddenly narrowed and dropped to search for Drina's hands.

Realizing the girl had read her mind and knew what she was up to, Drina quickly shot the snowball at her, but Stephanie was faster, whirling and ducking at the same time so that the ball missed her and hit the passenger window instead.

"Too slow," Stephanie taunted.

Drina shrugged. "That's all right. I'll get you when you least expect it."

Stephanie chuckled, unconcerned by the threat, and slid out of the SUV to walk around and join her. "He has a nice chest, doesn't he?"

He certainly did have a nice chest, Drina thought, and she'd been hard-pressed not to simply throw herself on top of it and drool all the way down to the top of his jeans when she'd seen it. But she'd restrained herself, and now merely shrugged, asking, "You noticed his chest, did you?"

"Not really. Mostly I noticed that you noticed," Stephanie responded with amusement.

Drina rolled her eyes with disgust. This being easily read business was going to become a serious pain in the arse at this rate, she decided.

"You played it cool, though," Stephanie praised her. "He didn't even have an inkling you were drooling inside."

"I wasn't drooling," Drina assured her dryly.

"Oh, yeah. You were," Stephanie said on a laugh.

Drina sighed. "All right, maybe a little inside." She shrugged. "What can I say? It's been half a millenniun since I've even noticed a man's chest."

Actually, it had been longer than that, she realized and hoped to God her hymen hadn't grown back in the intervening years.

"Oh my God! That doesn't happen, right?"

Drina blinked at that horrified exclamation and glanced at Stephanie with confusion. "What?"

"The nanos don't . . . like . . . fix your hymen after it's been broken so that every time you have sex it's like the first time?" she asked with a bone-deep horror that left Drina gaping.

"Good Lord, no!" she assured her. "Where on earth would you get an idea like that?"

Stephanie sagged with relief, and then explained, "You were just thinking you hoped yours hadn't grown back."

"Oh, I—That was—I was just having a sarcastic, self-deprecating minute in my head. Gees." She closed her eyes briefly, opened them again, and said solemnly, "Girl, you have to stay out of my head."

"I'm not in your head," Stephanie said wearily. "You're talking into mine."

Drina frowned, pretty sure she wasn't trying to talk into her head.

"So why don't they?" Stephanie asked suddenly, a frown tugging at her lips.

"Why don't who what?" Drina asked, confused again.

"Why don't nanos repair the hymen when it's broken?" she explained. "I thought their job was to keep us perfect and all."

"Not perfect. No one is perfect," Drina assured her. "They're programmed to keep us at our peak, the best we each can be as individuals."

Stephanie waved that away impatiently. "Right, but if you break a bone, they fix it. Why wouldn't they fix the hymen if it was broke?"

"Well—" Drina paused, her brain blank, and then shook her head helplessly. "I don't know. Maybe the nanos don't think the hymen is something that needs fixing. Or maybe the scientists didn't think to include the hymen as part of the anatomy when they programmed them," she suggested, and then grimaced, and added dryly, "I'm just glad as heck that they don't repair it."

"I know," Stephanie groaned. "That would be vile."

"Hmm." Drina nodded and gave a little shudder at the thought, but then glanced at her sharply. "Have you had sex?"

"No, of course, not." Stephanie flushed with embarrassment.

"Then why so horrified at the thought of the nanos replacing the hymen?" she asked, eyeing her narrowly.

Stephanie snorted. "I read. It's not supposed to be fun to lose your virginity."

Drina relaxed and shrugged. "It's different for different people. For some it's painful, for others not so much, for some there's blood and others not. It may be all right for you," she said reassuringly, and then frowned and added, "But . . . you know . . . you shouldn't rush out there to find out which it will be in your case. You have plenty of time to try stuff like that. *Plenty* of time," she stressed.

"Now you sound like my mother," Stephanie said with amusement.

Drina grimaced. She kind of felt like her parent in that moment. Certainly, she suddenly had a lot more sympathy for parents having to give the sex talk. Dear God, she couldn't even imagine that conversation.

"Fortunately for you, my mother already gave me that talk," Stephanie said with a grin.

"You're reading me again," Drina complained.

"I told you, I'm not reading you. You're kind of pushing your thoughts at me."

Drina frowned and turned to ask her to explain what she meant, but paused to glance toward the garage as one of the doors began to whir upward.

"Harper must be ready to go," Stephanie commented. "You should let me take the front seat."

"I should, should I?" Drina asked with amusement.

"Definitely," Stephanie assured her. "We don't want him to think you like him or start worrying about life mates and stuff. Wave me that way as we approach the car. That way Harper will think you didn't care to sit in the front with him."

Drina smiled faintly but just nodded. It couldn't hurt, and she didn't care if she was in the front or not anyway.

"And you should sit right behind him, not behind the passenger seat," Stephanie whispered as the garage door finished opening, and they saw Harper waving to them from the driver's seat of a silver BMW.

"Why?" Drina whispered back, using the excuse of closing the still-open door of the SUV to delay approaching the car.

"That way, every time he looks in the rearview mirror, he'll see you," she pointed out.

Drina peered at her with surprise. The kid was smart, she thought, and knew by the way that Stephanie smiled widely that she'd heard the compliment. Chuckling, she slid her arm around the girl and used it to steer her toward the car.

"You can sit in the front if you like," she said with amusement, steering her that way, and then breaking off to move up the driver's side of the car herself.

"You're sure you don't mind?" Stephanie asked with feigned concern, pausing beside the passenger door.

"Not at all," Drina said dryly and had to bite her lip to keep from laughing when the girl grinned at her over the roof of the car, out of Harper's view. Shaking her head, Drina opened the back door and slid in behind him.

"Thank you, Harper. This is really sweet of you," Stephanie said as she slid into the front seat. "Isn't it sweet, Drina?"

"Very," she agreed mildly.

"It's no problem," Harper assured them, smiling at Stephanie, and then meeting Drina's gaze in the rearview mirror and smiling at her as well. "Just tell me where you want to go, and we're there."

"Well, Drina insisted we had to stay in town because she doesn't know her way around, so we were just going to go to Wal-Mart. But with you driving, maybe we could go into London," Stephanie said in a rush.

"I don't think so, Stephanie," Drina said firmly when Harper hesitated. "It isn't just that I don't know the area. I think it's better that we stay in town until we're sure no one trailed you guys from New York. Here we at least have the house relatively close and can call Teddy Brunswick if we need help."

"But there are so many cool stores in London," Stephanie protested. "We could go to Garage or the Gap or—"

"I'll tell you what," Harper interrupted. "How about we try Wal-Mart today for the necessities, and then maybe later in the week we can venture out to London if you don't find everything you need here in town?"

Stephanie heaved out a sigh. "Oh, all right."

"Good. So, do up your seat belts, and we'll be on our way."

Drina smiled wryly at Harper's relieved tones and did up her seat belt, then sat silently in the backseat as he maneuvered the car out of the garage and past the SUV.

"If you're the daughter of Lucian and Victor's brother, how come your name is Argenis and not Argeneau?"

Drina blinked at the sudden question from Stephanie, caught a bit by surprise, but it was Harper who answered.

"Argenis is just basically the Spanish version of Argeneau. They're derivatives of the same root name," Harper said, sounding like a schoolteacher. "As each branch of the family spread out to different areas of the world, the name changed to fit the language of that area. Argenis in Spain, Argeneau in France, Argent in England, and so on."

Stephanie peered at Harper curiously. "So what's the root name?"

"I believe it was Argentum, which means silver in Latin," Harper said solemnly. "It was because their eyes are silver-blue."

"They named people for their eye color?" Stephanie asked with disbelief.

Harper chuckled at her expression. "Back then they didn't really have last names. They were mostly first names and then descriptors, like John the barber, or Jack the butcher, or Harold the brave and so on."

"So it was Lucian the silver?" she asked dubiously.

"Something like that," Harper said with a shrug.

"Hmm." Stephanie swung around to peer at Drina. "And you're a rogue hunter in Spain?"

Drina nodded.

"Is it different than being a rogue hunter here?"

Drina raised her eyebrows. "I don't know. It doesn't appear to be so far."

"They have different laws in Europe," Harper put in quietly.

"Like what?" Stephanie asked, turning back to him.

"Biting mortals is not outlawed there," Drina an-swered stiffly when Harper hesitated. She knew that was the reason for the hesitation. It was a bit of an issue between the North American council and the European one.

"You can bite people over there?" Stephanie frowned. "So Leonius wouldn't be rogue in Europe?"

"I said bite, not kill or turn. Trust me, Leonius would be rogue anywhere," she said dryly, and then sighed. "So long as they are discreet and don't unduly harm the mortal, immortals can bite mor-tals in Europe. Although," she added firmly, "while they haven't yet outlawed it, it is somewhat frowned upon by most, and the majority of immortals stick mainly to bagged blood."

"Have you bitten mortals?" Stephanie asked curi-ously.

"Of course," she said stiffly. "I was born long before there were blood banks."

"But since blood banks, have you bitten them?" Stephanie persisted.

Drina grimaced, but reluctantly admitted, "Only consenting adults."

Stephanie's eyes widened, and she squealed, "She means during sex."

Drina blinked. That hadn't been what she'd meant at all. She'd been thinking of the occasional formal dinners at the homes of council higher-ups, which sometimes included willing bitees for the guests to feed on. It was something she wasn't very comfort-able with anymore but was expected to participate in when forced to attend . . . and Stephanie should know that. She could read her mind. And she'd read it earlier, so knew it had been eons since she'd bothered with sex. Drina eyed Stephanie quizzically, wondering what the girl was up to.

"I don't know why everyone thinks it's so hot to get naked and sweaty and sink their teeth into each other," Stephanie was saying with disgust, and then she glanced at Harper, and said, "I mean, imagine you were alone with Drina getting busy. You're both naked and hot and she crawls onto your lap, her naked boobs jiggling in your face . . . Would you really want to plunge your fangs into them?"

"Er . . ."

Drina swung her gaze to the rearview mirror to see that Harper looked quite overset. His face was flushed, his eyes glazed, and then he suddenly swung the steering wheel and brought the car to a halt with a jerk.

"We're here," Harper choked out, practically throwing himself out of the vehicle and slamming the door with a resounding thud.

"You little devil," Drina muttered watching Harper stagger toward the store.

"Yeah, I'm good," Stephanie said with a grin. "Now he's thinking of having sex with you."

Drina turned her gaze to the girl, eyeing her thoughtfully. "You're kind of evil."

Stephanie took it as a compliment and grinned as she got out of the car.

Three

Harper stepped through Wal-Mart's sliding doors, and then paused as Stephanie sped past him to pull a cart from a small collection of them waiting directly ahead. Shifting uncomfortably, he glanced around, his gaze barely touching on Drina before it slipped away. "I can probably find something to entertain myself with in the video department if you girls would rather shop without me trailing you around."

"Oh, no," Stephanie protested. "It won't be as much fun without you, Harper. Besides, a guy's opinion is always vital when it comes to fashion."

"Vital, huh?" he said with a faint smile.

"Very vital. My dad always said no woman can tell another woman what looks best on her, only a man can," she assured him. "And Drina and I want to look our best in case we run into some hunky guys when she takes me to lunch."

"Lunch?" he asked with a frown.

"Oh." Stephanie frowned. "Well, she promised we'd go to lunch after shopping, but that was when we were going by ourselves. I suppose that's out now," she added, her head lowering with disappointment.

"I'll take you both to lunch," Harper said quickly when her lower lip began to tremble.

"Really?" Stephanie brightened at once. Beaming happily, she gave him a hug. "Thank you, Harper. Here, you can push the cart while Drina and I throw clothes in. It will give you something to do. Come on, Drina. I need scads of clothes."

"Hmm," Harper muttered, taking her place at the cart when she danced out in front of it to lead the way. He had the distinct impression he'd been played here, an impression that only solidified when Drina chuckled "sucker" in a soft voice as she followed Stephanie into the aisles.

Harper shook his head and followed the pair, sighing when he realized his eyes had seemed to fasten on Drina's behind and appeared unwilling to leave it. It was Stephanie's fault. That business about being naked and sweaty with Drina, getting it on, and her crawling in his lap, her breasts jiggling . . . Would he want to plunge his fangs into her? The girl's words had painted a picture in his head of the two of them entwined on the sheets of his bed, Drina straddling his lap facing him and his plunging more than just his fangs into her. It had been a rather invigorating image that had left him hot, flushed, flustered, breathless, and damnably excited. And hell yes, he'd have wanted to sink his fangs in her, as well as other things. The thought had so startled Harper that he hadn't been able to get out of the car, and away from the image, fast enough. Unfortunately, the image was following him.

He supposed it didn't help that he'd accidentally seen just how round and full those jiggling breasts would be if she were to crawl naked into his lap. The image of her on her hands and knees on the snowy driveway, top gaping and revealing her lovely curves, now flashed into his mind again.

Sighing, Harper forced his eyes from Drina's behind and up to her face with some effort as she paused to examine some item of clothing they'd approached. From the glimpse he'd got of her face in the rearview mirror, Drina hadn't looked nearly as affected by the image Stephanie had painted of them as he had. If anything, her expression as she'd peered toward Stephanie had been rather confused, though he wasn't sure why.

"What do you think, Harper?"

Blinking, he shifted his attention to Stephanie and raised an eyebrow uncertainly. "What do I think of what?"

"Of these," Stephanie said with a laugh, and held a pair of panties in front of Drina's groin. They were red silk with black lace trimming. "Do you think men would find her attractive in these? There's a matching bra too." She held that up in front of Drina's breasts next and peered at the effect with a tilted head. "I think they're gorgeous, but Drina says the material of the bra is too flimsy and her nipples would show through when it's cold. Do men mind nipple bumps?"

"I—" Harper stared, his mind suddenly on hiatus as he imagined Drina in the outfit, her nipples erect and pressing the material outward. "Don't—"

"See, he said 'I don't.' I told you men don't mind nipple bumps," Stephanie said with a laugh, and tossed the bra and panties into the cart.

Harper stared helplessly at the scraps of material and shook his head. He hadn't meant he didn't mind nipple bumps. Hell, he wasn't sure what he'd meant. Please don't do this to me, maybe. The girl was . . . well, he didn't know what to think of Stephanie. She had been quiet and sad-looking when she'd first arrived in Port Henry, but had blossomed a bit under Elvi's and Mabel's attention before they'd left. However, she appeared to have really come out of her shell with Drina's arrival and was being rather precocious. He didn't think she had a clue how her suggestions and words were affecting him, though. No doubt she was young enough that she really thought a man could just look at this stuff without it affecting him, but—

His gaze shot to Drina, and he wondered what she was making of all this. He'd been too busy looking at the material in front of her and imagining it on her body, to even take in her expression this time. Though he had a vague sense that she'd seemed embarrassed by the girl's behavior. She appeared unconcerned now, though, completely oblivious of his presence, her expression serene as Stephanie held up a black and red bustier in front of her. A bustier, for Christ's sake!

"You're so lucky to have the body to wear this stuff." Stephanie was sighing as he tuned in to what she was saying. "You have lovely breasts. I noticed when you were changing your clothes last night. I hope I have breasts like yours when I finish growing. They're full and round, just like those girls in the screamer movies."

"Dear God," Harper muttered, forcing his eyes and ears away from the pair as his mind again filled with the image of Drina's full, round breasts in the white lace.

Was this how females talked when alone together? Commenting on breasts and stuff as they stripped in front of each other? And if it was . . . well, that was one thing. But he wasn't a girl, and yet neither seemed troubled about having the discussion in front of him. What the hell did that say?

He supposed it said neither of them were thinking of him as a sexual male, and he guessed that was as it should be. Stephanie was too young to think of any male that way . . . he hoped. And it wasn't like Drina was his life mate. The woman was old enough she probably didn't bother much with sex despite Stephanie's efforts to gussy her up like a tart and send her out on the prowl for "hunky guys."

Harper was more than relieved when the women finished in the lingerie department and moved on to actual clothing. At least he was until Stephanie insisted Drina try on a slinky little black dress and model it for them in case she got the chance to go out and "kick up her heels" a bit.

The dress was nothing special . . . until Drina put it on. It looked to him as if Stephanie had given her the wrong size. Drina seemed to be busting out all over the place, her breasts overflowing the cups to the point of almost spilling out, and the slit up the front so high that Harper feared more than thigh would show were she to step up onto anything or sit in it.

"Perfect," Stephanie pronounced, jolting him out of his stupor.

He peered from Drina to Stephanie with disbelief. "Surely it's the wrong size?"

"Actually, it's just my size," Drina said, peering at herself in the mirror.

"But it's—" He paused, mouth open when she turned her back to him. Drina's behind was as generous as her bosom, and he couldn't help noting the way the material clung to her curves . . . or how short the skirt was. Were she to bend over, he was sure the skirt would climb halfway up her hips.

He'd barely had the thought when Stephanie said, "Maybe you should bend over, Drina. We need to be sure it's safe to do that in this dress."

Drina shrugged and bent at the waist as if to pick up something. The skirt didn't rise halfway up her hips as he'd feared, but high enough that he caught a glimpse of her white lace panties.

"It's okay," Stephanie decided. "It only shows a little panty when you do that."

"Then I won't bend over," Drina said dryly as she straightened.

Harper closed his eyes and just managed not to whimper. This was an experience he felt sure he would never forget . . . and definitely never repeat, he thought grimly. Women were crazy.

"I think we should probably get you some FM shoes to go with it when we go looking for winter boots," Stephanie announced, and Drina nodded as she slipped back into the dressing room to return to her jeans and blouse.

"FM shoes?" Harper asked blankly.

"It's what my sister calls high heels," Stephanie explained.

"Oh." He frowned and asked, "Is it a brand or—"

"No. It stands for something, but she'll never tell me what," Stephanie said with a grimace, and then shrugged. "Maybe Drina can tell us. She seemed to know what I was talking about. Oh look! Wouldn't these look darling on her?"

Harper stared at the package of thigh-high stockings Stephanie was now holding up and shook his head with bewilderment. It was like the girl was dressing a hooker Barbie. She seemed eager to get Drina in the slinkiest, sexiest items available. Not that Drina seemed to be fighting the effort. Although, to be fair, the black dress was the only outer clothing that fit that description. The rest of the clothes she'd chosen had been mostly sensible and comfortable jeans, T-shirts, and so on. But every bit of underclothing was downright rated X.

"Girls like to wear pretty things," Stephanie announced with a smile. "My sister, Dani, says it's kind of like a secret. Men don't know what we have on under our clothes. We may look like a librarian or tomboy on the outside, but underneath we can be as secretly sexy and pretty as we please." She turned back to the hose and smiled. "You should have seen the cute little pink panties and bra Drina was wearing last night. I suffered some serious envy when I saw them. I can't wait to wear stuff like that. They looked incredible against her olive skin."

Harper blinked, his mind filling with an image of Drina in pale pink panties and bra, and it did look incredible against her darker skin. Damn, he thought on a sigh as Drina stepped out of the changing room.

"I guess I'll get it. You never know when you'll need to dress up," Drina said lightly, setting the short, black cocktail dress in the cart. "What's left? Coats, boots, a hat, and gloves?"

"Yeah." Stephanie glanced down at the bomber jacket she wore and winced. "Tiny picked this up for me yesterday, which was really sweet, because if not I wouldn't have had a coat at all. But it's kind of big and really, just not my style."

"Hmm." Drina eyed the overlarge coat and nodded. "We can get you another one."

"Thank you!" Stephanie beamed and whirled to lead the way.

Harper began to push the cart after her. When Drina fell into step beside him, he cleared his throat, and commented, "Judging by all you've chosen, you don't appear to have brought much with you on this trip."

"Oh, well, I was only expecting to be at the wedding, spend a couple of days in New York, and then head back to Spain. I didn't count on this added bit," she explained wryly.

Harper nodded; he'd thought as much by the size of her suitcase when he'd seen it last night. "So they roped you in at the last minute?"

She nodded, but smiled. "I don't mind, though. So far it's been fun. Stephanie is . . ." Drina hesitated, and then shrugged. "She's really a sweet kid." She grimaced, laughed, and said, "Well, except for the part about being determined that I should find a nice Canadian farm boy to 'play with' while here."

"So that's what all this is about," he said wryly.

Drina nodded. "Ever since she read my mind and saw how my life has been all work and no play, she's been determined I should 'have fun.'"

"She's frighteningly good at reading minds," Harper said solemnly.

"Uncommonly good at it," Drina agreed, her expression troubled. "New turns can't usually read anyone yet, but she not only seems to be able to read new life mates, but non–life mates too and even those of us centuries or millennia older than her." She bit her lip, and admitted, "Actually, she says she's not reading minds at all, but that we're all talking into her head."

"Hmm." Harper frowned at the words.

"Oh, Drina! These are pretty, and they're so soft!" Stephanie cried, drawing their attention as she rubbed a pair of red gloves against her cheek. They had reached the outerwear section.

Forcing away the concern on her face, Drina

moved to join the girl, leaving Harper to follow. He did so more slowly, his mind consumed with Drina's words as he watched the two females consider the options in gloves, hats, and scarves.

He now understood Stephanie's apparent determination to dress Drina up in the hottest gear she could find. The kid probably felt guilty for the woman being roped into helping look out for her and wanted to repay her in some way. Or perhaps in reading Drina's mind she'd picked up on the soul-deep loneliness that most immortals suffered. Either way, it seemed her response was a desire to find Drina a boyfriend while she was here. The girl still thought like a mortal and didn't realize that such relationships weren't really very satisfying to their kind. To her, a female probably wasn't complete without a boyfriend on her arm. And apparently Drina was humoring the girl.

But the bit about Stephanie claiming not to read minds, but that everyone else was talking into her head was troubling. The truth was that unless an immortal had just found their life mate, their thoughts were usually more private, and they had to be read. While it was rude to do so, immortals did it all the time, which meant they all had to guard their thoughts when around others. But he'd never heard of someone experiencing what Stephanie claimed. Harper pondered what it might mean as the girls picked out hats, scarves, and gloves, and moved on to coats. It wasn't until Stephanie led them toward the boot section that Harper recalled her words while Drina had been in the changing room.

Moving the cart up beside Drina, he asked, "What are FM shoes?"

"What?" She glanced around with a start.

"FM shoes," he repeated. "Stephanie says that's what her sister calls high heels, but she didn't know why and suggested I should ask you. What does the FM stand for?"

"Ah." For some reason the question caused a struggle on Drina's face. It looked as if she was trying not to smile or laugh. Managing to fight off the urge, she turned and picked up a pair of impossibly high-heeled shoes from the row they were walking down and held them up. "These are FM shoes."

Harper peered at the shoes, black, strappy, and with heels that had to be six inches high. They were sexy as hell and would probably go well with the black dress she'd picked up earlier. "And the FM stands for?"

Drina cleared her throat and tossed the shoe, along with its partner in the cart, then announced, "Fuck Me," and turned to walk over to Stephanie.

Harper stared after her, stunned. For one moment he thought she'd actually been making a request of him, and he found he wasn't averse to the idea. But then his reason kicked in. Pushing the cart quickly forward, he gasped, "Are you serious?"

Drina nodded.

"Why?" he asked with amazement.

Her eyebrows rose, and then she leaned in and picked up one shoe. "Well, look at it. It's sexy as hell, could turn a guy on at twenty paces." She shrugged.

"But women actually call them that?" he asked with disbelief.

"It's what they are," she said with amusement. Seeing his lack of comprehension, her expression turned pitying, and she said, "You don't think we wear them because they're comfortable, do you? Because I can guarantee you they aren't. We pick them purely to attract the male of the species. The same reason we pick bustiers and anything else terribly uncomfortable but appealing to the male eye."

"Huh." Harper gave himself a shake. It had been centuries since he'd bothered reading a mortal woman's mind. Well, really, it had been centuries since he'd bothered with mortal women at all. He simply hadn't been interested until Jenny, and he hadn't been able to read her mind. Still, he supposed he shouldn't be surprised at these revelations. Even back then, women had done all sorts of things to attract mates: lead makeup, corsets, etc. They hadn't openly admitted that was what it was about, though. It seemed women nowadays were much more frank on the subject if they actually called high heels Fuck Me shoes. It occurred to him that the world might be a much more interesting place now than it had been.

"I'm sorry," Drina said suddenly, and patted his shoulder as if he might need soothing. "I guess we need to try to remember that this is all alien to you. I'm afraid we just keep forgetting you're a guy and have been thinking of you as one of the girls."

"One of the girls," Harper muttered, as she moved off to join Stephanie again. The thought was rather dismaying. It wasn't that he was interested in Drina and wanted her to think of him in that way, but—

"Christ." He breathed with disgust. Being considered one of the girls was damned lowering.

"That guy over there likes you, Drina."

Harper raised his gaze from the menu he'd been reviewing and followed Stephanie's gesture to a table where three men in jeans and T-shirts sat. One of them, a rugged-looking fellow of twentysomething was looking their way, his eyes sliding over Drina with definite interest.

"He doesn't even know me," Drina said with amusement, not bothering to glance up from her menu.

"Okay, he thinks you're hot," Stephanie amended with exasperation, and then taunted, "You should hear what he's thinking."

"Oh?" she asked mildly, turning the page of her menu.

"Yeah. He really likes the boots. I told you they were hot."

Harper just managed not to bend to peer under the table and get another look at the thigh-high boots. Stephanie had talked Drina into getting them, assuring her they would keep her warm over her jeans and be "hot" too. Drina had replaced her running shoes with them in the car on the way here. She'd lain across the backseat and kicked her legs in the air as she'd pulled them on over her tight-legged jeans in the back while he drove. She'd also switched her light coat for the much warmer long coat she'd bought and tugged on her new red hat and gloves. She was now properly attired for a Canadian winter.

"Oh, man, that's just gross," Stephanie said suddenly, and Harper glanced to the girl to see her wrinkling her nose with distaste.

Frowning, he followed her gaze to the "interested" mortal and slipped into the fellow's mind. His eyes widened incredulously at the guy's imaginings. He certainly did like the thigh-high boots. In fact, the fellow was imagining Drina in the boots and nothing else and doing things to her that . . . well, he wouldn't say they were gross, but they were disturbingly hot images and made him withdraw quickly from the guy's mind and scowl at him irritably.

"What are you going to order?" Drina asked Stephanie, no doubt to change the subject.

"A club sandwich and fries with gravy on the side," Stephanie answered promptly.

"Hmm. I guess I'll get the same," Drina decided, closing her menu.

"You eat?" Harper asked with surprise.

"On occasion," Drina said with a shrug. "Besides, we can't make Stephanie eat alone."

"No," he agreed on a murmur, lowering his gaze to his menu again and looking to see what a club sandwich was before announcing, "I'll have the same."

"So," Stephanie said once their waitress had left with their orders, "if you guys are both so old and both from Europe, how come you've never met before?"

Drina appeared surprised by the question and chuckled. "Sweetie, Europe is a big place. I'm from Spain. Harper is from Germany." She shrugged. "It's like suggesting someone from Oklahoma should know someone from Illinois just because they're from the United States, or that someone from BC should know someone from Ontario because they're both in Canada."

"Yeah, but you guys are immortals and as old as the hills. Don't immortals hang out together, or have a secret club, or something? You'd think you'd at least have met each other before this," she said, and then added, "Besides, I thought you guys move around every ten years or something. You haven't always lived in Spain, have you?"

"No," Drina admitted wryly, and shrugged. "Egypt, Spain, England, and then Spain again. Mostly Spain, though."

"Why?" Stephanie asked curiously.

"My family is there," she said simply. "And until recently, women didn't exactly wander the world on their own. They were expected to stay with family for protection."

"Even immortals?" Stephanie asked with a frown.

"Especially immortals," Drina assured her dryly. "You have to realize that we have it drilled into our head from birth not to draw attention to ourselves or our people, and an unattached female on her own would definitely have drawn attention through most of history."

"Oh, right," Stephanie murmured, and then her gaze shifted to Harper. "What about you? You aren't a girl."

The words brought a wry smile to his lips. After a day of being considered "one of the girls," it seemed that, at least Stephanie, was finally acknowledging he wasn't . . . if only for this conversation.

"I traveled more than Drina appears to have. I was born in what is now Germany, but have lived in many European countries, not England and Spain though. I've also lived in America and now Canada."

"So, if it weren't for Drina's having to help look out for me, you two might never have met."

"Perhaps not," Harper acknowledged, and found himself thinking that would have been a great pity. Drina was an interesting woman.

The food came then, and Harper turned his attention to the sandwich and fries placed before him. The brown sandwich, pale sticks, and brown gelatinous liquid in the small bowl on the side didn't look particularly appetizing. Harper had been a chef when he was much younger and felt presentation was important, but the food smelled surprisingly delicious.

Curious, he picked up his fork, stabbed one of the fries, and raised it to his lips, but paused when he saw Stephanie dipping hers in the small bowl of thick liquid on the side of her plate. Emulating her, he dipped his own fry in what he supposed was the "gravy on the side," and popped it in his mouth. His eyes widened as his taste buds burst to life. It was surprisingly good, he decided, and stabbed, dipped, and ate another before picking up half his sandwich and taking a bite of that as well.

"Aren't you going to finish your fries?" Stephanie asked.

Seeing the way the teenager was greedily eyeing her plate, Drina grinned and pushed it toward her, saying, "Go ahead. I'm done."

Stephanie immediately fell on the remaining fries.

Drina watched enviously as the girl gobbled them, almost sorry she'd given them up. But it had been a long time since she'd eaten, and she simply couldn't fit another bite in her belly. She'd been pushing it to manage half the sandwich and fries.

Her gaze slid to Harper and she noted that while he'd managed perhaps three quarters of his meal, he was slowing. His stomach wasn't big enough either.

"You should go out tonight."

Drina glanced to Stephanie with surprise to see her pointing a fry at her as she spoke.

"Seriously. It's been decades since you've gone out socially. You work and visit your family and that's it. You really need to get out and have some fun."

"I have fun," she assured her defensively.

"No you don't. I can read your mind, remember? You used to love to dance, but you haven't been dancing since those Gone-With-the-Wind-gowns were all the rage."

Drina bit her lip, wondering what the girl was up to now. She actually had been out since then. She had a couple of good female hunter friends back in Spain, and they often went to an immortal club called Noche and danced the night away to relieve some of the stress of the job. She didn't doubt for a minute that Stephanie had read that from her mind, so she was up to something. Again.

"You should drive into London tonight and hit a

bar and just let your hair down. Dance your feet off. It would be good for you."

"I can't drive," Drina reminded her dryly.

"Then Harper should take you," she shot back with satisfaction. "He needs to get out as much as you do. He hasn't gone anywhere in more than a year and a half except a couple of times when Elvi and Victor pretty much dragged him out."

Harper stilled, midchew, his expression becoming alarmed. "Oh, I don't know—"

"Yeah, I know, you'd rather hide in the house and go back to nursing your wounds," Stephanie interrupted. "But look how much better getting out today has made you feel."

Harper blinked.

"I really think it would do you both a lot of good. It's certainly better than acting like a couple of turtles."

"Turtles?" Harper asked with a frown.

"Yeah, you immortals all pull into yourselves and hide out at home rather than even consider a social life." She shook her head. "Seriously, I know you all have this thing about life mates and all, and I know you two aren't life mates, but that doesn't mean you can't have fun, does it?" She glared from one to the other, and then said, "If anything, it should free you up to have more fun. Drina, you're too old for Harper to read, and you're also too polite to read him, so you could both relax around each other. On top of that, because you *aren't* life mates, you won't be all worried about impressing each other and can just relax and enjoy each other's company and *have some fun*."

She let that sink in, and then sat back in her seat, and announced militantly, "Maybe it's because I'm new to this, but I plan to date like crazy before I settle down with any life mate. And you two should as well. You're both lonely and miserable. What can it hurt to go out and let your hair down?"

Drina stared at the girl, amazement sliding through her. Stephanie was frighteningly brilliant. By saying they weren't life mates, she'd just cleared the way for Harper to agree to an outing. And by saying that age was the reason Harper wouldn't be able to read her, she'd eliminated the possibility that he might try to read her, find out he couldn't, and panic. She'd basically just cleared away any protest Harper might come up with for spending time with her and freed him to do so if he wished without feeling guilty that he was enjoying himself when Jenny was dead.

"I do feel better," Harper said quietly, and sounded surprised by the realization. "I guess this change in routine did do me some good."

Stephanie nodded solemnly. "And really, you'd be doing me a favor. I'll feel awful if the only thing Drina sees of Canada is the inside of Casey Cottage and the local Wal-Mart."

"Hmm. That would be a shame," Harper murmured, and then pushed his plate away and nodded. "All right. We'll go dancing tonight at the Night Club in Toronto."

Drina blinked in surprise. Toronto was two hours away. Shaking her head, she said, "No. I can't be gone that long. I have to be back by bedtime for Stephanie."

"Anders is on nights," Stephanie reminded her. "I'm his problem then."

"Yes, but we're roommates so that no one can slip in and take you from your bed."

"And so I don't slip out and run away," Stephanie said dryly.

Drina scowled. So much for Stephanie's not knowing they knew about the possibility.

"It's okay though," Stephanie said quickly. "I'll just snooze on the couch in front of the television until you guys get back. That way Anders can keep an eye on me, and you can still get out for a bit."

"It's set then," Harper decided, glancing around for their waitress. "I'll pay this and we can head back to the house. I need to call to have my helicopter come for us and—"

"Helicopter?" Drina interrupted with surprise.

"Harper's mad rich," Stephanie told her with amusement. "But then so are you." She shrugged. "I guess when you guys live as long as you do, you eventually build up a fortune."

"Not everyone," Drina assured her.

"Whatever," Stephanie said, standing up. "I have to pee before we go."

Nodding, Drina pushed her chair back at once. Smiling at Harper, she murmured, "Thank you for buying lunch. We'll meet you at the car."

She waited long enough to see Harper nod before hurrying after Stephanie.

Four

There was a woman in the bathroom cleaning it. Drina offered her a polite smile and leaned against the wall while Stephanie tended to her business in one of the stalls, and then washed her hands at the sink. She followed silently as Stephanie then led the way outside, but as they approached Harper's car and she saw that he hadn't yet returned, she finally said, "Stephanie—"

"Please don't," Stephanie said quickly, turning to face her. "I know you're feeling guilty about what you think is our manipulating Harper, but it's for his own good. And we aren't tricking him into anything. We're just making him feel safe enough for his true feelings to grow without his guilt over Jenny's death getting in the way."

"But—"

"Please," Stephanie pleaded. "Please don't ruin everything. I like you. I like you both. The two of you deserve to be happy. Besides, I've had more fun today than I've had since—" She paused, a cloud crossing over her face before she ducked her head.

Drina sighed, knowing she'd nearly said before Leonius had attacked her, and wasn't at all surprised. From what she'd been told, the girl had been pretty miserable since the turn, struggling with her losses and the adjustments she'd had to make. But this day had been one full of fun and laughter. For all of them.

Drina closed her eyes briefly, then reached out to rub one hand lightly over the girl's upper arm. "I had a good time today too, and it's been a long time since I've been able to say that."

"I know," Stephanie whispered, and then lifted her face to smile crookedly. "Your surface memories of the recent past are pretty grim. You put on a good face and seem cheerful and happy, but your days are spent hunting bad guys and mourning unwilling turns you have to capture or kill. And I know you struggle every day with feeling guilty that you have to do it. You think that if you'd just tracked their rogue sires down a bit faster, they might have been saved before they were turned, or at least before they were made to do something that marked them for death." She grimaced. "It seems a pretty grim life."

"It is," Drina said quietly.

"Then why do you do it?"

She smiled wryly and shrugged. "Someone has to."

"But it kills you a little bit inside every day," Stephanie said quietly.

Drina didn't deny that, but simply said, "It kills

all rogue hunters a little bit inside every day. But for me . . ." She sighed and said, "Maybe, just maybe, my actions have prevented one or two other young girls, like you, from going through what you are." She smiled crookedly. "Surely that makes it worthwhile?"

Before she could respond, they both heard the restaurant door opening and glanced around to see Harper approaching.

"Sorry, I forgot I'd locked the car," Harper murmured, hitting the button on his key fob.

"That's all right. We just got here ourselves," Drina assured him, moving to the back passenger door as Stephanie opened the front door.

"Thank you for lunch and for taking us shopping today, Harper," Stephanie said moments later, when they pulled into the driveway at Casey Cottage. "I had fun."

"I'm glad." He murmured absently as he eased his car into the tight space on one side of the two-car garage.

Stephanie then turned in her seat to peer at Drina in the back, and said, "While you guys are out tonight, I'll check the Internet and look for things for us to do tomorrow."

"Okay," Drina agreed easily, undoing her seat belt.

"Things to do tomorrow?" Harper asked, but the vehicle had stopped, and Drina was already slipping out, leaving Stephanie to answer. However, she got out just as quickly, and Harper followed, repeating the question as he closed the door. "What do you mean, things to do tomorrow?"

"Well, it wasn't just that we needed warmer clothes and stuff that made us go out today," Stephanie explained, walking around the front of the car toward the stairs into the house. "We were worried about waking up everyone if we stayed in. That will still be a problem tomorrow, so we'll have to find someplace to go or something to do to entertain ourselves." She paused at the top of the steps with a hand on the door and pursed her lips. "I guess we're going to be pretty limited without a car, though." Sighing, she shrugged and pulled the screen door open. "I'll figure out something."

Stephanie started into the house then, and Drina was directly behind her, but Harper caught her arm and drew her to a halt. The moment the door closed behind Stephanie, he asked with concern, "Do you think it's wise to take her away from the house?"

"She's not a prisoner, Harper. We can't keep her locked up in the house. Besides, she was sent down here to live as normal a life as possible," she pointed out, and then added, "And I did call Lucian first to make sure it was all right. He's pretty sure they weren't followed from New York, and she's safe. Apparently Anders and I are just a precaution and babysitters until Elvi and Victor return."

"Oh," he murmured, releasing her arm. "Well that's good news. That she's safe, I mean."

"Yes," Drina agreed, and turned back to the door, only to back up a step when it suddenly swung open and Stephanie reappeared, her coat already off but her eyes wide.

"We forgot our clothes!" she squawked with disbelief.

Drina laughed at her expression and turned away to slip past Harper and off the stairs. "Close the door; the garage isn't heated, and you aren't wearing your coat. I'll get the bags."

She was at the trunk of the car before Drina realized she didn't have keys, but Harper was already there beside her, handling the matter. They each took half the bags and carted them into the house. Stephanie was immediately on them, taking as many bags as she could handle and traipsing out of the room to dump them in the dining room before returning for the rest.

"I put the kettle on to make cocoa," she announced as she gathered the rest of the bags and turned away again. "Hurry up and get your boots and stuff off. We can have cocoa and cookies while we sort through all this and decide what you should wear tonight, Drina. I think it should be the black dress and FM shoes with those fishnet stockings."

"What fishnet stockings?" Drina asked with surprise, but Stephanie had already rushed out of the entry again.

"The ones she threw in the cart while you were in the changing room," Harper answered for her, his voice dry.

"Oh," Drina murmured, and wondered if she'd have the nerve to wear the outfit she'd bought today. She'd only really allowed Stephanie to convince her to buy the dress and shoes to make sure Harper was thinking about what she would look like in them. But really, they weren't quite her style. The dress was a little too low cut at the neckline, and a little too high at the thigh, and the shoes looked like they'd be killer to wear. Fortunately, she did have a dress and shoes of her own with her. Although she had to admit it was a bit conservative since she'd brought it for the wedding. It wasn't really Night Club material either . . . at least not if the Night Club was anything like Noche.

Sighing, she hung up her coat, and quickly shucked the new, ridiculously high-heeled, thigh-high boots that she'd also allowed Stephanie to talk her into. She then padded into the kitchen, leaving Harper still working on the laces of his second boot.

Stephanie was pulling down mugs from the cupboard, presumably for the cocoa, but Tiny was also there. The big mortal was bent over and peering into the oven at something that was emitting really delicious smells.

"You're up early," Drina murmured, blinking as she took in his present garb. The man wore flowered oven mitts and a matching apron. He should have looked ridiculous, but since he was wearing only jeans and his bare chest was barely covered by the apron on top . . . well it was oddly sexy, she decided with a slight shake of the head.

"I'm mortal," Tiny reminded her with amusement. "Daytime is my time."

"Yes, but I thought you and Mirabeau—"

"Tiny and I conked out around four in the morning and were up by noon," Mirabeau announced, entering the kitchen from the living room. Her expression was grim as she asked, "Where were you guys?"

"We went shopping and out for lunch," Stephanie announced happily, busily dumping a pale brown powder into the five mugs she'd collected.

When Mirabeau raised a cold eyebrow in her direction, Drina said, "Just to Wal-Mart, and I called Lucian first to be sure it was all right." She then added, "I apologize for not leaving a note, but I thought you were day sleepers and expected we'd be back long before anyone woke up."

"See, I told you there was nothing to worry about, Beau," Tiny chided gently as he retrieved a tray of little circles from the oven. "Now stop looking at Drina as if she murdered your kitty and come have a cookie."

Mirabeau blinked at Tiny's words and then relaxed. She even managed a smile for Drina. "Sorry. I was just worried when we got up, and you were all gone. The only reason I didn't have Lucian on the phone and Teddy Brunswick out looking for you was because Tiny checked the garage and saw that Harper's car was gone."

"I should have left a note, and will in future," Drina assured her.

"And your cell number too," Mirabeau said at once, moving over to slide an arm around Tiny and press a kiss to his bare arm. Her voice was somewhat distracted when she added, "We should have exchanged numbers the minute you guys arrived last night. Then I could have called you at least."

"I'll write mine down now," Drina decided, and

moved to the refrigerator, where a magnetized note-pad took up a corner on the front. She immediately scribbled down her number on the pad, and then turned to hand the pen to Mirabeau, saying, "I don't know Anders's number, but we can have him put his here as well when he gets up, and then anyone who wants it on their phone can do so, but it will be on the fridge if anyone needs it."

Nodding, Mirabeau slid away from Tiny, took the pen she offered, and then pulled a cell phone out of her back pocket.

"Both our numbers are new. We lost our phones in New York, so Lucian sent us new ones," she ad-mitted on a grimace and began to punch buttons, presumably in search of her phone number.

"My phone's in my back pocket, Beau," Tiny rum-bled as he began to slide cookies off the metal cookie sheet and onto a plate.

Mirabeau immediately moved over to slide her hand in and dig out his phone. Drina turned away to hide a smile when she saw that while Mirabeau was retrieving the phone with one hand, she hadn't been able to resist gliding her other hand under the top of his apron and over his bare chest.

"What smells so good?" Harper asked, coming into the kitchen from the pantry.

"Chocolate chip pecan cookies," Tiny announced, his voice gruff as Mirabeau retrieved her hands and his phone and turned back to the refrigerator.

"That sounds interesting," Harper decided, and moved forward to peruse the little discs. "Can I have one?"

Tiny paused and glanced at Harper with surprise, "Well, yeah sure, that's why I made them."

Nodding, Harper took one and lifted it to his mouth to try a bite. Eyes widening as he swallowed, he pronounced, "Mmmm. Good."

Tiny stared at him silently. When his gaze then slid to her, Drina promptly turned away to begin collecting the Wal-Mart bags from where Stephanie had set them. But she heard him say, "Have another." And she glanced over her shoulder to see Tiny watching the man closely.

"Thanks." Harper took a second cookie, and glanced to where Stephanie was hovering over her cups of cocoa. "Can I help you with that?"

"Well, it's ready except for the water, but if you'll pour the water in when the kettle boils, I could help Drina carry the bags up to our room."

"Okay," he said agreeably.

"Thanks." Stephanie grinned at him and rushed around the counter to Drina's side.

"I'll help with the bags while you boys oversee the food and drink," Mirabeau announced, as Drina straightened and headed for the stairs. She had just started up when she heard Tiny murmur, "So you're eating again, Harper?"

"Oh, yeah, I started a year and a half ago when I first came to Port Henry and met Jenny."

"Your life mate?" Tiny asked.

"Yes, meeting a life mate reawakens old appetites, of course, and I guess they don't just die if the life mate does. They'll go away again eventually, but it will take a while I suppose."

"But I didn't think you'd been eating since Jenny died," Tiny said mildly.

Drina paused on the stairs, waiting until Harper answered with, "I guess I was too depressed to be bothered, but going out with the girls today perked me up some, and my appetites are back."

"Hmmm," Tiny murmured, and Drina continued up the stairs just as Stephanie and Mirabeau came out of the dining room and started up the stairs behind her.

"Okay, spill," Mirabeau said firmly as soon as they were in the room Drina and Stephanie were sharing.

"Yes, Drina, show her what you got," Stephanie said lightly, dropping her bags and hurrying to close the door behind Mirabeau.

"I didn't mean—" Mirabeau began.

"She knows," Drina pointed out on a sigh. The kid seemed to know everything. There probably wasn't a thought in this house the girl didn't hear.

"I just wanted to close the door so the guys don't hear," Stephanie said in a hushed voice as she moved past Mirabeau to Drina's bed. Sprawling on the twin bed, she smiled at Mirabeau, and said, "Marguerite picked Drina for Lucian to send just as she suggested Tiny and you bring me here."

Mirabeau's eyebrows rose as she recognized the significance of that. "Harper's your life mate?"

"It would seem so," Drina said wearily, dumping the nearest bag on the bed and beginning to sort through the clothes that spilled out.

"Christ. That means we have another distracted

hunter guarding Stephanie," Mirabeau muttered with disgust. "What was Lucian thinking sending you here if—"

"Because he doesn't care if I'm distracted."

"What?" Mirabeau asked with surprise.

"He planned to send someone named Bricker down here to replace me the moment Harper and I acknowledged we were life mates, but it turns out there's been a sighting of Leonius in the States, which means you guys weren't followed. Stephanie's safe, and Anders and I are just—" Drina snapped her mouth closed as she realized what she was about to say, but Stephanie finished for her.

"Babysitters," the girl said with amusement, and then reassured Drina, "It's okay. I'm not upset."

"Huh." Mirabeau muttered and leaned against the dresser drawers at the foot of the bed. She was silent for a moment as she took it all in, and then glanced to Drina and asked, "So what's all this nonsense Harper was spouting downstairs about his reawakened appetites being leftovers from Jenny?"

"He believes it," Stephanie said simply, sitting up to help Drina sort the clothes they'd bought.

Mirabeau narrowed her eyes. "Why? Hasn't he tried to read you?"

Drina shrugged. "Probably. But I'm older than him by quite a bit. He wouldn't have been able to read me anyway."

"And you've tried to read him?" Mirabeau asked.

"The minute I met him," she admitted quietly. "And I can't."

"Why haven't you told him?" she asked at once.

Drina took in Mirabeau's grim face with a sigh. It looked like she had some explaining to do.

"The girls are taking a while," Tiny commented as he helped carry the cookies and cocoa to the dining-room table.

"They're probably *oohing* and *ahhing* over what Stephanie and Drina bought today," Harper said with amusement. "Speaking of which, a bit of advice; if Mirabeau decides to take Stephanie shopping— just hand over the keys and let them go. You'll save yourself some humiliation and several shocks."

"Humiliation and shocks?" Tiny asked, a smile pulling at his lips.

"Hmm. I spent the day being considered 'one of the girls' and learning things I never wanted to know about women," he said dryly.

"Like what?" Tiny asked curiously.

"Do you know what they call high heels?" Harper asked, not expecting him to know.

"Ah, yes," Tiny sat back with a nod. "Good old FMs."

"You knew about that?" he asked with surprise. "Do you know what FM stands for?"

Tiny nodded again, and then explained, "My best friend most of my adult life has been a female . . . and, come to think of it, she's probably treated me more like a girlfriend than a guy friend," he admitted with an unconcerned chuckle.

"Hmm." Harper shook his head. "Well, I've never been treated like a girlfriend in all my life. It was a bit lowering."

"Nah." Tiny shook his head. "It's a compliment. It means they don't see you as sexually threatening. You're a friend rather than a man friend."

"And that's a compliment?" Harper asked doubtfully.

"It is if you're only interested in being a friend," he reasoned, and then shrugged, and added, "But I suppose if your interests lie in a more sexual relationship, then it's probably less flattering. Fortunately, I never had that kind of interest in my friend, Jackie. She's more like a combination buddy and sister type for me."

"Jackie? Vincent's wife? The one who is flying in at the end of the week to help oversee your turn?" Harper asked. The big man had called Jackie last night to tell her he would be turning soon. Apparently, his friend had insisted on being there for it, so they'd had to set a date and time. The end of the week had been the decision.

"Yes." Tiny smiled faintly, and then they both glanced toward the stairs as they heard a door open and the chatter and clatter of the girls returning. Harper smiled, finding himself oddly eager to see them again. The day just seemed brighter with the girls around.

"You look gorgeous." Stephanie sighed where she lay on her bed, hugging her pillow.

Drina surveyed herself and thought that she looked like a prostitute on the loose.

"You do not," Stephanie and Mirabeau said as one, making her scowl and turn to the older woman.

"It's bad enough her reading me, but you too?" she asked with disgust.

Mirabeau grinned and shrugged. "You're an open book at the moment. It's hard not to."

Drina scowled and turned back to the mirror to sigh at her reflection, but her mind was on the conversation that had taken place in this room earlier in the afternoon. Much to her surprise, once Drina and Stephanie had explained things, Mirabeau had decided they were doing the right thing and had offered to help.

Actually, that had been something of a relief. Drina had found it increasingly difficult not to feel guilty about the head game they were playing with Harper as the day had worn on. But Mirabeau's assurance that it was probably the smartest move had made her feel a little better.

Now, however, she stared in the mirror at a woman she hardly recognized and wondered what the hell she was doing.

"This is the style nowadays," Stephanie assured her, sitting up on the bed, her expression earnest.

"She's right," Mirabeau agreed. "This is what they wear at the bars and clubs."

"So, everyone dresses like prostitutes now? What's it called? Hooker Chic?" Drina asked dryly, tugging at the low neckline of the black dress she'd somehow been convinced to wear after all.

Mirabeau chuckled at her acerbic words. It was Stephanie who said, "Stop fussing with the neckline. It isn't that low. You're just used to more conservative clothes."

Drina couldn't argue that point. She'd always been self-conscious at what she considered a too generous chest and so tended toward high necklines or even turtlenecks.

Sighing, she started to turn away from the mirror and immediately paused to peer down at her high heels. "I won't be able to dance in these."

"Then kick them off before you step on the dance floor," Mirabeau suggested. "I've seen women do that."

"Is that the helicopter?" Stephanie asked, suddenly leaping off the bed and hurrying to the window as they became aware of a distant whir. Pulling the curtains aside, she peered out at the sky, and then gave an excited little hop. "It is!"

"Time to go," Mirabeau said cheerfully, moving to open the bedroom door.

"I hope I don't have to walk far in these," Drina muttered, following her.

Releasing the curtains, Stephanie laughed and hurried after them, saying, "At least you won't have to worry about blisters. The nanos will heal them as quickly as they form."

Drina didn't bother to respond; she was too busy worrying about the curving staircase ahead and making it to the ground floor without taking a header. Seriously, she really shouldn't have bought these shoes or the dress. She should have bought something she would be comfortable in. But who knew Stephanie the great puppet master-cum-cupid, would maneuver Harper into taking her out tonight?

"Never underestimate the great Stephanie," Mirabeau said with amusement from in front of her.

"Stop that," Drina snapped. Good Lord, she definitely didn't like being read.

Mirabeau just laughed, but she managed to subdue her amusement as they reached the main floor and headed into the dining room.

"Oh good, the helicopter is here and—"

Drina tore her eyes away from watching her feet and glanced to Harper in question when his words died abruptly. He was staring at her, his mouth open, her coat in one hand and the other half-lifted toward the window as if he'd been gesturing outside to where the helicopter was. He looked rather stunned. She wasn't sure that was a good thing. He'd already seen her in the dress. It shouldn't elicit this effect, whatever this effect was. Horror was her guess.

"It's not horror," Stephanie hissed with exasperation behind her. "It's awe. While he saw the dress, he didn't see the dress, stockings, heels, jewelry, makeup, and hair. You've taken his breath away."

"Here's your coat," Tiny announced, taking the long faux leather coat from Harper's unresisting hand and crossing the room to hold it open for her.

"Thank you," Drina murmured, slipping first one arm and then the other into the sleeves.

"You're welcome," Tiny said cheerfully, and she swore his eyes were twinkling as he shifted his gaze from her to Harper, who was still silent but had closed his mouth and lowered his arm. "Well, you two kids have fun."

Drina smiled wryly at the man, though she couldn't have said whether it was at his calling them kids when they were both pretty much ancient, or at the suggestion they have fun when she was positive that was impossible.

"Right," Harper said, snapping to life as she reached his side. "The helicopter landed just across the street in the schoolyard." His gaze dropped to her heels and turned, concerned. "Can you manage in those shoes? It's icy out there."

"Maybe you should wear the thigh-high boots, instead, Drina," Stephanie suggested suddenly. "Those are FMs too, but would have more traction. They'd also be warmer."

"Thigh-high boots would work with that dress," Mirabeau decided. "In fact, they'd be sexy as heck with it."

"The shoes are fine," Drina insisted, flushing with embarrassment at all the attention. Everyone in the room was now staring at her legs in the fishnet stockings. Fishnet, for God's sake! The only thing she could think of that would be sluttier was the thigh-high boots.

"Well, I suppose Harper can carry you if you find it too slippery," Stephanie said cheerfully.

"Right. The boots then," Drina snapped, tossing a glare at the teenager as she moved out into the pantry to get them. She almost tried to don them right there, leaning against the wall, but gave up that idea when she nearly fell over just trying to remove the shoes.

Sighing with exasperation, she carried the boots

back into the dining room and sat down to quickly remove her shoes. She then tugged on first one boot, and the other, trying to ignore just how much leg she was flashing while doing so. Drina then stood up and moved back to Harper's side.

"All set," she said with forced cheer.

Harper tore his eyes away from her boots, swallowed, nodded, and then took her arm and ushered her to the door, muttering, "Don't wait up."

She was crossing the deck when Drina decided she was glad to be wearing the boots after all. It was cold as the dickens, and the boots at least kept her legs from freezing. They were also easier to walk in than the shoes, which were probably an inch taller. Not that the boots didn't have high heels too, but they were at least manageable. She'd felt like she was on stilts in the shoes.

Drina eyed the helicopter as they crossed the street. She then glanced around, noting that traffic had slowed to a stop, and people were looking out the windows of the surrounding houses. As transportation went, it definitely wasn't your low-profile choice. By her guess, every phone in town would be ringing before they'd lifted off.

Heck, half of them were probably already ringing, she thought wryly, as they ducked to rush under the blades to the helicopter door.

Five

No one had mentioned how long the trip to Toronto would be by helicopter, and Drina wasn't wearing a watch, so couldn't check, but it didn't seem to take long. Though that might have been because she was busy gazing wide-eyed down at the passing lights. She'd expected they would land in another school-yard once they reached Toronto, so was a bit startled when they set down on the top of a building.

It obviously wasn't their destination, however. After riding down in an elevator, Harper led her through a huge, majestic lobby and outside to the curb, where a car waited. Drina sighed as she settled against the warm, cushioned seats. She listened absently as Harper spoke to the driver, and then they were moving.

"The Night Club doesn't do much in the way of food," Harper explained as he settled back in the seat next to her. "So I booked a table at a restaurant for supper. I hope that's all right?"

"Of course," Drina said with a smile. "Actually, now that you mention it, I am rather hungry."

"So am I. Now we just have to hope that this restaurant is good," he said wryly. "I called my vice president for suggestions of where to go, not thinking that as an immortal he doesn't eat. He assured me this place is good, though, for what that's worth."

"Your vice president?" Drina asked curiously.

"I have a frozen-food business," he admitted with a self-deprecating grimace. "Silly, I suppose, for an immortal to run one, but I was a cook when I was much younger, and while I eventually lost interest in eating, I never really lost interest in food itself," he admitted, sounding embarrassed. "So my business down through the centuries has always been in some area of food service or other. Pubs, restaurants, and finally, frozen entrees. We've branched out to wine as well the last decade or so."

"Oh, well that's—" Drina paused and glanced out the window as the car slowed and pulled to the curb.

"It wasn't far, but I thought with it being so cold tonight, a car might be the better bet," he explained, and then leaned forward to say something to the driver. She caught what sounded like there was no need for the man to get out and get the door, and something about calling when they were done here, and then Harper opened his door and slid out. By the time Drina slid across the seat, he had turned back and was holding out his hand.

Smiling, she clasped his fingers and lifted one

booted leg and then the other out to the sidewalk, trying not to panic as she felt her skirt slide up her legs. That concern was forgotten, however, as she felt the slippery surface of the sidewalk under her boot. Holding her breath, she stood up, relieved when her feet stayed under her, and she didn't do anything as unglamorous as fall on her butt on the icy concrete.

Harper ushered her a step away from the door, and then turned back to close it. The moment he'd turned away, she gave her skirt a quick tug to put it back where it belonged. By the time he turned back, she had finished and was smiling calmly.

He ushered her inside, and Drina glanced around as he spoke to the maitre d', noting the low lighting, the crisp white linen, blood red candles, and what she would bet was real silver on the tables. Almost all of which seemed occupied. Then Harper was taking her coat and handing it along with his own over to a smiling young man in a black tux who whisked them away as another young man, similarly outfitted, led them through the quiet restaurant to one of the few unoccupied tables she could see.

"Thank you," Drina murmured, accepting the menu offered to her. She then glanced around again as the fellow left. The restaurant was busy, but the atmosphere subdued, soft music playing unobtrusively in the background and the dinner guests speaking in soft tones. A far cry from the restaurant where they'd had their lunch that day. There the music playing had been some form of rock or pop, played loudly enough that people had to speak up to be heard over it. This was nicer, Drina decided, and smiled faintly as she turned her attention to her menu.

"So," Harper said moments later, as their waiter left with their orders. "You know about my little business. How about you? Have you always been a hunter?"

Drina smiled wryly at the "little business" bit. She doubted men with little businesses had helicopters, BMWs, and diamond-encrusted watches like the one Harper was wearing this evening. But she didn't comment on any of that, and merely said, "No."

Harper raised an eyebrow. "No?" he asked with disbelief. "That's it?"

"No, Harper?" she suggested mildly, but knew her eyes were twinkling with amusement and gave up teasing him. "Okay. Let's see . . ." She considered her past, and then smiled wryly and shook her head. "Well, I was a perfume maker, Amazone, concubine, a duchess, a pirate, a madam, and then a hunter."

Harper's eyebrows had slid up his forehead as she rattled off her résumé. Now he cleared his throat and said, "Right, let's start at the beginning. I believe that was a perfume maker?"

Drina chuckled and nodded. "My father first settled in Egypt, my mother was Egyptian. It's where I was born. Women had a lot more freedom there. We were actually considered equal to men, well mostly anyway. Certainly more equal than in other cultures," she added dryly. "We could own businesses, sign contracts, and actually work and make a living rather than be a burden to our fathers or male relatives."

"And you grew up to be a perfume maker," Harper murmured.

"My mother wanted me to be a seshet, a scribe," she explained with a grimace. "But I was fascinated by scent, how the blending of them could create another wholly different aroma and so on." She smiled, and added, "It turns out I was very good at it. The rich came from far and wide to buy my scents. I made a very good living, owned my own large home and servants and all without having to have a man at my side. It was the good life," she said with a grin that faded quickly. Heaving a sigh, she then added, "But the Romans arrived and ruined everything. Those bloody idiots invaded everywhere and brought their more archaic laws with them. Women were not equal in Roman society." She scowled, and then a smile began to tug at her lips again. "I couldn't run a business under their rule, but I could fight. I became a female gladiator. Amazones they called us."

"After the Amazons I suppose?"

Drina nodded, and said dryly, "The Romans were as lacking in imagination as they were intelligence."

Harper chuckled at her snide words, and she smiled.

"I wasn't a gladiator long. It just wasn't very challenging. The mortal gladiators were slower, weaker, and easy for me to defeat. It felt like cheating. I did try to avoid 'to the death' fights. That would have just been, well, like slaughtering sheep," she said with distaste.

Harper nodded with understanding, and then

they both fell silent and sat back as their waiter returned with the bottle of wine Harper had ordered. The man opened and poured a small amount in Harper's glass for him to try, and when he nodded approval, quickly filled both glasses. He assured them their meal would follow directly, and then slipped away.

"So beating up mortal gladiators was no fun, and you gave it up to become . . ." He arched an eyebrow. "A concubine, was it?"

Drina chuckled at his expression. "Well, not just like that. Some time passed." She paused to take a sip of wine, smiled as the smooth flavor filled her mouth, and then swallowed, and said, "In retrospect, I think the concubine gig was my rebellious stage. I did behave and live with my family, playing the dutiful daughter for a while before that. But it was very hard. After having tasted the freedom of living and ruling my own life, to suddenly be reduced to a dependent child was very frustrating." She blew out an irritated breath at the memory.

"Ah," Harper nodded with understanding. "Yes, I suppose it would be."

"Perhaps, had I started out living in that sort of society and hadn't tasted freedom, I would have handled it better," Drina said thoughtfully. "But I wasn't, so I didn't take well to being ruled by a man. At least not with Stephano doing the bossing."

"Your father?" Harper asked.

"No, my eldest brother. He was named after our father. Our parents died when the Romans first invaded, and Stephano then became the "head of the family." She grimaced. "He and I are like oil and water. Or we were. We get along well enough now, though." She grinned. "But boy did he pitch a fit over the concubine thing. He even called in Uncle Lucian to deal with me."

Harper's eyebrows rose. "I'm surprised Lucian bothered to intervene."

"Well, it wasn't just the concubine thing. I was a couple of centuries old by then, and I suppose my being a concubine wouldn't have bothered him if I hadn't stepped over the line." She hesitated, and then sighed and said, "As you probably have experienced, mortals become boring as lovers and partners after a while."

He nodded solemnly. "Easily read and controlled, it's hard not to give in to the temptation to do so."

"Yes, well . . ." Drina grimaced. "I'm afraid while I was seen as a concubine, I was really playing puppet master with my lover and kind of ruling the country through him. At least until Uncle Lucian caught wind of it and came to give me hell."

Harper started to laugh, and then asked, "Who was he?"

Drina shook her head at once. It was just too embarrassing to admit. She'd nearly caused a civil uprising with her messing about, which was why her uncle had intervened. "Perhaps I'll tell you one day, but not tonight."

"Hmm, I'll hold you to that," Harper assured her. Drina shrugged.

"So, next was duchess, I believe?" he asked.

"Yes, that was sometime later. I was suitably

chastened after the concubine business. Enough to
behave for a while again. We moved to Spain in that
time, and the Spanish were as bad as the Romans
when it came to women's place in society. But eventually I grew weary of Stephano bossing me about
again. And then I met a very handsome and charming duke, who quite swept me off my feet."

"You've had a life mate?" Harper asked with surprise.

Drina shook her head. "No. But unlike most
people, his thoughts were as lovely and charming
as his words. He was an honest man."

"A rarity," Harper murmured solemnly.

"Yes. I quite liked him, and he truly loved me and
asked me to marry him, and I agreed, promising
myself I wouldn't control him or do anything like I
had with . . . er . . . when I was a concubine."

"And did you?" he asked curiously.

Drina delayed answering by taking another sip of
wine, but when a knowing smile began to tug at his
lips, she gave up trying to think of a way of avoiding the question, and defended, "It's very hard not
to when you know you're right, and he's just being
a stubborn git."

Harper burst out laughing again, and she shook
her head. "Anyway, he was only a duke, so it wasn't
like I was ruling a country and risking civil riots,
but still I felt bad about it every time I did take control. I also felt bad because I was keeping him from
having an heir, which I knew he wanted."

"You didn't wish to have a child with him?"
Harper asked curiously.

Drina frowned and shook her head. "It wasn't that I didn't want to. But it seemed cruel. Our child would be immortal, and aside from the increased risk of revealing what we were, he or she would have to leave when I did. It seemed cruel to give him a child, and then take him or her away."

When he nodded in understanding, she sighed and ran her finger around the rim of her wineglass. "Even with just myself to worry about, it became increasingly hard to hide what I was. I claimed a bad reaction to sun on my skin to explain why I avoided it, but I still needed to slip away to hunt every night, which was much more difficult than I'd expected . . ." She blew out a breath and shrugged. "We were only together a year or so before the duchess had to die."

"How did you manage that?" Harper asked quietly.

"Oh, Uncle Lucian helped me out," she said wryly. "The man always seems to show up when you need him. It's like a sixth sense with him or something."

"I've heard that about him," Harper said and asked curiously, "What did he do?"

"He arranged for a message claiming that Stephano was deathly ill and asking for me at a time when my husband was expected at court. Lucian assured him he'd see me safely there and had booked passage up the coast on a ship. Then he bought a ship, manned it with immortals, and my husband rode with us to port to see us off.

"It was surprisingly emotional," she admitted with a frown. "I mean, I knew I wasn't going to die, but I would be dead to him and never see him again, and I was quite overwrought. Of course, he put it down to concern for my brother and was very sweet and tender. He stayed to watch us sail off." She fell silent as she recalled that morning, and found herself having to blink away a sudden, surprising well of tears. She had been fond of many mortals over the ages, but Roberto had been a special man. She'd loved him dearly and for years had regretted that he hadn't been a possible life mate.

Shaking her head, she finished quickly, "Uncle Lucian had purchased the ship with the sole purpose of sinking it. The ship went down, supposedly with all hands on board, and I, along with everyone else, was presumed dead."

"And then you were back to living with your brother," Harper said with a grimace that suggested he knew how little she would have enjoyed that.

"Not for terribly long," she said with satisfaction. "Just long enough to decide what I wished to do next."

"Which was . . ." He paused, apparently going back through his memory to the list she'd rattled off earlier, and then said uncertainly, "Pirate?"

Drina chuckled. "I was a privateer really, but it's the same thing, just that it was sanctioned by the government. As captain, I had a letter of marque allowing me to attack and rob vessels belonging to enemies of Spain. Royal permission to plunder."

"You were the captain?" he asked with a smile. "And were you Captain Alexander or Alexandrina?"

She smiled. "Alexander, of course. Well, just Alex.

But they thought me a man, or most of them did. As you can guess, few Spanish men would have worked a boat with a female captain, so I dressed as a man. I was very butch," she assured him with a teasing light in her eyes, and then wrinkled her nose. "Or at least I thought I was. It was most disheartening when I read in their minds that most of them thought me fey and probably gay."

Harper threw his head back on a laugh loud enough to draw several glances their way. Drina didn't care, she just smiled.

"I imagine you were a very good pirate," he said finally, and she chuckled.

"I'm not sure if that's a compliment or not."

"A compliment," he assured her. "You're clever enough, and had the fighting background for it."

Drina nodded. "Yes, we were very successful. But I eventually grew tired of watching my men die."

Harper arched an eyebrow as he picked up his wineglass.

She shrugged and picked up her own glass. Turning it in her hands, she said, "They were all very skilled, of course, and I insisted they train daily, but they were mortal. They weren't as fast or strong, and didn't have the "healthy constitution" or quick healing I enjoyed." She sighed. "I lost a lot of good men over the years, and finally decided enough was enough. It was time anyway. They were aging, I wasn't, and I had taken a wound or two that should have been fatal but wasn't." She grimaced. "When the fighting comes from every side, it's impossible not to take injury."

Harper nodded in understanding. "How did you explain that away?"

"It was pretty tricky," she said wryly. "The first wound I took was a sword to the back. One of the buggers snuck up behind me while I was dealing with two others and—" She shrugged. "Fortunately, it was near the end of the battle, and one we won. I woke up in my cabin with One-eye, the ship's cook, sitting beside me, his mouth scrunched up as if he'd sucked a lemon." She laughed at the memory. "He'd dragged me from the battle while my first took over leading the men to finish the battle. He'd carried me to my cabin, stripped away my jacket and shirt to tend my wound and discovered I had breasts. He was more horrified by that than the length and depth of the wound," she said dryly.

Harper laughed.

"One-eye didn't admit this," she continued, "but I read his mind, and it seems he was so sure he must be seeing things when my breasts were revealed that he grabbed me through my pantaloons in search of my 'equipment.' Much to his dismay, there wasn't any," she said wryly, and Harper's laughter deepened.

"How did you handle that?" he asked finally, as his laughter waned.

Drina smiled wryly. "Well, it took some talking and a bit of mind control, but I managed to convince him not to tell anyone. I suppose I could have just erased the memory and sent him off the ship, hired another cook, but he was a good man. A bit older than the others, more wizened, but a good man.

"Fortunately, he felt I was a good captain, so agreed to keep the secret, and the whole thing was so upsetting to him that he didn't seem to notice that I should have died from the wound.

"One-eye kept an eye on me after that, though, watched my back in battle and wouldn't let anyone else see to my wounds on the rare occasion that I took one." She took a sip of wine, and then added, "I only ever let him bind me if I couldn't manage myself, and then only once directly after receiving the wounds. It was to be sure he didn't notice how quickly I healed. He, however, thought it was because I was shy of his seeing my body, and I let him think that.

"For the first few wounds, he was so flustered by tending a woman that he practically closed his eyes while he did it." She chuckled. "Actually, he was surprisingly missish about it for a pirate. I think it was only because I was his captain." She shrugged. "But eventually he got more used to it, and then I took another wound that would have been fatal to a mortal, and that time he did notice."

"How did you explain it?" Harper asked.

"I didn't. What could I say? I just muttered that I'd always been strong and a fast healer and left it at that, but he started watching me more closely and started putting things together."

"Like what?"

"Like the fact that I stayed in my cabin all day, leaving the helm to my first, and came out to man the helm myself only at night, doing so with an unerring sense of direction, as if I could see through the darkness," she said dryly. "That I only approached ships at night to attack them. That I was uncommonly strong, especially for a woman, and that I was as nimble in the rigging at night as they would be during the day, while they had to feel their way blindly in the dark.

"Ah," Harper said with a grimace.

She nodded. "Then he followed me down into the hold of the ship one night when I went to visit the prisoners in search of blood to replace what I'd lost from a wound."

Harper didn't appear surprised by her words. Before blood banks, all of them had been forced to feed on mortals. Still, she felt she had to explain, and said, "I tried never to feed on my own crew, and even with prisoners I was careful not to take too much blood, feeding on several rather than one or two. I wiped their memories that I was ever in the hold, and our prisoners were always treated well. I was careful."

"But he followed and saw," Harper murmured.

"Yes." She sighed unhappily. "He took that even worse than my being female. I did have to erase his memory then. We were already headed for port to off-load the prisoners, but I put him ashore as well. I gave him enough money that he wouldn't have to work again and sent him on his way." She shifted unhappily. "Privateering just wasn't the same for me after that. And, as I say, I was tired of losing my men."

"So you retired from pirating," Harper said quietly.

"Yes." Drina took another sip of wine and

shrugged. "It was time for a change. Fortunately, I'd made a fortune, definitely enough to keep me in dresses for a couple of centuries."

Harper opened his mouth to speak again, but paused as their waiter returned with their meals. They both murmured "thank you" as their plates were set before them.

Drina eyed the dish she'd selected and felt her stomach growl at the delightful aromas wafting from it. It was something called chicken fettuccini. She'd chosen it because it was listed as the chef's special, and because it had been so long since she'd eaten that she wasn't sure what was good or not. But this certainly smelled delightful.

"It smells amazing," Harper murmured, sounding awed, and she glanced to his identical plate and nodded with agreement.

They fell into a companionable silence as they both dug in, but Drina found herself continually smiling as she ate. She was enjoying herself, enjoying Harper's reactions to her tales, his laughter, his shock . . . It was nice, and she decided she was going to have to thank Stephanie for arranging it.

Six

Drina sat back in her seat with a little sigh that was half regret and half satisfaction. She had enjoyed the food and was full, but regretted not being able to finish it. It was really good.

"So," Harper said, setting down his own fork. His expression was also full of regret as he pushed his half-eaten meal to the side, but he smiled as he glanced to her, and said, "I believe you had just finished regaling me with your pirating career and were about to explain how you landed as . . . a madam?" He arched an eyebrow. "Another rebellious phase?"

Drina grinned. He was trying not to sound shocked or affected in any way by that career choice, but she could see he wasn't taking it as calmly as he'd like her to think. Shrugging, she said, "Surely you must be bored with tales of my life by now. You should tell me more about—"

"Oh no," Harper protested at once. "You can't stop just before the best part."

She grinned at his expression, and then shrugged. "After I let go of the men and sold my ship, I decided to settle in England as a wealthy widow. At least that was the plan, and I did at first," she assured him, and then added, "Really, the madam bit was something of an accident."

"Right," he drawled. "You were an accidental madam."

Drina chuckled at his expression. "As it happens, yes I was. One night, I was wandering along, hunting for a snack and minding my own business, when I happened upon a young woman being beaten." Her smile faded at the recollection. The girl, Beth as she later found out her name was, had been half-dead when Drina had come upon the scene, but the man beating Beth had seemed determined to finish the job.

Shaking away the memory of Beth's poor battered body, she continued, "I took exception and ended it. Then I picked her up and she directed me to her home. But it turned out it was a brothel, and the man I'd stopped had been their protector." She said the last word with distaste, for he hadn't been anywhere near protective of any of the women under his care. The group she'd found at that house had all been terribly young, half-starved and each bearing the scars and marks of past beatings.

Drina sighed. "Well, Beth, the girl I'd saved, told the others what I'd done. Half of the women were furious that I'd killed their "protector—"

"Killed?" Harper asked, one eyebrow flying up.

Drina grimaced. "It was part accident and part self-defense. He didn't care for being tossed about by a female and pulled a knife. That rather irritated me, and I tossed him up the alley." She shrugged. "He landed on his knife."

"Ah." Harper nodded.

"Anyway, as I say, half of them were furious I'd killed him, and the other half just didn't seem to have the energy to care either way. Then Mary, a rather mouthy bit of goods, announced that since I'd killed their man, I was now their protector." Drina smiled faintly at the memory. She'd been rather dismayed at the time but had felt responsible for the women and hadn't known what else to do. So, she'd become a madam.

"According to Mary I wasn't a very good madam," she admitted with amusement. "I mean, I kept them safe and made sure none of their clients hurt them, but I didn't take any of their money. In fact, it cost me money instead," she admitted with a grin. "And as far as Mary was concerned, that made me a failure as a madam."

Harper chuckled, but asked with interest, "So you just hung about and looked out for them for nothing?"

"At first," she said slowly. Sighing, she admitted reluctantly, "But after a particularly nasty encounter with three drunk clients who tried to abuse one of the girls . . . well, I was injured. And healed," she said dryly.

"They sorted out what you were," he guessed.

"One of the risks of spending too much time with mortals," Drina said dryly. "Fortunately, the women took it much better than One-eye had. In fact, they were surprisingly accepting, and most just seemed relieved."

"Relieved?" Harper echoed with surprise.

Drina nodded and explained, "Well, I looked out for them but would never take their money. It turns out this had left them feeling beholden, and not one of them was comfortable with that. But now they felt they had something to offer me."

"To feed on them," Harper breathed, sitting up.

Drina nodded solemnly. "I refused at first, but Beth sat me down and explained that I was being terribly selfish in refusing their kind offer."

Harper started to laugh. "They had your number."

"Perhaps," Drina admitted with amusement. "But it wasn't what she said so much as what she didn't say. I realized that they were afraid. I was the best protector any of them had had. I didn't beat or rape them, didn't even take a cut of their money and had suffered a few injuries to protect them and yet expected nothing from them in return. It confused them. They didn't understand why I did it."

"Why *did* you do it?" Harper asked.

Drina considered the question. "Because I could, and no one else would."

"I think there was more to it than that," Harper said quietly. "You were your own woman and in charge of your life in Egypt until the Romans invaded, and it seems to me that you spent a good part of your life after that fighting to get that independence and freedom back. You managed to regain some small measure of it as a gladiator, then some more from ruling a country as a puppet master/concubine, became a duchess to escape your brother's rule, and then pretended to be male to run your own ship." He nodded. "I think you felt for those women. I think you were trying to free them from the tyranny of a male-dominated world, allowing them the independence to earn and keep their own money, and protecting them from those who would have abused and taken advantage of them. You saw yourself in them and were trying to give them what you'd always fought for."

Drina shifted uncomfortably. He'd seen her pretty clearly, and it made her feel naked. Trying to lighten the atmosphere, she teased, "Or perhaps I just secretly always wanted to be a prostitute."

"Did you?" he asked, surprised at the suggestion.

"No. I was well tired of sex with mortals by then," she said on a chuckle, and smiled wryly. "You're probably right about my motivations, but even I didn't understand them then." She turned her wineglass on the table, and admitted, "Originally, I tried to get them out of the business, but none of them were interested. They didn't see any other life for themselves." She sighed and shook her head, re-experiencing the confusion and frustration she'd felt at the time. "Not one of those women had wanted to be prostitutes. Each had dreamed of a husband and family, a happy life. They were, every one of them, forced into it, a few by circumstance, but most by the man they had called their "protector.""

Once in that life, society considered them garbage, as if in a matter of moments they'd somehow changed and become less."

"As happened with you when Rome invaded Egypt, and you were no longer allowed to run a business," he pointed out. "As if with the invasion, you had become less intelligent, or skilled, and were suddenly a child who needed a man to look out for her."

"I suppose," Drina admitted. "Though, as I say, I didn't see the correlation then. And I didn't suddenly feel less with the invasion, but they all seemed to feel they were all now less or damaged." She sighed. "Anyway, when Beth gave me her little talk, all I could do was reassure her that I wanted nothing and wouldn't suddenly abandon them. But, of course, her experiences in life didn't suggest that was likely. It didn't for any of them, and they were afraid and frustrated because of it. In their minds, there was nothing to stop me from simply pulling up stakes and leaving at any time. They didn't trust that I wouldn't, and the possibility left them constantly terrified. Once I realized that, I agreed to their offer."

"To feed from them?"

Drina nodded. "It turned out to be a good thing all the way around."

"How so?" he asked curiously.

"The women had always been on edge, fluctuating between being overly nice and snapping at me and each other," she began, and then paused and wrinkled her nose. "Frankly, it was a bloody cathouse at times. But once I agreed to feed from them, some sort of balance was restored. They felt everyone was getting something, so it would all be all right. They relaxed, the house gained a much more pleasant atmosphere, the women even became like family rather than fighting all the time. It was nice," she said with a reminiscent smile. "And, of course, I didn't have to hunt at night anymore, which was handy. Everyone was happy."

"Everyone?" Harper queried, and she chuckled at his wry expression.

"Well, everyone but my family," she admitted on a laugh.

Harper nodded, not surprised. "I didn't think your brother would be pleased to have his sister running a brothel." He grinned and tilted his head, asking, "Did he call on Lucian for help with you again?"

"Of course," she said dryly. "When his many letters and a personal visit to try to force me to sell the brothel and come home failed, Lucian was his next ploy. And Lucian even caught a ship and came all the way from the Americas, where he was living. He sailed into England to look into the matter."

"And?" Harper queried, leaning forward with interest.

"He read me, read my girls, and then turned to Stephano and surprised us all by announcing that I was old enough to make my own decisions. I wasn't doing anything wrong. He was proud of what I was doing for these women, and Stephano should be too, but whether he was or not, it was time he stopped interfering and let me be." Drina lowered her head to hide the tears that had swum into her eyes at the memory.

Bloody things, Drina thought. She didn't know why the memory of Lucian's approval made her teary. It was ridiculous really. She stilled when Harper covered her hand on the table and gave it a comforting squeeze.

"He was right."

Drina smiled faintly, and then sighed with disappointment when he withdrew his hand and picked up the wine bottle to pour more of the pale liquid into both their glasses. Setting the now-empty bottle down, he then glanced around, relaxing when their waiter immediately appeared at the table.

"So how long were you a madam?" Harper asked once the waiter had nodded to his request for more wine and slipped away.

She picked up her glass and took a sip before answering. "Quite a while, actually. The women all knew what I was, so my not aging didn't matter. I was never seen entering or leaving the brothel without a veil, and I didn't stay there all the time. I had a big brawny fellow act as bodyguard for the women on occasion so I could travel, and when I traveled, no one knew I was a madam." She shrugged. "Of course, as time passed, some of the girls left, either to marry, or to work a respectable job. One or two saved every penny they made and set out to start their own business, but Beth, Mary, and several others worked until they got too old. Then I shut the doors and bought another, smaller, house, which I turned into a retirement home for the half dozen who remained.

"They were so excited," she recalled with a soft smile. "It was far enough away that they could tell their new neighbors that they were retired widows or whatever they chose. They could be respectable, make new friends among the respectable matrons around them, and enjoy their waning years among the family they'd made in each other."

"It sounds like a happy ending," Harper said, smiling.

"It should have been," Drina agreed, her own smile dying.

Harper stilled, concern entering his expression. "What happened?"

"I set them up, saw them settled, and then left to travel, promising to visit frequently. But it was almost two years before I returned." She shrugged helplessly. "I didn't mean to stay away so long, but time slipped away from me."

"It tends to when you live as long as we do," Harper said, as if trying to mitigate the guilt he could sense in her words. "What happened to your girls?"

"Nothing until just before I returned. According to Beth, they made friends in the area and were all happily enjoying their new home and retirement . . . but then another immortal happened upon the women. His name was Jamieson. I don't know if that was his first or last name. Beth just called him Jimmy." Her mouth tightened. "He was rogue."

"Oh no," Harper murmured, reaching for her hand again.

Drina turned her hand over under his and their fingers closed around each other's, and then she said wearily, "I don't know if he was just passing through the area and came across one of them, read her mind, and saw her history with me, or what, but something made him pick them for victims."

When she paused again, Harper squeezed her fingers gently in sympathy. Drina shook her head, and said tightly, "He installed himself in the house and turned them all the same night in one horrible blood orgy. I guess it was horrendous; screaming old ladies watching each other being bled, and then having his blood forced on them, followed by the convulsions, the agony, the screaming." She shook her head, trying hard not to think about how it must have been for those women she had come to care a great deal for. She continued grimly, "One of the women didn't survive. Her heart couldn't take it, and she died during the turn. But Beth, Mary, and the remaining five survived."

"The one who died may have been the lucky one," Harper muttered, though she saw a haunted look in his eyes and realized she'd inadvertently reminded him of his Jenny.

Trying to pull his attention back from the ghost of his previous life mate, Drina quickly continued, "They woke from the turn confused and terrified, and were informed that now that he'd made them young and beautiful again, he owned them and they would do his bidding."

"He wanted them to prostitute for him?" Harper asked with a frown.

Drina shook her head. "They were to lure mortal men to the house with the promise of sex. But once there, these men would be robbed and fed on until dead."

"Christ," Harper muttered. "He couldn't think to get away with that. Someone would notice the sudden increase in number of missing men in the area."

"Yes, of course, but rogues are generally suicidal and want to be caught and put out of their misery anyway," Drina muttered.

"How did the women react to all of this?" Harper asked with a frown. "Surely they didn't go along with it?"

Drina cleared her throat. "Beth said that none of them wanted to. That Mary stood up to him when he told them his plans."

"Mary the mouthy one," Harper murmured, apparently recalling her earlier words.

"Mary the mouthy one who was too brave for her own good," Drina said quietly. "She told him they wouldn't do it. He could go to hell and they were going to find me and I'd stop him."

"Bet he didn't take that well," Harper guessed, sounding pained.

"He ripped her head off on the spot," Drina said grimly.

"Oh, Christ." Harper sat back in his seat with disgust, but still held on to her hand. If anything, his grip on hers was tighter, as if he was trying to infuse her with his strength to deal with the memory.

"The others immediately agreed to whatever he wanted at that point," Drina said quietly.

"I wonder why," he muttered dryly.

"So he sent them out to find men and bring them back," Drina continued. "The moment they were away from the house, Beth tried to talk the others into fleeing. They could find me, she said. I'd fix this." She sighed, feeling the pinch of guilt that she hadn't been able to fix anything in the end.

"Did they listen?" Harper asked quietly, sitting forward again.

Drina shook her head. "They were too afraid. They didn't know where I was, and he might come after them. She should go by herself, they said. They'd do what he said and wait to be rescued." Drina blew out her breath, and turned her wineglass on the tabletop with her free hand. "Beth fled, but she didn't know where to go to search for me, and she needed blood. She ended up returning to the original brothel to hide. She knew I hadn't yet sold it, and couldn't think where else to go. She hid inside for two weeks, feeding on rats, birds, and any other animal who got close enough to the house."

Harper's eyes widened incredulously. "She couldn't survive on that."

"No," Drina agreed on a sigh. "She was in a bad way by the end of the two weeks, but his turning of her had been so traumatic and she had always been kindhearted, she couldn't bear the idea of feeding on a mortal."

"What happened at the end of the two weeks?" Harper asked.

"She stayed inside during the day, but ventured out at night in search of small animals and such.

She was chasing a rat around the side of the house toward the street when a carriage passed. My carriage."

"You were back?"

Drina nodded. "I was on my way to the new house, but I was thinking of putting the old one up for sale and just wanted to see what shape it was in. I wasn't going to stop. I planned to visit the girls first. I just wanted to see how it looked and that it was still standing and hadn't burnt down or something while I was gone. So, I had the curtains open to look at it in passing. Beth recognized me through the window and shrieked."

Drina closed her eyes as she recalled the sound. She would never forget it. It had been an inhuman wail, full of pain, rage, and need. The sound had brought her head sharply around, and she'd spotted Beth standing there, pale and ragged.

"I didn't even recognize her," Drina whispered. "She was a plump, well-kept old woman when last I'd seen her, and this creature was a filthy, emaciated, young redhead. But I saw the glowing eyes and the state she was in and made the driver stop at once. I didn't realize who it was until I stepped down from the carriage and she threw herself at me babbling insanely about headless Mary and the others."

"I still didn't understand what had happened. She was half-mad with blood hunger and wasn't making any sense. I tried to get her to the carriage, saying I'd take her to the retirement house, but she went crazy at the thought and the only way to calm her down even a little was to promise I wouldn't take her there. I took her into the old house instead, and then set out to get her blood."

Drina shook her head. "It was an ordeal. She was repulsed and horrified at the thought of feeding on anyone, and I had to control both her and the donors. It was a slow process. She needed so much blood. I had to go out and bring back several donors one at a time, then control them both, keeping the donor from suffering any pain and unaware of what was happening, while also controlling Beth's horror and making sure she didn't take too much. And the whole time I was terrified that I'd simply have to kill her in the end anyway, that her mind was too far gone to be salvaged."

"Was it?" Harper asked.

Drina smiled wryly. "It's a funny thing about people. The ones who seem strong and mouth off the most, or bully others, are usually the ones most terrified and weakest inside. And the ones who seem quiet and speak their fears, appearing the weakest, are often the strongest under it all."

"Yes. I've found that too," Harper said solemnly. "So our Beth came out all right?"

She smiled faintly at his calling her "our Beth," but nodded. "Yes. I kept bringing her blood donors through the night. Let her rest for most of the day, and then began bringing in donors again that evening and night. She was coming around by the time dawn arrived on the second day, but I insisted she rest and we would talk after. She slept straight through the day and most of the early evening, and I stayed and watched over her. When she woke, she was quiet and calm and much better. She told me everything." Drina blew her breath out on a sigh. "I immediately set out for the retirement house. I tried to get Beth to wait at the brothel while I took care of it, but she insisted on coming with me.

"I should have insisted harder," she said dryly. "I thought I would only have to handle the rogue, but in the two weeks since Beth had left, he'd infected the other women with his madness.

"Some of the things he'd made them do to the men they lured back to the house on his orders were . . ." She shook her head at the memories she'd read from their minds as she'd entered the house, a house that had been charming and comfortable when last she'd seen it, but was now a blood-spattered nightmare, littered with dead bodies, some of which had been rent to pieces. Her mouth tightened. "They weren't salvageable.

"They attacked the minute we entered, which I hadn't expected. I was remembering the women the way they'd been, but they weren't those women anymore. He said attack, and they came at us as if we were strangers who meant less than dirt to them. Beth and I were outnumbered, but we were also at a disadvantage because we weren't mad, knew these women, and they were like family. Or had been," she corrected on a sigh, and then admitted, "I think Beth and I both would have died that day if council enforcers hadn't arrived to save our bacon."

"The council was on to them?" Harper asked.

"Yes, fortunately," she said. "But it would have been hard for them not to be. There was absolutely no caution being used. A lot of men, women, and even children from the area had disappeared. Several of the missing had been seen following the women into the house. And the smell coming from inside was rather atrocious. They might as well have painted 'Look here' on the front door." She shook her head. "The enforcers were apparently arming themselves in carriages across the street when we rode up and, as Scotty put it afterward, 'traipsed in as if attending a tea.'"

"Scotty?" he asked, pouring them both more wine.

"He was the lead enforcer on the raid. Now he heads up all the enforcers in the UK," she explained, and then grinned. "He was most put out with us that night."

Tilting her head to the side, she mimicked a very bad Scottish accent, mangling it horribly with her laughter as she did. "Ye should ha'e sent a message round to the council to handle it, not danced in there yersel'es like a pair o' idjits. Ye cuid ha'e got yersel'es killed, ye silly arses . . . And wid ha'e twoo had we no been here to pull yer fat oot o' the fire."

Harper chuckled with her, and then tilted his own head, and asked, "Is being saved by Scotty and the other rogue hunters the reason you became one yourself?"

"Partly, perhaps. They were pretty impressive. But I think we mostly joined up to make sure that what happened to the girls didn't happen to anyone else."

"We?" he asked, and then his eyes widened. "Beth?"

Drina nodded. "She's my partner. We joined together. Trained together. Were partnered when we finished training and work together still."

"In England?"

"No. Neither of us wanted to be there anymore. For Beth, England was a bad memory. As for me, well, the whole incident had rattled me. I'd always thought of myself as immortal, and while that's what we call ourselves, we aren't really. But that night in that house was the first time I was made to face it." She swallowed, and then explained, "When the enforcers crashed in, Beth and I were both pinned to the ground by the women, and Jimmy was about to hack off our heads. In fact, he was in the process of doing so to me when Scotty rushed him. It knocked him to the side and he only half scalped me, but it was enough. I stopped calling myself immortal that night. We are vampires."

He didn't argue, merely squeezed her hand again, and Drina continued, "That was the first time in all my adventures that I actually feared losing my life. And it had the strangest effect. I suddenly wanted to see my family again, live close to them, spend time with them. But I didn't want to leave Beth behind by herself. She was a baby vamp and needed training, and she had no one." Drina shrugged. "We stayed to watch the house burn after the hunters were done inside, then went straight to the docks, and I booked us both passage on a ship back home to Spain. We talked on the journey, and more while visiting my family, and she decided to join as well. We joined the Spanish branch of the rogue hunters once she'd adjusted to being an immortal. We joined together, trained together, and as I say, we were paired up after training and are still partners."

"She's more than that," Harper said quietly.

Drina nodded. "My brother welcomed her into our family. She's like a sister and carries the name Argenis now."

"A sister or an adopted daughter?" Harper asked solemnly, and Drina smiled.

"A bit of both I suppose," she admitted on a chuckle. "But don't tell her that, or she'll squawk."

He chuckled and she smiled and slid her wine-glass away, but then said, "Well I've monopolized the conversation nicely. Your turn. I know you were a cook once and own a frozen-food concern now, but what else have you done?"

Harper grimaced. "Believe me, my life hasn't been nearly as exciting as yours. It would bore you to tears."

"I doubt it. And my life wasn't all that exciting. It just sounds like it in the recounting."

Harper snorted with disbelief, and then glanced around in question when their waiter appeared. The man smiled gently and slid a small leather folder onto the table before quickly retreating. Harper glanced at the folder and opened it to reveal a bill, then glanced around, his eyes widening.

"What?" Drina asked, and peered around as well. They were the only guests left in the restaurant. The remaining tables were empty and cleared and workers were quietly setting chairs upside down on the tables, she supposed so that the floor could be vacuumed.

"I think we're holding them up," Harper said, pulling out his wallet.

"It would seem so," she murmured, glancing at her watch. "What time do they close?"

"Half an hour ago according to the waiter's thoughts," Harper answered wryly, setting a credit card in the folder and closing it.

"Oh dear," Drina murmured, finding the man and casting an apologetic smile his way as she asked, "Is he very upset?"

"Surprisingly not. But I'll leave him a big tip anyway to make up for it." He pulled his phone out and was talking quietly to his driver when the waiter took the folder away. By the time he'd hung up, the waiter was back with receipts and slips for him to sign.

The waiter might not be upset by their staying so late, but apparently he was still eager to go home, she thought with amusement, as Harper quickly filled in the tip amount and signed the bottom. Not that she blamed him.

A cold blast of wind slapped at them as they stepped out of the restaurant, and Drina huddled into her coat, grateful she'd bought the long, heavier one today and wasn't still wearing the lighter coat she'd worn to fly to Canada.

"The car should be along soon, but maybe we should stay close to the building for cover," Harper said, urging her back toward the wall beside the door.

"It's snowing," Drina murmured, eyeing the flakes whirling wildly around them with a frown.

"Yeah, here I'll block the wind." Harper turned to

face her and stepped up close, offering his body as a shield.

"Thank you," Drina murmured, fighting the urge to sway toward him.

"Where's your new scarf?" he asked with a frown. "Did you leave it in the restaurant?"

"No," she said, slipping her hands out of her pockets to catch the lapels of his leather coat and hold him in place when he started to pull away as if to rush back into the restaurant to fetch it for her. "I'm afraid I forgot it."

"And your hat and gloves too," he muttered, covering her hands with his gloved ones.

Drina smiled wryly. "I'm not used to needing them. Spain never gets this cold."

"No," he said, and then fell silent, his eyes seeming frozen on her lips.

Drina stilled, nearly holding her breath. She was sure he wanted to kiss her. When a moment passed without his doing so, she used her hold on his lapels to draw him nearer, whispering, "It's cold."

"Yes," he growled. He released her hands and let his drop to slide around her back, pulling her closer still. "Does this help?"

"A little." She sighed, squeezing even closer. She could hear his heart pounding, a quick tattoo, and slid one hand from his lapel to glide it up to touch his face and then onto his ear. Caressing the cooling skin gently, she whispered, "You're cold too." Then she leaned up on her tiptoes and blew her hot breath against his ear before whispering into it, "Does this help?"

Harper muttered something she didn't quite catch,
and then he turned his head and claimed her lips.
Drina immediately slid her hands into his hair and
let her mouth drift open, inviting him in . . . and all
hell broke loose. It was as if she'd torn away chains
that had bound and gagged him. She found herself
suddenly pressed hard against the wall behind her
by both his hips and his hands at her shoulders,
and then he was undoing her coat, his hands almost
tearing at the buttons in his eagerness to reach what
was inside. And all the while his mouth devoured
hers, his tongue invading and exploring.

Drina responded in kind, digging the nails of
one hand into his scalp while the other dropped
around to clasp his behind and urge him on as he
ground his hips against her. They both gasped with
relief when he managed to get the last button of her
coat undone and jerked the lapels apart. When his
hands immediately moved to cover her breasts, she
moaned and arched into the touch.

They froze when the door opened beside them.
Harper tore his mouth from hers, and they both
turned to stare blankly at the waiter, who had frozen
halfway out the door. The mortal's eyes were wide
and his expression amazed as he peered through
the glass door at them. Their waiter.

"Oh," Harper muttered, and then, seeming to
realize he was still clutching her breasts, released
them at once and stepped back from her, only to
step closer again when the wind caught her open
lapels and began to whip them about. "Here."

He quickly pulled the sides closed, then glanced around almost desperately. Relief rushed across his face when he spotted the car at the curb, and he caught Drina's arm and urged her quickly toward it, muttering, "Have a good night," over his shoulder.

Seven

Drina nearly fell into the car when Harper opened the door. She quickly scrambled across the seat, her eyes flashing to the driver and then skittering away as she wondered how long he'd been there and what he'd seen. Then Harper was inside, and they were pulling away. A glance out the rear window showed the waiter still standing frozen in the open restaurant door, staring after them, and Drina shook her head and turned to face front, her hands automatically doing up the buttons of her coat.

Once done, she felt a little less scattered and glanced nervously to Harper. Spotting the frown on his face, she bit her lip, worried about what he was thinking. It seemed to her that giving him time to think too much was probably a bad thing at that point, and she opened her mouth to say something, anything, but he was quicker.

"I'm sorry."

Drina smiled. "Don't be. It's not your fault the waiter came out." He blinked at her words, and she quickly added, "Now it's your turn. You said you were a cook?"

Harper hesitated, but then relaxed back against the seat. "Yes."

"Was your father a cook too?"

"No. He was a baron with a large holding of his own, as well as one he gained on turning and marrying my mother. He wanted me to take over running Mother's holding, but I had other interests."

"Food," she suggested.

Harper nodded, and then chuckled, the last of the tension slipping from him. "I *loved* food. So much so, I think had I been mortal, I would have been four or five hundred pounds by the time I was twenty. I spent all my time in the kitchens, following our cook around and learning all I could. Not to mention sampling every little thing that went through it.

"By the time I was old enough to leave the nest, I had decided I wanted to be the greatest cook ever. Of course, to be the greatest cook, I had to have access to every possible ingredient there was, which meant I needed to work for someone wealthy enough to find and purchase those ingredients. I left home and went straight to the home of the wealthiest person I knew of. Emperor Elect Maximillian."

Drina's eyebrows rose, and a smile tugged at her lips. "Straight to the top, huh?"

Harper nodded wryly. "I presented myself in the kitchens, sure they would be glad to have me. Unfortunately, the head cook was less than impressed. He wanted nothing to do with me, but with a little persuasion, I managed to convince him to give me a position."

"What kind of persuasion are we talking here?" Drina asked with amusement. "The mortal or immortal variety?"

"Immortal," he admitted ruefully. "But, only enough to convince him to give me the lowest position in the kitchen. I wanted to prove myself and work my way up to chef."

"Ah," Drina said, and then asked, "and you did?"

"Yes." He smiled faintly. "It took me a lot of years though, and then I only got to be his head chef for a couple of years before I had to move on."

"The not aging can really be a pain," she said with sympathy.

"Hmm." He nodded, and then shrugged. "It turned out all right. He gave me the medieval version of an employer reference and wished me well. I spent the next fifty years or so cooking in royal palaces in various countries, extending my knowledge and honing my skills.

"Eventually, however, I grew tired of working for someone else and wanted to open my own business. As much as I love cooking, it wasn't going to make me the money I needed to do that, though, so I had to hang up my spoon for a bit. I tried various things, but the most successful was working with a band of mercenaries. Much to my surprise, I turned out to be a natural on the battlefield."

"Why would you be surprised?" she asked with

a smile. "Immortals are naturals in battle. We're stronger, faster, and hard to kill."

"Yes, but you also need skill, or you're likely to lose your head, and I'd spent most of my life in the kitchens. Even as a youth, I shunned practice in the yard with the men to trail the cook around," he said solemnly. "However, I found that I was a natural in battle. And I turned out to be a whiz at planning for successful attacks and defenses, which turned out to be not much different to planning a large feast."

"What?" she said with disbelief, and he nodded solemnly.

"It's all in the details," he assured her with a grin, and Drina burst out laughing. He watched her with a smile, and then said, "Actually, my knowledge of castle kitchens came in handy during sieges. I knew what they were likely to have on hand and how long it would last and so on." He shrugged. "I did well for myself. Well enough that I made the money I needed to start my own pub. And that did well enough that I was able to start a second and so on, and then I moved on to restaurants, and then hotels."

"How did you end up moving from restaurants to hotels?" she asked with surprise.

"Well, I had opened one of my restaurants on the main floor of a hotel in Paris. The restaurant earned a reputation and did a booming business, but at the same time the hotel was beginning to flounder. I was considering moving the restaurant elsewhere before the hotel folded altogether, but I was becoming a bit bored. I had lost my interest in food after a couple of centuries, and it took a lot of the joy from cooking. The moment I had noticed that happening, I'd hired the best chefs I could find to take over the actual cooking in my establishments, but it left me basically a pencil pusher. I needed a challenge, so rather than move the restaurant, I decided to buy the hotel and see if I couldn't make it a successful concern again.

"I renovated it floor by floor, and the restaurant handled the room service. We built a reputation, and the hotel started to flourish as well. So I opened another, and then another.

"Everything rolled along nicely, but I soon grew bored again, and then in . . . I think it was the 1920s," he murmured, then shrugged it away as unimportant and continued, "I read an article about a brand-new technique for preserving food."

"Frozen food," Drina said with amusement.

Harper nodded. "I got in on the ground floor. We started with vegetables, and then branched out to entrees, and, as I said, we recently added wine to what we do." He smiled wryly. "See, I told you that my history wasn't nearly as exciting as yours."

Drina shook her head. "I don't know. It sounds exciting enough. Truth be told, my life wasn't nearly as exciting as it sounds in the recounting. I mean titles like gladiator, pirate, and madam sound exciting I suppose, but in reality they were just another day in the life. Being a gladiator was hot, sweaty, bloody labor, hacking away at other gladiators. Being a pirate wasn't much different than being a sailor. It was night after night of hauling rope, raising sails, and steering into a storm with the occasional battle to get the blood going. And as a madam, I mostly greeted the men at the door like a Wal-Mart greeter, reading their minds as they entered the establishment to be sure they had no nefarious plans. Then I sat about, reading or playing cards until the evening ended, and the men left. The only excitement that occurred there was when the occasional fellow got too rough, or tried to make one of the girls do something she didn't want to. And then that was a momentary adrenaline rush as I saw them off the premises."

She shrugged wryly. "If I've learned anything in all my years, it's that nothing is as exciting or glamorous as it sounds. I suspect if you read the minds of movie stars and rock stars, you'd probably find their lives were a daily grind with the occasional fan frenzy to scare the crap out of them and get the blood going."

Harper smiled. "You're surprisingly sensible for one who has been so rebellious most of her life."

Drina shrugged. "We all live and learn."

Harper nodded, and glanced around as the car slowed. "We're here."

Drina leaned forward, stretching her upper body in front of his to peer curiously out the window at the very uninteresting building they were stopping in front of.

"Nondescript like our clubs in Europe," she commented, placing her hand on his shoulder as if to keep her balance.

"Yes," Harper agreed, sounding a tad husky.

She turned her head and smiled at him, close

enough to kiss, as she said, "I suppose it's to avoid attracting mortals."

"Yes," he repeated, this time in barely more than a whisper. His head began to move forward, and Drina moved her own head closer, and then they both froze as the front door slammed shut. Harper glanced past her to the now-vacant driver's seat, then out the side window, and sighed. "Right, we're here."

Drina straightened as the driver opened the door on Harper's side. She then followed him out of the car and into the cold night. Harper paused long enough to give instructions to his driver before hustling her to the door of the Night Club.

A wave of heat and sound hit them as they entered and Drina peered around curiously, not at all surprised to find it looked like any club in any city. They were in a large room with shadowed booths around the edge of a lit dance floor. Loud music blared from all corners. Harper started to lead her to one of the few empty booths, but she caught his arm and leaned up to ask, "Is there a lounge area? Somewhere quieter, where we can talk when not dancing?"

Nodding, he changed direction at once and led her to a set of swinging doors. They pushed through into another room, this one wholly made up of tables and booths and much quieter once the doors swung shut behind them. They chose a booth along the wall.

Sliding into one side, Drina smiled as she shrugged out of her coat. "We can always go in there to dance as we like, but it will be easier to talk in here when we want a break."

"Smart thinking," Harper said, hanging his own coat from a hook at the end of the booth. He then took her coat to hang it beside his.

He slid in across from her, murmuring an apology as his feet nudged hers, then glanced around as a waitress appeared. He smiled at her, but then glanced to Drina, and asked, "Do you know what you want? Or would you like to check the menu?"

For answer, she picked up a narrow menu in a holder at the end of the table and opened it, saying, "It's probably better to see what they have in case the selection isn't the same as in Spain or the names are different."

Harper nodded and turned to the waitress, but she was already slipping away, saying, "I'll give you a minute."

Drina laid the menu on the table and turned it sideways so they could both see it. They each leaned forward, head to head to look it over, but then a beeping came from Harper's coat. Frowning, he straightened and reached in the pocket to retrieve his phone.

Drina politely pretended she couldn't hear what he was saying, not that there was much to hear. He said, "Hello," listened briefly, and then sighed, and said, "I did wonder about that. All right. Well, there's nothing we can do about it." Another silence followed, and then he said, "I'm not sure. I'll have to call you back on that."

Drina glanced at him in question as he hung up, and Harper grimaced.

"It seems it's officially a blizzard out there," he announced apologetically. "That was my pilot saying they've shut down the airport and are advising people to stay off the highways. He thinks they'll be closing those soon too, but whatever the case, it isn't safe to take the helicopter back to Port Henry tonight."

Drina stared at him blankly for a minute, and then reached for her own phone.

"We can try driving back tonight, but we'd have to leave right away if you want to give it a go," Harper said, as she began to punch in the number for Casey Cottage. "Otherwise, we aren't leaving until tomorrow sometime, and then only if the storm lets up."

Drina bit her lip and nodded to acknowledge his words, then stilled as the phone picked up on the other end.

"Drina?" Mirabeau said by way of greeting.

"Yes, I—"

"Listen, a big storm hit here an hour or so after you guys left. They just shut down the 401 from London to Woodstock, and I suspect the rest of the highway will soon follow. I'm thinking it probably isn't safe for you guys to fly. You two better not try to come back tonight."

"What about Stephanie?" Drina asked with a frown. "I'm supposed to sleep—"

"She's sound asleep on the sofa with the TV on. We'll leave her there for now. If she wakes up and wants to go to bed, I'll go up with her. It's not a problem. Although, that probably isn't even necessary tonight. Leonius isn't in the area, and she isn't likely to try running away in a blizzard, especially with them shutting down the highways. Even if she managed to slip away, there aren't any buses running to take her anywhere."

"Right," Drina murmured. "I guess it's best we not try coming back then."

"Definitely," Mirabeau assured her. "Don't worry. Everything is good. You and Harper just get a hotel room or something and stay in the city until this clears."

"I have an apartment here in the city. We can stay there," Harper announced, apparently having caught the gist of the conversation. He punched a stream of numbers into his phone and turned it toward her so she could read from the small screen. "This is the number, give it to her and tell her to call if there are any problems."

Drina read off the numbers to Mirabeau, passed along the message, and then echoed her good night and hung up.

"Well," she murmured.

"Yes," Harper said.

They stared at each other for a moment, and then Drina caught movement behind his head, and glanced past Harper to see the waitress slowly making her way along the row of booths, taking orders as she moved in their general direction.

"Well," she said again, turning her gaze to the menu, "let's see what we have here."

She ran her eyes slowly down the list of available blood blends, murmuring each aloud as she went, and then paused as she reached—"Sweet Ecstasy."

"It's a dose of blood from someone who's taken the drug ecstasy," Harper murmured. "The impact on immortals is supposed to be pretty powerful. They say it's like immortal Spanish fly."

Drina smiled. "I know. Beth swears by it. She says it's reawakened her flagging interest in sex and that she has the best sex ever on it."

Harper's eyebrows rose. "Does she?"

"Yeah." Drina chuckled, her gaze dropping back to the menu as she admitted, "She's always pestering me to try it, and I've always kind of wanted to, but I've never been with anyone I liked and trusted enough to try it with." She glanced up and met his gaze, and added, "Until now."

Harper stared back silently, their gazes locked until a shift in air drew their attention to the fact that someone was standing at the end of the table. He didn't even glance over to ensure it was the waitress, but simply growled, "Two Sweet Ecstasies."

"Okie dokie," the waitress said cheerfully, and slipped away.

The silence drew out for a minute, and then Drina said abruptly, "Let's dance."

She didn't wait for a response, but promptly slid out of the booth and started back toward the door to the dance section of the club. She didn't have to glance around to see if Harper was following. Drina could feel the heat coming off his body and pouring along her back. The man was practically on her heels and stayed there all the way into the next room and onto the crowded dance floor.

The music was a dance mix, fast and pulsing, the rapid heartbeat of a lover. Drina let it flow through her, allowing her body to move as it would to the sound. She knew Harper was right there with her but didn't even look at him. Instead, she closed her eyes and moved. When the music slowed three songs later, and he caught her hand to pull her into his arms, she went willingly. The instant electricity between them told her they wouldn't need any Sweet Ecstasy, but she hadn't expected they would. Still, when she spotted their waitress moving through the room toward them with a tray holding two drinks, she waved at the woman and smiled as she approached.

"They were going warm," the waitress explained, pausing beside them.

"You're a gem. I was getting thirsty," Drina said with a grin. She then grabbed her drink and downed it in one go as Harper reached for his own drink.

"Another?" their waitress asked with a wicked grin as Drina lowered the now-empty glass.

"Oh definitely," she said on a laugh as she set the empty glass back on the tray.

"Make it two," Harper suggested, and then quickly downed his own and replaced it on the tray.

"You got it," the woman said cheerfully, and swung away.

Smiling, Drina slid her hands around Harper's neck as he drew her back into his arms.

"Stephanie was wrong about you not dancing since 'Gone-With-the-Wind-dresses' were in fashion," Harper said with amusement as she shifted against his body to the slower beat. "You know how to move to modern music."

"Beth and I often hit the clubs with some of the

other hunters after work. It's good for blowing off steam," she admitted, and then said, "You don't do so bad yourself. You're disproving that old saying about white men not being able to dance."

Harper chuckled. "I don't know about that."

"I do," she assured him, and then deliberately moved close enough that their hips met, and added, "Beth says that's a sure sign that a man is good in bed. Are you good in bed, Harper?"

Harper's laughter caught in his throat, and his eyes flared silver-green. Then he caught her by the back of her head and kissed her. It was no slow, gentle melding of mouths, but as if their earlier embrace had never been interrupted, and they were just continuing that. His mouth was hungry, hot, and hard, devouring rather than exploring, demanding with no sign of tentativeness. He wanted her, bad, and didn't care who knew.

It wasn't the Sweet Ecstasy. That couldn't possibly have kicked in yet, Drina knew. She tightened her arms around his neck, meeting his need with her own, and moaned into his mouth when his hands slid up her sides to the level of her breasts. He didn't grab them as he had outside the restaurant, but kept them at her sides, allowing just his thumbs to feather along the sides of her breasts and then under them in a tantalizing caress that had her nipples hardening with hope that they could feel that touch. They didn't. Instead, his thumbs slid back up again in another mostly innocent caress to join his fingers at her sides. Harper wasn't so far gone down the road of need that he'd forgotten where they were, she realized, half-relieved and half-disappointed.

Her disappointment was mitigated a great deal when his leg slid between both of hers, and he dropped one hand down to press her bottom forward so that his thigh rubbed against her with every step. He didn't remove his hand at once but let it dip lower, curving it briefly under her bottom and letting his fingers brush lightly between her legs in a caress that had her breath hitching in her throat. It was the swiftest of touches, and then his hand slid back up to her waist, but it was effective. The blood now roared in her ears, the strobing lights suddenly seemed blinding, and she was abruptly weak in the knees and sagging against him, flat out riding his thigh, which only intensified everything.

Drina didn't realize the music had changed again until Harper broke their kiss and spun her away from him. Sound came crashing back, and she blinked her eyes open to see the others moving to the more frenetic beat. Harper drew her back then, not turning her to face him but pulling her up against his chest so that her bottom now pressed into his groin. He slid his arms around her waist, one atop the other directly below her breasts, and bent his head to her ear to whisper, "You're trembling. Are you cold?"

The words were soft and teasing, and he nipped at her ear as he said them. Then he let one hand drift down over her stomach to her pelvis, where he pressed gently, and murmured, "Shall I warm you?"

Drina couldn't have responded had she wanted. He was still moving them to the music, which was good because if he'd stopped, she would have simply stood there like an idiot. But while she was sure anyone looking would simply see two people dancing, it didn't feel like dancing. It felt like foreplay.

"Our waitress is coming with our drinks. Shall we go sit down?" he asked by her ear, and Drina nodded at once, hoping she would regain some equilibrium if he wasn't holding her.

Harper shifted his hold, not releasing her but moving her into his side so that his arm was around her back, and he could usher her off the dance floor.

Drina spotted their waitress almost at once. She'd come to a halt halfway between the doors to the lounge and the dance floor, but now turned and moved back to the doors, leaving them to follow. By the time they pressed through the swinging doors, she was setting their drinks on their table and melting away.

Harper ushered her to the table, and Drina slid in, then moved farther over to make room for him when he started to slide onto the bench seat beside her rather than claim the opposite bench as he had earlier. The moment they were both settled, he caught her chin in his hand and turned her face up to his for a kiss. This time it was a quick, hard one, almost a brand of possession, and then he released her and reached for his Sweet Ecstasy.

He took a healthy swallow, and then set it back and rested his arm on the edge of the table in front of her. Following his lead, Drina reached for her own glass and took a drink. It was as she was setting it back on the table that she felt something feather across her right nipple. Glancing down, she saw that he'd extended his fingers, the tips feathering over her hardened nipple visible through the thin material of her bra and dress.

As she watched, he did it again, just extending his fingers and letting the tips brush across the excited nub. Drina bit her lip and glanced around, but the way he'd positioned himself blocked anyone from seeing what he was doing. When she met his gaze, he asked, "Do you enjoy being a hunter?"

Drina blinked, her brain slow to absorb the idle question. Finally, she nodded.

"Yes." The word came out in a husky whisper, and she cleared her throat before adding, "Sometimes it gets disheartening, but mostly I feel like I'm helping people, if only by stopping rogues from hurting anyone else."

"They're lucky to have you," he said quietly, and then raised his hand to run one finger along the edge of her neckline, following the V-neck over the curve of her breast and down to where the material met between her breasts. "What do you do for fun besides dancing?"

Drina licked her lips and forced her attention from what he was doing to try to answer the question. "I find reading relaxing, and—" She paused and bit her lip, her body going still as he leaned forward and nuzzled her ear.

"And?" he prompted, his breath tickling across flesh suddenly alive with nerve endings.

"And what?" she breathed, turning her face to find his lips.

Harper kissed her, a long, lazy kiss this time, his tongue sweeping in and then withdrawing before he drew back. His hand drifted away from her neckline, and he reached for his glass again.

Drina shivered at the loss of his touch and reached for her own drink.

"The way you move on the dance floor is incredibly sexy. I found myself watching you and wondering if you were wearing one of the new bra and panty sets Stephanie helped you pick out today."

She'd just raised the glass to her lips and her eyes shot to his over the rim. His expression was casual, as if they were discussing the weather, but his eyes were fierce. She took a gulp of her Sweet Ecstasy and merely nodded as she swallowed.

He smiled and set his glass down, then returned his fingers to her neckline, running the tips lightly along the edge again. "Which one?"

Drina hesitated. She then smiled slowly, and said, "I think I'll leave you to find that out for yourself."

Harper met her gaze and held it, but she felt a tugging at her top, and then he looked down. She did as well to see that he'd caught the neckline with one finger and eased it the slightest bit to the side, revealing the edge of the red lace bra with its black trim. When she looked back to his eyes, she found them burning silver.

"My favorite," he breathed, his eyes glowing and Drina almost released a nervous laugh. That was what Stephanie had said when she'd insisted she wear them tonight. "Harper really liked these. You should wear them."

Drina took another drink and managed not to squirm on the seat as he slid his finger under the edge of the bra and ran it lightly downward, brushing tantalizing close to a nipple that positively ached now. She didn't breathe again until he withdrew the finger and let the top of her dress slip back into place.

Harper turned to pick up his drink again. Another swallow left half the drink remaining. He set it back, and then turned to face her again. Her glass was now half-empty as well. Another half to go for each of them, and surely they could leave? If he didn't suggest it, she would, Drina decided. This was driving her crazy.

"You're wearing the matching panties too, of course."

Drina blinked at the abrupt comment and glanced down as his hand landed warm and heavy on the top of her thigh. She had the mad urge to repeat the words "I think I'll leave you to see for yourself," and imagined him sliding under the booth and between her legs to do just that, but then gave herself a shake. They were in a public club. Well, not really public. More private, for immortals only, though they got the occasional mortal straggling in. At least they did in Spain.

"Are you?" he asked, leaning forward to nip at her ear, his hand slipping a little farther up her thigh with the movement.

"Yes," she breathed.

"I'm glad," he whispered. "I can't wait to see them on you."

She couldn't wait to show him, Drina thought faintly, her fingers clenching around her glass as his fingers began drawing lazy circles on the top of her thigh through her skirt.

"I can't wait to take them off you," he whispered, whirling his tongue inside the delicate shell of her ear as the lazy circles he was making on her thigh moved down the side of her leg now to her inner thigh.

Drina closed her eyes, aware that her breathing had grown shallow and rapid. His fingers had somehow slipped under her skirt, and his bare skin was on hers, sending tingles along her thigh in both directions. Forcing her eyes open, she glanced down to see that the handy-dandy slit in the skirt had given him access. As she watched, his hand slid farther up her inner leg, pushing the material ahead of it.

Harper nipped lightly at her ear, sucked the lobe into his mouth, and drew on it slowly, then released it, and asked, "Do you want to dance anymore?"

Drina gave the faintest shake of her head.

"Then maybe we should drink up and go to my place," he suggested, his fingers reaching and brushing, light as a feather, against the material of her panties.

Drina gasped in a breath. Her eyes started to close, but she forced them open and lifted the glass to her lips, drinking a good portion of it as she wondered when this had all slipped from her control to his . . . or if she'd ever really been in control. She'd thought she was seducing him earlier, but the tables had turned. Had it been her challenge on the dance floor? Asking if he was good in bed?

Setting her glass back, she turned her head, caught him by surprise, and took his lower lip in her mouth, sucking it as he'd done to her ear. When his fingers then brushed against her again, more firmly, she released his lip on another gasp, her mouth opening slightly on the sound. Harper immediately thrust his tongue inside as his fingers quickly shifted the lace of her panties aside so that he could run his thumb across her core.

It was too much, and Drina had to fight not to cry out or straddle his lap right there in the booth. She could have wept, though, when he suddenly withdrew his fingers, allowing her panties to slip back into place.

Harper broke their kiss just as abruptly and turned to pick up his drink. He downed it in one go, set the glass back and slid from the booth, removing his wallet as he went.

"Finish up, and I'll pay the bill." His words were gruff, his jaw set, but she knew it wasn't anger making his expression tight.

Breathing out slowly, Drina tried to calm herself as she watched him slip through the tables toward the bar. He pulled out his phone as he went. Calling for the car, she realized as she watched him press it to his ear. The car that would take them to his apartment where they would . . .

Cripes, what was she doing? she wondered with sudden panic. It had been centuries since she'd—

Raising her glass to her lips, she gulped down the last swallow, wishing it was Wino Reds or something with some punch to it rather than a drink full of pheromones. She didn't need to be any more horny; she needed some bloody Dutch courage. Literally.

Shaking her head, she slid out of the booth, and then had to grab the table to stay on her feet as her legs quaked beneath her. Cripes, she was a mess. Over two thousand years old and quivering like an untried virgin. This was pathetic, she decided, reaching for her coat. She slid it on, and then nearly jumped out of it and her skin both when a hand landed on her shoulder.

Harper had returned, she realized, glancing around and managing a smile.

"The car is on the way," he said, grabbing his own coat and tugging it on.

Drina mumbled what might have been a "Good" or could just have easily been an "Oh God," and then he had his coat on, had caught her hand, and was leading her through the tables toward the exit.

"Have fun, kids," someone sang out.

Drina glanced around to see their waitress standing aside and smiling as they passed, and then Harper was tugging her through the door.

Snow and wind hit her in the face as they stepped into the darkness. Drina squinted against it and followed half-blind as Harper led her around the building to a narrow alley leading toward the back. The wind died abruptly once he pulled her into the cover it offered, and Drina sighed with relief. She wasn't used to this northern climate.

She turned to say as much to Harper, but never got the words out. His mouth was suddenly on hers, his hands and body pushing her back against the cold, hard bricks of the building as his body plastered itself to her front. What followed was an explosion of passion like she'd never experienced in all her life. It washed over her like the fallout from an atom bomb, only to turn and roll through her again, and Drina merely grabbed at his arms and held on as he drove his tongue into her and urged the sides of her coat apart so that he could run his hands over her body.

His hands molded her breasts, her waist, slid down the front of her thighs and then around to their backs before rising to clasp her behind the upper legs and lift her against the wall until their faces were level. Once he had her where he wanted her, he used his hold to spread and raise her legs around his hips.

Drina instinctively hooked her booted ankles behind his waist, helping to take her weight as he pinned her against the wall with his hips. It freed his hands, and he immediately reached one hand to her breasts, using it to tug her neckline and bra aside, baring one to the night air.

Drina gasped as cold curled around her nipple, but then he broke their kiss to lower his head and latch onto it, his hot moist breath bringing on a heat that had her moaning and squirming against the wall. When his teeth grazed the tender nub, she cried out and raised her face to the night sky. Cold flakes flurried around them, landing on her eyelids, cheeks, and lips, and her breath came in small gasps, forming mini clouds that floated heavenward.

When she felt his hand brush against her thigh, moving upward, Drina closed her eyes and held a breath that shot out on a cry when he found her core. Digging her nails into his shoulders, she thrust her hips away from the wall, into the caress, and twisted her head to the side, suddenly gasping for breath, as he slid her panties aside to touch her again.

"Christ," Harper growled against her breast, and then raised his head to growl almost helplessly, "You're so hot and wet."

Drina opened her eyes and lowered her head to meet his gaze, and then moaned as his fingers moved across her tender flesh again.

"I want you," she gasped, writhing under his touch.

The silver in Harper's eyes spiked, and he claimed her mouth again.

His fingers retreated then, but she felt his hand moving between them and knew he was undoing his pants. She kissed him more frantically with the anticipation of what was coming, and then a car horn honked.

They both froze for a heartbeat, and then Harper broke the kiss and they both turned to stare blankly at the back end of the car just visible at the curb. Harper dropped his head to her chest with a groan. He gave it a slight shake and straightened again. His hand moved briefly between them again, presumably doing up what he'd undone, and then he caught her at the waist and eased back.

Silently cursing the driver for being so damned prompt, Drina unhooked her ankles and allowed her legs to drop back down to support her. Harper held on for a moment as she found her balance in the thigh-high boots, and then he released her to quickly tug her dress back into place before catching her hand and leading her out of the alley to the car.

Harper had grabbed her right hand with his left, and didn't let go as he ushered her into the car but followed and closed the door, all while gripping her fingers. He continued to clasp them firmly as he leaned forward to speak to the driver and as he sat back.

Drina peered at their entwined fingers, and then glanced up to his face, worry fluttering through her as she noted that he was staring out the window, his expression grim. She fretted over what was going on in his head for the duration of the ride, but couldn't think of anything to say to distract him. Her body was still humming from what had nearly taken place in the alley, which, now that she was able to think a bit, would have been a catastrophe, she thought with a grimace. Harper may be putting the reawakening of his "appetites" down to residuals from Jenny, but the truth was they were life mates, and it was said life mates often fainted after sex during the first year or so. They could have been lying there unconscious in the snow for who knew how long had the car not arrived. Okay, so maybe she didn't mind that the driver was prompt after all, she thought wryly.

Eight

Harper stared out the window, Drina's hand warm and soft in his. He couldn't seem to let it go; it was a lifeline keeping him tethered as his mind suggested the most incredible and impossible things, the wildest of which was the suggestion that she was his life mate. He'd nearly taken Drina there in an alley, up against a wall, during a freaking blizzard, for God's sake.

Harper wanted to think it was the Sweet Ecstasy, and it just might have been, he acknowledged, but what had happened in the bar itself was plaguing him. On the dance floor and then at the table, when he'd touched her it had caused him pleasure, and not the "it-pleases-me-to-please-you" kind, but actual physical pleasure. Tingles of awareness and excitement had shuddered through his body with every caress he'd given her, urging him on to do things he'd never even considered prior to this night.

While the way he'd turned his back to the rest of the club had hidden what he was doing, touching her the way he had in their booth, with people all around, had been madness. But even worse, he'd wanted to do more, and wasn't really sure how he'd managed not to. It had taken great effort. He wanted to touch her now too and was holding her hand to keep from grabbing her by the waist and pulling her onto his lap. He wanted to push her coat and dress off her shoulders, remove her bra, and feast on her flesh. But mostly he wanted to tug her skirt up, rip her panties off, and sink himself in all that warm, moist heat he'd found between her legs. And he didn't particularly care whether the driver was watching while he did it.

Harper had never wanted anyone as badly as this, never felt such a bone-deep need. Not even for Jenny. The thought shamed him. Jenny was dead, she'd died leaving few to grieve her, just himself and her sister, and yet he couldn't remember her face and now wanted another woman with more passion than he'd ever felt for her.

It's the Sweet Ecstasy, Harper assured himself.

But the Sweet Ecstasy wouldn't allow him to experience Drina's pleasure, another part of his mind argued, and he'd definitely felt tingles race through his body when he'd extended his fingers and let the tips brush across her nipples. The first time had been an accident. He hadn't realized his hand rested that close to her. But the excitement that had coursed through him had made him do it again, and more.

Perhaps it was just the excitement of what he was

doing, combined with the Sweet Ecstasy. Because there was no way Drina was his life mate. He'd just lost one, and if there was one thing he'd learned, life wasn't kind enough to throw him another so soon.

I am eating again, though, Harper thought, his mouth tightening. But he'd already explained that away to himself satisfactorily . . . along with his eager libido. Both were just a result of his appetites being reawakened by Jenny, his true life mate. They simply hadn't died with her death, they'd just been superseded by grief and depression for a while, but now he was getting out again and feeling better, and they were making their presence known once more. And Drina was a beautiful, sexy woman. Any man would desire her if he had the least interest in sex at all.

Oddly enough, while that explanation had sounded reasonable earlier in the day, it wasn't sounding as reasonable to him at the moment. Especially since he'd never experienced this kind of passion with Jenny.

His mind immediately tried to shy away from that thought, but Harper forced it back. He hadn't felt this depth of passion for her. He'd felt some, but she'd always kept him at arm's length, never letting him even kiss her. So it had remained a seed, never blossoming like his desire for Drina had the moment his mouth had closed on hers.

The Sweet Ecstasy, he decided. That was the only thing that made sense. Only it could create a passion so overwhelming it surpassed what he'd experienced with his life mate.

Still, the excitement he'd felt when he'd touched Drina bothered him. He needed to test it, Harper decided. He needed to touch her without her touching him in return to confuse the matter. And he needed to do it somewhere normal and boring, where there was no chance that the situation and possibility of getting caught might inflame his passions.

His apartment, of course. There was nothing more pedestrian than an apartment or home. Certainly it was more pedestrian than a public booth or alley. Once they got to his place, he would calmly and methodically caress her and prove to himself that he wasn't experiencing her pleasure. He would even avoid kissing her to ensure he wasn't excited, he decided. At least, he would until he had reassured himself that he hadn't been experiencing the shared pleasure that immortal couples raved on about.

It would be hard, Harper acknowledged with an inner grimace. He had two Sweet Ecstasies roiling through his blood, which wasn't likely to make it easy. But he would prevail.

"Is this your building?"

Harper's eyes refocused at Drina's question, and he saw that the car was easing to a stop in front of his apartment building. Taking a breath, he nodded, and then opened the door before the driver could get out. He welcomed the frigid blast of air that hit him as he slid out of the vehicle, pulling Drina behind him. The arctic air would help to cool his ardor further, Harper assured himself, and didn't rush to the building after closing the door to the car but moved through the swirling snow at a sedate pace.

* * *

Drina returned the smile the guard at the door gave them as they entered. Her gaze moved curiously over the large, luxurious lobby as Harper led her to the last of four elevators. She wasn't surprised at the swank to the place. The man had arranged for a helicopter to pick them up for the evening. She'd already known he had money. Not that it mattered to her. She was no slouch in that area either. Her time as a privateer and some sensible—as well as a few lucky—investments since had ensured she would never need to worry about money.

The elevator was silent and fast, and it seemed like they'd barely entered before it was sliding to a halt at the top. Harper led her out into a hall, still holding her hand, and she glanced around, and then came to a stop as she realized they weren't in a hall, but a foyer.

Harper turned, an eyebrow rising in question.

"I take it the whole floor is yours?" she asked wryly.

"Yes." He smiled faintly. "That's my private elevator."

"Right," Drina said with amusement. "And yet you stay at Casey Cottage with only a room to call your own?"

"It's a nice room," he said with a shrug, and added solemnly, "and all the wealth in the world isn't as comforting as friends in times of need." Harper then grinned, and said, "Besides, the rent for the room is cheap."

Drina chuckled and pulled her hand free of his to

remove her coat. The apartment was toasty warm, too warm for the coat. Harper quickly shrugged out of his own coat and moved to the closet to grab two hangers. He hung up his own, and then took hers, set it on the hanger, and hung it up as well. He closed the door and turned toward her, only to pause.

Drina's eyebrows rose, and then she followed his attention to see that when she'd removed her coat, she'd tugged her gown off one shoulder, and it now hung down her arm, leaving a good portion of one red and black bra cup exposed. She almost tugged it back into place, but then just didn't. Why bother? She didn't plan to wear it long, she decided, and turned her gaze back to Harper, not at all surprised to see the silver coming back to life in his eyes. They had been almost pure green by the time they'd gotten into the elevator, all the earlier passion apparently washed out by the passing moments of the ride here, or perhaps the cold as they'd walked to the building. Now they were beginning to glow silver again, and it made relief course through her. He'd been so silent in the car, she'd worried—

Her thoughts scattered, and she held her breath as Harper suddenly closed the space between them. She expected him to take her into his arms and kiss her. At least it's what she was hoping for, but instead he moved behind her. Drina started to turn, but he caught her shoulders and turned her himself, but so that her back was fully to him again.

"Look."

Drina peered where he was pointing to see them reflected in the mirrored surface of the sliding closet doors: a tall, fair-haired man in a charcoal suit, and a shorter, dark-haired and olive-skinned woman in a black dress. The moment she was looking where he wanted, Harper's hands slipped from her shoulders and she felt them at her back, and then her dress loosened as he slid the zipper down.

Drina swallowed, fighting the urge to turn to him again. He obviously didn't want her to. She didn't know why, but was willing to play along . . . for now, she decided.

His gaze met hers in the mirror again, and then his hands appeared, one at her shoulder and the other catching the already fallen arm of her dress and tugging both down until the dress dropped away to pool around her feet. It left her in the red and black lingerie and the thigh-high boots, and Drina had to admit she looked damned good. Hot even. A little like a dominatrix maybe, but still hot. She would have to thank Stephanie, she decided. That thought scattered when Harper skimmed his fingers lightly up her arms, raising goose bumps and making her shiver. She gave up her quiescence then and tried to turn, but Harper slid one arm around her waist, holding her in place.

"Watch," he whispered by her ear, his breath bringing on another shiver.

Drina returned her attention dutifully to the mirror and forced herself to stay still. The moment she did, he began to move, his eyes burning as he withdrew his arm until his hand was flat on her stomach. He then raised it to slide over one breast as his other hand appeared to cover the other. Holding her that way, he pulled her back against his chest, his fingers beginning to knead and squeeze her through the flimsy material of her bra as he lowered his head to press a kiss to her neck.

Drina tilted her head back on a moan and covered his hands with hers to urge him on, but he stopped at once.

"No."

She blinked her eyes open with confusion and met his gaze.

"Watch, don't touch," he growled by her ear.

Drina hesitated, but then let her hands drop again. The moment she did, he began to caress her once more through her bra, and then he let one hand drift away and slide down her belly and between her legs to cup her there. A groan rose from her throat, and Drina had to fight not to close her eyes and give in to the sensations his touch evoked. But she wanted to see now. The sight of his hands on her was incredibly erotic.

Harper continued to caress her through the silky red material for a moment, tweaking the nipple of the breast he held and rubbing her panties against her core until her breath was coming in little pants, and then he suddenly withdrew both hands to find the back of her bra. When it slipped away to join her dress on the floor, his hands replaced it, and Drina leaned her head back against his shoulder, watching through half-closed eyes as he fondled her.

"Beautiful," he growled, biting her ear almost painfully.

Drina shook her head slightly though she couldn't

have said if it was in denial of the compliment or out of sheer frustration. She wanted to touch him, and being forced to stand there quiescent while he played with her was becoming unbearable.

"Harper," she growled in warning, but froze as one of his hands suddenly slid down again, this time slipping inside her panties and between her legs to dip unerringly between her folds to find the bud hidden there.

She heard a sound halfway between a cry and a moan and realized it was coming from her, and then he withdrew his hands and moved in front of her. Drina immediately felt relief course through her, but before she could reach for him, he was urging her backward. She stepped out of the circle of her gown, but he continued to urge her back until she came up against a wall.

Harper then dropped to his haunches before her. Kneeling at her feet, he leaned forward to press a kiss to the skin above one boot. He then peered up the length of her body and watched her face as he reached for the waist of her panties and began to draw them down.

Drina stared back, lifting first one booted foot and then the other so he could remove the delicate cloth. He tossed it on her growing pile of clothes and moved his mouth to the skin above her other boot, this time licking along the rim to the inside of her thigh, his head forcing her legs farther apart before his mouth began to travel up.

"Harper," she gasped, grabbing for his head as her legs began to tremble. He braced her with his hands at the backs of her thighs, using his hold to urge her legs even wider to allow his lips to travel farther up until he reached what he was searching for. The moment his mouth closed over her most tender spot, she cried out and threw her head back, damned near knocking herself out when it slammed into the wall.

Stars danced behind her closed eyes, but she didn't get the chance to worry overmuch about it; Harper was pushing everything away with his actions, driving everything but pleasure from her mind and building the pressure until she was nearly sobbing with need.

Drina was teetering on the edge, wave after wave rolling through her and pushing at her when he suddenly straightened in front of her.

She blinked her eyes opened and peered at him, then grabbed for his shoulders when he suddenly caught her behind the legs and raised and spread them as he had in the alley. Pinning her against the wall with his body, Harper urged her to wrap her legs around his hips.

Instinct alone had Drina obeying the silent order. Certainly, she wasn't capable of much in the way of thought. Her eyes slid past his shoulder to find their image in the mirror, and she saw that his coat jacket was gone, his shirt untucked, and his suit pants hanging low on his hips. She wondered when he'd removed the jacket and undone the pants, but then he was sliding into her, and she just didn't care.

Drina cried out and closed her eyes, no longer interested in watching . . . or anything else outside of the force building inside her. The world could have crumbled and fallen away around them, and she wouldn't have cared as he pounded into her, sending wave after irresistible wave of unbearable passion searing through her body and brain until it exploded bright and hot in her mind. It then receded, leaving darkness.

Drina woke to find herself sprawled naked in the silk sheets of a king-sized bed and alone. Sitting up, she peered around the darkened room, making out furniture, blackout blinds, and several doors, but no Harper.

Frowning, she slid her feet to the floor and stood up. She started toward the nearest door, hoping it led somewhere besides a closet, but stumbled on something on the floor and paused to glance down at her boots. She stared at them blankly for a moment, some part of her brain working out that Harper must have removed them for her while she was unconscious, and then continued forward again.

The first door she tried was an en suite bathroom. The second was a closet, but the third led out into a hall, and she padded down it on silent, bare feet, only pausing when it ended at a set of four steps down into a large open living room. Eyebrows climbing up her forehead, she ran her eyes over the huge fireplace, the elegant black and white furnishings, and the wall of windows that surely stretched fifteen or twenty feet to the ceiling at one end of the room. That's where her gaze stopped.

Harper stood in the center of the wall of windows, dressed in his shirt and pants, staring out over the lights of the city. She would have bet a lot of money that he wasn't seeing anything outside, however. There was a moroseness about his pose and expression that convinced her he was lost in thoughts, and not pleasant ones.

"We're life mates."

Drina stiffened at the grim announcement. Apparently, he'd heard her approach despite her silence. Or perhaps he'd simply seen her, she realized as she spotted her reflection in the glass. And then his words sank in.

Crap. He knew.

Of course, she supposed she should have expected as much. As it was fabled, life mates did apparently faint after sex. No doubt he had too, though it appeared he'd recovered more swiftly than she had. And she'd obviously been deep in it. He'd not only carried her to bed but tugged those boots off without her stirring. She'd been out like a light.

Sighing, Drina continued forward, crossing the room toward him. "Most people would be happy about it."

"I am," he said, and she snorted in disbelief.

"You don't sound happy," she pointed out, pausing beside him and considering his face. "And you definitely don't look happy."

"Did you know?" Harper asked.

Drina turned to peer out the window. "Yes. I tried to read you the night we met, and then there was the eating and . . ." She shrugged.

"And you didn't say anything."

Drina sighed. "Marguerite said you might have

some trouble accepting it, and it was better to let you figure it out on your own."

"Marguerite," he muttered wryly.

"She said you feel guilty about Jenny's death and have been punishing yourself."

"It was my fault," Harper said wearily.

"I know you feel that way, but—"

"It's true," he barked. "If she'd never met me, she'd still be alive."

"Or she might have had a heart attack jogging. I mean, it was her heart that gave out, wasn't it? Some unknown defect she had?"

"Still, it was the turn that—"

"Harper, I do understand," Drina interrupted quietly, and he turned on her sharply.

"How the hell could you understand? Have you killed a life mate?"

Drina's eyes narrowed, and she said dryly, "Not yet, but there's still time."

He blinked in surprise.

"Don't yell at me. I know you're upset and hurting, but don't take it out on me," she said firmly. "It's one thing to punish yourself for what you think is your fault, but I won't be your whipping boy."

Sighing wearily, Harper ran a hand through his hair and turned away, muttering, "Sorry. I shouldn't have snapped."

"No, you shouldn't. And whether you want to believe it or not, I *do* understand your guilt over Jenny. I have my own guilt."

"For what?" he asked with surprise.

"Hello. Were you listening when I told you my history? I'm pretty sure I mentioned Beth and the girls in detail." Mouth flattening, Drina turned to peer out the window again. "I'm pretty sure Jimmy only picked them for victims because of their connection to me. If I'd never entered their lives, they might have lived to a ripe old age and never endured the horrors that twisted them at the end."

"That wasn't your fault," he said quietly. "You can't blame yourself for that. You did your best for them."

"Just as you did your best for Jenny," she pointed out. "But the fact that we were doing our best, and had no idea how that might play out, won't make either of us feel less guilty."

Harper turned back to the window and sighed wearily.

They stood like that for a minute, and then Drina shifted restlessly. "Marguerite said that you are so determined to punish yourself that you might do something foolish like avoid me to keep from ac-knowledging we were life mates."

"A little late for that," he muttered.

"Only because you weren't given the opportu-nity," Drina said with certainty, and then added, "She said not to confront you with it, and to let you realize it for yourself, but to be prepared for you to try to push me away once you do realize it . . . which, of course, you're doing."

"I'm not pushing you away," Harper denied, glancing around with surprise.

Drina rolled her eyes. "Oh, please, I'm standing here not six inches away, naked as the day I was born, and it feels like there are miles between us."

She felt his eyes glide over her, and held her breath, hoping he'd bridge the emotional gulf he'd created between them, but she wasn't terribly surprised when he turned away and looked out the window again.

"I just need time to adjust to this," he muttered, leaning one arm on the window and pressing his forehead to it.

"Right," Drina said. Her temper was stirring, but her voice was calm as she asked, "What exactly are you adjusting to?"

Harper straightened and frowned. "I need to wrap my brain around it, is all. This has taken me by surprise."

She nodded. "And how long will that take?"

He shrugged helplessly, and then said miserably, "I don't know."

"Fine," she snapped, finally unleashing the rebellion stirring within her. It was a familiar sensation for Drina, and she turned on him, and said coolly, "Well, first off, I resent that in punishing yourself, I too will be punished. And second, I should warn you, I don't intend to take that punishment for very long. You may want to wallow in your guilt and shun what we could have, but that doesn't mean I intend to wait around forever for you to 'adjust.' You have two weeks. Once Victor and Elvi return, and I leave here, I'm asking Marguerite to actively look for another possible life mate for me. One who will actually want me." She smiled coldly into his stunned face, and added, "And I'm sure she will manage it.

After all, I'm your second possible life mate in two years. With Marguerite actively looking, it might not even take that long."

Much to her relief, Drina saw alarm flash across his face at the suggestion. Perhaps there was hope for them, she thought, but merely turned on her heel and started back across the living room, adding, "Now, if you'll excuse me, I've got two doses of Sweet Ecstasy still coursing through me and don't intend to suffer any more than necessary. I'm going downstairs to give the doorman the night of his life. It won't be as satisfying as it would have been with you, but you're obviously more interested in wallowing in your guilt than me . . . and beggars can't be choosers."

Drina wasn't terribly surprised to hear him curse. Nor was she surprised to hear the quick patter of his footsteps as he gave chase. She didn't speed up or break into a run, simply continued on, making it all the way across the room and up the four steps to the hall before he caught her arm and jerked her back around with enough force to bring her crashing up against his chest. Catching his hand in her hair, he dragged her head back and slammed his mouth down on hers. She could feel his resentment in that kiss, his anger that she wasn't going to sit sadly sighing and patiently waiting for him to fight his demons until he felt he'd suffered enough that he could allow them to enjoy this gift they'd been given. She could almost hear his conscience battling with his desire as he struggled between what he wanted and what he felt he deserved.

Drina stayed completely still and unresponsive as she waited to see which side would win, but when the caress turned from anger to passion, she knew his conscience had lost this round. The moment it did, she relaxed and reached for the buttons of his shirt.

"You'll drive me crazy," Harper muttered, tearing his mouth from hers to trail it along her neck.

"Probably," she agreed, finishing with his buttons and turning her attention to tugging his shirt out of his pants. Pushing it off his shoulders then, she ran her hands over his muscled chest and sighed with pleasure, teasing, "For a cook, you have a good body."

"Thank the nanos," he muttered, sucking in a breath when her fingers skimmed down his belly to work at his pants. He caught her hands as she finished with the fastening and began to slide the zipper down, then waited until she'd raised her eyes to his in question before asking, "You wouldn't really have gone downstairs and—"

"I never make idle threats," Drina interrupted, dropping to her knees before him.

"Good to know," Harper muttered, as she shook his hands from hers and finished what she'd started, drawing the zipper down.

Drina caught her fingers in the waist of pants and boxers, and pulled them down, smiling as he sprang free. Reaching out, she closed her fingers around him, her eyes closing at the shaft of excitement it sent shooting through her own body.

Shared pleasure. Another symptom of life mates.

This was really her first chance to experience it. Prior to this, Harper had insisted on doing all the—Drina's thoughts died as she realized there was no way he couldn't have known they were life mates earlier in the night. He would have experienced this both at the bar and afterward. What did that mean? He hadn't run at the first touch. Was there more hope for them than she'd been led to believe?

Her ponderings scattered as he spoke.

"Maybe we should move to the—" Harper's words choked off as she leaned forward and ran her tongue lightly along the side of his growing erection, sending little licks of excitement through them both.

Bracing his hands on both walls of the hall, he muttered, "Next time," and then groaned with her as she took him into her mouth.

The ringing of a phone drew Drina from sleep and had her shifting grumpily.

"Yes?"

Blinking her eyes open at the sound of Harper's voice, she peered at his chest, which she presently nestled on, then raised her eyes to his face. They were in his large king-sized bed. He'd obviously woken first, as usual, and carried her there again because they'd been in the kitchen when unconsciousness overtook her. Drina had gone there in search of food, but of course Harper hadn't even lived here for a year, and while he had told her he had a cleaning service come in weekly anyway, he hadn't eaten in centuries before the trip to Port Henry, so hadn't had food in even then.

There hadn't been a crumb in the kitchen. No blood either. Fortunately, Harper had woken and come to find her as she'd realized that and managed to distract her from both hungers with a different one. Really, kitchen counters were the perfect height for such a distraction.

"I'll call you back," Harper said, glancing to her when she began to draw invisible circles on his chest. He reached out to set the phone in its cradle, then turned, rolling Drina onto her back and coming down on top of her with his face at chest level.

"Who was that?" she murmured, stretching beneath him and smiling as she felt something hard press against her leg.

"The pilot," he mumbled, catching her hands and pressing them down on either side of her head as he nibbled his way along her collarbone. "The storm's over. We can fly now."

"Oh." Drina sighed with keen disappointment that this idyllic period was over. "We should go."

"We will," he assured her, his mouth moving lower now, making a beeline for one breast. "After."

Drina hesitated, but her sense of duty made her shake her head. "I should—"

Harper released one hand to cover her mouth, then lifted his head and peered at her solemnly. "It's midafternoon. We can't land in the schoolyard until evening. It's a school day."

"Oh," she said, and then smiled slowly. "Well, in that case . . ."

Turning abruptly, she caught him by surprise and managed to roll him onto his back again, and immediately rose to straddle him. Smiling down at his surprise, she said, "You should feed me."

Harper peered at her for a moment, his eyes narrowing in calculation, and then he heaved a reluctant sigh. "Yes, I suppose. I *am* hungry."

Drina blinked and managed to hide her disappointment. She'd rather hoped for some protest, maybe a little wrestling session, and then round six of mad passionate sex . . . or maybe it would have been round seven. She'd lost count. It didn't matter anyway, it seemed Harper was more hungry for food than her.

Forcing a smile, she started to slip off of him, to stand beside the bed, and then cried out with surprise when she was caught around the waist and tugged back onto the bed.

Drina landed on her back on the mattress, and he was immediately coming down on top of her again. Harper did seem to like to be the one in control in the bedroom, she'd noticed. Oddly enough, Drina found she didn't mind, which was kind of unexpected when she considered that she had spent most of her life struggling for independence and control in the rest of her life. But then, perhaps that was why. It was nice to lay down the burden and let him steer the boat, especially when it was such a pleasant journey.

"I thought you were hungry?" She laughed, as he set about pinning her legs with his own and pinning her hands down by her head again to be sure she couldn't roll on top again, or even move really.

"I am," Harper assured her, and then bent his

head to flick the tip of his tongue repeatedly over one hardening nipple, before adding, "And we *will* eat. After."

"After," Drina agreed on a moan as he stopped teasing and finally closed his mouth over her nipple.

Nine

Drina glanced over the dark schoolyard they were hovering above and then to Casey Cottage on the corner across the street. She stared at the lit windows of the house, wishing with all her heart that the storm had continued, and they hadn't had to return. It wasn't because she didn't want to see Stephanie, Mirabeau, and Tiny, or even Anders, but the closer they'd gotten to Port Henry, the more grim Harper had become. She very much feared the passion and laughter of the last twenty-four hours would soon be nothing more than a memory as Harper sank back into his guilt.

"Idiot man," she muttered under her breath as the helicopter touched down, and then she sighed and moved along the seat toward the door when Harper shifted to open it. He got out first, and turned, raising his hands to help her out.

Drina hesitated, taking in his impersonal expression, then got out, her teeth grinding together when he took her elbow to usher her away from the helicopter.

Like she was an old crone rather than the life mate he'd made love to seven times in the last twenty-four hours, she thought bitterly. It was a noticeable difference from the affectionate way he'd slid his arm around her waist and tucked her to his side as they'd made their way to the helicopter in Toronto. She could actually feel the ghost of Jenny Harper slipping between them, cold and clammy.

Infuriated by that fact, Drina searched her mind for something to say or do to stop what was happening, but in the end she simply slid her booted foot to the side, tripping him. She then allowed herself to fall with him when he went crashing toward the ice. Harper did what she expected and caught her to his chest, turning as they fell, so that he took the brunt of the impact.

"Oh, I'm so sorry! My foot slipped on the ice," Drina lied, raising herself up on his chest and shifting "unintentionally" on his groin to peer into his stunned face. "Are you all right?"

Harper struggled briefly to regain the wind that had been knocked out of him, and then nodded. "I'll live."

"Oh, my poor Harper. Thank you for saving me from the worst of the fall," she said, and kissed him. It was no, "my hero" peck. It was an "I-ain't-wearing-these-bloody-painful-FM-boots-for-nothing-buddy," devouring of his mouth.

Much to Drina's satisfaction, Harper only managed to hold out for a moment before his arms closed around her, and he took the lead. She knew she'd won this round when he rolled her in the snow and began to yank at the buttons of her coat to get at what was underneath as he ground his hips against her.

"All right, you two, cut it out, or I'll have to arrest the pair of you for lewd behavior. There are kids watching, you know."

Harper tore his mouth from Drina's and glanced around to stare blankly at the man crossing the schoolyard toward them. "Teddy."

"It looked like you took a hell of a spill, and I rushed over to see if you two were all right, but it's pretty obvious you recovered quickly enough," Teddy muttered, pausing beside them and offering Harper a hand.

Sighing, Harper accepted the assistance. Once on his feet, he turned back to help Drina up. She glanced around as she rose, noting that, as had happened when they'd left, there were faces peering out of nearly every window of the surrounding houses, and several of them *were* children.

So, her plan hadn't been the best, Drina thought with a shrug. At least it had worked. If nothing else, she was now pretty sure that she just had to keep hammering at Harper's walls with sex. As her life mate, he would find it hard to fight their attraction. So, every time the ghost of Jenny Harper slipped between them, and he threw up a wall, she would use sex to tear it down, Drina decided. She could handle that.

"Good Lord, girl!"

Drina blinked her thoughts away at that exclamation and glanced to Teddy Brunswick to see him eyeing her boots with dismay.

"It's no wonder you can't stay on your feet. Those boots are for looking at, not walking," the chief of police muttered. Shaking his head, he took her arm as if afraid she wouldn't be able to stay upright long on the heels, and then he urged her forward.

"They're fine," Harper said quietly, slipping his arm around her waist and drawing her against his side. It was a possessive act and one that sent a stream of warmth through her, as well as the hope that they would overcome his guilt and work things out after all.

Teddy chuckled. "Well hell, Stoyan, I'm not surprised you like them. If those aren't a pair of FMs most red-blooded men would like to lick, I don't know what are."

"You know about FMs?" Harper asked with surprise over Drina's head.

"I may be old, but I'm not brainless," Teddy said dryly, and then paused to glance both ways as they reached the road.

Drina bit her lip to keep back a chuckle at Harper's disgruntled expression, and asked, "You were at the house, Teddy. Is everything all right?"

"Fine as far as I know," Teddy assured her, urging them to cross the street. "I was just stopping by to check on things on my way home. I wanted to ask about Tiny's turning too and had just pulled into the driveway when your helicopter showed up, so I waited to walk in with you."

"Tiny's turning tonight?" Harper asked tensely, and Drina didn't need to read his mind to know he was thinking of Jenny's turn. The ghost had returned, but with Teddy there, she couldn't trip Harper and throw herself on him again. She would have to be patient.

"Not tonight, no," Teddy said. "But I'm sure it will be soon. Anders brought the blood down for it, and Leonius isn't in the area, so there's no worry of his attacking while everyone is distracted . . ." He shrugged, and then added sensibly, "There's no use in waiting. I'm sure it will be in the next day or two, and I want to be on hand when it happens in case they need extra help."

"Right," Harper muttered grimly.

"So how was your outing in Toronto?" Teddy asked, as they started up the driveway to the house. "Heard you got snowed in."

"Yes, but it was still nice," Drina said quietly when Harper remained silent. "In fact, I'm almost sorry we had to return."

"Uh-huh." Teddy nodded. "So you two are life mates?"

Drina turned on him sharply. "Did Stephanie and Mirabeau tell you—"

"They didn't tell me a thing. You two just have that new-life-mate glow about you. I've seen five new life-mate couples now, not counting you two, and recognize the look."

"Six," Harper said tightly.

"What's that?" Teddy asked.

"You've seen six new life-mate couples," Harper explained.

"No, I don't think so," Teddy said with a frown and began to count them off. "Now, let's see, there's Victor and Elvi, DJ and Mabel, Alessandro and Leonora, Edward and Dawn, Mirabeau and Tiny . . . That's five."

"You forgot—"

"Oh wait, you're right, I forgot Lucian and Leigh. They were still brand-spanking-new life mates when they came down here that first time," Teddy said with a nod. "So it *is* six. And you two are seven."

"I meant Jenny and I," Harper said firmly, unable to leave the woman out.

"Hmm." Teddy was silent as they traveled along the side of the garage toward the deck, but then said, "Well, here's the thing. You two weren't like the others."

Harper looked startled by the words, and it was Drina who asked, "What do you mean?"

"Well, sure enough Harper seemed eager, but Jenny was another kettle of fish. She treated Harper like she did poor old Bobby Jarrod when they were in high school. The boy was crazy for her," he explained. "Over the moon, and they even dated for a while, but she kept him at arm's length, treated him real cool." He shook his head with distaste. "Everyone knew she was just using him for free tickets to the movies. He was an usher at the Cineplex in London," he explained.

Drina glanced to Harper to see how he was taking this, but his head was bowed, and she couldn't see his expression.

"The biggest favor she did for Bobby was tossing him over for that idiot Randy Matheson when he showed her some interest." Teddy shook his head. "Now there was a troublemaker. She always went after troublemakers. And Randy's name fit him to a T, let me tell you. Never seen a more randy teenager. I caught those two parking on back roads all around the county until she tossed him over for some London fellow with a rich daddy and an allowance big enough he could afford to rent himself a motel room rather than grope in cars. I wasn't sorry about that at all. Chasing off bare-arsed teenagers just gets old pretty quick."

They'd crossed the deck and reached the door of the house by then, and Teddy paused to turn back to Harper, saying, "I never would have told you all that had Jenny lived, and I didn't say it when she died because I knew you were hurting, but now that you're happily settled with Drina here, and enjoying that new-life-mate glow like the others, I have to tell you I think you made a lucky escape there. I don't know all the ins and outs of this life-mate business, but while Jenny might have been a possible life mate for you and agreed to the turn, I don't think her heart was in it. I kind of got the feeling she just saw you as another Bobby Jarrod."

Turning away, Teddy opened the screen door and raised a hand to knock but paused as Mirabeau opened the door from inside.

"Beau," Teddy greeted, stepping inside.

Mirabeau smiled, then glanced past Teddy to Drina and Harper and waved them in. "Come on you two. It's cold out."

Forcing a smile, Drina stepped inside, wishing she could drag Harper somewhere to talk and find out what he was thinking. But there didn't appear to be much of a chance at the moment. She would have to figure out a way to get him alone and talk to him later.

"Decided to come out of hiding now that Drina and Stephanie have gone to bed, did you?"

Harper stiffened at that greeting from Anders as he stepped off the stairs and turned the corner into the dining room. The hunter sat at the table, a deck of cards spread out before him in what appeared to be a complicated version of solitaire. Harper frowned at the man, not appreciating that one of the few times the Russian chose to speak more than a word or two was to call him out on his behavior.

"I wasn't hiding," he lied, turning to walk along the L-shaped counter separating the kitchen from the dining room. Moving to the refrigerator, he opened it, his eyes sliding from the bags of blood to the available food inside.

"Right," Anders said dryly. "You just like four-hour showers."

Harper scowled into the refrigerator, and then grabbed both a bag of blood and a bowl of some sort of leftover. He wasn't sure what it was, but he was hungry. He'd heat it up and see what it tasted like.

The dinner he'd had with Drina was the first time he'd eaten in a while. He hadn't a clue what he would like, so everything was an experiment just now.

"Your avoiding her hurt Drina," Anders growled.

Harper set the bowl on the counter with a sigh and lowered his head. He shouldn't be surprised that his fleeing the minute they'd got their coat and boots off, and then not returning downstairs would hurt her, he supposed, but he hadn't been thinking of her. He'd been thinking of—

"A dead woman," Anders said grimly, reminding him that his thoughts were easily read at the moment.

"She was my life mate," Harper said quietly.

"*Was* being the operative word. She died. Fate had other plans for you. Now you have Drina. It's a damned lucky turn of events for you. Some never find a second life mate, and those who do usually have to wait centuries. And Drina's already immortal, another bit of luck since you've already used your one allowed turn. It would be foolish to throw this good fortune away."

Harper stared out the back window of the house, frustration coursing through him. Everything Anders said was true, but he couldn't seem to rid himself of the clawing guilt. He'd managed to forget it for a while in Toronto, but the closer they'd gotten to Port Henry, the more he'd felt like a philandering husband returning from an elicit rendezvous with his secretary.

Harper closed his eyes. Jenny was dead and in the grave because she'd been willing to turn and be his life mate, and he was off laughing and playing with another woman. He felt like he was dancing on her grave.

But that wasn't even the worst of it. The thing that really ate at him was that he couldn't even remember what Jenny had looked like anymore. That wasn't because of Drina's arrival. He hadn't been able to recall her face for a while now. Her image had faded from his mind almost before she'd been in the ground. It was wrong. Shameful. She'd died to be with him and deserved better than that.

"And what does Drina deserve?" Anders asked, obviously still in his thoughts.

Harper turned and scowled at the usually uncommunicative man. "What do you care?"

"I don't," Anders said with a shrug, moving cards around on the table. "If you want to throw away a good thing when fate is kind enough to give it to you, go for it."

"Thank you," Harper said dryly, turning back to the counter.

"But I'll tell you this," Anders said in a conversational tone. "If it had turned out that Drina could have been a life mate to either you or me . . . you'd be dead. I'd have killed to claim her. Most immortals would. So I'm thinking you're either a fool or seriously fucked up. Either way, she's better off without you."

Harper whipped around to gape at him, but Anders didn't even glance up from his cards and continued matter-of-factly playing his game as he added, "I'm doubting she'll see it that way, though.

This'll eat at her, distract her from what she's supposed to be doing, and a distracted hunter usually
ends up a dead hunter."

Anders paused to glance to Harper, and added,
"That's all right, though. You'll have two life mates'
deaths on your hands and can completely submerge
yourself in guilt and misery, right?"

"Gin," Stephanie said triumphantly, laying her
cards on the table.

Drina tore her gaze from the ceiling and reached
for a card from the deck.

"Hello. I said *gin,"* Stephanie said dryly, making
Drina pause and blink at her in confusion. Heaving a heavy sigh, the teenager shook her head. "You
aren't even paying attention, Dree."

"Sorry," Drina muttered, and then a small smile
tugged at her lips, and she set her cards down,
saying, "Beth calls me that."

"Dree?" Stephanie asked, collecting the cards and
beginning to shuffle them again. "She's your partner, right?"

Drina nodded, suddenly wishing Beth were there.
She could use some advice at the moment.

"Harper's avoiding you," Stephanie murmured
sadly as she began to deal cards.

"It would seem so," Drina said on a sigh, her
eyes sliding to the ceiling again. He'd been avoiding her ever since their return the night before.
He'd escaped to his room to shower and change the
moment they'd gotten their coats and boots off and
hadn't left it until she and Stephanie had retired

for the night. She'd heard him come down from the third floor and descend the creaky stairs.

Now it was midmorning, and he was apparently still sleeping. Or hiding in his room. She didn't know which but suspected it was the latter.

"What are you going to do about it?" Stephanie asked quietly, finishing dealing and setting the remaining cards on the table.

Drina shook her head. She'd lain awake most of the night trying to figure that one out, and she'd been fretting over it since rising with Stephanie this morning and still didn't have a clue. It was hard to know what to do to drag him out of his gloom and preoccupation if he was going to just hide in his damned room.

Oh, she knew what she wanted to do. Drina wanted to go to his room, climb into his bed, and wipe the memories of Jenny from his mind with hot, live-life-mate sex. Unfortunately, she had responsibilities here. She had to spend the nights with Stephanie to be sure the girl didn't take it into her head to run off to her mortal family, and she had to spend the days watching out for her until Anders took over. That left only the evening hours for her to do anything, and Drina suspected Harper was going to use the presence of the others to keep her at arm's length, or—

Her thoughts scattered to the four winds, and Drina stiffened as she heard footsteps moving along the landing above them and then start down the stairs.

"It's him," Stephanie whispered, sounding excited, and Drina glanced at her with surprise. Before she could ask how the girl knew it wasn't someone else, Harper came around the corner and into the kitchen.

"Good morning, ladies," he greeted, crossing straight to Drina and bending to press a kiss to her forehead.

"Morning," Drina whispered huskily, surprise and relief leaving her wide-eyed as he straightened.

Harper paused halfway upright, his gaze caught by hers, then bent to kiss her again, this time on the lips.

"Oh geez, gag," Stephanie said with disgust, as the kiss turned carnal. "Really, Harper? At least Dree is imagining dragging you upstairs to the privacy and comfort of a bedroom and not throwing you on the table to have her way with you."

"The table?" Drina asked breathlessly when Harper immediately broke their kiss.

"Sorry. A stray thought," Harper muttered, straightening.

Stephanie snorted. "More like a full-blown fantasy. I mean, it was pretty detailed." Standing, she moved around the table, heading for the stairs. "I'm going to brush my hair and change my clothes if we're going out. That gives you two about ten minutes to get it out of your system, so I'm not stuck with a couple of frustrated horndogs all day. But no pressure," she added on a laugh as she swung out of the room and started upstairs.

"We're going out?" Drina murmured, turning her gaze back to Harper.

"I thought I'd take you girls to the city for lunch and some shopping," Harper admitted, catching her hand and dragging her from her chair.

"Oh," she breathed, stumbling after him through the kitchen and into the pantry. "What are we doing?"

Harper came to a halt in the small pantry, turned to catch her by the waist, and lifted her onto the counter in front of the window overlooking the backyard.

"What—?"

"You heard her. We have ten minutes," Harper muttered, catching the hem of her T-shirt and tugging it upward to reveal another of her new bras, this one a pale pink that stood out against her olive skin. Pausing, he breathed, "Damn, I think I have a new favorite."

"Harper," Drina protested on a laugh, grabbing for his hands as he tugged one cup aside to free a breast. "Stop, we can't."

"Ten minutes," he reminded her, bending forward to latch onto the nipple he'd just bared.

"But we'll pass out, and she'll find us naked on the pantry floor," Drina groaned, releasing his hands to grab his head instead. Unfortunately, while her mind was being sensible—at least a tiny part of it was—her body wasn't like-minded, and instead of forcing his head away, she laced her fingers through his hair, silently urging him on.

"Damn," Harper breathed, letting her nipple slip from his mouth. He remained still for a moment, and then straightened and slipped her breast back into her bra.

Drina nearly groaned aloud when he then tugged her shirt back down, but she knew it was for the best.

"We'll just have to manage it with our clothes on."

She blinked with confusion. "What?"

"We'll stay dressed," Harper announced, and then stepped between her open, jeans-clad thighs and kissed her.

Drina didn't have a clue what he was up to, but his tongue was now in her mouth, his hands finding and caressing her breasts through her T-shirt and bra, and she found it hard to think about anything but the sensations now flooding through her.

When he moved closer and ground his hardness against her through her jeans, Drina groaned and dug her nails into his T-shirt, dragging it upward. Harper immediately broke their kiss, and muttered, "Clothes on," as he trailed kisses across her cheek to her ear.

"Clothes," she echoed without comprehension, and released his T-shirt, only to move her hands around to reach for his belt buckle.

Harper immediately released her breasts and stepped back to lift her off the counter. That snapped Drina out of it a bit, and she opened her mouth to protest, but then bit her lip in surprise when he suddenly turned her so her back was to him, and growled, "Hands on the counter."

"What?" she asked with surprise.

"Hands on the countertop," Harper ordered, his own hands moving around her waist and up to cup her breasts again through her clothes. It immediately reminded her of his apartment and his doing this in front of the mirrored closet doors. The erotic memory of their reflection filled her head and ratcheted her mounting excitement by several degrees.

Drina ground her teeth and leaned on the counter, her head bowing as one of his hands slid down between her legs, both caressing her through her jeans and pressing her bottom back against his hips and the hardness growing there.

When Harper suddenly used his hand at her breast to pull her upright and back against his chest, Drina leaned her head back on his shoulder. Closing her eyes, she covered his hands with hers and moaned as he nearly lifted her off the floor with the hand between her legs in his effort to affect her through her thick jeans.

"Eight minutes," he breathed, nipping at her ear.

A breathless laugh slipping from her lips, Drina opened her eyes, and then blinked as she spotted movement in the backyard. She squinted against the bright sunlight pouring through the window, trying to make out what she'd seen, then gasped and stiffened as Harper stopped cupping her between the legs and shifted his hand to slide it down her pants. Slipping under the waistline of both jeans and panties, his fingers dove unerringly between her legs, intensifying everything for them both.

"Oh God," Harper muttered against her neck, his caress becoming frantic as their mingled pleasure and excitement bounced between them in growing waves.

"Yes," Drina gasped, eyes closing and hips rotating to his touch, so that she ground back against him with each movement. She was clawing at his hands now with excitement, her only thought reaching that peak they were racing toward, and then he slid two fingers inside her and sank his fangs into her neck at the same time, and Drina screamed as pleasure exploded over them.

"So tell me again about that mouse Drina saw that made her scream and faint?"

Drina turned in the front passenger seat of Harper's BMW to make a face at Stephanie in the backseat. "All right, smarty-pants. You can read our minds and know there was no mouse. Get over it."

"Well, even if I couldn't read your minds, you don't really think I would have bought that whole mouse story, do you?" Stephanie asked with amusement. "I mean, seriously, a hunter who faints at the sight of a tiny mouse?"

Drina shook her head and turned to face forward again. As usual, Harper had woken from their postcoital faint before her. He'd been trying to rouse her when Stephanie had found them on the pantry floor. She had no idea why he'd even bothered to make up the mouse story when the girl could read them so easily, but he had. As one would expect, it hadn't gone over.

"It wasn't exactly a postcoital faint, was it," Stephanie said dryly. "I mean coitus is—"

"Stephanie!" she barked, swinging on her with horror.

"Well, it wasn't," Stephanie said defensively. "Harper didn't actually insert part A into part B.

Well, I suppose there was some insertion, but of part F not—"

"How do you know that?" Drina interrupted her teasing sharply.

Stephanie rolled her eyes. "We've been through this. I can read your mind, remember?"

"Yes, but I wasn't thinking of it," Drina said at once, aware that Harper was glancing from the road, to her, to Stephanie in the rearview mirror with a troubled frown.

Stephanie shrugged. "You must be. Otherwise, how would I know what you two did?"

Drina stared at her silently, more than troubled. She hadn't been thinking of what she and Harper had done. She'd been thinking of the after, the waking up on the floor. Yet Stephanie apparently knew what had happened between her and Harper and obviously in detail. It should embarrass her, but she was too concerned by what the girl's apparently pulling—not just thoughts, but—actual memories from her mind could mean to worry about embarrassment.

Usually, for an immortal to access someone's memories, they had to get the person they were reading to recall them. Stephanie apparently could access them whether the person was thinking of them or not.

"You think I'm a freak now," Stephanie said unhappily.

"Not a freak," Drina said quietly. "Apparently very gifted."

The girl relaxed and smiled a little at that. "Gifted?"

"Very," Drina murmured, and turned in her seat to face front, doing her best to keep her thoughts as blank as possible. Stephanie's abilities weren't normal, but she didn't even want to get near that thought in the girl's presence. She needed to think, but away from Stephanie.

She also needed to find a chance to talk to Harper, Drina thought on a sigh. While she was glad he wasn't avoiding her this morning, he had last night, and his blowing hot and then cold was leaving her uncertain and worried about the future. She had started out her journey to Port Henry determined to be patient, but that was before she'd met and spent time with him. The more Drina got to know Harper, the more emotionally invested she became, and she'd started out pretty invested to begin with for the simple reason that he was her life mate.

The moment Drina had walked into Casey Cottage, tried to read him, failed, and acknowledged that Marguerite was right, and he was her life mate, she'd thrown in half her emotional chips. But with every conversation they had, and every experience they shared, she was throwing in more chips, and Drina was afraid of getting hurt here if his guilt proved too strong for him to put aside.

"Are you feeling all right, Stephanie? You look pale."

Harper glanced to the girl at Drina's words and frowned as he noted her pallor.

"I'm fine, hungry is all," Stephanie mumbled. "Can we stop and get a sundae or something on the way out? That'll settle my stomach."

"I don't think it's food you're hungry for," Drina said solemnly. "We've been at the mall for hours now, and you're a growing girl. You need to feed."

"I'll get the cooler out of the trunk and put it into the backseat before we leave. She can feed on the way back," Harper murmured, ushering them toward the exit nearest to where he'd parked.

"I don't want to feed," Stephanie complained, sounding as cranky as a five-year-old.

"I said you *need* to feed. *Want* doesn't come into it," Drina said firmly.

Harper couldn't help but notice this made Stephanie's lower lip protrude rebelliously. He suspected they would have a fight on their hands getting the girl to feed at this rate, and then noted the way she was rubbing her stomach, and said, "It will make your cramps go away."

"Whatever," Stephanie snapped, leading the way outside in a stomp.

"She just needs to feed," Drina murmured, excusing her behavior as if worried Harper might think badly of the girl.

"I know," he assured her, and then, finding it adorable that she would defend the girl like a mother bear with a cub, Harper slipped his arm around Drina's waist and drew her to his side to kiss her forehead. "You're going to be a good mother."

She turned a stunned face to him, then quickly looked forward again, and Harper smiled wryly. He supposed she hadn't yet considered the possibility of children. Not that he had, either. He hadn't really considered much at all yet.

Anders's words the night before had shaken Harper sufficiently to send him back to his room and into bed, where he'd lain contemplating the possibility of losing Drina to death. He'd been so wrapped up in his own emotional struggles, he hadn't even considered how it might affect her. Oh, certainly, she'd made him consider that if he didn't claim her, he might lose her to some possible alternate life mate, but that had seemed a far-off thing. Harper supposed, in his arrogance, he'd also imagined that he would have a chance to win her back in that distant future if his actions drove her away now.

But Anders's words had made him worry about her actually dying, killed as a direct result of her emotional upheaval and distraction. The possibility had scared the crap out of him and made him face what was important here. Jenny was dead, and while he felt responsible, there was nothing he could do to bring her back or rewrite what had happened. He had grieved and been wracked by guilt for a year and a half now. How much longer would his conscience demand he suffer for a death he never imagined, let alone intended? Did he really feel he needed to lose Drina, even temporarily, to make up for the loss of Jenny? And did he really want to risk losing her permanently to death just to satisfy that conscience?

The answer had been no, and Harper had finally gone to sleep around dawn having decided he wasn't going to avoid her anymore. It was time to put his guilt aside and embrace his good fortune, because he was definitely one lucky son of a bitch to be given a second chance at the brass ring of happiness with a life mate, especially so soon after receiving it the last time.

Harper wasn't foolish enough to think it would be easy. Deciding not to feel guilty was a first step, but he knew he would have to fight on occasion to keep to that decision. However, he was determined and felt sure he could do it . . . for Drina.

"Hurry up you two. Gawd, you're as slow as snails," Stephanie complained, shifting restlessly beside the car.

Harper heard Drina sigh with exasperation at the teen's moodiness and briefly tightened his arm around her waist in sympathy. He then dug his keys out of his pocket.

"You two get in. I'll get the cooler," Harper said, moving toward the back of the vehicle.

It was Drina who'd thought to bring blood along. Which was another reason he felt sure she'd be a good mother. It hadn't even occurred to him that Stephanie needed to feed more often than they did. As he lifted the cooler out of the trunk, he smiled at the thought of Drina with a little Drina in her arms. Or a little Harper, he thought as he closed the trunk and moved around to open the back passenger door and set it on the seat behind his own. Or both even. He grinned as he closed the back door and moved to open the driver's door.

"How am I supposed to feed? I don't have any straws," Stephanie snapped, as he slid behind the steering wheel.

"We'll stop at a drive-thru and buy a couple of drinks. You can use the straws," Harper said calmly, starting the engine.

Stephanie muttered under her breath, but didn't comment otherwise and Harper shifted the car into gear, then reached out to place his hand on Drina's leg as he steered them out of the parking lot. Her thigh was as hard as steel at first, telling him Stephanie's behavior had put her on edge as he'd suspected, but some of that tension left under his massaging fingers, and by the time he steered the car into the line at a fast-food drive-thru, she had relaxed considerably.

"What do you want?" Harper asked as he nosed up to the speaker. "Coke?"

"Whatever," Stephanie muttered.

"Coke it is," he said cheerfully, and quickly ordered three.

The moment Harper received and passed over the drinks, Drina passed Stephanie hers along with the straw from a second one. She then set the third drink in the holder for him, and took the lid off her glass to drink from the cup itself.

They were silent for a bit, Harper glancing in the rearview mirror occasionally to see that Stephanie actually was feeding. The fact that she went through three bags one after the other, stabbing the straws viciously into them and then grimly and steadily sucking back the thick red liquid, told him how badly she'd needed the blood.

They were nearly to Port Henry by the time she'd

finished the third one, and Stephanie heaved an audible sigh as she scrunched up the empty bag and tossed it back into the still nearly full cooler.

"Feel better?" Drina asked, turning in her seat to smile tentatively at the girl.

"Yeah," Stephanie admitted, sinking back in her seat with a sigh, and then, sounding embarrassed, she muttered, "Sorry if I was cranky."

Drina shook her head. "I should have kept better track of the time and thought to feed you sooner."

Stephanie smiled wryly. "Well, it's not like you're used to having kids around. Everyone in your family is old."

Harper glanced to Drina to see a cloud of worry cross her face and guessed this wasn't something she'd told the girl but another sign of Stephanie's skill at pulling information from their minds. It was growing increasingly obvious that Stephanie had some mad skills, beyond anything he'd encountered before.

Turning back to the road, he saw that they were approaching the first set of stoplights on the way into Port Henry. He eased his foot down on the brakes . . . and then applied more force when nothing happened.

"What's wrong with the brakes?" Stephanie popped into view in the rearview mirror as she abruptly sat up. He had no idea how she knew, probably a stray thought from his mind, he supposed, but didn't have time to work it out.

"The brakes?" Drina asked with confusion.

"Hold on," Harper ground out, reaching for the

emergency brakes and cursing when that had no effect. He tried to shut off the engine then, but knew it was too late; they were already flying into the intersection on a red light . . . and a semi was roaring toward them from their right, unaware of their problem and rushing to make his green.

The next moment seemed to pass both with the speed of a heartbeat, and crawl by like a slow-motion hour for Harper. He was vaguely aware of the girls' shouting, of roaring Drina's name himself and reaching desperately for her, and then the truck barreled into the passenger side and the scream of tearing metal joined the chaos. Blood, pop, and glass exploded through the interior of the car, and they were slammed about, and then moving sideways, screeching up the road on burning rubber and then rims, propelled by the semi. That seemed to last forever, though it was probably only a minute or two before the semi driver managed to stop his vehicle, and consequently the car as well, and then everything went silent and still.

Ten

Harper opened his eyes and stared at the ceiling over his bed, then a vision of Drina covered in blood filled his mind, and he sat up abruptly.

"Settle down, boy. You're safe," Teddy Brunswick said, hefting himself out of a chair beside the bed.

Harper stared at the man blankly, the crash replaying in his head; blood splashing, glass flying, and the smoke from burning rubber all filled his vision, accompanied by the sound track from hell. Shouts, screams, screeching metal, shrieking brakes, and then dead silence and stillness.

He recalled being dizzy from hitting his head. Barely holding on to consciousness, Harper had turned instinctively to Drina and moaned at what he'd found. Her bloodied body had appeared partially encased in metal, and what wasn't—including her face—had been shredded by the flying glass.

"Drina?" he growled, shoving aside the memory

along with the blankets that had been covering him, and shifting to get up.

"She's alive. You know you people don't die that easy," Teddy said grimly.

Harper relaxed a fraction, but continued to his feet, asking, "And Stephanie?"

"They're both in their room being tended to by Beau and Tiny," Teddy assured him, reaching out to steady Harper when he swayed on his feet. "I'm thinking you need blood. Your head wound didn't look too bad, but you lost consciousness and have been out all night. Your nanos probably used up a fair amount repairing whatever damage was done."

"All night?" Harper muttered with surprise.

Teddy nodded. "I was surprised myself. Once we cleaned away the blood, there didn't seem much wrong with you compared to the girls, but the knock your head took must have caused some internal damage that needed repair or something. We fed you a couple of bags of blood, but didn't want to give you too much and cause other problems." He frowned, and asked, "If I go fetch a bag for you, will you sit your arse down and wait for me to get back before trying to—?"

"I need to see Drina," Harper interrupted impatiently, staggering past the man.

"That's what I figured," Teddy said on a sigh, and caught his arm to help him to the door. "I'll see you down to the girls' room then before I fetch that blood."

Harper muttered a "thanks," but then remained silent for the rest of the walk down the hall, the flight of stairs, and up the second floor hall to the girls' room. He knew he definitely needed blood by the time they reached it. He was unsteady on his feet and exhausted by then. Obviously, there had been more damage done inside his head than it had appeared, but then his brain had probably bounced around inside his skull like jelly in a bowl during the accident.

Teddy reached past him to open the bedroom door, and Harper staggered eagerly forward, almost desperate to see for himself that Drina was all right. He spotted an exhausted Mirabeau and Tiny sitting in chairs by the window, and then his gaze dropped to the first bed, and he let out the breath he hadn't realized he'd been holding. Drina was pale, but otherwise appeared fine, with no sign of the shredded skin or smashed body he recalled in his memory.

Of course, she was under the covers, so there might be injuries still mending, but she would heal, he assured himself, his gaze now moving to Stephanie. She had been seated directly behind Drina on the impact side as well, and had no doubt taken equally severe injuries, but like Drina, the girl appeared pale and still but otherwise fine. There was an IV stand between the two single beds; two bags of blood hung from it, each with tubing. One long tube dropped down, and then curved into Stephanie's arm, the other trailed down from the second bag and led into Drina's.

"Sit down before you fall down," Teddy said gruffly, urging him to the bedside as Tiny and Mirabeau stood up.

"How are you feeling?" Mirabeau asked, coming around the bed toward him.

"I'm no expert on your people, but I think he needs blood," Teddy answered for him as he forced Harper to sit on the side of Drina's bed.

Mirabeau nodded and turned back toward the windows, but Tiny was already opening a cooler that sat under the window ledge and retrieving a bag.

"What happened?" Harper asked as he accepted the bag, and then clarified, "After the accident. How did you get us out?"

"I was first on the scene," Teddy said grimly. "Got the call in my car and headed right over. Didn't realize it was you three at first. Between injuries and the burst bags of blood all three of you were unrecognizable." He grimaced at the memory. "I thought it was people at first and as good as dead, but then you moaned Drina's name, and I took a second look. Once I realized it was you three, I blocked off the road and called the house, then started trying to get you all out. I thought we'd need the Jaws of Life, but then Beau and Anders got there and started pulling the metal away like it was toffee. Even so, it took a long time to get Stephanie and Drina out. They were both a damned mess. Never seen a body so mangled, let alone two, and it was hard to tell where flesh ended and metal began," he added with a shake of the head. "Never want to see anything like that again so long as I live."

"I had no brakes," Harper said fretfully, his old familiar friend, guilt, creeping over him as he wondered if there was something he could have done to prevent the crash.

"Yeah, I know," Teddy said, surprising him, and then explained, "I took witness reports, and when they kept saying you didn't even try to stop, I knew something was wrong. I had the car towed down to the garage to be looked over. The mechanic, Jimmy, called me just a few minutes before you woke up and reported that the brake lines were cut."

"Cut?" Harper asked with a frown, and then muttered, "We didn't have any trouble on the way into London. It must have been done in the parking lot while we were in the mall."

"Most likely," Teddy agreed. He then added, "The news, though, immediately made me wonder if that Leonius feller didn't track down the girl here after all."

Mirabeau shook her head at once. "Leonius wouldn't try to kill her. He wants her alive for breeding."

"Breeding?" Teddy squawked, his dismayed eyes shooting to the fifteen-year-old.

Mirabeau nodded, her expression tight. "To replace the sons he lost taking Stephanie and her sister. He wouldn't have tried to kill her," she said firmly. "It couldn't have been him."

"I don't know," Tiny said slowly, and when the others turned to him in question, he pointed out, "He'd know that a car accident probably wouldn't kill her. And this Leonius sounds pretty twisted. He might enjoy torturing and tormenting her, along with anyone else he could, before taking her."

"The more I hear about this animal, the less I like," Teddy muttered, staring at Stephanie with troubled eyes, no doubt still contemplating that some madman wanted to use the child as a broodmare.

"Where's Anders?" Harper asked suddenly.

"He was watching over you with me," Teddy informed him. "Just before you woke up, he left. In fact, I think it was the sound of the door closing that woke you."

As if having heard his name, the door to the bedroom suddenly opened, and Anders entered, phone in hand. His gaze skated over Harper, flickering as he noted that he was up and about, and then the immortal handed his cell phone wordlessly to Mirabeau.

They all fell silent, simply listening. Not that there was much to hear. Mirabeau said, "Hello," and then listened briefly, said "Yes, Lucian," and hung up.

"Well?" Teddy asked as she handed the phone back to Anders.

"We're to switch to feeding them blood. It's faster than the IVs. Lucian wants Stephanie and Drina back on their feet as quickly as possible," she said grimly, standing to move to the cooler and retrieve two bags of blood. Pausing then, she glanced to Tiny apologetically, and added, "And he wants you turned by nightfall."

Tiny frowned. "But Jackie wanted to be here for it, and she and Vincent won't be here for another couple days."

"I know. I'm sorry," she said regretfully.

Tiny sighed and nodded. He took one of the bags

from her, but as she moved up beside Drina's bed, asked, "Did he say why?"

"He wants us all at top speed as quickly as possible and prepared for anything," Mirabeau answered, bending over Drina. She opened the unconscious woman's mouth and massaged her upper gums to force her fangs out. The moment they slid down, Mirabeau popped the bag onto them.

"Hold this for me," she said to Harper, and when he reached out to hold the bag in place, Mirabeau turned, took the other bag back from Tiny, swung toward Stephanie, and then paused, a blank look covering her face. Stephanie didn't have fangs.

"Will she swallow it if you pour it down her throat?" Tiny asked, seeming to recognize the problem.

"I don't know," Mirabeau admitted on a sigh.

Tiny hesitated, but then shrugged and moved around to the other side of Stephanie's bed. Sitting on the edge, he slid an arm under her neck, raising her so that her head draped over his arm. Using his free hand, he then caught her jaw and pulled it open before glancing to Mirabeau. "From what I understand, she won't choke or drown from it. Even if it gets in her lungs, the nanos will probably retrieve it to use. You may as well try."

Mirabeau hesitated, but then nodded and stepped forward. She held the bag over Stephanie's open mouth and stabbed at it quickly with one fingernail. Blood immediately began to gush out.

Drina had a serious case of dry mouth. It felt like she'd gone to sleep with glue in her mouth. A most unpleasant sensation, she decided, smacking her lips together with a grimace and rolling over in bed only to bump up against something hard.

Opening her eyes, she stared blearily at the wide dark expanse before her, slow to recognize it as a man's chest in a dark shirt.

"You're awake."

That mumble from above her head made her lean back slightly and peer up to find Harper lying facing her on his side. He was looking sleepily down at her, and the relief on his face was obvious. Her head was nearly tucked under his chin, or probably had been when she'd first rolled over, she realized, and smiled at him.

"Hi," Drina said, and frowned at the sound that croaked out of her parched throat.

"You need more blood." He rolled away and sat up, then stood and moved around the bed and out of sight. Drina had to shift onto her back to follow him with her eyes as he moved to a set of coolers by the window. He opened one, retrieved a bag of blood, and returned, but, when she realized they were in her room, she turned her attention to the bed beside her own.

Seeing Stephanie sleeping in the next bed, she half sat up, whispering with confusion, "What are you doing in here?"

"You don't remember the accident?" Harper asked, sinking to sit next to her on the mattress.

Drina opened her mouth to say no, but paused as memory came crashing in. She sucked in a breath as horror washed over her in the wake of the memories, and then fell back on the bed with a guttural sound, her eyes running briefly over Harper to be sure he was wholly intact, and then to Stephanie again. She looked fine. Unmarked and pink-cheeked, her breathing even.

"She'll probably wake up soon too," Harper murmured, offering Drina the bag of blood he'd retrieved.

Drina sat up and shifted up the bed to lean against the headboard, then accepted the blood.

"What happened to the brakes?" she asked, recalling Stephanie's saying something about them just before the accident.

Harper waited until she popped the bag of blood to her fangs before saying grimly, "The brake lines were cut."

Drina frowned around the bag in her mouth.

"There's some worry it's Leonius playing nasty games before he tries to take Stephanie," he admitted. "So everyone's on high alert. Lucian wants you and Stephanie on your feet and Tiny turned as quickly as possible. He called Alessandro and Edward and asked them to bring their mates and come help out till the turn is done," he added, and then seeing her confusion, explained, "Edward and Alessandro are the other two immortals who came in answer to the ad Teddy and a friend of Elvi's named Mabel, put in the Toronto papers for a vampire mate for her."

Drina immediately nodded. Harper had told her how he'd landed in Port Henry during their twenty-four hours in Toronto. While she hadn't recognized the names when he'd mentioned them a moment ago, she knew who the men were and knew that they'd become good friends to Harper this last year and a half.

"Alessandro, Edward, and their mates arrived a few minutes ago," Harper informed her. "Teddy, Tiny, and Mirabeau went downstairs with Anders to greet them and coordinate everything. Until then, we'd been feeding you and Stephanie bag after bag of blood, trying to rush you through the healing. They were administering it intravenously before that."

Drina grimaced, suddenly understanding the dry mouth. The slower the blood entered the body, the slower the healing was, but it was also less painful. When the blood was fed through the fangs bag after bag, it hit the system fast and sent the nanos into a frenzy of healing that hurt like hell. She'd probably been screaming her head off until the worst of the healing was done.

She turned and glanced toward Stephanie again.

"They were pouring it down her throat," Harper said quietly. "It seemed to work just as well."

Drina nodded and pulled the now-empty bag off her fangs.

"Do you want another?" Harper asked, getting up.

"No." Drina smiled wryly. "I think I'm probably good for blood, but water would be nice."

He leaned to the side at once and picked up a glass of the clear liquid from the bedside table.

"Thank you," she murmured, accepting it. Drina

was very happy to see that her hand didn't tremble as she raised the glass to her lips. She wasn't suffering any lingering weakness. At least she didn't appear to be, she thought as she drank half the water down in one go. Drina paused to breathe and smile at him, and then downed the rest of the glass before handing it back.

Harper set it on the table, then reached out to slide his hand into the hair at the back of her neck and pulled her forward to press his forehead to hers. "I'm sorry."

Drina nodded solemnly, bumping her forehead on his nose as she did. "You should be. You should have spun the wheel so your side of the car took the impact and saved Stephanie and me all this."

Harper pulled back with amazement. "Crap, I didn't think of that."

"Idiot," Drina chided, rolling her eyes. "Honestly! I was joking. I wouldn't have wanted that any more than you wanted my getting injured to occur. This wasn't your fault. And we're all fine. That's the important thing."

A small smile tugged at his lips, and Harper suddenly leaned forward to kiss her. Afraid her breath was less than pleasant at the moment, Drina froze, but if it was bad, Harper didn't seem to care. When he deepened the kiss, she sighed and allowed him to ease her back on the bed.

"Geez, guys, really? Right there in the bed beside me?"

That husky growl from Stephanie made them both stiffen, and then Harper straightened, bringing Drina upright with him again. They turned to peer at the girl together.

"How are you feeling?" Drina asked quietly, as Harper released her.

"Thirsty," Stephanie said on a sigh, sitting up as well and rubbing sleep from her eyes.

"Blood thirsty or water thirsty?" Drina asked at once.

Stephanie hesitated, and then sighed and admitted, "Maybe both."

Harper immediately stood to return to the cooler and brought back a bag for the girl, only to pause. "We don't have straws. Mirabeau was just stabbing the bag and letting it pour down your throat."

Stephanie immediately tipped her head back and opened her mouth, apparently willing to go that route to get what she needed. When Harper hesitated, Drina realized what the problem was and stood to take the bag from him. He had no nails. She did. She positioned the bag over Stephanie's mouth and quickly stabbed the bag, then squeezed to force the liquid out more quickly as the teenager swallowed over and over.

"More?" Drina asked when it was empty. When Stephanie paused to consider, but then shook her head, Drina tossed the bag in a garbage pail that had been positioned between the two beds, picked up a second glass of water from the bedside table, and offered it to her.

"That was some crash," Stephanie muttered as she accepted the glass.

"The brake lines were cut," Drina said quietly as Stephanie took a drink.

"Nice," the girl said dryly, and glanced to Harper. "So who have you pissed off besides Drina?"

"He didn't piss me off," Drina said at once, and when Stephanie snorted, added, "Well, perhaps I was a bit frustrated after we returned from Toronto when he seemed to be avoiding me, but I wasn't pissed off . . . much."

Harper chuckled and slid his arm around her. "Well, don't worry. I've come to my senses. I won't be dragging my feet or avoiding you from now on, so you won't be pissed off or frustrated again." He smiled wryly, and added, "At least not about that."

"So you're ready to accept her as a life mate?" Stephanie asked with a grin.

"Do I have a choice?" he asked dryly. "She just is."

"Hey! You're blessed to be my life mate," Drina snapped, punching him in the stomach for the crack, and with more than just a teasing force behind it.

Harper winced and shook his head. "I don't know. A lifetime of your fiery Spanish temperament? I think it's more a curse than a blessing."

"Don't listen to him, Dree," Stephanie said with amusement. "He's just winding you up. It used to bother him that Jenny was such a cold fish. He likes your passion."

"Really?" Drina asked with interest, but her eyes were on Harper, noting the way his eyes had widened with surprise, as if he'd just realized the truth of those words himself.

"Oh, good, you're up."

Drina glanced over her shoulder to see Mirabeau entering the room.

"How are you two doing? Do you need more blood?" Mirabeau asked.

"I think we're good at the moment," Drina answered for both herself and Stephanie.

"How about food then?" Mirabeau asked. "Alessandro and Leonora brought a big batch of spaghetti and a bunch of garlic bread for everyone, and we're going to eat before we start Tiny's turn."

"Is there Parmesan cheese?" Stephanie asked.

"Freshly grated," Mirabeau assured her.

"Yum." Stephanie was off the bed at once and hurrying for the door.

Smiling wryly, Drina started to follow, but slowed, her smile widening when Harper caught her hand in his. It seemed he'd meant what he'd said. He'd come to his senses and wasn't going to fight their being life mates.

Drina paused at the head of the bed in Mirabeau and Tiny's room, and then glanced around to watch the rest of the crew file in. There was Mirabeau and Tiny of course, Stephanie, Anders, and Teddy Brunswick, and then came the people she'd never met until little more than half an hour ago—Alessandro and Leonora Cipriano, and Edward and Dawn Kenric.

Alessandro and Leonora, both olive-skinned and sporting long, dark hair, were similar enough in looks that they could have been brother and sister, but a brother and sister would never find any and every excuse to touch each other. Nor would they look at each other the way these two did, devouring each other with bronzed brown eyes full of love and desire.

In contrast, Edward and Dawn Kenric were fair-skinned and fair-haired. They were also more conservative in behavior. They still shared the same touches and exchanged passionate looks, but only when they thought no one else was looking.

Harper had told Drina that Edward had been the most arrogant, annoying bastard he'd ever known, until he met Dawn, but that finding her had changed him considerably, and he now actually called him a friend.

Altogether, what they had was a small army in that room, Drina thought grimly as she took in their numbers. That being the case, she wasn't terribly surprised when Tiny suddenly said, "Surely it isn't necessary for all of you to be up here? Shouldn't some of you be downstairs watching the doors and windows?"

"Most of us will go downstairs once your turn is under way," Edward said, reminding the mortal of what they'd apparently decided earlier. "Then we'll take turns watching over you until it's finished."

"Yeah, but why are so many here for the start?" Tiny asked with a frown. "We don't need this many people, surely? Even little Stephanie here could probably bench-press me with one hand."

Seeing the distress on Mirabeau's face, Drina said, "Maybe, but you're a big guy, Tiny, and pretty strong for a mortal. Once the nanos hit, you'll be even stronger. And in pain . . ." She shrugged, leaving the rest unsaid but thinking they'd be lucky if he didn't toss someone out a window in his distress.

"Don't worry, son. It will be all right," Leonora

Cipriano crooned and moved over to hug the big man and pat his back as if he were a five-year-old who needed soothing.

Drina glanced to Harper in question, and he murmured, "She's eighty-six or thereabouts, just turned the summer before last."

Drina nodded with understanding. The woman might look twenty-five now, but in her head, she was still the grandmotherly old woman she'd been before her turn. To her, Tiny was just a boy.

"Well, let's get to it," Teddy said bracingly, as Leonora released Tiny and stepped back to Alessandro's side.

"Right." Tiny glanced to Mirabeau, and seeing the worry on her face, reached out to caress her cheek. "It's all right, Beau. By this time tomorrow, it will be over. Or maybe the next day," he added with a frown. "Marguerite told me that different people take different lengths of time to turn."

"That's true," Harper murmured.

Tiny nodded and glanced around. "So, you'll need some rope, right?"

"All taken care of," Kenric announced. "We brought chain. Speaking of which, we left it in the garage. I'll go get it."

"Chains?" Tiny asked, eyes widening as the Englishman hurried out of the room.

"Si," Alessandro began, nodding. "The Lucian, he say is best we—"

"Rope is sometimes used, but chain is better," Leonora interrupted, slipping her hand into her husband's and giving a shake of her head when he glanced to her in surprise. She then turned back to Tiny, and added, "They used rope for me and I snapped the tie on my right wrist before the end of the turn and I was just an old woman, so when Lucian suggested chain, it seemed a good idea."

"Right," Tiny repeated weakly, but he was starting to look a bit gray around the gills, and Mirabeau was beginning to wring her hands with worry as it was brought home to her what a dangerous endeavor the turning could be.

Edward hadn't dallied about collecting the chain. Leonora had barely finished speaking when he returned with several lengths of heavy-duty chain made up of large, thick links. Even Drina had to bite her lip when she saw it. An elephant would have had trouble snapping them.

"Well, let's get started," she said with forced cheer, thinking it was better just to get it done than to delay. The more time he had to think, the more anxious Tiny would get.

"Do I need to change or anything? Or do I just lie down?" Tiny asked, and the uncertainty in his voice caught her ear.

"You might want to take off your shirt if you're especially fond of it," Drina murmured. "And change your pants if you like those as well."

Tiny didn't ask questions, he merely shrugged out of his T-shirt. Apparently he wasn't overly fond of the joggers, though, because once his shirt was off, he simply lay down on the bed.

It was Teddy who asked, "Why? What's going to

happen to his clothes? He's not going to hulk out or something, is he?"

"No," Drina assured the older mortal with amusement. "But the nanos will force out any impurities through his skin. It's hard to get the clothes clean afterward."

"I'll say," Stephanie muttered with disgust. "I was wearing my favorite top when I turned. I washed it six times before I gave up trying to get the stink out." She grimaced, and then added, "The bed I was on was ruined too. They hadn't thought to put one of those bed-protector things on before laying me in it."

Tiny was immediately hopping off the bed as if it were hot coals. Without a word, he tugged the blankets and sheets up at one corner to reveal a bed protector underneath with one side plastic, the other cloth. He didn't return the bedding then, but pulled the sheets off completely and tossed them in the corner of the room, leaving only the protector, muttering, "No sense ruining Elvi's sheets."

Edward immediately moved forward with the chains and quickly half tossed and half slid the first under the metal frame. Alessandro pulled it out the other side, and then moved to the foot of the bed as Edward repeated the process there. Once done threading chain under the bed at both the top and bottom, Alessandro straightened and nodded with approval. "Bella. Is good."

Tiny grunted something of a response and climbed back onto the mattress protector.

Drina moved toward the two coolers Anders had

moved to the room earlier. "Did Lucian send any—"

"The green cooler," Anders interrupted before she could finish, and Drina closed the red cooler she'd just opened, which held only blood, and moved to the second, green cooler. Opening it, she nodded as she spotted the little medical case inside. She knew it would contain needles and ampoules of various drugs. They wouldn't prevent Tiny's experiencing the pain, but would dull it somewhat and keep him from getting too active during the worst of it. Unfortunately, they couldn't be administered until after the turn had started. The dosage would kill a mortal without the benefit of the nanos in their system. She straightened and opened the case to reveal the items lined up inside.

"Are those the nanos?" Tiny asked warily.

"No," Drina answered. "These are drugs to help you through the turn."

Tiny frowned, and Stephanie—obviously reading his thoughts—piped up, and said, "Oh believe me, you do want the drugs. They don't do much, but they're better than nothing at all."

Leonora and Dawn nodded in solemn agreement. They were the only immortals there besides the teenager who had been turned. The rest of them had been born immortal and avoided this necessity. Tiny knew that as well and peered from one solemn face to the other, before clearing his throat, and asking, "So what can I expect here?"

When the older women hesitated, Stephanie grimaced, and said honestly, "It's gonna hurt like the dickens, Tiny. It feels like you're being torn apart from the inside out and I guess that's kind of what the nanos are doing." She breathed out a little sigh, and then added, "But the nightmares are the worst part."

Tiny raised his eyebrows. "Nightmares?"

"Or hallucinations or whatever," Stephanie said unhappily. "I was in a river of blood. It was burning, the flames leaping all around me, and I was caught in a current and being dragged downstream. I couldn't get out, and these mutilated and bloated corpses kept floating by while I just screamed and screamed. And then the current pulled me under, and I was choking on the burning blood." She shuddered at the memory. "And then I woke up, and it was over."

"I had the same nightmares," Leonora said with surprise.

"Me too," Dawn announced. She then murmured, "I wonder if it's your brain trying to understand what's happening inside your body."

Drina didn't comment but thought it a possibility. Every turn she'd ever talked to had had the same, or similar, nightmares. Rivers of blood, fire, corpses floating past, and then being pulled under either by the corpses in the water with them or by the current itself, followed by the sensation of drowning on the blood they inadvertently swallowed as they screamed. It was always the same with little in the way of variation.

"Why don't we just leave it for now and do this another time," Mirabeau said with a frown.

Tiny glanced at her with surprise, noted her shaky

expression, and reached out to take her hand. "It's okay, Beau," he murmured. "Better to get it done. If it's the price of being with you . . . better just to get it done."

He pulled her hand to his lips and pressed a gentle kiss to it, then glanced from Anders to Drina in question. "So where is the shot with the nanos? Give it to me and let's get it over with."

Drina felt her eyebrows rise and glanced to Mirabeau in question.

"We haven't discussed the turn and what takes place," the woman admitted on a sigh, though Drina supposed she needn't have bothered. Tiny's question had given that away.

"Well?" Teddy barked. "Where's the shot? Give it to the boy. Don't make him sit here worrying over what's coming. Just get it over with."

"There is no shot," Drina said quietly.

"No shot?" Tiny and Teddy echoed as one.

"Beau has to give you her nanos," Harper explained solemnly.

When Tiny glanced to Mirabeau in question, she hesitated, but then opened her mouth, let her fangs slide out, and lifted her wrist to her mouth.

"What are you doing?" Tiny asked, catching her arm to stop her. "You don't have to bite yourself."

"Yes, I do," Mirabeau said quietly.

"No you don't," Teddy said at once. "Tiny's right. This isn't a damned vampire movie. Drina there has needles. She can just pull some blood out of you and shoot it in Tiny, and, hey presto, it's done."

"That won't work," Drina assured him. "It would

just be blood. No nanos would be in it. Or, at least, not enough to start a turn."

"What?" the old man asked with disbelief. "How would that be possible?"

When Drina sighed, it was Harper who explained. "Think of the nanos like rats in a pet-store cage. The shop owner opens the cage and reaches in, and all the rats run to the corners of the cage to avoid being pulled from their nice safe home. Nanos do the same when anything punctures our skin, whether it's a needle, or a knife, or fangs. They are programmed to keep their host body at their peak, and they can't do that unless they stay in the body. That is why you will not find nanos in tears, urine, sperm, or any other material that naturally leaves the body. So if you stick a needle into any one of us, the nanos would immediately evacuate the area to avoid removal."

"No, no, no," Teddy said firmly. "From what I understand, our Elvi was turned when some vampire fellow was injured in an accident and bled into her mouth."

"A wound such as the one you're talking about, or like Mirabeau ripping her wrist open, is like someone tearing away the side of the rat cage and turning it to dump the contents. It's large and unexpected. The nanos in that area will be caught by surprise and get swept along in the blood that flows out. At least at first," he added dryly. "If the wound isn't big enough, or she's too slow pressing it to his mouth, she will have to do it twice, or even more, to give him enough nanos to get the process started."

"Barbaric." Teddy grunted and shook his head. "I

don't know why you just don't mix up a batch of those damned nanos and keep them for turning people."

"Because no one's been able to replicate the process," Drina said dryly.

"What?" Teddy peered at her with amazement. "You people made them. You should be able to make more."

"Not us," Drina said with amusement. "Our scientists did, and they tested them out on guinea pigs first."

"You mean none of your scientists tried it themselves?" Teddy asked with disbelief. "I find that hard to believe. It was their idea, and they'd surely want to be young and healthy forever too. It's probably why they came up with them in the first place."

"Perhaps," Drina said mildly. "But apparently they weren't willing to risk trying it themselves until they'd perfected them on others, and Atlantis fell before they decided they were perfected." She shrugged. "They all died in the fall. We have today's scientists trying to replicate the process, but they haven't yet been successful."

"Is this how you two were turned?" Teddy asked Dawn and Leonora with horror.

Both women nodded silently.

"Barbaric," Teddy repeated with disgust, and then sighed and glanced to Mirabeau. "Well, then I guess you'd best get to it."

She nodded, but Tiny was still holding her arm, and he asked uncertainly, "Are you sure you want to do this, Beau? It sounds painful."

"Not as painful as the turn," she said solemnly.

"And I'd go through this and a lot more to keep you as my life mate."

Tiny sighed and reluctantly released her wrist with a nod. Mirabeau didn't hesitate or give either of them a chance to reconsider or agonize. The moment he released her arm, she whipped it up to her mouth. Her fangs were out by the time her wrist reached her teeth, and she bit into it as viciously as a dog, not just puncturing the flesh, but tearing into it and then ripping away a good-sized flap so that it hung from her arm like a torn pocket. Even as blood began to spurt from the open wound, she was turning it to press against Tiny's mouth.

"I'll get bandages," Harper muttered, and headed for the door to the adjoining bathroom.

Drina nodded absently, but her attention was on Tiny. Despite knowing what was going to happen, the violence and suddenness of it all appeared to have caught him by surprise. He instinctively tried to pull away when Mirabeau pressed the wound to his mouth, but caught himself almost at once and allowed her to do it. Still, he choked a bit as the blood coursed into his mouth, no doubt unable to subdue his natural repulsion at the thought of drinking anyone's blood.

"You have to swallow. Try to relax," Drina said quietly. Tiny met her gaze over Mirabeau's arm. Seeing the distress in his eyes, Drina instinctively slid into his mind to help, soothing his thoughts and making his body relax, so that he could swallow as much of the blood as possible before the nanos made the bleeding stop.

Inside his head as she was, Drina knew when the gushing began to slow. It quickly reduced to a trickle, and when it stopped altogether, she released her control of him.

Tiny immediately removed his mouth from Mirabeau's arm and sank back on the mattress.

"Are you all right?" Mirabeau asked with concern, hardly seeming to notice that Harper had returned with bandaging and was tending to her wound. "Tiny?"

Nodding, he raised his head and forced a smile. "I'm fine. You?"

His gaze slid to her wrist, but there was nothing to see now that Harper had bandaged it. Still, he grimaced at the swath of white and then sighed and asked, "How long does it usually take to start?"

"It differs for different people," Harper murmured, setting the roll of cotton bandaging on the bedside table. "With some it starts right away, and with others it takes a while before they notice a difference, and then it's sometimes just a slow onset that builds up."

"How do you feel?" Mirabeau asked worriedly.

Tiny smiled wryly as he took in the circle of concerned faces around him. But shrugged. "Fine. I don't feel any different. I guess I'm going to be one of those slow-buildup kinda guys. I—" He paused, eyes suddenly widening, and then began to convulse on the bed.

Eleven

'Chains,' Harper barked, as Tiny went into convulsions, and the room was suddenly a hive of activity as the group broke off into pairs. Leonora and Alessandro threw themselves at Tiny's right leg, Edward and Dawn took his left one, Mirabeau and Anders went for the right arm, and Harper hurried around the bed to join Drina at Tiny's left arm as Teddy and Stephanie tried to squeeze their way up between the others surrounding the bed to help.

Even with two immortals to a limb, it was a struggle to get Tiny chained down. His body was thrashing wildly, jerking his limbs about. It wasn't until Teddy gave up trying to help hold one of Tiny's legs to implement an alternate plan that they made any headway.

Harper saw the old mortal straighten and move around the people crowded around the bed. Even so, he wasn't at all prepared for the sight of the man suddenly grabbing up Stephanie, and pretty much tossing her on top of Tiny's chest. He then quickly climbed onto the bed, and dropped to sit on Tiny right next to her. The two hung on for dear life as the mountain of a man bucked and thrashed beneath them, managing to stay put and weigh him down, easing his movements long enough for the others to get the chains in place.

The moment Harper managed to get the wrist he and Drina were struggling with locked up, she reached around and grabbed up the bag of drugs she'd let drop. She quickly prepared a shot and jabbed it into Tiny's arm, pushing the plunger home. Still, it took a moment after that before Tiny's struggles eased.

"Well," Teddy sighed, mopping his brow as he climbed off of Tiny. Tucking the hankie in his pocket, he turned back and helped Stephanie off as well, muttering, "That was exciting. Like riding a wild bronco."

Harper smiled faintly at the man. "It was fast thinking on your part to sit on him."

"I couldn't see what else to do." Teddy shook his head and glanced from face to face before saying, "I suppose it's a little late for this, but it seems to me it would have been smarter to chain him up before feeding him the blood."

Drina grimaced. "It seems cruel to chain them up before necessary, and usually you get a little more warning than this. They don't go into it this quickly as a rule."

"Right . . . well . . ." He shook his head again and strode to the door, muttering, "I need a drink."

"She's a good kid."

Drina turned from peering at Stephanie, who had fallen asleep in a chair in the corner, and nodded at Mirabeau's words. They had decided to divide into four-hour shifts. Harper and Drina were taking the first shift with Mirabeau to watch over Tiny. Stephanie was there as well, mostly because the teenager had refused to leave. She seemed to like Tiny and had watched over him anxiously until exhaustion had overcome her, and she'd dozed off in her chair. She'd done so about five minutes before Harper had fallen asleep in his own chair beside Drina.

Dawn, Edward, and Anders were going to take the second four-hour shift, with Anders administering the drugs Drina had been giving Tiny every twenty minutes to half an hour since the ordeal had started.

Leonora, Alessandro, and Teddy were supposed to take the third shift. For that one, Leonora, who it turned out had been a nurse before retiring some twenty years ago, would take over administering the drugs.

Mirabeau was supposed to rest during the second and third shifts, but Drina suspected the woman would insist on staying by Tiny. It was what she would have done if it were her life mate lying there.

"She seems to be fond of you and Tiny," Drina murmured finally in response to Mirabeau's comment. Stephanie had brought up the other couple a lot during the last few days. It was always Beau this, and Tiny that.

"The same is true of you two," Mirabeau said quietly. "But then I think she's desperate to connect to someone. She's pretty alone right now."

Drina nodded and glanced back to the girl again.

"She has a lot of questions," Mirabeau murmured, drawing her attention again. Meeting her gaze, Mirabeau grimaced, and explained, "She doesn't really know a lot about what she is now. She only had her sister to ask, and Dani would go to Decker to get the answers and, with them being new life mates, they would invariably get distracted and never get around to answering her, so she kind of gave up asking. The only other immortal female she's had much contact with until now was Sam, and Sam and Mortimer are new life mates too, so—"

"Sam isn't turned."

Both women paused and glanced toward Stephanie as she made that announcement, alerting them to the fact that she was now awake.

Mirabeau peered at the girl blankly for a moment, then said, "Sure she is. Sam and Mortimer have been together since last summer. Mortimer would have turned her right away."

Stephanie shook her head and stretched. "Sam refused because she didn't want to leave her sisters behind in ten years."

When Mirabeau frowned at this news, Drina asked with amusement, "Mortimer's the head of the North American Enforcers, right?"

"Yeah, under Lucian," Mirabeau murmured.

"And you're an enforcer?" Drina asked.

Mirabeau nodded.

"So, haven't you met this Sam? I mean, if she lives at the enforcer house, and you're an enforcer, you'd have to go there quite a bit. Surely you would have met her and realized she was mortal?"

Mirabeau frowned, and it was Stephanie who answered, saying with amusement, "Beau's been avoiding the house ever since I got there. She goes straight to the garage when she has to meet with Mortimer. And Sam pretty much arrived on the scene just days in front of Dani and me, so I doubt she even met her more than once thanks to trying to avoid me."

Mirabeau looked alarmed, and quickly said, "It wasn't you, Stephanie."

"I know," Stephanie said, some of her humor slipping away. "It was just my situation. Losing my family and all. It reminded you of losing your own, and so you tried to avoid me to avoid thinking of it."

Drina glanced to Mirabeau curiously. "You've lost your family too?"

"It was a long time ago," Mirabeau said quietly, her gaze moving back to Tiny when he stirred restlessly. She reached out and brushed her fingers along his cheek. Her touch seemed to soothe him.

"Dree's parents were killed when Rome invaded Egypt, but she has all her brothers and sisters still," Stephanie announced.

"How do you know that?" Drina asked with surprise.

"You just thought it," Stephanie said with a shrug.

Drina just stared at her. She was pretty sure she hadn't just thought that though she supposed it could have been stirred in her subconscious. Still—recalling the accident, she asked, "You were reading Harper's mind during the accident? It's how you knew there was something wrong with the brakes?"

"I told you, I don't really read you guys. You shout your thoughts at me," she said, looking uncomfortable, and then admitted, "Except Lucian. Him I actually have to concentrate a bit to read."

"Concentrate a bit?" she queried, eyes narrowing.

"Yeah." She shrugged. "With most people, mortals and immortals alike, it's like a freaking radio playing on full volume, and I can't turn it down or shut it out. But with Lucian, I actually have to concentrate to hear what he's thinking. Anders is kind of like that too."

"Anders?" Drina asked sharply, aware that her voice had been sharper than she'd intended. Lucian was still relatively new in the life-mate game, and new life mates were known to be easily read, which could explain away what Stephanie was saying. However, Anders was old and mateless. Even Mirabeau probably couldn't read him. Yet, Stephanie, who had only been an immortal for six months, could.

Drina glanced to Mirabeau and saw the troubled expression on her face and knew without a doubt that it reflected her own expression.

"Well, we already knew you had mad skills when it comes to reading thoughts," Harper said mildly, apparently awoken by their discussion. His hand covered Drina's and squeezed gently in warning.

Getting the message, she tried to blank out the worry from both her mind and expression and noted Mirabeau's suddenly clearing her own expression as well. Harper continued, "You're a whiz at reading minds. Have you noticed any other new skills since your turn?"

"Like what?" Stephanie asked, looking uncomfortable.

"Anything that is different now that you've been turned," Harper said easily. "Some edentates have special talents other immortals don't. Maybe you're one of the gifted ones."

She bit her lip briefly, but then admitted tentatively, "Well, I know when life mates are around, and usually who is whose. Like I knew Dawn and Edward were mated and Alessandro and Leonora were each other's mates before you guys introduced them even though Dawn was helping Leonora in the kitchen while Alessandro and Edward set the table."

"Really?" Drina asked with amazement. "How?"

"There's this kind of electricity between them, and this energy that comes from them," she said, and then frowned and tried to explain, "The closest thing I can compare it to is what comes from cell phones and satellites and stuff. I sense these kind of . . . waves or streams of something coming from cells and satellites. It's the same kind of thing that flows between life mates. Like a million nanos are sending out text messages back and forth between them."

Frustration crossed her face, and she said, "I don't know how to describe it any better than that. But anyway, I knew the minute you got here, Dree, that you were Harper's because both your nanos started buzzing."

"I wonder if that's how Marguerite zeroes in on finding life mates for each other," Mirabeau said thoughtfully. "Maybe she picks up on these waves too."

"But Marguerite can find them without their being in the same room. I was in New York, and Harper was here in Canada when she decided I would suit him. She wouldn't have sensed waves between us," Drina said with a frown.

Stephanie shrugged. "Well, she probably recognized that the sounds are the same from both of you."

"Sounds?" Harper queried gently.

She looked frustrated again. "I don't know what to call it. Frequencies maybe."

"Marguerite can't be finding life mates by zeroing in on these frequencies," Mirabeau realized suddenly. "Tiny is mortal. In fact, most of the life mates she's put with immortals have been mortal. There wouldn't yet be nanos in the mortal to communicate with."

"True," Drina murmured, then glanced to Stephanie and said, "Were you able to tell that Tiny and Mirabeau were life mates?"

She nodded.

"How?" Mirabeau asked.

"The electricity you each give off is the same."

"Electricity?" Drina asked with a frown. The girl had mentioned electricity and energy earlier, but she'd thought she'd just been using two different terms to try to describe one thing.

"Yeah. Well, I call it electricity," she said with a sigh that spoke of her frustration with not knowing the proper terms for what she was trying to explain.

Drina supposed it was like trying to explain color to a blind person. The teenager struggled to try to make them understand, though.

"It's energy too, but different than the waves thing. This energy is more physical, like a shock wave. It makes my hair stand on end on the back of my neck. It's not so bad when there's only one life-mate couple around, but tonight, with so many mated couples here in the house"— Stephanie grimaced—"it's like my finger is stuck in a plug socket."

"That doesn't sound very pleasant," Drina said with concern.

"It isn't," she said wearily. "But then neither are all the voices in my head. It's easier when there are only a couple of you around at a time. With so many of you in the house, it's like several radio stations playing at the same time, all with a different talk program on. It gets maddening and exhausts me."

"You should have said something," Mirabeau said with a frown.

"Why?" Stephanie asked, almost with resentment. "It's not like you could do anything about it."

"We don't know that," Mirabeau said at once. "Maybe if you went up on the top floor, and the rest of us stayed on the main floor, it would make it better."

"She can't be left alone," Drina reminded her.

"Besides, it wouldn't matter as long as I'm in the house with you all," Stephanie assured her. "The floors and walls don't seem to stop it, at least not inside. Although going outside helps muffle it quite a bit if you're all inside. I'm not sure why, though."

"This is an old Victorian house with connected double outer walls," Harper said quietly, and when Drina raised an eyebrow, he explained, "If you've ever looked at the bricks on the outside of the house, each row has three or four normal-sized or uniform bricks and then a small end piece, then more normal sized and another small one and so on. It's because they built an outer wall and an inner wall. The small bricks are actually ones that connect the outer wall to the inner. It made for good insulation or something . . . or perhaps just sturdier buildings. But that was how they were built when this house was erected." He shrugged, and then suggested, "The double brick, and then plaster on top of that probably creates more of a barrier for whatever Stephanie is picking up."

"I don't suppose you guys would let me just step out on the deck for a couple of minutes?" Stephanie asked hopefully. "Even a few minutes respite would help."

Drina exchanged a glance with Mirabeau and knew at once that the other hunter, like herself, wanted to say yes but just couldn't. Especially when they were on high alert. They had to consider Stephanie's safety first.

"That isn't necessary," Harper said suddenly, sitting upright in his seat. "The porch off Elvi and

Victor's bedroom was an add-on sometime after the house was built. They've insulated it and put in an electric heater, but the wall between it and Elvi's room is the original double-walled construction. It's as good as standing outside in that regard except it's heated, furnished, and has a television and music system and everything." He smiled, and explained, "Elvi and Victor spruced it up a bit to use it as their own private living room, for when they feel like getting away by themselves."

Mirabeau smiled. "Well that sounds perfect; why don't you two take Stephanie out there and watch a movie or something?" When Drina hesitated and glanced toward Tiny, Mirabeau glanced at her watch, and said, "It's only fifteen minutes until the next shift, and Tiny seems quiet enough for now. We should be fine."

Drina checked her own watch and said, "It's time for his next shot in five minutes. I'll get it ready and give it to him before we go." Standing, she glanced over her shoulder to Stephanie, and suggested, "Why don't you run down and get us some snacks or something? Maybe pick a move from the DVD collection in the living room."

"On it!" the girl said, cheerful now, apparently at the prospect of a respite from the constant voices and energy. She stood and rushed out of the room.

Silence fell briefly in the room as Drina prepared a needle; and then Mirabeau said solemnly, "This isn't good."

"No," Harper agreed on a sigh.

Drina didn't comment. She knew what they were

referring to. Stephanie's abilities. Harper had tried to sway it like they were a good thing, a special ability she'd been blessed with, but the truth was it might be a curse.

There were very few edentate in their society, most were from the time of the fall of Atlantis or shortly after. Very few had come afterward for the simple reason that male edentates never turned mortals. If they found a mortal life mate, the council assigned an immortal the task of turning that mortal rather than create another edentate with the flawed nanos. Any offspring they then had took on the mother's blood and nanos and would be immortal as well.

The same was true for female edentates, except if they did have children, that baby would take on its mother's blood and nanos and so would be edentate.

The council hadn't outlawed edentates having children, but most refused to do so for fear of having to watch their progeny die or be killed as a mad thing. There had been a few born, but not more than a handful since the fall of Atlantis. They were rare. Between that and the length of time since the no-fangers had been believed to be wiped out, little was known about the madness that turned an edentate into the dreaded no-fanger. It was usually assumed that in a turn, the madness was evident as soon as the turn was done, that the turnee came out of it screaming mad. However, there were rumors and legends that suggested it might not be that abrupt, that they could still come out of the turn seemingly fine, but then shortly thereafter go mad, driven there by something, though the tales had never specified what that something might be.

Drina had always disregarded the rumors as ghost stories told around a campfire, but now wondered if constantly being bombarded by people's thoughts and these energy waves and the electricity Stephanie spoke of might not be the cause. She hoped not. She liked Stephanie and wouldn't want to have to see her put down like a rabid dog.

"Lucian will have to be told," Mirabeau said quietly, when Drina didn't comment, and then added, "Maybe he knows a way to help her."

Drina tightened her lips and bent to give Tiny his shot. Once Lucian was told . . . If there was something he could do for her, she didn't doubt he would. But if there wasn't, she also didn't doubt that he wouldn't hesitate to put the girl down.

"She needs to be taught to block thoughts," Drina said grimly as she straightened. "Nobody has bothered because new turns usually need to be taught to read thoughts, not block them. But teaching her how to shield herself from other immortals' thoughts might help considerably. I'd rather try that first than tell Lucian just yet."

"To tell the truth, so would I," Mirabeau admitted quietly. "But if Lucian comes down here and reads that we knew there was something amiss and didn't say anything . . ."

"I'll take responsibility for the decision," Drina announced, turning to dispose of the needle she'd just used, and then a thought suddenly struck her, and she smiled as she pointed out, "You're not technically on duty anymore anyway. Anders and I are on the job now, and you and Tiny were relieved."

"Yeah, but we've kind of been roped back in because of the brakes being cut," Mirabeau pointed out reluctantly.

Drina frowned. "Did he actually say you were back on duty? I thought he just said to get Stephanie and me back to peak and get Tiny turned because he wanted everyone prepared."

A slow smile curled Mirabeau's lips. "Actually, you're right."

"Then you're not on duty," Drina decided. "It's my problem. And I'm not telling him."

Mirabeau smiled, and then worry began to pluck at her lips. "He'll be so pissed at you."

Drina gave a short laugh. "Uncle Lucian's temper doesn't worry me. Well, not much anyway," she admitted wryly, and then pointed out, "I work for the European council. I'm only here as a favor. He really has no jurisdiction over me."

"Nice," Mirabeau said with a grin, and then glanced to the door as it opened.

"I got popcorn and some sodas for each of us, and I picked three movies," Stephanie announced, bouncing into the room, her arms full. "An action flick, a horror, and a comedy. I figured we could vote on which to watch." She glanced over her shoulder as they heard footsteps on the stairs, and added, "The others are coming to relieve us. Are you two ready?"

The porch Harper had mentioned was rectangular, running along the side of the house away from the road on the second story. The upper half of the three outer walls were made up mostly of windows, but there was also a heavy-duty door with a relatively new dead bolt. It led down to the deck, and Drina vaguely recalled seeing a screen door on the outside while crossing the deck on one pass. As for the windows, they were old-fashioned, tall and narrow with wooden frames that swung open rather than raised or slid to the side as more modern windows did. Their screens had been removed for the winter season and were stacked against one wall. Seasonal caulking of some sort had been run around each window to prevent a draft from slipping through, but while the walls themselves may have been insulated, the windows were not, and it was quite chilly when she, Harper, and Stephanie stepped out into the porch.

"It warms up in here pretty quickly," Harper assured them as he moved to turn on a heavy-duty electric heater in one corner.

Drina nodded and glanced around as Stephanie dumped her cache of goodies on a coffee table between the couch that sat under the wall of windows and the television that sat opposite it against the house wall. A frown drew Drina's lips tight as she considered the vulnerabilities, and then she said, "Stephanie, go get yourself a bunch of pillows and maybe a comforter. Whatever you think you'll need to make a comfy nest on the floor. I don't want you in front of the windows."

"Okay," Stephanie said easily, either not minding the nesting idea or not willing to cause a fuss and risk losing this opportunity to be away from the others. "I'll bring enough that you guys can join me if you like."

"I didn't think of the windows," Harper said apologetically, glancing around at them as Stephanie slowly walked to the far end of the room, taking in what could be seen of the surrounding neighborhood.

It was probably a charming view during daytime, and wasn't bad at night either. However, with the lights on in the room, they were on display to anyone who cared to look up toward the windows.

"It'll be okay," Drina murmured. "We'll just make sure Stephanie keeps her head under the window ledges and maybe turn the lights out so only the television screen casts light. That's more fun for horrors anyway."

"Horrors, huh? Is that what you're voting for?" Harper asked by her ear, and she turned in surprise to find he'd crossed the room to join her. When he caught her by the hips and drew her to rest against him, she smiled and slid her arms around his neck.

"Actually, I like actions, comedies, and horrors in equal measure," she murmured as he nuzzled her ear.

"What about porns?"

A startled laugh slid from Drina's lips, and she pulled back to peer at him. "I'm afraid I've never seen one. They just seemed uninteresting when I hadn't bothered with sex in so long."

"I've never seen one either," he admitted with a grin, and then his voice deepened as he added, "Except for the ones that have been playing through my head since the day you arrived in Port Henry."

"Really?" Drina asked with interest, leaning her upper body farther away, which inadvertently pressed her hips more tightly against his. "And what happens in those porns that play through your head?"

"Oh, many things, but mostly I lick, nibble, and kiss my way from your toes to the top of your head, and then turn you over and do it again," he growled, and then lowered his head to kiss her.

Drina opened to him at once, her body pressing eagerly forward in response to his words. They'd sparked a heat in her that was never far from the surface anyway, and she found the image he'd created filling her mind as she ran her hands over his chest, and then down to find the growing hardness between them.

Harper growled into her mouth and pressed her back against the window, his own hands moving over her body through her clothes before settling on her breasts and squeezing almost painfully, evidence of his own excitement.

"I love your body," he muttered, tearing his mouth from hers to explore her neck and ear, as he let one hand skate down between her legs. "You should be naked all the time."

Drina laughed breathlessly and removed her hand from his erection to catch his hand as she reminded him. "Windows everywhere and Stephanie returning."

Harper groaned by her ear, but stilled and sagged against her.

"Besides," Drina added on a sigh, "you're just stoking a fire we can't do a damned thing about since I'll be rooming with Stephanie again tonight."

"Damn," he breathed with frustration.

"On the bright side," she added with forced cheer, "if you were to go to bed the same time as Stephanie and me, you and I might finally get to experience those shared dreams everyone talks about life mates having."

Harper pulled back suddenly to peer down at her with surprise. "How come we haven't had those yet?"

Drina smiled wryly. "Well, I'd guess because the first night I went to bed you probably didn't hit the hay till near dawn, just before Stephanie and I woke up. And then we were together in Toronto and didn't sleep much at all other than brief faints." She paused and raised her eyebrows, before saying, "And I don't know about you, but I didn't sleep much at all last night." She frowned then, realizing that she didn't know how long she'd been out after the accident. Twenty-four or even forty-eight hours may have passed since then, she realized, and said, "I mean, the night we got back from Toronto."

"Neither did I," Harper admitted, and then smiled. "Shared dreams. Mmmm. That could be very interesting. I can put you back in those sexy thigh-high boots of yours and nothing else, or maybe team them up with a maid's apron."

"A maid's apron?" she asked with disbelief.

"Mmmm." His smile turned into a leer. "A very tiny French maid's apron that covers barely anything, and you can be bent over dusting something with your beautiful tush poking up, and I can come up behind you and ravish you like some wicked lord of the manor."

Drina laughed, albeit a bit breathlessly, and shook her head. "You're an old pervert."

"Yes," Harper acknowledged without apology. "Sad but true. However, in my defense, I didn't used to be until you arrived on the scene. So it must be some naughty vibe I'm getting off you."

"Oh now, don't blame me," she said on a laugh. "You probably had just as perverted ideas in your shared dreams with Jenny."

Harper blinked, and Drina bit her lip as she realized what she'd said. Bringing up the ghost probably wasn't the best thing to do, she thought on a sigh, but rather than coming over all guilt-ridden, Harper frowned, and admitted, "I never had shared dreams with Jenny."

Drina relaxed, relieved that he wasn't turning morose on her, and shrugged. "Perhaps she wasn't sleeping close enough for you to have them."

"I don't know," Harper said slowly. "Alessandro made some comment once about the wild dreams he'd shared with Leonora while he was courting her, and she lives across the street. Well, they both do now," he added, and released her to point out the window. "The corner house there."

Drina turned to follow his pointing finger. Noting the pretty gingerbread house, she asked, "And where did Jenny live?"

Harper turned her and urged her the length of the porch to look out over the backyard, then pointed

to the right a bit to the row of buildings backing this one. There was a midsize house directly
behind Casey Cottage and right next to it a smaller
white one, both facing onto the next road. It was the
smaller one he was pointing to. Drina stared at it.
The backyard of Casey Cottage was perhaps the
length of two cars or a bit more, but the distance was
definitely shorter than that between this house and
the one across the street. With the front yards, side-
walks, and then streets, Leonora's house was a good
ten or fifteen feet farther away than the little white
house where Jenny had apparently lived.

"Maybe not all life mates have shared dreams,"
she said finally, not sure what other explanation
there could be.

"Okay, I got enough pillows and comforters for all
of us," Stephanie announced gleefully.

Drina turned toward the door and burst out
laughing when she saw Stephanie stepping into
the porch, dragging a large, bulging comforter apparently stuffed with pillows and other comforters
behind. She'd gathered the ends and pulled them
over one shoulder, but the sacklike carrier she'd
made dragged on the floor behind her. She looked,
for all the world, like a skinny blond Santa in jeans
and a T-shirt.

"Here, let me help you with that," Drina and
Harper said as one, and moved toward her.

"No, no, I got it," Stephanie assured them. "You
two shove the coffee table out of the way, so we can
start nest building."

Smiling at the girl's much more cheerful mood,

Drina turned to help Harper shift furniture around to make room.

"So did you check out the movies?" Stephanie asked, as they finished situating the comforters and pillows.

Drina smiled faintly, knowing the girl probably already knew the answer. She seemed to know everything they thought and did.

"Drina voted for horror," Harper announced. "Lights-out-huddling-on-the-floor-in-the-dark horror. But we can always do that second if you have another preference. First choice should go to you since you had to fetch everything for this excursion."

"No that's good. My first choice is horror too," Stephanie said happily, grabbing the movie in question and opening the DVD case as she crawled over to the television and DVD on her knees.

"I'll get the lights," Drina said, hopping up and moving to the door, but then pausing to wait for Stephanie to get everything going.

"All set," Stephanie announced, finishing up, and then dropping back amid the nest they'd built.

Drina flipped the light switch off and moved to join Harper and Stephanie on the floor. Stephanie had taken the near edge of the nest, leaving a spot between herself and Harper who had claimed the far end, and Drina settled into the spot, smiling when he slid his arm around her shoulders.

"It warmed up in here pretty quickly like you said, Harper," Stephanie commented, as the FBI warning rolled offscreen and the movie trailers began. She pushed away the comforter she'd automatically pulled over herself as she spoke, and Drina glanced around, noting that it *was* much warmer than when they'd first entered the room. She almost pushed the comforter aside herself, but Harper caught her hand to stop her.

When she turned to him in question, he merely smiled and gestured that she should look toward the screen.

"Harpernus Stoyan, if you can't behave yourself and go and turn all Roman hands and Russian fingers under that comforter, you're going to have to sit on the couch," Stephanie snapped, sounding for all the world like a stern schoolteacher.

Drina burst out laughing at Harper's exaggerated groan, suddenly understanding what he'd been up to. She then pushed the comforter aside and shifted herself up onto the couch behind them to remove temptation, and said, "That's okay, I'll sit up here. I had nowhere to put my soda anyway sitting between the two of you."

"Oh, I didn't think of that," Stephanie said, glancing down to the can on the floor beside her. Harper's can too sat on the floor at his side since the two were on either end of the nest, but, in the middle, Drina hadn't had anywhere to put hers and would have had to hold it through the movie. Now, however, she settled on the couch in the corner behind Stephanie, far out of Harper's reach and temptation, and set her can on the end table beside the couch.

"Can you reach the popcorn?" Stephanie asked with concern, as Harper used the remote to skip through the commercial trailers.

"Just put it between the two of you, and I can reach down," Drina assured her.

Stephanie did as she suggested, and then they all fell silent as the movie began. It started with a bang, of course, or actually an axing, and Drina rolled her eyes at the antics on screen. Truly, she liked horrors because they were always rather comedic to her. It never failed to amaze her how mortals could paint their own kind so damned stupid. She'd lived a long time and met enough mortals to populate a small nation but had never met a female mortal she thought would be stupid enough to go creeping out into a dark yard at night, unarmed and in a skimpy nightie, to investigate after hearing or seeing something there that disturbed or scared her.

And while Drina had dipped into enough male mortal minds to know that the majority of them seemed to think about sex with every fifth or sixth heartbeat, she was quite sure even they wouldn't think it clever or exciting to drag a female away from the safety of the herd to indulge in a quicky when dismembered bodies of friends or partygoers were falling around them like snow in a Canadian winter.

Seriously, at one time she had actually considered it insulting to humans as a whole, but lately she'd started to find it an amusing reflection of the lack of intelligence of the moviemakers. Between that and the fact that a great majority of movies today appeared to be remakes, it made her wonder how the devil they made any money at all in Hollywood.

Drina almost groaned aloud as one of the characters locked themselves in a windowless bathroom to escape the axe-wielding psycho killer who simply axed his way through the door while the girl trembled in the tub waiting to die.

Couldn't she even find something, anything, to try to hurt the guy with? Granted, perhaps not everyone kept scissors or other deadly items in their bathroom, but there was shampoo to squirt in his eyes and blind him, or even conditioner to squirt on the floor just inside the door so that the killer might slip and fall when he finally entered. That would at least give her the opportunity to race past and make a run for a smarter escape route. Surely anything was better than just standing there wailing and squealing and waiting to die with her boobs jiggling about? And it wasn't like she didn't have time to think while watching him slam the axe repeatedly through the door.

Shaking her head as the wailing, screeching, jiggling girl got the axe in the head, Drina reached for her drink, and then paused as motion in the backyard caught her eye. Frowning, she squinted, trying to make out what she'd seen. From her position, all she could see was the very back of the yard, and she'd thought she'd seen motion out there and a brief flash of reflected light.

Stephanie gasped in horror, and Drina glanced back toward the girl to see her cuddling a pillow and watching the screen wide-eyed as another character pretty much threw himself under the axe, or into it as the case may be.

Drina glanced back out the window, briefly, but

then stood and stepped over Stephanie, heading for the door.

"I'm going to the bathroom," she said quietly.

"Do you want us to pause it?" Stephanie mumbled, eyes glued to the screen.

"No, I won't be a moment," Drina said, and slipped quickly from the room.

Twelve

Drina walked quickly into Elvi and Victor's bedroom and right past their en suite bathroom, headed for the door to the hall. She didn't have to go to the bathroom, of course. She'd only said that to keep from worrying Harper, and fortunately, Stephanie had been too wrapped up in the movie to read her and call her on the lie.

Not that there was anything to worry about, Drina thought. She'd probably just seen a neighborhood cat or something skulking across the yard or over the fence. But she was going to check it out anyway.

Armed and *not* in a nightie, she thought with a wry shake of the head as she hurried up the hall to the stairs and down to the first floor. Teddy, Alessandro, and Leonora were in the living room talking quietly while they awaited their shift sitting with Tiny and Mirabeau. They glanced over at the sound of her descending the stairs and Teddy immediately came out of the room.

"Problem?" he asked.

Drina shook her head. "I thought I saw something in the backyard, and I'm just going to take a quick peek around. I probably won't even leave the deck."

"I'll come with you," he said, moving to follow, but she shook her head as she walked into the pantry to don her coat and boots.

"There's no need. In fact, it's better if you watch from the window. If there *is* trouble and you're with me, we could both be taken out. If you watch from inside, you can shout the alarm and warn the others, so they aren't taken by surprise," she pointed out sensibly. "Besides, it was probably just a cat skulking about or something. There's no sense both of us getting cold."

"Alessandro can come watch from the window to give the alarm if anything happens," Teddy said grimly, dragging on his coat as she pulled on her boots. "I'm not letting you go out there by yourself. I'm police chief of this town, and if there's trouble, I'm going to help take care of it. You're not going out there on your own," he finished stubbornly.

"What? Are you trying out for the role of the cop in a slasher movie?" she muttered with disgust, thinking they were usually just as stupid as the other characters in the movies.

"What?" he asked with bewilderment.

Drina straightened with a sigh, and said solemnly, "Look, Teddy, you're being very brave and strong to want to accompany me. Unfortunately, you're also being stupid. If there is a problem out there, you could only be a detriment rather than a help in this situation."

He puffed up indignantly. "I know you immortals are stronger and faster and all that nonsense, but I have a gun and wouldn't hesitate to use it."

"Which makes you even more dangerous," she said firmly. "Any immortal worth a spit could take control of you and make you turn the gun on me before I even realized they were there." He blanched at the possibility, and she added gently, "The best thing you can do in this situation is watch from the window and shout to alert the others if there is a problem. That isn't a reflection on you. It doesn't mean you are weak and helpless. It is the smart thing to do, and you're a smart man. So act like it and stop letting your pride make foolish decisions for you. And please try to remember I'm basically the immortal version of a cop. I am trained for this. I'm not some helpless female creeping out in her nightie."

Confusion flickered across his face, telling her he didn't recognize that reference either, but Teddy heaved a disgusted sigh, and nodded. "All right. But give me a signal if you see anything, anything at all."

"I will," she assured him, dragging on her coat and hat before turning back to the closet to retrieve one of the large suitcases Anders had stored in there when they'd thought they were basically babysitting. Opening it, she rifled through the contents, noting that a couple items were missing. Anders was already armed and she should have thought to arm herself before this, she knew. It was that old "new-life-mate" distraction thing getting in the way, Drina thought on a sigh as she retrieved a quiver of arrows, a crossbow, a gun, and a box of drug-laced bullets that should knock out any rogue for at least twenty to thirty minutes . . . enough time to secure them for pick up.

"Christ," Teddy muttered, eyeing the arsenal she'd revealed.

"Did you think we went after rogues armed with just our charming smiles and good sense?" Drina asked with amusement as she strapped the quiver to her back for easy arrow retrieval, and then quickly loaded the gun.

"I don't know. I guess I never really thought about it," he admitted quietly, and then shook his head. "And I suppose you're good with both those weapons?"

"With our eyesight, better than the best mortal sniper in the world," she assured him, and then added wryly, "Having more than two millennia to practice and perfect the skill doesn't hurt either."

Teddy nodded solemnly, and then followed her into the kitchen. He paused at the window, though, and she glanced back to see him already peering fretfully out into the darkness. He didn't glance around as she opened the door, but said gruffly, "Be careful out there."

"I will," she assured him, and slid outside.

It wasn't as cold as it had been before this, and Drina wondered idly if this was the first sign that winter might be coming to an end here, or just a slight reprieve. Whatever the case, the snow on the deck was a bit slushy under her boots, so it was actually warm enough to bring on some melting, and the night was as still as death, with no wind to aggravate things. The one thing she'd noticed while here was that the cold that seemed bearable on a calm night, became completely unbearable if a wind kicked up. She'd also learned that it played havoc with something called the windchill factor, which as far as she could tell just meant it felt even colder than it really was.

Gaze skimming the backyard, Drina moved to the edge of the deck and paused at the bench that ran around it. She squinted, searching the dark shadows, automatically turning off the safety on her gun as she did, but didn't see anything. Of course, she'd taken long enough to gear herself up that whatever she'd seen could have climbed up onto the roof by now, she thought a bit irritably.

The possibility made Drina glance back toward the house, her eyes searching out the roof. Of course, she couldn't see all of it from that angle, so sighed and moved to the stairs to descend into the yard and start toward the back fence. She glanced back occasionally to see how much of the roof she could now make out, but was nearly to the back fence before she could see all of it.

There was nothing to see. No raccoons, hungry enough to break from their winter sleep and go in search of food, and no rogue creeping about, looking for a window to slip through.

Which didn't mean they hadn't moved around to

the front of the house, Drina thought, and moved closer to the house until she was sure Teddy could see her, then pointed at herself, made a walking signal with her fingers, and then gestured toward the road-side of the house.

Teddy seemed to understand and, in response, pointed to himself, and then pointed in the same direction, which she presumed meant he would follow her progress via the ground-floor windows. Drina turned and started around the house, crossing the driveway, and then walking along the sidewalk beside the house to get to the front. She kept glancing up toward the roof as she went, spotting Teddy at various windows as he followed her progress, but also scanning the roof to be sure there was nothing and no one creeping up there.

At the front of the house, Drina paused at the wrought-iron gate and took a good long look at the yard and house. She noted Teddy's presence at the front-door windows, but as in the back, the roof at the front was empty. She was about to turn away and head back around the house to return inside, when a rustling caught her ear and made her freeze.

Turning slowly, Drina searched the front yard more carefully, checking every nook and crevice. She frowned when she spotted movement in the shadowed snow in the corner of the yard in front of the upper and lower porch. Whatever was moving was too small to be human. She hesitated, but curiosity won out and she opened the front gate and stepped inside.

The worry about rogues gone now, Drina started across the yard, another concern rearing its head. It might be a poor abandoned, hungry, and freezing cat rooting in the snow for food. Drina liked animals, often more than mortals and immortals, and wasn't above bringing the poor little bugger a bowl of milk or something to help it see its way through winter. Or if it looked uncared for, maybe even letting it sleep in the garage for the night, where it would be protected from the elements. She could always take it to an animal shelter in the morning.

"Oh, what a cutie," she murmured, slinging the cross bow over her shoulder by the strap as she got close enough to better make out the animal. It was a chubby little sucker, white and black and digging away as if scratching at kitty litter. As she moved closer, she crooned, "Here kitty, kitty."

The cat stilled at her call, growled, and stomped its feet like a child throwing a tantrum. It made Drina chuckle as she continued forward, and she bent forward, trying to make herself smaller and less threatening as she continued to call, "Here kitty, kitty," hoping to lure it to her.

Animals were so adorable really; cute, cuddly, affectionate. In the darkest part of the front garden though it was, she could still make out that it was hunkered down to the ground, looking oddly flat and wide. Not starving then, but—

Drina stopped abruptly, a choked sound slipping from her throat as the damned thing lifted its tail and somehow pissed at her. She was a good eight or ten feet away still, and the damned thing hit her right in the face and chest and—

Dear Lord, the smell was the most god-awful stench she'd ever encountered. Drina staggered back, wondering with horror what the hell the animal had been eating that its urine would smell so damned foul. That was followed by the wonder as to whether it was some damned mutant to be able to pee out its butt at her, but they were brief thoughts that flashed across her mind, and in the next moment were gone, replaced with dismay as her eyes began to sting as if someone had shoved burning hot pokers in her eyes.

Gagging and choking, Drina stumbled and fell on her butt and rolled to the side. Her hands rose to cover her burning eyes, and moans were gargling from her mouth.

"Drina?"

She hadn't heard the front door open, but she heard Teddy's shout and the stomp of his feet as he raced down the front steps.

"What the hell—Dear God, it's a skunk!" His approaching footsteps stopped abruptly on that almost falsetto squawk, and then continued more cautiously, appearing to curve to the side a bit rather than approach directly, as he muttered, "Shoo! Shoo you little bugger. Don't make me shoot you, you damned varmint. Christ, you've been sprayed. I can smell you from here. Oh God Almighty. What the hell were you thinking playing with a skunk? For Christ's sake. Shoo!" he repeated. "Damn, did it get you in the face? Shoo!"

Drina was lying still now, curled on her side with eyes closed, waiting for the nanos to fix whatever the heck the cat urine had done and listening to Teddy with confusion. She couldn't tell from one moment to the next who he was addressing, herself or the cat, and she hadn't a clue what he was talking about, except he seemed afraid of the little beast that had done this to her. Not that she blamed him really, considering the agony she was in, but the creature wasn't much bigger than a kitten, and Teddy did have a damned gun and—cripes her eyes hurt.

"Shoot the damned thing," Drina growled, deciding maybe she didn't like animals so much anymore.

"I'm not shooting it. It'll wake up the whole damned neighborhood. Could give one of the old biddies in the retirement home across the street a heart attack, and—"

"Then throw a damned snowball at it," she demanded furious.

"Teddy? What's happening?" Leonora's voice called out from the general vicinity of what Drina guessed was the porch.

"Why is the bella Alexandrina rolling on the snow?" Alessandro's voice sounded next. "Is she making the snow angels?"

"No, she's not making the damned snow angels," Teddy muttered with exasperation.

"Oh dear, is that a skunk?" Leonora asked.

"No," Alessandro gasped with horror. "No the smelly cat!"

"I've told you, Alessandro darling, they aren't cats."

"They look like the cats. Like the big fluffy cat

she's been stepped on and flattened to a big fluffy pancake cat," Alessandro argued.

"Well, perhaps a little," Leonora conceded.

"I hate the smelly cats," Alessandro vowed, and Drina thought she heard a shudder in his voice. "They smell like—Like that!" he cried, as the smell apparently reached him. "Make her to go away, Teddy!"

"How the hell am I supposed to make it go away, Alessandro?"

"Throw the ball of the snow at it," Alessandro said, and Drina nodded. It was exactly what she'd suggested.

"He can't do that, dear," Leonora said soothingly.

"Why not?" Alessandro demanded.

"Because the damned thing has nowhere to go," Teddy snapped. "Drina's in the way. It's trapped in the corner of the garden. Throwing snowballs at it will just piss it off and make it spray again, and I have no intention of getting sprayed."

"Then you must to get the bella Alexandrina out of the way," Alessandro said with distress. "We must to get the smelly cat to go away."

"Drina, pull yourself toward my voice a few feet. I can help you up and out of its way then," Teddy called.

"Pull myself?" she asked with disbelief, and then demanded, "Come here and help me. I can't even see."

"I can't. You're too close to the skunk," Teddy explained. "Just pull yourself this way."

"Where the hell is Mr. Big Brave Police Chief who

was willing to take on a rabid rogue?" she asked dryly. "A rabid rogue, by the way, who could twist you into pretzel shapes and laugh while he did it?"

"Rabid rogues are one thing, skunks are another entirely," Teddy said dryly. "Just pull yourself over here and—"

He fell silent as the sound of smashing glass sounded.

"What was that?" Drina asked sharply.

"It came from the back of the house," Teddy said sharply, and then she heard Harper shout and Stephanie scream, and Teddy barked, "Wait here."

"What? Wait!" she cried, then cursed and forced her hands from her eyes to try to see as she heard his footsteps rush away. She could hear Leonora and Alessandro moving away as well but couldn't see a damned thing. Opening her eyes merely brought on the pain again and forced her to close them once more. Though she thought this time they hurt a little less. Maybe.

Adrenaline rushing through her, Drina started to roll onto her stomach to get up, ignoring the growl the action immediately caused from the corner of the yard. Worried sick about Harper and Stephanie, she merely snarled, "Go ahead and spray me again, bitch! My eyes are closed, and I can't smell any worse than I do now."

Drina staggered to her feet and stumbled blindly toward where she thought Leonora's and Alessandro's voices had been coming from earlier. She'd only taken a couple of steps when she stumbled into what felt like a snow-covered boulder and fell face-first in the snow. Releasing a string of curses she'd learned while a pirate, Drina started to scramble back to her feet, then froze as a faint waft of smoke reached her nose. Lifting her head, she sniffed the air, but whatever she'd smelled was gone. All she could smell was some horrible combination of rotten eggs, burning rubber, and very strong garlic. She could hear the hungry rush of flames, though, coming from what she thought was the side of the house.

Gritting her teeth, Drina didn't bother trying to get up and risk running into something else but began to crawl forward on her hands and knees. She'd only moved a foot or so when her senses made her pause and stiffen.

Drina's head rose like a deer scenting the air for danger though she apparently had no sense of smell at the moment, and it was sound she was testing the air for. Someone was there. She knew it. She could feel their presence in the prickling along her spine.

Her first instinct was to go for her gun, but she no longer had that. She must have dropped it when she'd fallen back after being sprayed, Drina realized. Christ, she was a blind idiot, crawling around in the dark without a damned weapon, she thought bitterly, and then recalled the crossbow hanging from her shoulder. Not that it would be much use since she was presently blind. She might as well be wearing a stupid nightie and wailing please don't kill me.

"Screw that," Drina muttered, and immediately fell back to sit in the snow, reaching back to snatch an arrow from the quiver and slinging the crossbow

around at the same time. She was practiced enough
at the task that even blind she managed to arm the
crossbow in a heartbeat. The problem then became
where to aim the damned thing, but she lifted the
weapon and strained to hear any sound that would
give away the person's location.

When Drina turned in the general direction of the
side of the house, or what she thought was the side
of the house where the cornered skunk had been or
still was, there was a sudden flurry of sound that
definitely wasn't the skunk. Whatever made it was
big, human-sized big, judging by the thud of footsteps as they fled in what she thought was the direction of the gate.

Drina followed the sound with her crossbow, and
when her instincts screamed to release it, loosed her
arrow. She heard a grunt, but the footsteps didn't
slow, and she cursed under her breath, suspecting
she'd only winged whoever it was.

Drina sighed, but rearmed the crossbow just in
case and listened blindly for another moment before
she heard approaching sirens.

"Fire trucks," she muttered, beginning to shuffle
backward on her butt in the direction she thought
the stairs were, using one hand and her legs to move
herself. The entire time, she continued to point her
crossbow blindly in the general direction of where
she thought the yard's front gate was.

"Well, they put out the fire," Teddy Brunswick announced wearily, stomping his feet on the mat as he
entered his kitchen and began to remove his coat.

Drina glanced to him from the stool Anders had silently set beside the back door for her . . . as far from his own position at the far end of the attached dining room as he could get her without sticking her outside. Her vision was still blurry, but she could see well enough to make out the way the police chief's nose wrinkled as he caught her scent. She also didn't miss how quickly he scooted out of the kitchen and into the dining room, straight across the room to the desk against the far wall, where Anders was busily punching away at Teddy's computer keyboard. He was searching the Internet for suggestions to remove skunk spray from a person.

Sighing miserably, Drina glanced toward the ceiling, wondering how Harper and Stephanie were. They had been placed in one of the two bedrooms upstairs in this tiny, two-floor house of Teddy's. Dawn, Leonora, and Alessandro were tending to them. Tiny had been moved to the second bedroom, with Mirabeau and Edward continuing to oversee his turning.

Teddy had arranged to have them brought here to his home while the fire trucks were still working on putting out the fire at Casey Cottage. It had taken two ambulances and his deputy's car to transport them. Everyone else had gone in the ambulances, and Drina had been the only one in the police car. While she hadn't yet been able to see at that point, she was sure she'd heard the deputy making muffled sounds that could have been either gagging or weeping. Either was possible considering how she smelled, and the fact that the deputy had been in such a rush to get her where he had to take her that he hadn't thought to put anything down on his seats before ushering her quickly into the back of his car. His car could very well carry that horrible smell forever for all she knew. Drina could certainly understand if he'd been sobbing over that.

It turned out the sound of breaking glass they'd heard had been a rock crashing through one of the windows in the second-floor porch. It had been followed by a Molotov cocktail that had shattered just inches from the blanket. The fuel inside had splashed across the blankets, pillows, and Harper and Stephanie. The two had apparently come staggering out of the room in flames.

Edward and Anders had heard their shouts and were the first to reach them, with Teddy, Leonora, and Alessandro hard on their heels. They'd somehow doused the flames eating away at Harper and Stephanie, and then—afraid the fire would move through the entire house—had gotten everyone out, along with as much blood as they could grab.

Drina had been the last one anyone had thought of, which she didn't mind since she wasn't seriously hurt or anything, but the whole thing had been incredibly frustrating and frightening. She'd been worried sick about Stephanie and Harper and as useless as a baby as she dragged herself to the front porch and inside. It was the firemen, charging into the house, who had found her using the door frame to pull herself to her feet in the foyer, shouting frantically for Harper and Stephanie. One of the men had led her through the house to the back door and out into the yard with the others.

"Damage?" Anders's voice made Drina leave her self-pitying thoughts and tune in to their conversation.

"Surprisingly little," Teddy said, and did sound surprised. "Apparently the house is double-walled brick, and that helped prevent the fire from spreading from the porch to the rest of the house. Both the upper porch and the one below it are write-offs, of course, and the hallway between the porch and Elvi and Victor's room took some damage before the firemen arrived. There was a good bit of smoke damage, though," he added with a grimace. "And the fire chief said no one can stay there for a bit due to the possibility of hot ashes starting the fire up again and something about toxic air and residue through the house."

She saw Anders nod acknowledgment.

"Did you call Lucian?" Teddy asked.

"No. He likes full reports, so I waited for your return," Anders said, and then punched more keys and Drina heard a sound she recognized as a computer printer kicking to life.

"What's this?" Teddy asked, and his blurry figure moved over to peer down at whatever printed. "Hmm. Carbolic soap, vinegar, and tomato juice."

She saw his head swing her way and sat up a little straighter. "Is that how to get rid of this damned smell?"

Drina had already removed her clothes and now sat there in the kitchen in the rattiest old sheet

Anders could find in Teddy's linen closet. It was almost gauze thin and frayed on the edges, wrapped around her twice or three times and tucked into itself above her breasts. She still smelled horrendous, though. Along with her clothes, the skunk— or smelly cat as Alessandro called it—had gotten her in the face, neck, hair, and hands when he'd sprayed.

"Yes," Teddy murmured, and then shifted. "I have some vinegar, but she'll need more than I have, and I don't have any tomato juice at all. I can get both at the twenty-four-hour grocery store, but it says here you have to get the carbolic soap at a drugstore and they just recently reduced the hours on what used to be our twenty-four-hour drugstore. It closes at 10 P.M. now."

Drina turned to peer at the clock on the kitchen wall and squinted to read the time. When she saw that it was 10:03, she could have wept. Did she have some rotten luck or what?

"We'll have to wait till it reopens in the morning," Teddy said unhappily.

Drina turned to take in the men's expressions. Neither Teddy nor Anders looked happy at this news, but she was so miserable about it herself, she had little energy left to care about how they were feeling. It wasn't just that she was tired of stinking to high heaven, but Anders insisted, and rightly so, that she should stay in the kitchen and not spread her smell through the rest of Teddy's house. This meant she was stuck right where she was, on the hard vinyl barstool in the kitchen. There would be no creeping upstairs to watch over Harper, no checking on Stephanie, no looking in to see how Tiny's turn was going. She supposed she'd even be sleeping there on the kitchen floor, like the family dog, if she slept at all.

It was not being able to go up to Harper that bothered her the most, though. Drina wanted to be at his side, nursing him back to health as he'd done for her when she'd woken after the accident.

"Well . . ." Her gaze slid back to Teddy at that muttered word to see that he was shuffling sideways toward the doorway to the hall. Avoiding her gaze, he mumbled something about checking on the others, and ducked quickly out of the room.

"Calling Lucian," Anders announced, following quickly.

Drina watched them go, suspecting it would be the last she'd see of them until the drugstore opened in . . . oh, ten or twelve hours was her guess . . . it seemed like a lifetime at that point.

"I don't know what the hell Drina thought she was doing playing with the damned thing."

Those gruff words drifted through Harper's consciousness, the sound of Drina's name, stirring him from sleep.

"She probably didn't know what it was, Teddy," Leonora Cipriano's calm tones said soothingly. "There aren't any in Europe."

"That is because we no would suffer the smelly cat," Alessandro announced firmly.

"No, you'd most likely transport them somewhere

else." Teddy sounded irritated. "That's probably how we got the little beasts ourselves. You guys put them all on a boat and sent them over here to North America a couple of hundred years ago."

"The English maybe would do such a thing. Is what they did with the criminals, so maybe they would send you the smelly cats. But no the Italians. We would no be so cruel."

"Well, I don't know what the hell it was doing out this time of year anyway," Teddy said. "I thought they hibernated."

"They go into a torpor, not a true hibernation," Leonora explained quietly. "And it was probably hungry. They will sometimes wake up and come out in search of food if it warms a bit, and it did warm up quite a bit last night." There was a pause, and then Leonora said, "I just feel sorry for the poor little thing having to sit down there in the kitchen all by herself like some sort of outcast. She looked so miserable when I went down to ask Anders if he'd managed to reach Lucian yet."

"Had he?" Teddy asked sharply.

"No, I'm afraid not. He said he's left several messages, though. I'm sure Lucian will call soon."

There was a gusty sigh, and Teddy said, "Well, he'd better. You're all welcome to stay here, of course. But this is a small house. I only have the two bedrooms. You'll all be sleeping in shifts until he calls and gives some sort of instruction."

Harper was having trouble following the conversation. What the hell was a smelly cat and who had been playing with it? For that matter, what was wrong with playing with a cat? And what was that about Lucian and instructions?

Harper forced his eyes open and turned his head to peer toward the voices and found he was in bed in a room he didn't recognize and that Alessandro, Teddy, and Leonora were having their rather strange little discussion by the door.

Movement beside him in the bed drew his attention, and Harper turned his head the other way to find Stephanie lying beside him. Her eyes were open, and she looked much less confused than he felt.

"Drina was sprayed by a skunk," Stephanie explained quietly, apparently reading his confusion. "Alessandro calls them smelly cats."

"Ah." Harper sighed and supposed he should have recalled as much. He had a vague recollection of hearing the name "smelly cat" before from the man, but it had been sometime ago.

"You're awake," Teddy said grimly.

Harper turned his head to watch the trio approach the bed.

"How do you feel?" Leonora asked, bending to smooth his hair back from his forehead and check his eyes for he knew not what.

"Better than I did earlier," he said dryly, recalling the "earlier" in question. Roaring flames, bubbling skin, the stench of burnt meat, and knowing it was his flesh. Being engulfed by fire was a most unpleasant and terrifying experience. It wasn't something he'd soon forget.

Leonora moved around the bed to Stephanie now

and repeated the same question and actions; feeling her forehead he realized now, not just brushing hair back, and checking her eyes, perhaps to see if they were clear or how much silver there was in them. It could be a good gage of many things, including passion levels and blood levels.

Harper heard Stephanie murmur that she was fine. He didn't believe her for a minute. He had no doubt the poor kid was traumatized. Hell, he was traumatized, and he wasn't a teenager who until just recently had been mortal. Fire was one of the few things that could kill their kind. If they hadn't gotten out of that room and found help to douse the flames, they could have died there.

The thought disturbed him and made him shift unhappily. "Where's Drina?"

"Er . . . She was sprayed by a skunk," Teddy said with a grimace.

"Yes, Stephanie said so, but where is she?" What he really wanted to know was why the hell she wasn't there with him. He'd nearly died, dammit. He wanted her with him.

"Well, she's down in the kitchen at the moment."

"They won't let her out of the kitchen because they don't want her to smell up the house," Stephanie told him, no doubt plucking the explanation from someone's head. He didn't care whose.

"She's very worried about you, though," Leonora reassured him. "She wanted to be here with you both. She's probably fretting herself sick down there."

The words soothed him somewhat but not completely, and Harper sat up and started to get out of bed, pausing when the blankets covering him fell away revealing a Port Henry Police T-shirt and black joggers.

"Your clothes were pretty much just charred bits melted into your skin. They fell away with the damaged skin as you healed. Teddy was kind enough to loan you those and help Alessandro dress you while Dawn and I dressed Stephanie," Leonora explained quietly.

He glanced back to Stephanie to see that she wore a similar getup. Grunting, he stood, his gaze sliding over a garbage bin brimming with empty blood bags. They were really going through them. In fact, he wondered that they'd had enough to deal with the accident, Tiny's turn, and now this.

"Leonora opened up the blood bank, and she and Edward brought back a bunch more blood," Teddy announced, catching where his gaze had gone.

Harper nodded. Leonora had insisted on coming out of retirement after her turn and taken a position at the local blood bank, which had distressed Alessandro no end. Not that he really minded having a wife who worked. It was just distressing to him because they were still new turns, and Leonora's position meant she had to leave their bed more frequently than he'd liked when she'd taken it on. Especially when he was wealthy enough that she needn't work at all if she chose.

"Thank you," he murmured to Leonora, heading for the door.

"Wait for me," Stephanie said, throwing the covers aside to follow him.

Harper slowed as he headed out of the room, but not much. He wanted to see Drina. He wanted to take her in his arms and never let her go. A man got a lot of things straight when he was forced to face his own mortality, and Harper had realized some things. He loved the damned woman. He'd come to love her fire, her passion, her wit, and her strength. And he was glad as hell she hadn't been in that room when the firebomb or whatever it was had come flying through the window.

"A Molotov cocktail," Stephanie said behind him, as he started down the stairs. He only realized she was naming whatever it was that had exploded all over them, when she explained, "The memory of the fire chief saying that was one of Teddy's surface memories . . . Thank you for dragging me out of the porch."

Harper slowed at her quiet words and turned to slip his arm around her shoulders affectionately, muttering, "My pleasure."

Stephanie slipped her own arm around his waist and squeezed briefly, then slid past him on the stairs and hurried the rest of the way to the main floor, turning right at the bottom as if she knew where she was going. Harper followed since he didn't have a clue of the layout of the house, and they turned into a dining room, where Stephanie paused abruptly, her mouth dropping.

Harper followed her gaze, spotted Drina slumped miserably on a stool in the kitchen at the opposite end of the house and started toward her at once. Relief coursed through him just at the sight of her. He was passing Stephanie when she made an odd sound that had him glancing toward her. He frowned as he realized that her mouth hadn't dropped open in surprise; the girl was heaving.

Slowing reluctantly, he asked, "Are you all—" And then he came to a shuddering halt as the smell hit him. His head jerked back to Drina with horror just as her head came up.

She peered at them blankly for a second, and then relief lit up her face like a Christmas tree. She promptly leapt off her stool and rushed forward, clutching what appeared to be a ratty old sheet around her as she hurried to him.

"Oh, Harper, Stephanie. Oh thank God!" she cried. "I've been so worried."

Despite himself, Harper took a quick step back at her approach, but then caught himself and forced himself to stand still. He also stopped breathing, however, holding his breath in a desperate bid to keep from gagging as the woman he loved threw herself at him and hugged him.

Drina held him tightly and for a very, very long time. At least it seemed a very long time to him as he continued to hold his breath, but then she finally pulled pack to peer up at him happily. Her smile was wide, her eyes glowing . . . until she saw his face. Concern immediately replaced her relief.

"You're terribly flush," she said with a frown. "Have you had enough blood? Maybe you should lie down for a bit. Are you—Harper, you're turning purple!"

"I'm fine." He sighed on an exhale and pulled her

to his chest again so that she wouldn't see his face as he inhaled another breath. Dear God, he thought as the toxic fumes wafted from the love of his life to fill his mouth and lungs. Oh Good Lord in heaven, he moaned inwardly, barely managing not to whimper aloud.

"I wanted to come up—" Drina began, and then paused as she peered past him. "Stephanie? What are you doing way over— Oh."

She deflated like a punctured balloon, and then flushed with mortification and—avoiding Harper's eyes—scurried quickly back to her stool. She crawled back onto it, her shoulders slumped and every line of her body speaking of misery. Her voice was much subdued when she said, "I'm glad you're both all right, and that you came down so I could see for myself. You can both go back upstairs now with the others, though, if you like. I understand."

Harper turned to see that Stephanie had moved over to a desk holding a computer, about as far as she could get and stay in the room. He supposed that and the girl's dismayed expression were what had recalled Drina to the matter of her scent.

Sighing, he glanced back to Drina, and then forced himself to move across the room to join her. With every step, he assured himself that his senses would deaden to the scent quickly, and he could bear it till they did. Still, he couldn't help holding his breath as he approached and stood in front of her.

"What—?" she began when he appeared before her. But when Harper simply caught her upper arms and pulled her against his chest, she fell against him with a little sniffle that told him how much it meant to her. He suspected his Drina did not cry often, if at all. A weepy woman would never have passed for a male pirate, and he doubted gladiators could afford the luxury of weeping, either.

Harper heard her inhale and glanced down curiously to see that she had her nose pressed to his chest and was trying to inhale his scent. He wondered that she could smell anything over her own stench, so wasn't terribly surprised when Drina sighed miserably, and mourned, "I can't smell you. I love your scent, but I can't smell you."

Harper didn't have a clue what to say to that, and really, speaking would mean releasing the air in his lungs and taking in another. He desperately wanted to avoid doing that until absolutely necessary, so was grateful for the distraction when the door beside them suddenly opened, and Anders entered, bags in hand.

Drina was out of his arms and on Anders at once. "Did you get everything?"

"Dear God, woman! Get back. You stink," Anders barked.

Harper scowled at the man. It was no more than Drina was doing, however. He wasn't surprised her moment of sniffly misery had passed and her naturally fiery nature had reasserted itself. This was more the Alexandrina Argenis he knew.

Eyes narrowing, Drina moved closer instead of getting back as Anders had ordered, and then hissed up at the Russian. "And you're the most miserable SOB I've ever encountered, so I guess we all have our crosses to bear." She snatched the bags from him, and then turned away adding, "The difference is I'm about to bathe away this smell, but when I come down, you'll still be a miserable SOB."

Harper found a smile pulling his mouth wide as he watched Drina make her exit, walking out of the room with her eyes blazing and head high, as regal as any queen.

"Damn, she's magnificent," he breathed, positive he must be the luckiest bastard on the planet to have found her.

"Glad you think so," Anders said dryly. "Then you can take these instructions up to her so she doesn't screw it up and use the stuff in the wrong order or something."

Harper glanced down at the paper the hunter shoved at him, noting the title *Instructions on How to Remove Skunk Odor from a Human*. He glanced back to Anders and smiled widely. "I'll even help her follow the instructions."

"I'll bet you will," Anders said dryly.

Thirteen

Drina closed the bathroom door behind her with a kick of her heel, set the bags of soap, tomato juice, and vinegar on the bathroom counter, and then turned to the tub, only to pause with a frown. Was she supposed to just pour all this stuff in the tub, or was she supposed to add water or what? She hadn't a clue. She needed the instructions.

Clucking with irritation, Drina turned back to the door, annoyed with herself because she was about to ruin a damned fine exit by having to scurry back and beg for the instructions. Muttering under her breath, she pulled the door open and found Harper there, hand upraised as if he'd been about to knock.

Smiling crookedly, he lowered the knocking hand and raised the other, revealing the instructions.

"Thank you," Drina breathed, taking the sheet of paper with a relief that was not proportional to the moment. She knew then that her exhaustion was definitely making her overemotional. She'd sat on that stool all night, nodding off a time or two from sheer exhaustion, but only for a second each time before her swaying body had brought her abruptly back awake.

"Do you want some help?" Harper asked quickly when she started to close the door.

Drina paused in surprise, and then smiled wryly at his pained expression and shook her head. "Thank you for offering. It's very sweet, but I know I smell like the worst backed-up drainage system ever and wouldn't even inflict this on Anders."

"I came prepared," he said quickly, bringing her to a halt again. This time the door was almost closed, and she had to pull it back open. When she peered at him quizzically, Harper opened the hand he'd had fisted to knock, revealing a clothespin resting in his palm.

Drina released a startled laugh and shook her head. "You—"

Her words caught in her throat when he suddenly covered her mouth with his. Lifting it a moment later, Harper said gently, "I believe the expression is for better or worse. Besides, in a few minutes, it will be all better and no worse."

She chuckled at the way he wiggled one eyebrow lasciviously and backed into the bathroom to let him in. "All right. You can read the instructions to me."

Drina handed him back the instructions after a quick glance at the first one. She then moved to the tub to put in the stopper.

"Take off the clothes you're wearing," Harper read

out as she straightened. He then caught the back of her sheet and whipped it away.

Drina gasped, and then turned to prop her fists on her naked hips and give him a feigned scowl. "I read the first instructions. It said take off the clothes you were wearing *when sprayed*."

"True, but you can't bathe in the sheet anyway, so I thought I'd be helpful," he said, his eyes appreciating her pose and nakedness.

Drina snorted at the claim, and then grinned with amusement when he glanced around, closed the toilet seat, and sat on it, then attached the clothespin to his nose, pinching it closed, as he considered the instructions again.

"Fill a tub with water and get in," he read, his voice now nasal.

Chuckling, she turned back to the tub and turned the taps on full. Drina then glanced over her shoulder to catch him eyeing her derriere in a manner that probably wouldn't go under the listing of "helpful." Shaking her head, she asked, "What do I put in first? The tomato juice or—?"

"Neither," he interrupted, managing to tear his gaze from her derriere and back to the sheet. "It says to wash first with just soap and water, that sometimes if you only got a light spray, it's enough."

"My spraying wasn't light," she said dryly. It had been a nice hard steady stream. The little beast had probably been saving up all winter to douse someone. Lucky her for being the recipient. "And Teddy said a bath wouldn't help by itself, or I would have done it last night."

"I'm just reading the instructions," he said with an apologetic shrug.

"Right," Drina muttered. The tub was only half-full, but she stepped into it and sat down anyway. While the water continued to run, she picked up the bar of soap on the side of the tub, dunked it in the water, and began to lather it up and apply it to herself.

Harper said something she couldn't hear over the sound of the rushing water. Busy lathering her chest and neck, Drina simply lifted one foot out of the water and used her toes to turn off the tap before turning to him to ask, "What was that?"

He was staring rather blankly at the taps.

"Harper?" she asked with a frown.

"You turned it off with your toes," he muttered.

"Yes," Drina said, and tilted her head uncertainly. She'd done it automatically and hadn't realized it was odd, but his expression was . . . well, she wasn't sure what his expression was. His eyes were wide though, and he was now staring at her feet at the end of the tub with a sort of fascination.

"What talented little feet you have," he murmured finally, his gaze shifting back to her face. "What else can you do with them?"

Drina opened her mouth, closed it, and then narrowed her eyes. "Are you having another one of your perverted little fantasies like the maid apron and boots?"

"Uh-huh." Harper nodded, his eyes sliding over her naked breasts above the water.

Drina chuckled and turned to begin soaping herself again, saying nonchalantly, "I can do all sorts of things with my toes and feet."

Harper released a little sigh and set the instruction sheet on the side of the sink, then slid to his knees beside the tub and reached for the soap. "Let me help soap you up."

"No way." She laughed, holding the soap out of his reach. "Back on the toilet, mister. You can help later, when I smell better."

He sighed but did as instructed and simply watched silently as she soaped every inch of her skin, and then rinsed it away.

"I haven't been able to smell for hours now," Drina said on a sigh as she sniffed at her arm. "But I don't think it worked."

Harper caught her hand and pulled it to his nose for a sniff, then bit his lip and shook his head.

"Right," she muttered, pulling the plug on the water and standing up as the tub began to drain. "So what's the next step?"

"Wash with carbolic soap," he read, and stood to search the bags on the counter for the item in question.

Drina glanced impatiently down at the half-drained water, and reached to turn on the shower. It didn't make sense to wash the smell away and then sit in the smelly water full of stuff you just soaped off. She would shower this time.

"No fair," Harper complained when she pulled the tub's shower curtain closed after taking the soap he handed her.

Drina chuckled but simply continued with her

plan, standing outside the spray of water to thoroughly soap herself up, and then moving under it to rinse herself.

"Now?" she asked a few moments later, jerking the curtain open enough to stick her hand out for inspection.

He sniffed and then shook his head apologetically. "Better, but . . ."

Drina sighed and turned off the shower. "Next?"

"Fill a bucket with equal parts water and vinegar and use a rag to wash yourself with the mixture. Scrub hard, but not to the point of pain," Harper read, and then glanced around with a frown. "We don't have a bucket."

"Look under the sink," she suggested.

He opened one of the cupboard doors and made a sound of triumph. "A cleaning bucket."

"Good enough," Drina decided, stepping out of the tub and using the ruined sheet to dry herself while Harper quickly rinsed the bucket, dumped a large bottle of vinegar in, then refilled the vinegar bottle with warm water and added that as well.

He reached under the sink again then, and sorted through a stack of washcloths before settling on the rattiest of the bunch, which wasn't truly very ratty. He dropped it in the water and glanced to her. "Shall I—?"

"Sit," she said firmly, urging him aside. Drina then began to clean herself with the pungent solution, first dunking her hair in the pail, wringing it out as thoroughly as she could, and then scrubbing at her face and working her way down. She was aware of Harper's fascinated eyes watching every move and just couldn't resist playing it up a bit, moving the cloth over her breasts more lovingly, and then setting her foot on the toilet seat between his thighs to wash one leg, leaving herself open to his view as she did.

Really, she hadn't got sprayed on the legs and this wasn't necessary at all, but Drina thought the smell was finally beginning to recede, she was feeling better, and really it was fun, she acknowledged to herself as she switched feet on the toilet seat, giving him the same open view from a different angle. This time she washed *everything*.

"I think it's starting to work," Harper growled, his hands reaching for her, and Drina immediately jumped back.

"Starting is good, but I want it gone," she said firmly. "What's next?"

Harper stared mournfully at the crux of her thighs for a moment, and then turned back to the sheet of instructions. "Pour the tomato juice all over your body and wash yourself with it as well, scrubbing again." He glanced up. "It's the last step. After that it's wash with soap and water again, probably to remove the tomato juice."

He set the sheet down and stood to move past her to the bags on the counter. "Get in the tub, and I'll pour the juice over you."

Drina stepped into the tub. She then bent to put the stopper back in to keep the fluid in the tub in case he missed a spot pouring it on her, like under her chin, or her ears or—good Lord—just anywhere the spray may have gotten.

"Head up, eyes closed," Harper ordered, when she straightened and turned back.

Drina did as instructed and gasped as cool liquid poured over her head and face and splashed down over her, then blinked her eyes open in surprise when his hands were suddenly moving over her breasts.

"It missed a couple spots as it poured over you," he explained huskily, moving the cool red liquid around and over her breasts . . . repeatedly, first with his hands, and then with the cloth.

Drina bit her lip and clenched her fists to keep from reaching for him as Harper spent what seemed an endless amount of time, and half the jugs of tomato juice Anders had purchased, ensuring her breasts were spray free.

Her toes were curling in the red liquid now pooling in the tub, when he finally said, "Turn."

Drina turned her back to him, and sucked in a breath as the cool liquid poured over her head and back. He again used his hands to direct the tomato juice around, this time paying special attention to her behind. His fingers sliding over the curves, under the curves, and then dipping briefly between her legs, making her brace her hands on the cold tiles to keep her balance as she gasped, "I'm pretty sure I didn't get sprayed there."

"Yes, but you were sitting in the first batch of tub water when you cleaned the surface stuff away, and it may have gotten everywhere. Best to do a thorough job," he said, sounding cheerful and a bit breathless himself. His fingers slipped away as he turned to switch the empty jug for a fresh one, and then he repeated the process, once again ending between her legs.

Drina bit her lip as his fingers ran over her, sure Harper was punishing her for her earlier teasing when she'd been using the water-and-vinegar solution. On a bright note, though, as her life mate, she knew he was punishing himself as well since he too was experiencing the excitement he was stirring in her.

"Last bottle." Harper's voice was gravelly now, but she was amazed he could speak at all. She didn't think she could, and then the cool liquid was pouring over her for the last time, little red rivulets running over her shoulders and down her arms.

This time Harper didn't waste time moving the liquid over her derriere but immediately slid his free hand between her legs as he poured. Drina curled her fingers against the tile surround of the tub and moaned. When the bottle was empty, and he retrieved his hand to turn and set the jug on the counter with the others, she turned and leaned weakly back against the cool tiles, glad to still be on her feet. She'd begun to worry her shaking legs would collapse under her by the end.

Harper turned back and eyed her, then stepped to the edge of the tub, caught her arm, and pulled her forward for a kiss that did little to settle her excitement. His hands moved over her briefly as he thrust his tongue into her mouth, and then he broke the kiss and stepped back to begin removing his T-shirt.

"Going to scrub my back?" she asked huskily,

sinking back against the tile again as the T-shirt hit the floor.

"Your back, your front, your top, your bottom, and everything in between," he assured her, and reached for the waist of his joggers, only to pause as a knock sounded at the door.

"Drina?" Stephanie's voice called. "I'm sorry to bother you guys, but this is the only bathroom, and I really have to go."

Drina bit her lip as Harper closed his eyes on a sigh.

"You don't have to get out of the tub, Dree," Stephanie added now. "Just pull the shower curtain closed if you want. I don't mind. But I really, really have to go."

"One second, Steffie," Drina said finally when Harper bent to retrieve his T-shirt and quickly pulled it back on. He leaned forward then to kiss her again, a quick, hard one, and then tugged the shower curtain closed and turned to open the bathroom door.

"Sorry, Stephanie. Go right ahead," Harper said as he slid from the room.

Drina sat down in the tub with a little thump, grateful to get off her shaking legs. She heard Stephanie enter and a rustle as the girl announced, "Teddy sent up some joggers and a T-shirt for you. I'm putting them on the counter."

"Thank you," Drina murmured, picking up the washcloth. She soaked it in the tomato juice in the tub and began to scrub herself as her nerve endings slowly began to calm.

"The tomato juice and stuff must have worked. It only smells a little in here now, and I think that's from the sheet." Stephanie's words were accompanied by a rustling Drina supposed was the girl preparing to "go."

"Yes, I think it worked. I can actually smell the tomato juice now, and I haven't been able to smell anything for hours," Drina said.

"Lucian still hasn't called Anders back," Stephanie announced, and Drina suspected the girl was just talking to try to hide the sounds as she relieved herself. "You don't think Lucian will make us go back to Toronto now that Casey Cottage is temporarily uninhabitable, do you?"

Drina heard the worry in the girl's voice and frowned, but the suggestion worried her as well. It would be harder to hide Stephanie's abilities—and trouble handling them—from Lucian if they were in Toronto . . . and Drina was worried about what he would do. She wanted to help the girl learn to block the voices and perhaps deal with the electricity and energy she claimed to feel around life mates, and had spent a good portion of her night in the kitchen considering how to do that. The problem was that it was the complete opposite of what new turns usually needed to learn, and she had no idea how to go about it.

Realizing she shouldn't be thinking about this with the girl so close, Drina pushed the thought from her head, and said, "I don't know, sweetie. But if so, I'll be with you. Don't worry. And it would probably only be temporary until Casey Cottage was habitable again."

"Right," Stephanie murmured. She was silent for a minute, and then said, "Sorry to interrupt your bath."

"You aren't interrupting," Drina said with amusement, scrubbing the tomato-soaked cloth over her leg.

"Yeah, but I mean, you probably want your privacy and stuff."

Drina chuckled at the suggestion. "Steffie, when I was young in Egypt, servants would help me with my bath. They would pour water over me and so on. And in Spain, I always had a maid who helped me bathe. Well, until that went out of fashion. I am not bothered by your being here."

"Really?" Stephanie asked curiously. "Did they have soap in Egypt?"

"Not the hard bars used today. Ours was a cream made up of lime, oil, and perfume."

"That sounds nice." Stephanie sighed. There was a rustle, and then the flushing of the toilet, followed by the squeak of the taps being turned.

Teddy needed some oil on that, Drina thought absently as she continued scrubbing.

"Well, I guess I'll go back downstairs," Stephanie announced, turning off the taps. "Do you want to play cards or something when you come down?"

"Sure," she said easily. "I'll be down in a minute."

"Okay." Drina heard the bathroom door open and thought Stephanie was leaving, but she suddenly said, "Oh, I forgot, Teddy went out to pick up sandwich fixings before heading to the police station. I was going to make myself a Kitchen Sink sandwich. Do you want me to make you one too?"

Drina stilled and asked uncertainly, "What is a Kitchen Sink sandwich?"

Stephanie chuckled. "That's what my dad calls them because it includes everything but the kitchen sink. It's tomatoes, lettuce, onions, radishes, green peppers, cucumber, cheese, mayo, Italian dressing, and ham or whatever. It's basically like a sub sandwich, but on bread."

Drina was actually salivating by the end of that long list of ingredients. "That sounds delicious."

"Oh, it is," Stephanie assured her on a laugh. "So you want one?"

"Yes, please."

"Okay, see you soon."

The door closed, and Drina promptly unplugged the stopper and switched the shower on. She was suddenly in a hurry to get downstairs and try this Kitchen Sink sandwich.

"I hear that Lucian finally called."

Drina glanced up from her cards and smiled at Teddy as he settled at the table with his plate of pork chops, potatoes, and salad. Leonora had made dinner tonight with Drina, Harper and Stephanie basically getting in her way as they tried to help. Everyone else had eaten two hours ago, but Teddy had just gotten home. She suspected the poor man had worked late to avoid coming home to his presently overcrowded house. She couldn't blame him.

"Yes, he called just before we sat down for dinner," she said finally, and then smiled apologetically. "Lucian's going to make arrangements, and

then call back. I'm not sure what's going to happen."
She discarded so that Harper could take his turn,
and then added, "Tiny should be waking up soon.
He's calmed considerably and hasn't needed to be
drugged for the last couple of hours. That usually
means they're through the worst of it."

Teddy nodded as he started to eat.

"Does that mean Leonora, Dawn, Alessandro,
and Edward will go home soon?" Stephanie asked,
reaching for a card when Harper finished and discarded.

"Yes," Drina said, and then added wryly, "In fact,
I suspect they'll leave the minute Tiny opens his
eyes."

"Oh," Stephanie murmured, but Drina could see
the relief on her face and knew it was for two rea-
sons. One, while everyone was being really consid-
erate, they were all exhausted, the house was just
too small, and they were getting on each other's
nerves. On top of that, though, she knew Stephanie
would be relieved to have four less life mates in the
house. Drina and Harper had been playing cards
and board games with the girl all day to try to distract her, but she didn't think it had helped much. It
would have been nice if they'd been able to take her
out to Wal-Mart or a restaurant or something to give
her a break from the energy and voices bombarding
her, but all the vehicles were still back at the house,
and Teddy had been at work. They'd been stranded
here in his house in the country, which might be for
the best until they sorted out who was behind the
attacks. They were guessing Leonius, and Teddy

and his deputy had been asking around about any sightings of strangers in town, but no one had seen anyone fitting his description.

"Teddy, I think I'm going to have to make another run to the blood bank," Leonora said, entering the dining room. "As a new turn, Tiny will need a lot for a while, and Stephanie's still growing, so she needs a lot as well. I don't want them running low after we leave."

Teddy glanced around with a frown. "How is the supply holding out? Do we need to hold a blood drive?"

Leonora considered briefly, and then shook her head. "No, we should be fine. Well, so long as there aren't any more incidents, we should be fine."

Teddy nodded and glanced back to his plate, then pushed it away with a sigh. "I'll take you now and warm this up when we get back."

"It's after eight o'clock, Teddy," Harper said quietly. "Finish your dinner, I'll take her." Harper stood, then paused, and frowned. "I forgot, I don't have—"

"Use my car," Teddy interrupted, withdrawing keys from his pocket. "You'd best use my boots and coat too."

"Thanks." Harper grabbed the keys, then glanced to Drina before asking him, "You don't happen to have an extra pair of boots and another coat Drina can borrow, do you?"

"In the closet," Teddy answered, pulling his plate back in front of himself.

"Can I come too?" Stephanie asked, as Drina stood to join Harper.

"Only got the one extra coat," Teddy announced around a mouthful of pork chop.

"It's probably better you stay here anyway," Drina said apologetically. "We'll be right back."

Stephanie looked so despondent that Drina asked, "Is there anything you want us to get while we're out? We could stop at a store on the way back."

"Chocolate," Stephanie announced at once. "And Coke. And maybe you could stop at the house and pick up my coat on the way back?"

"Good thinking," Harper said as he led Drina out to the front hall and the closet beside the front door. He handed Drina a coat and pair of boots, then pulled out the same for himself. "We can pick up our coats and boots too while there and stop borrowing Teddy's."

"And you can drop me off so I can collect the SUV," Anders announced, jogging lightly down the stairs behind them, already in coat and boots.

"Also good thinking," Drina decided, as the other hunter moved past where they were donning their gear and slid out the front door. It would be better not to be dependent on Teddy for transport. The man had enough responsibilities in this town and didn't need them being any more of a burden than necessary.

"Maybe we should pick up my car, too," Harper murmured, apparently thinking along the same lines.

"Your car is toast." Drina reminded him quietly of their accident.

"Oh, right." He frowned, and then said, "Well,

Victor said I could borrow his car while they were gone if I needed it. We could pick that up."

"That's probably a good idea," Leonora commented as she stepped into the entry to take her coat from the closet. "We could go to the house first. I can drop you two and Anders off there, and go on to the blood bank alone. Then you'd just have to stop at the store on the way back to get Stephanie her treats."

Harper immediately stuck his head into the dining room, and asked, "Would you mind if Leonora drove your car, Teddy?"

"Nope. She's had her license longer than I've been alive," he said easily. "I was only going to drive with her so she didn't have to go alone. But if she doesn't mind . . ." He shrugged.

"She will no be alone," Alessandro announced, coming down the stairs to catch the conversation. "I too will go."

"Sounds like a plan," Harper said wryly, quickly pulling on his coat and dragging on his boots. When Drina straightened from completing the same task, he took her arm and urged her around Alessandro and Leonora toward the door. "We'll go heat up the car and give you two some room to get your stuff on."

He didn't wait for a response but urged Drina outside. She stomped out onto a small porch, her feet sliding about in the overlarge but warm boots. The coat was too big as well, but also did the job, protecting her from the cold night.

Harper kept a hand on her arm as they descended the stairs and headed for the driveway in front of the house. Watching her tramp forward through the snow, he asked with concern, "Are you going to be all right in those?"

Drina grimaced as his hand tightened on her arm, preventing her from falling when her feet slipped about inside the boots, and the boots slid on the slippery snow. "For now. But tomorrow I think I will have to visit Wal-Mart again."

Harper nodded, and then said, "I suppose Stephanie won't be able to come?"

"I'm not sure," she said on a sigh. "I'd think Lucian would want her restricted to the house after these attacks, but since the last one took place in the house . . ." She shrugged unhappily.

"Yeah," Harper murmured, then they both glanced toward the house as the front door opened and Leonora and Alessandro came out. Harper whistled, and when Alessandro stopped and glanced his way, he tossed them the car keys, saying one of them may as well drive since they were essentially just dropping everyone off.

Fourteen

Casey Cottage was dark and silent when Leonora dropped them off. Anders didn't waste any time but got immediately into the SUV he and Drina had driven down in. He started the engine and was backing the vehicle out almost before Alessandro had cleared the driveway. Drina shook her head at the man's impatience. Really, he was so rude sometimes, she thought, as Harper ushered her up the sidewalk along the garage.

The house was heavy with the smell of smoke when they entered, and Harper heaved a sigh as he closed and locked the door behind them. "I hope the insurance people can get this cleaned up and back in shape before Elvi and Mabel return. They'd be heartbroken to see it like this."

"Yes," Drina murmured, reaching instinctively for the light switch and glancing around with surprise when Harper caught her arm to stop her.

"It's probably better not to," he said quietly. "The wiring may have been damaged in the fire. If we turn on the juice, it might spark something and get it going all over again."

"Oh, of course." Drina let her hand drop when he released it and shrugged. "It's probably for the best anyway. It's doubtful anyone would be watching the house now it's uninhabitable, but there's no sense advertising we're here."

"No," he agreed.

Drina glanced around. It was a clear night, dim moonlight creeping through the windows. With their night vision, they didn't really need the lights anyway.

"Maybe we should collect some clothes too while we're here," Harper suggested, bending to slip off his snow-covered boots. "They'll probably reek of smoke from the fire, but a good wash or three might take care of that."

"My own clothes," Drina said on a sigh as she shrugged out of Teddy's coat and laid it over the radiator. She didn't mind going without a bra and panties so much, but had spent most of the day tugging up the joggers Stephanie had brought to her. They had a drawstring, but she'd only been able to tighten it so far. The darn things were loose enough they kept dropping to ride her hips rather than staying at her waist, where she would have preferred them.

Harper tossed his own coat over the radiator next to hers and chuckled as she stepped out of Teddy's overlarge boots without undoing them. He then caught her hand and headed for the curving staircase. "I'm sure Stephanie would appreciate it too. The poor kid has no hips yet and has had to hold her pants up since she put them on."

"I'll pack her things too," Drina murmured, as he led her upstairs. When he reached the landing and turned left rather than right toward the bedroom she shared with Stephanie, she asked, "Where are we going?"

"We'll start with my clothes and then stop for clothes for you and Stephanie on the way back down," he announced.

"Or I could gather Stephanie's and mine while you get yours. It would be faster," she said with amusement, but Harper shook his head at once.

"I'm not letting you out of my sight until this business is finished and I don't have to worry about your getting hurt in sudden attacks."

"But Stephanie isn't with us," Drina pointed out gently, as he turned left at the end of the landing to head for the stairwell leading to the third floor.

"No, but you are," he said at once.

"Yes, but Leonius isn't interested in me," she pointed out, and Harper came to a halt and turned to peer at her solemnly.

"Drina, you're an incredibly vibrant, sexy, and beautiful woman. If he's been watching us, he's seen you, and if he's seen you, he might be tempted to take you as well as Stephanie. Hell, he might even decide not to bother with her and just take you. You'd be incredible breeding stock."

Drina blinked. That had all been really sweet right

up until the bit about her being incredible breeding stock, she decided. That last part just hadn't sounded as flattering as she suspected he'd meant it to be. Or maybe other women would find it flattering, and she was an oddball for taking umbrage at being talked about like a broodmare.

She opened her mouth to point out that it was unlikely anyone even knew they were in the house, so they should be safe, but paused as she noted that Harper's gaze had slid past her to the door to Elvi's room and that a haunted look had entered his eyes.

Frowning, she glanced toward the door and stilled when she noted the dark stain on the hall wall beside it where the paint had been charred . . . as if something on fire had leaned or slumped there. Her gaze then dropped to the floor and she saw large charred spaces—two of them, one larger, one smaller. That must have been where Anders and Edward had encountered Harper and Stephanie and doused the flames consuming them, she realized, and released a slow breath.

Turning back, Drina stepped forward and kissed Harper. He remained still under the caress, but she kept at it, nibbling at his closed lips, and then trailing her mouth to his ear, then his neck, her mind working frantically. She liked this house, she liked the town too, and she liked Teddy. She also liked the other life-mate couples she'd met here, but especially liked Stephanie. Drina wanted to be able to visit the girl here on occasion, but would never inflict that on Harper if coming here would stir bad memories for him. She needed to try to replace his bad memories of the fire with new, more pleasant memories, and this was the only thing she could come up with. Drina wasn't sure if it would work, but she was going to give it her damnedest, she decided, nipping and kissing his neck as she began to tug his T-shirt upward so she could play her hands over the skin of his stomach and chest.

"Drina?" he said uncertainly as if coming out of a fog.

She lifted her head and kissed him then, relieved when Harper slowly began to kiss her back. Even so, Drina wasn't sure she'd fully reclaimed him from his ghosts until she slid her hand down to find him through his jogging pants and felt a shaft of pleasure stir between her own legs.

"Let's go to my room," he muttered, breaking their kiss and reaching for her hand.

"Next time," Drina promised, evading his fingers and dropping to her knees, her eyes never leaving his face.

"But—" Harper began, and she saw his gaze flicker to the wall several feet behind her, but then his gaze jerked back to her on a sucked-in breath as she tugged his joggers down and clasped his growing erection. When she took him into her mouth, he let that breath out on a moaned, "Next time."

Harper woke up crumpled on the hardwood floor with Drina's head in his lap. He lifted his head to peer at her and smiled faintly, but the smile faded as he peered at the marks on the wall beyond her. He stared at them for a moment, recalling how they had got there, then let those memories fade away and looked at Drina.

He knew exactly what she'd tried to do, and he loved her for it. It had even worked for the most part. At least, Harper thought it had. When he'd first seen the charred mark on the wall, and then the others on the floor, his instinct had been to abandon the idea of getting clothes and rush Drina back downstairs. Or at least go wait for her downstairs while she collected clothes for herself and Stephanie. He'd wanted to be away from it and the bad memories it roused in him.

Now, however, while he wasn't exactly happy when he looked at them, Harper didn't feel an immediate need to get away, either.

Drina stirred sleepily, her hand tightening around his shaft, and Harper bit his lip and closed his eyes as the damned thing began to awaken too. Honest to God, he was bloody insatiable where she was concerned . . . and short on staying power. Not that new life mates were supposed to have great quantities of that, but seriously, there were things he wanted to do to her that this shared-pleasure business really put a kibosh on. He just couldn't keep their excitement level down long enough to get to them.

For instance, he wanted to tie her to his bed and kiss and lick his way from the tips of her toes to her nose, and then kiss her as he plunged himself into her. But he doubted he'd make it halfway up her thighs before they were both screaming and fainting.

And that was another thing, Harper thought

with disgruntlement. He had never fainted in his life, and while he knew it was this whole life-mate, mind-blowing-sex business, it was still damned demoralizing to be fainting like a breathless virgin at the end of every encounter. And he couldn't even blame her for exciting him too much or driving him wild with passion until he lost control.

Well, perhaps he could this last time, Harper acknowledged with a smile. Drina had definitely been the one in control of this last round, and she *had* driven him wild with passion, so fast and so hard that he'd performed no better than an inexperienced fourteen-year-old with a high-priced hooker. He swore she hadn't been on her knees two minutes before he'd been throwing his head back and screaming like a madman . . . only to wake up on the floor in a heap.

Which was precisely why he normally tried to take control of the situation. It was an effort to slow it down and try to make it last longer than two grunts and a gasp. Unfortunately, so far that wasn't working. It didn't mean he wouldn't keep trying, though, Harper thought wryly. Drina deserved for him to make slow love to her, to be appreciated and—

These thoughts paused abruptly as another occurred to him. Why did she let him take control in the bedroom? Drina was a woman who had fought for independence and control her whole life, yet she'd never once protested his taking the lead when it came to passion.

Harper dropped his gaze down to her and frowned, now worried that his doing so might be taking away from her pleasure. Well, not pleasure exactly, because he knew damned well that she enjoyed it as much as he, but Drina might resent it at the same time. He scowled at the thought, and then a creak drew his gaze to the stairwell. There was nothing there. The sound had just been the house settling, he supposed. But it made him realize how reckless they'd been indulging themselves here in the hall. While Stephanie wasn't there, Leonius might decide to add Drina to his list of desirable females. Allowing themselves to get caught up in a passion that left them passed out and vulnerable just hadn't been that smart. The least they could have done was move to his room, where the door could be locked, he thought and began to sit up.

Rustling and the sounds of drawers opening and closing drew Drina from sleep. Blinking her eyes open, she sat up slowly and peered around what she knew must be Harper's room. He had said it was a nice room, and he hadn't been kidding. It really was lovely, with the bed, closet, and chest of drawers in one corner and the rest of the room taken up with a little sitting area complete with television, music system, and bookshelf as well as a love seat, chair, and then a small dinette set.

It was like a small bachelor apartment, she thought, her gaze sliding to where Harper was quickly dragging clothes out of the chest of drawers and packing them away in a suitcase. Drina watched him for a moment, and then slid her feet off the bed to sit on the edge.

"Oh, you're awake." Harper smiled at her, then closed the drawer, shut his suitcase, and quickly carried it to what she presumed was the door to the rest of the house.

Drina stood up to follow him, thinking they were leaving, but stopped after a couple of steps when he merely set the case down by the door, and then turned back.

Smiling, he walked back to her and slid his arms around her waist.

Drina relaxed against him with a little sigh, and then asked with annoyance, "Why is it you always wake up before me? I'm older than you. Surely I should wake up first?"

Harper chuckled at her complaint and bent to kiss her nose. He then countered, "Why do you always make me so crazy with passion that I ejaculate far too soon, and then swoon like a girl?"

"I'm not too pleased about the fainting bit either," she assured him. "It's rather alarming. I didn't even faint when those damned corsets were all the rage, and they wore them so tight you couldn't breathe." She grimaced, and then leaned back, and met his gaze as she added, "As for the other, I don't think it's too soon."

"No?" he asked with a smile, his hands sliding up and down her back.

Drina shook her head, and then smiled and admitted, "Well . . . there are some things I'd like to do to you that I don't think we're going to get to for a decade or so until this new-life-mate madness passes, but . . ." She shrugged. "I guess I can be patient."

"Decade?" Harper asked with a grimace. "I thought it was a year or so before it slowed down?"

"So they say," she agreed. "But I'm not holding my breath."

Harper grinned, and then bent to kiss her. It started out a sweet, gentle kiss, but soon turned more carnal. When Drina pressed close and wrapped her arms around his neck, he began to back her up, then turned them and fell back on the bed so that she landed on top.

Breaking away on a laugh as they bounced, Drina sat up to straddle him and grinned wickedly. "Now I have you right where I want you."

"I thought that might be the case," Harper admitted solemnly, and when Drina stilled and eyed him quizzically, he explained, "It occurred to me that you're a woman who has fought for independence and control all your life, and yet in this area I keep taking that control from you. I don't want you to hate me, so it's time I gave up the reins and—" He paused with surprise when she suddenly covered his mouth.

"First off," she said softly, "I don't hate you for being dominant in the bedroom."

She felt his mouth move under her hand and lifted it.

He was smiling crookedly, and now that he was free to speak, said, "I'm glad to hear it."

"Secondly," Drina began, smiling back. "As it happens I . . ."

When he raised his eyebrows at her pause, she sighed and shrugged her shoulders helplessly.

"Surprised as I am to admit it, I don't appear to mind. I don't understand it myself," she added in a rush. "I mean, I noticed in Toronto that you liked to be in control, and since I'm all about control, I wondered myself why it didn't bother me, but . . . it doesn't. I even like it. It kind of turns me on." She frowned, and then admitted, "Which really rather bothers me."

Harper smiled gently at her confusion, and then raised a hand to brush her hair behind one ear, murmuring, "Or maybe you're just tired of having to be in control all the time and are enjoying a break."

"That's possible," she admitted wryly, and then warned, "Which means it may change."

"I sincerely hope so," Harper assured her and when concern flittered across her face, he said, "I'm sure it will change for me too. We have time immortal ahead of us, Drina. Change is good."

Relaxing, she nodded. There would be times when he was dominant and times when she was, and times when neither was, she supposed. There might even be times when they wrestled each other to be on top. But that would probably be fun too. Definitely never boring, she decided.

"Take off your T-shirt."

Drina blinked her thoughts away at his words— which had most definitely been an order, not a request—and met his gaze.

"Take it off," he repeated. "I want you naked."

She smiled faintly, aware that her nipples were tightening, and moisture was pooling low in her belly, then sat up straighter, reached for the hem of her T-shirt, and slowly began to pull it up and off.

She swiveled her upper body slightly to toss it to the floor, then turned back and simply waited as his eyes slid over her breasts, taking note of her already erect nipples. The sight made his eyes begin to glow.

"Now take off your pants," he said gruffly.

Drina hesitated, and then slid backward along his thighs to get off the bed and stand up. He immediately sat up, and she was aware of his eyes following her every move as she slipped her thumbs under the waist of her joggers and began to ease them down. When she bent forward to finish the job, he reached out with one hand to fondle her breast briefly, and she paused as excitement jumped through her. The moment she stopped, Harper stopped and withdrew his hand.

Devil, she thought affectionately, and finished removing the joggers. She then straightened.

"Come here."

Drina stepped forward, stopping just short of their knees touching. He took her hand then, and she swallowed as the slow pulse of excitement beating through her gained an echo.

"Someday, I'm going to tie you to the bed and lick every inch of your body," Harper said quietly.

Drina closed her eyes as the words evoked an image in her head that had the pooled liquid in her lower belly overflowing and sliding toward the apex of her thighs. Who knew she was secretly into bondage? she wondered faintly, and then opened her eyes with a start as his free hand suddenly slid between her legs.

He smiled at the wetness he found there, and then

watched her face as his fingers moved across her slick skin. Drina bit her lip to keep back a moan as pleasure shimmered through her in double waves and wasn't at all surprised to see that his jogging pants had formed a tent. It looked like it was going to be another one of those "too soon and swoon like a girl" encounters, she thought. If they even got to the encounter part of it. She was already on the verge of exploding.

Really, Drina decided, new life mates were just pathetic . . . and then she stopped thinking as he released her hand to reach for one breast as his mouth moved to latch onto the other.

"Here, try this on."

Drina set down the suitcase holding her and Stephanie's clothes next to his by the door to the garage. She then glanced at the bomber jacket Harper was holding out. It was the coat Tiny had bought for Stephanie and that they'd replaced on their shopping trip to Wal-Mart. It had been a bit large on Stephanie, but Drina was bustier and it would probably fit. Certainly, it would fit better than Teddy's borrowed coat.

When Drina took the offering, Harper turned back to the pantry closet and began to dig through items on the top shelf. Leaving him to it, she shrugged out of Teddy's coat, slung it over the suitcases so they wouldn't forget it, and pulled on the bomber in its place. She then stepped in front of the full-length mirror that hung on the wall across from the door to the garage.

The coat wasn't quite her style, but as expected, it fit. It would do until she could replace it, Drina decided, and then blinked in surprise as Harper stepped up behind her and pulled a white wool hat over her head. He took the time to tuck her hair under it, and then smiled at the results in the mirror.

"It's cold out," he said for explanation, then held up a pair of flat-heeled, black leather boots. "Try these. They're Elvi's, but I'm sure she wouldn't mind, and they look like they'll fit."

The moment she turned to take the boots, Harper moved back to the closet to continue his search for treasure. Drina slid her feet out of Teddy's huge boots, and leaned against the wall to try on one of Elvi's, smiling when she found it fit almost perfectly. It was perhaps half a size large but didn't slide around on her feet as Teddy's boots did.

"Good?" Harper asked as he shrugged out of Teddy's other coat and tossed it on the suitcases as well before pulling on his own.

Drina nodded and set to work pulling on the other boot. "Very good. Thank you."

He smiled faintly and turned back to the closet to quickly find his own boots and switch them for his borrowed ones, then collected Stephanie's boots and new coat.

"Is there anything else we need?" Harper asked as he closed the closet door and carried Teddy's boots over to the suitcases.

Drina considered the question, but shook her head. "Not that I can think of. We can always come back if something comes up."

Nodding, Harper snatched his car keys from the key rack beside the door and began to gather his suitcase and Teddy's borrowed clothes. He managed everything but one pair of boots and her suitcase. Drina picked those up and followed him out into the garage.

They quickly stowed everything in the trunk of Victor's car, then got in.

"Chocolate and Coke?" Harper asked as he hit the button to open the garage door, and then started the engine.

Drina opened her mouth to answer, but paused as the garage lights automatically came on, and she recalled his worry about using electricity and sparking another fire.

Harper grimaced, but then sighed and simply shifted the car into gear and pulled out into the driveway. He hit the button to close the door then, and they glanced back to watch it lower and the lights go out.

Frowning, he eyed the house warily, muttering, "I don't think the garage is probably on the same circuit as the porch. At least I hope not. And I'm not an electrician, so might be completely wrong about the possibility of a fire, but . . ."

"Why don't we sit here for a minute to be sure nothing happens," Drina suggested. "Better to be safe than sorry. I'd feel awful if we left, and something happened."

Harper nodded and shifted the car into park, then drew one leg up and turned sideways in the seat so that he could see both her and the house. Reaching out, he took her hand in his and drew it onto his knee. He began to toy with the fingers as he asked, "Do you think Lucian will want you and Anders to take Stephanie back to Toronto?"

Drina sighed and leaned back in her seat. "Stephanie asked me something similar earlier, but I don't know. We can't stay here until the house is repaired, so he probably will unless he finds somewhere else in town for us to stay."

They were both silent. Drina was wondering what Harper would do if that happened. Would he want to come with her? She thought so, or hoped so, but—

"Maybe he'll replace you now that there is a threat and you're a distracted new life mate like Mirabeau and Tiny," Harper commented, sliding his thumb back and forth over her palm. He glanced to her, and asked, "Would you stay here if he did that?"

Drina hesitated. She wanted to say yes. Truthfully, she wanted to pull him back inside the house, drag him to bed, and simply stay there . . . forever. However, she couldn't do that. As for saying yes, while she wanted to with all her heart, she didn't feel she could. She had assured Stephanie that she would be with her if she had to go back to Toronto and didn't want to let her down.

Aside from disappointing the teenager, though, Drina was worried about what would become of the girl once in Toronto in close proximity to Lucian. If he decided she could go no-fanger and was a possible threat, he might . . . Well, at the very least, he would probably insist she remain at the enforcer house, and the kid would be miserable there, with no chance at any kind of normalcy. Drina didn't even want to think about the worst of what he could do.

Harper released her fingers suddenly and turned to shift the car into gear again. "We've waited long enough. I guess we'd better get Stephanie's stuff and head back to the house."

Drina glanced around with surprise. She hadn't realized she'd sat in thought so long, but judging by the disappointment in Harper's voice, she'd been silent quite a while. And she hadn't answered his question. Which, judging by his closed expression, he was taking as a no.

She needed to explain her promise to Stephanie, Drina realized, but before she could, Harper reached out and turned the radio on. He also cranked it up several notches so that loud music filled the car. Rather than try to shout over the radio, Drina let it go for now. She would explain when they got back to the house . . . and then she would ask him to come to Toronto with her if Lucian did order them back. They could decide from there what to do after that. There was no doubt in her mind that she wanted to be with him. The question was where that would be, and it was something they both had to decide on.

Fifteen

"There you two are. We were about to send out a search party."

Drina paused in the front entry of Teddy's house and turned to glance into the dining room. Her eyes slid over the three people seated at the table but widened as she found the speaker.

"Tiny," she said on a grin. "You're awake."

"Yeah." He smiled and stood to move out of sight toward the kitchen, but his voice was loud as he asked, "Coffee?"

"Yes please," Drina said, her gaze sliding back to Teddy and Mirabeau at the table as Harper said he'd take one too.

"He woke up shortly after you guys left," Mirabeau said, positively beaming with relief and happiness.

Drina smiled at the woman, and then turned to

remove her coat and boots and stow them away even as Harper did.

"Teddy took Alessandro and Edward and the girls home shortly after Tiny woke up," Mirabeau announced, as Drina set the bag from the corner store on the table and settled in a seat. "So it's down to the six of us."

"Speaking of the six of us, where is Stephanie?" Harper asked. "We bought the stuff she wanted."

Drina grimaced. They'd spent longer at the house than intended. It was after midnight. The girl had probably gone to bed. Although if so, it was somewhat surprising that Mirabeau was here at the table. The thought made her frown as she asked, "Did she go to bed?"

"No. Anders took her out for a burger," Mirabeau answered.

"What?" Drina asked blankly.

Mirabeau nodded. "We were playing cards, then Anders got a call and left the room to take it. When he came back in, Stephanie was complaining about how long you guys were taking and said she wished she could call you and maybe have you pick her up a burger on the way back. He offered to take her out to get one."

Tiny smiled faintly, and added, "The kid couldn't get out of here fast enough."

Drina frowned. She wasn't surprised Stephanie would jump at the chance to get out of the house. She'd been stuck in here for twenty-four hours and had been stuck inside Casey Cottage before that. She was probably going a bit stir-crazy. Still, Drina couldn't help thinking it was a bad idea to take the girl anywhere considering the attacks on her.

"It'll be fine," Mirabeau said soothingly. "Anders isn't stupid. He'll take her straight there and back. Besides, we're out in the middle of nowhere here, and I checked the road as they were getting in the truck. There was no one watching."

Drina relaxed and nodded. Teddy's house was out of town, a strip of land between two large fields. There was nowhere to hide out here to watch the house unobserved. Wondering how long she had before bed, she asked, "So how long ago did they leave?"

"An hour ago," Teddy said, when Mirabeau paused uncertainly.

"It can't have been that long," Mirabeau protested with a frown.

"I checked my watch when they left," Teddy said quietly.

"They should be back by now," Harper pointed out with concern.

Drina reached automatically for her back pocket and her phone, but paused as she recalled she was wearing joggers. Her phone should be—She cursed as she realized it would have been in the back pocket of the jeans she'd been wearing when she was sprayed. Only she'd emptied her pockets before handing over her jeans to be bagged and tossed, and there had been no phone there. It must have fallen out when she was rolling around on the front yard of Casey Cottage, she thought.

"I'll call Anders," Mirabeau announced, retrieving

a phone from her own pocket. She'd just started to punch in numbers when they heard a vehicle pulling into the driveway. Mirabeau stood and walked to the window, relaxing as she peered out. "It's the SUV."

Everyone at the table seemed to relax at the news.

Mirabeau had just sat back in her seat when Anders burst into the house and appeared at the dining room door. "Is she here?"

Drina raised her eyebrows. "Who?"

"Stephanie."

Drina stilled at that hissed name, foreboding slipping through her.

"She was with you," Mirabeau said, as if he might have forgotten it.

Anders cursed and turned back to the entry.

Realizing he was about to leave again without explaining himself, Drina stood and rushed around the table to stop him. "Just a minute. What's going on? Where is she?"

Anders paused, but then sighed and turned back, running one hand through his hair with frustration. "I don't know. I stopped for gas, filled up, went in to pay, and when I came out, she was gone."

"She probably just went to use the bathroom or something," Teddy said soothingly as the tension in the room ratcheted upward. Standing, he moved to the desk and pulled out a phone book. "Which gas station was it? Esso or the Pioneer by Wal-Mart?"

"Neither," Anders answered. "The other one. I don't remember the name."

Teddy turned to peer at him blankly. "What other one? We don't have another one."

"The one up by the highway," Anders said. "It doesn't matter anyway, I did check the bathroom."

Teddy let the phone book lower to the desk. "Why the hell would you go all the way out there? The other two are half the distance."

Anders muttered something Russian under his breath and turned away again. "I'm going back out to look for her."

"The hell you are." Drina caught his arm and pulled him back around. "What's going on, Anders? Where were you taking her?"

"I can't tell you," he said grimly.

"Why not?" Mirabeau demanded, joining them.

"Because Lucian said not to."

Drina blinked in surprise at those words, then narrowed her eyes. "You were taking her to Toronto."

He didn't confirm that, but he didn't deny it either, and she knew she was right.

"Why didn't Lucian want Drina to know that?" Harper asked, crossing to join them as well with Tiny on his heels.

"Because she would have felt she had to come too, and he wants her to stay here with you," Anders said dryly.

Drina felt Harper peering at her but was too busy worrying over what Anders had said and what it would mean for Stephanie. Being in Toronto, closer to Lucian, and without anyone who cared about her. Drina knew Stephanie's sister, Dani, was somewhere down in the States right now, playing bait, and Mirabeau and herself were here in Port Henry. The kid would have been on her own.

"Well, she couldn't have gone far without a coat. She was probably in the bathroom while you were in the store and in the store while you checked the bathroom. It's not like she'd walk back, Anders," Teddy said, picking up the phone. "It's too damned far and cold for that. She's probably standing around in the gas station waiting for you to come back."

"No, she ran away," Drina murmured, and Mirabeau nodded solemnly.

"What?" Anders frowned. "Why the hell would she run away?"

"Because she likes it here, and you were taking her back to Toronto, where she was miserable," she said dryly.

"She didn't know that. I hadn't told her yet. I was going to after I got on the highway."

"You didn't have to tell her," Mirabeau assured him. "She would have read it from your mind."

Anders didn't laugh at the suggestion. His mouth tightened, and he said, "I made sure I didn't even think about it. There was nothing to read."

His words told Drina that he knew about Stephanie's special abilities, or at least knew part of it. He knew she could read his thoughts even though he was old and not a new life mate, but didn't know it wasn't restricted to surface memories. Which meant Lucian knew. She saw Anders's eyes narrow on her and sighed as she realized how he'd known. He was reading her thoughts even now and had probably read them before, both from her and Mirabeau.

"It doesn't matter," Drina said wearily, moving

past him to get to the closet and retrieve the bomber jacket.

Anders turned toward the door again. "I'll go back out and look for her again."

"Wait for us," Mirabeau said, reaching past Drina to grab her own coat and Tiny's. "You can drop Tiny and me at Casey Cottage. Our SUV is still there. We can help search too."

Drina had started to shrug into Stephanie's bomber, but paused and glanced to Harper uncertainly when she realized she'd just assumed he'd be willing to search for the girl and hadn't asked. "I'm sorry. Would you mind if we—?"

"No, of course not," he said solemnly. "Hand me my coat."

Sighing with relief, she passed his coat over, then grabbed her boots and moved back into the dining room to don them. Teddy was hanging up the phone as she entered. When she glanced his way in question, he shook his head, and then sat down at the desk and opened the phone book again.

"I'm going to make a few calls," he announced. "Get the clerks at Tim Hortons and the corner store and anywhere else still open to keep an eye out for her, and then coordinate a search party. Report in here if you see or hear anything."

Drina nodded and sat down to quickly don her boots. By the time she finished, Mirabeau, Tiny, and Anders had left, and Harper was straightening from donning his own boots in the entry.

"Ready?" he asked.

Nodding, Drina led the way outside and to Victor's borrowed car.

"Where do we start?" Harper asked as he started the car. "The gas station by the highway?"

Drina frowned and considered briefly, but shook her head. "Anders is probably heading back to the gas station, so there's no use trying there."

"I don't know," Harper said as he backed out of the driveway. "Stephanie might hide from Anders because he was going to take her to Toronto, but I don't think she'd hide from you. She might come out if she saw us driving around."

"Do you think so?" Drina asked, hoping it was true.

"Definitely," he said solemnly.

Teddy hadn't been kidding; the gas station was a hell of a distance out of town. It seemed to take forever to get there, but Drina spent the whole journey scanning the streets and anybody they passed, growing increasingly desperate to find Stephanie as she considered what could happen to her on her own.

Drina wasn't worried about perverts or mortal sickos attacking the girl. With her increased strength and speed, Stephanie was pretty much mortal proof. Actually, any mortal foolish enough to look at the petite blonde and see her as a victim, would find they were very much mistaken. But someone had been attacking them, and if it was Leonius . . .

The thought of what might happen to the girl if he got his hands on her was worrying Drina sick.

They saw Anders at the gas station, but no Stephanie, so set out to drive around the surrounding area, scanning fields and businesses, and then houses and yards as they got closer to town and a more urban area.

"Is there anywhere she would go? Somewhere she liked or . . . just anywhere you think she might go?" Harper asked some two hours later. They were driving in circles now, recovering old ground and seeing nothing but the others out searching for Stephanie.

Drina started to shake her head, but paused, and murmured, "Beth."

"Beth?" Harper glanced to her with a frown. "Beth of the madam days Beth?"

Drina nodded. "I was just thinking that when Beth ran from Jimmy, she went straight back to the empty brothel. The last place she'd been safe and called home."

"Casey Cottage," Harper said, getting it at once. He turned at the first corner, and Drina closed her eyes and sent up a silent prayer that they'd find her there, safe and sound and well. However, it appeared no one was listening to prayers that day because a thorough search of Casey Cottage turned up nothing.

"I guess it's back to driving around."

Harper frowned at the weariness in Drina's voice as he ushered her out of the house and across the deck. She sounded exhausted, and he wouldn't be surprised if she was. Surely she hadn't slept much on that stool of hers the night before while waiting for the drugstore to open. But he suspected most of the exhaustion was caused from worry. She was beginning to lose hope.

"I need more gas, and the one by the highway is the only one open at this hour," he said, as they walked along the side of the garage to the driveway. "We'll head back there and start another circuit."

Drina nodded, not looking terribly encouraged.

Harper opened the car door for her, but when she went to get in, he caught her arm. "We'll find her, Drina. We won't stop looking until we do."

Drina let her breath out on a sigh, then leaned forward and kissed his cheek, whispering, "Thank you." She looked just as calm and strong as she had all night, but there was something in her voice that told him while she appreciated his effort to encourage her, it hadn't really worked. Harper watched her slide into the car and wished he could do something to make her feel better. But the only thing likely to do that was finding Stephanie.

Where the hell was the girl? he asked himself as he closed the door and walked around to get in the driver's side. Unfortunately, he didn't have a clue.

They were quiet on the drive back to the gas station, both of them scanning the passing scenery for Stephanie. They were nearly to the station when Harper said, "Maybe we should call the house and make sure no one's found her."

Drina glanced at him with surprise. "I'm sure they would have called if they had."

"Oh right," Harper muttered, and then suggested, "Still, if she's causing a fuss about leaving, they might be a little distracted and forget to call."

"That's possible," Drina said slowly, and then straightened a little, and asked, "Can I use your phone?"

He pulled his gaze from the road to glance at her with surprise. "Where's yours?"

"I lost it the night of the fire," she admitted.

Harper grimaced and turned his gaze back to the road before admitting, "So did I. It was in my back pocket." It was probably a melted mess by the end, he supposed.

"Neither of us has a phone?" Drina asked with amazement, and then smiled slightly, and said, "Then they couldn't call us. She could have been at Teddy's for hours."

Harper glanced at her, worried about her getting her hopes up only to have them dashed, but said quietly, "We can call from the gas station. I know Teddy's house number."

Drina hung up with a little sigh, and stood for a minute, waiting for her disappointment to ease. Harper had given her Teddy's number and suggested she call while he pumped gas. But Stephanie wasn't back at the house, and no one had even reported a sighting of her, "Not the gals at Timmy H's, or Val at the twenty-four-hour Quicky mart, nobody." Teddy had sounded as frustrated as Drina felt.

"No joy, huh?"

Drina glanced to the skinny, sandy-haired gas-station attendant behind the counter. His nametag read Jason. "No joy?"

"No luck," Jason explained, his Adam's apple bobbing with the words. "No one's seen her?"

"Oh, no," she said on a sigh, pushing the phone back toward him. "Thank you for letting me use the phone."

"No problem," he said easily, turning away to set it back where it belonged on the counter behind the till he manned. "Least I could do since we didn't have a pay phone. It's hard to find those anymore. They become more scarce as cells get popular."

"Yes," Drina murmured, her gaze dropping to the chocolate bars lining the front of the counter. As upset as she was, her body was getting hungry. Harper must be too.

"It's hard to figure why no one's seen her though. A new car seems to pull in here every ten minutes with people out scouting for her. Teddy must have half the town searching," Jason said, turning back. "If she's on foot, someone should have seen her by now. Maybe she thumbed it."

"Thumbed?" Drina asked blankly.

"You know." He held out his hand, fingers curled into a fist and thumb up. When she still looked blank, he added, "Hitchhiking. She must have hitched a ride or something." Jason smiled faintly when her expression cleared. "Your accent . . . you're not from around here, huh?"

Drina shook her head, and murmured, "Spain."

"Cool." He nodded. "Always wanted to go. Someday I will."

"Were there any other cars here when Anders was getting gas?" she asked suddenly.

"Anders," Jason said blankly, and then his expression cleared, and he said, "Oh, you mean the cool black dude who lost the girl?"

Drina nodded.

"Well, yeah, some old dude was in here paying for his gas and getting junk food. A real asswipe," he added with a sneer. "He saw your Anders guy get out and start pumping, and says to me, "You better lock up the till and door, boy. That nigger's probably here to rob you." Jason snorted. "Racist old prick. I checked the security tape after he'd left and, sure enough, he was the thief. Pocketed at least three chocolate bars when I turned my back to get the lottery tickets he wanted."

Drina stilled. "Security tape?"

"Yeah." He waved toward a corner of the store. "My boss put them in last year. Said it would keep the insurance down."

Drina peered at what looked like a rounded mirror in the corner and considered the direction it was pointing.

"That Anders guy asked about them too, but there aren't any outside, and it doesn't show the pumps. There's only the one inside, so he didn't bother with it. But you can check out the security tape if you want."

Drina hesitated, but then decided she might as well. They hadn't been able to find Stephanie by driving around. Perhaps there was something on the tape that might be useful. "Yes. Please."

"Come around," he invited, waving toward the end of the counter.

Drina walked around the long counter and came up behind it as Jason knelt to start typing on a keyboard under the counter next to where he stood. There was a very small computer screen next to it.

"What are you doing?" she asked, as he typed, tapped at a mouse, and typed again.

"I'm pulling up the program and punching in the time I want so it will start replay there," he explained, and muttered, "A late-night *Two and a Half Men* rerun was on so it was between eleven and eleven thirty."

"A late-night *Two and a Half Men* rerun?" she echoed with confusion.

"A comedy show on television. I watch it instead of the news," he explained, gesturing to a small television on his other side. "It passes time while I'm sitting here twiddling my thumbs."

"Oh." She nodded, and then glanced to the door as Harper entered.

Apparently, he was done pumping gas.

"What's going on?" he asked, as the door closed behind him.

"Security video," she answered, and he came around the counter to join them.

"There," Jason said with satisfaction, and an image popped up on the computer screen of the store.

Drina noted the miniature Jason slumped in the corner watching his little television. Her gaze started to shift to the background, but Jason fiddled with the mouse a bit, and the image sped up.

When a beer-bellied older man entered the store on the screen, he hit a button, and the image played at normal time again.

"That's the asswipe," Jason announced.

"Asswipe?" Harper echoed with amusement.

"Racist shoplifter," Drina explained, but her attention had shifted to the background. It was true you couldn't see the pumps, but she could see the parking lot in front of them and the exit sign.

"See, I told you he lifted three bars."

Drina glanced to the man shoving something in his pocket while Jason worked at the lottery machine, but then her attention shifted back to the background as the nose of a vehicle appeared halfway up the left edge of the screen. The SUV, she was sure, and was proven right when Jason said, "That's the Anders guy's truck, and now the asswipe's making his crack about locking up the till and store."

Drina nodded but continued to watch without comment.

"Then he just stood there in the store for a bit like he was afraid to go out, like your Anders guy would rob him or something," Jason commented with disgust. "There, Anders must be heading in to pay 'cause that's when the guy scooted out."

They watched the old man leave the store. Three seconds later, Anders entered and waited as Jason punched buttons and jiggled things on the cash register.

"I had trouble ringing him up. This is a new system, and it's kind of glitchy," Jason muttered, sounding both annoyed and embarrassed.

"Stop!" Drina barked suddenly, and Jason started, and then scrambled to grab the mouse and pause the image for her.

"What?" he asked, glancing at the screen uncertainly. "He's just signing the slip."

"Back it up, but just a little," Drina said. He hit his mouse, it started to rewind, and Drina said, "Stop," again.

Jason's hand was on the mouse, and he paused it at once, but frowned. "I don't see anything."

Harper had apparently seen what she had. He leaned past Drina and pointed to the car on the street. It had just pulled out of the gas-station exit. "She's in the backseat."

Jason leaned closer and squinted. "I see a smudge that could be a head, but—"

"It's her," Drina assured him. She'd been watching the car when it had driven into view, headed for the exit. The backseat had been empty as it cruised to a stop at the street. Then it had turned onto the road, and a head had popped into view. It had to be Stephanie. "She hitched a ride."

"That explains why we haven't been able to find her walking the streets," Harper muttered. "We should call Teddy and give him a description of the car and the license-plate number. He can pass it to everyone."

"Good thinking," Jason said, grabbing his mouse again. "I'll make the image bigger and see if we can read it."

"No need, I've got it," Drina assured him. "Can I use the phone again?"

"Well, yeah, sure, but—" He fell silent as she turned sideways to pick up the phone on the counter behind them. Then he bent to squint at the screen again. Shaking his head, he glanced to Harper, and said, "There's *no way* she can see the license plate, let alone read it."

"She has very good eyes," Harper said solemnly, as Drina punched in Teddy's number.

"Man, that's not good eyes, that's whacked, superscary sci-fi eyes," Jason assured him, and then frowned, and said, "You look familiar. Are you—" He stopped suddenly and slapped himself in the forehead. "You're that vamp guy who rents a room next door to my buddy Owen's place."

Drina saw Harper wince and bit back a smile, but then Jason turned to her, his eyes widening farther.

"Oh, whoa, that means you're probably one of the vamp chicks staying there. Aren't you?"

"Owen is the son of Elvi's neighbor," Harper explained to her, then in answer to the question said, "Yes."

"Damn," Jason muttered, not even sparing Harper a glance. He then added mournfully, "I shoulda known. You're too hot to be human."

Drina just shook her head and turned her back to him. She *was* human, and she definitely was not too hot to be anything. In fact, she didn't consider herself hot at all. She was really rather average. But she was immortal, and for some reason mortals tended to find them attractive. Beth had a theory about it. Since she drew a lot more attention from mortal men now that she was immortal, Beth suspected it was another little trick of the nanos, making their bodies create and release extrastrong pheromones to attract prey.

Drina had no idea if it was true or not and didn't much care.

Teddy's voice sounded in her ear, and Drina forced her mind to the task at hand. She quickly relayed what they'd found, giving him a description of the car and the license-plate number. He made her repeat all the information, promised to pass it on to the others, and then quickly ended the call. She suspected he was eager to get moving on it. This was the first lead they'd had after hours of frustrating, resultless searching.

"Thank you, Jason," Drina said sincerely as she turned back from the phone. "We appreciate your help."

"No problem," he said, but she couldn't help noticing that he was looking at her differently. Earlier, he'd been friendly and open. She'd been able to tell that he was attracted to her, but he'd been more natural. Now, however, he was looking at her like she was some exotic creature who had unexpectedly flown into his workplace . . . a sexually attractive exotic creature. Drina added the last thought as she noted the way his eyes had dilated and kept dropping downward over her body.

"Right," Harper said dryly, taking Drina's arm and urging her back around the counter. "We'd best go help look for the car."

There were two islands with two pumps each, and Harper had parked on the outside of the second island, farthest from the store itself. They had just passed the first island and were approaching the second when Jason suddenly yelled at them from the store door, "Hey, you forgot to pay!"

They both stopped at once, and Drina was chuckling at Harper's irritated mutter as they turned back, when Jason yelled, "Look out!"

Drina instinctively started to glance around, but Harper was already pushing her to the side. Staggering, she grabbed at the gas pump to keep her feet and glanced back to see Harper throwing himself forward and to the ground, his hand outstretched as if he were a baseball player trying to catch a ground ball. The only thing missing was the baseball glove . . . and the ball, she thought as she saw the flaming bottle land in his open palm.

Harper immediately closed his eyes and briefly lowered his forehead to the cold pavement as if in thanks, then lifted his head and pulled the burning bit of cloth out of the top. He crushed it between his palm and the ground to put it out, then started to rise, holding the bottle like it was a venomous snake.

"Are you all right?" Drina asked, hurrying to his side, her eyes scanning the direction the bottle had come from. There was nothing to see, however. Whoever had thrown it was gone.

Harper nodded as he straightened beside her. "Sorry I pushed you."

"Don't apologize," she said at once. "I didn't even see it."

"I spotted it as soon as Jason yelled. It was like a recurring nightmare," he said dryly.

Drina squeezed his arm sympathetically, and then glanced around as Jason rushed to them.

"Man oh man, that was—*Man*!" he yelled, reaching them, his eyes round holes of shock and awe as he eyed Harper. "Man, you—That was—It was like, *woooooo*." He flew his hand threw the air in an arc as if emulating the bottle's trajectory. "And you were like *waaaaah*." Mouth open, he mimicked Harper diving for the bottle, and then shook his head, and said, "Man, you kick ass. That was freaking *amazing*!"

Drina bit her lip and glanced from the young mortal to Harper to see him looking slightly embarrassed by the kid's adoration. Clearing her throat to get Jason's attention, she asked, "Did you see who threw it?"

Jason shook his head, "No, sorry, no. I just saw this firebird flying at the two of you and shouted and—" His gaze shifted back to Harper. "Wow, man. You could play for the Jays. We'd kick ass *every* game."

"Yes, well, here, maybe you could dispose of this." Harper handed him the bottle of fluid, and when Jason nodded and took it, he reached for his wallet and pulled out three twenties. As he handed them over, he said, "Sorry about forgetting to pay."

"Oh, no problem," Jason said at once. "I knew it wasn't on purpose. We just got distracted with the security video. But, hey, this is too much," he added, keeping two of the bills and offering the other back. "You only got forty bucks worth."

"Keep it," Harper said, urging Drina toward the car. "And thank you again."

"Yeah, thanks! Hey, you two have a good night. And stay safe, huh?" Jason called as he turned back toward the store, and then Drina heard him mutter, "Man, that was something else. *Wow*."

"You have a fan," she said, as they got in the car.

Harper grimaced as he started the engine, but said, "He's a good kid. A total geek, but he has the good sense to recognize a goddess when he sees her."

"A goddess?" Drina asked on a laugh.

Harper nodded and shifted into drive to head out of the gas station. "He was sure your name must be Aphrodite or Venus."

"Right," she snorted.

"But he kept your clothes on in his head," Harper announced, and added wryly, "Which raised him in my estimation. Like I said, a good kid."

"And he saved us from a great deal of pain," Drina added, her voice becoming more subdued.

"Pain?" he asked dryly. "Try saved our lives and his own too. If that bottle had landed, the whole damned place probably would have exploded. Those were gas pumps."

Drina nodded and reached over to squeeze his legs. "He helped, but you did the saving. Nice catch," she added quietly.

"That was desperation," Harper said on a sigh as he pulled out onto the road. "I didn't really notice the bottle, but I saw the flaming, fluttering cloth coming at us like a bird on fire and . . ." He shook his head. "It was the last thing I saw in the porch before it became an inferno. That time I didn't know what it was and wasn't quick enough to stop it. This time I was."

Like a recurring nightmare, she recalled his words and squeezed his leg again. But then frowned and glanced out the window, before announcing, "We have a problem. Two, actually."

"Only two?" Harper asked dryly.

Drina smiled faintly, but said, "Stephanie wasn't there. The attack was on us. It may not be Leonius."

"Except that you're about Stephanie's height, wearing her coat, and your hair is tucked under a hat so you could easily have been mistaken for her," he pointed out.

Drina glanced down at the bomber she wore and frowned as she realized he was right. That made her mouth tighten, and she said, "Which means we have a different set of problems."

"That he doesn't seem to be that concerned about keeping her alive for breeding since the explosion could have killed her," Harper guessed.

Drina nodded.

"What's the other?" he asked.

"Stephanie must have controlled the driver of the car."

Harper took his foot off the gas, allowing the car to slow as he sought out her eyes. "You think so?"

"What would you do if someone suddenly popped up in the backseat of the car?" she asked quietly.

Harper's head went back a bit as realization struck him. "The car didn't slow, stop, or jerk to the side. It just continued smoothly up the road." He frowned. "I didn't know she could control mortals already."

"Neither did I," Drina said on a sigh. "And she shouldn't be able to."

"No," he agreed, taking one hand from the steering wheel to cover hers on his leg. He was silent, considering this, and then said, "She could make him take her wherever she wanted."

"Yes," Drina agreed.

He thought for a minute, and then asked, "Where does her family live?"

"Windsor." Marguerite had told her a bit about Stephanie in New York—what she'd been through, where her family was from, etc. Marguerite seemed to feel bad for Stephanie, but then so did Drina.

Harper nodded and pulled a U-turn on the empty road, heading back the way they'd come. The highway entrance was just beyond the gas station.

"Do you want to call Teddy before we leave the area?" he asked, as they approached the gas station.

Drina shook her head. "We'll call from Windsor if we find her there."

"It's more than two hours away," he warned.

Drina bit her lip but shook her head. "Anders will call Lucian, and he'll have someone in the area head right over. I'd rather Stephanie wasn't faced with strangers to deal with this."

Harper nodded and squeezed her hand with understanding. They drove past the gas station and took the on-ramp to the highway.

Sixteen

'That's it," Harper murmured, slowing and pointing to a large two-story redbrick building.

"Don't stop. I don't want to scare her off if she's here," Drina said quietly. "Drive around the block. We'll find somewhere to park and walk back."

Harper eased his foot down on the gas, speeding up a bit to cruise up the road. At the corner, he turned right, then slowed to a stop as they passed the mouth of an alley that ran behind the houses.

"What do you think?" he asked quietly. "We could park on the road here and walk up the alley."

Drina nodded silently and unbuckled her seat belt as he parked. Her gaze slid out the window to the lightening horizon. It had taken them far longer than the expected two hours to get here to Windsor and it was almost seven o'clock. There had been an accident on the highway. Emergency vehicles had blocked off the highway, stopping traffic completely while they'd removed the injured and the cars and cleaned up the mess.

They'd actually hit the city half an hour ago, but then they'd had to find a pay phone and phone book to look up the McGills. There had been a handful listed, but Drina hadn't known Stephanie's father's name so they'd had to check almost all of them. As it turned out, Stephanie's family's phone number wasn't listed, but eventually they'd hit a McGill who was related and Drina had pulled the address of the family home from the mind of the grumpy man who had answered the door. Now here they were, hours after they'd set out.

Drina hoped to God she hadn't made a huge mistake by not calling Teddy's house and letting Anders call Lucian. If anything bad had happened because she'd made that choice, she'd never forgive herself, she thought, as they got out of the car.

They were silent as they walked up the dark alley, counting houses as they went and watching for the two-story redbrick. Drina didn't know what to expect or even what to do once they got there. Now that they'd reached Windsor, she was beginning to wonder if Stephanie really would have come this way. She must have known they'd think to check here. And if she *had* come here, would she have approached the house? Walked up and knocked? Was she inside even now, in the bosom of her family?

They slowed as they spotted the house ahead. At least three of the second-floor lights were glowing in the early-morning darkness, but they couldn't see the first floor yet. The neighbor's garage blocked their view of the McGills' backyard. They had barely passed the garage in question when Harper caught Drina's arm and drew her to a halt. He needn't have bothered. She too had spotted the slender figure hugging the tree in the McGills' backyard and had been about to stop herself.

Drina released a slow breath, a good deal of tension sliding out of her as she took in Stephanie's lonely figure. It looked like she hadn't approached the house but had simply stood in the cold, dark night watching it . . . in nothing but joggers, a T-shirt, and a thick woolly sweater, Drina noted, taking in what the girl was wearing. The kid must be freezing, she thought with a frown, then sighed and turned to gesture to Harper to wait here.

When he nodded, she turned and started silently forward. Drina was perhaps six feet behind Stephanie, when the girl said, "It took you long enough to get here."

Drina stopped, and then grimaced and continued forward at a more natural pace.

"What took you so long?" Stephanie asked, as Drina paused a little beside and behind her.

"There was an accident on the highway, traffic was stopped for hours," Drina explained, and then smiled wryly, and asked, "You expected me to figure out you'd come here?"

Stephanie shrugged. "Where else would I go?"

"How long have you been here?"

"Hours." Stephanie leaned her head wearily

against the tree and sighed. "I've just been standing here watching the house."

Drina shifted her gaze back to the McGills' home. There were lights glowing on the ground floor too, she saw, but all the activity was in the kitchen. She could see into the room quite clearly through a pair of sliding glass doors that led out onto a deck. The vertical blinds were open, revealing a dining-room table and a kitchen beyond. There were three kids and a man who she guessed was Stephanie's father at the table. An adult female, no doubt her mother, and more kids, older ones, were moving around the kitchen, pouring coffee and toasting toast.

"The blinds were closed, but Mom opened them when they got up. She likes to watch the sun rise," Stephanie said quietly.

Drina focused on the mother, but said, "You controlled the man from the gas station and made him drive you here."

"Yes," she said simply.

"You didn't tell me you could control people already," Drina said quietly.

Stephanie shrugged. "I didn't really know until I tried tonight."

Drina closed her eyes. If making a man drive her two hours to Windsor was her baby step at mind control, the kid was scary skilled. It just made her worry more for her. Pushing that thought aside, she said, "I'm surprised you just stood out here and didn't go in."

Stephanie smiled bitterly. "I was going to. That was the plan on the way down here. I'd come home, and Mom would put her arms around me and tell me she loved me and that everything was going to be all right. And Dad would call me his little girl, which I always used to hate, but would kill to hear now."

The yearning in her voice was painful to hear, and Drina had to swallow a lump in her throat. Stephanie was just a kid. She wanted her family. She'd asked for none of this. Clearing her throat, Drina asked, "What stopped you?"

"I'd just be messing up their lives," Stephanie said with a shrug. "I know Lucian did something to them to make them forget me. I'd just mess that up."

"They haven't forgotten you, Stephanie," Drina said firmly, shrugging out of her coat and moving closer to drape it over her shoulders. The nanos would be using up blood at an accelerated rate keeping her from freezing in this weather, and they didn't have any blood to give the girl. Sighing, she rubbed her arms briefly, and added, "Lucian just sent people to veil their memories and probably alter them a bit."

"I know the veiling bit is so they don't suffer so much from losing Dani and me, but how did they alter their memories and why?" she asked quietly.

"They would have made their memories of your faces fuzzier, more vague, so that they wouldn't recognize you if they came across you accidentally."

"Accidentally?" Stephanie asked dryly. "You mean so they wouldn't recognize me if I came knocking."

"No," Drina assured her. "If you walked up to the door, and knocked and said, 'Mommy, it's me,

Stephanie,' the veil would be torn. They would re-member. But if they happened to see you on a street, or bumped into you in passing and never spoke, chances are they wouldn't. That's why it's done. So that you aren't accidentally revealed to be alive."

"So if I walked up right now and knocked on the sliding glass door, I could make them remember me?" she asked, staring at the people in the house.

"Yes," Drina admitted.

"But you'd stop me from doing that, wouldn't you?"

Drina hesitated, and then shook her head. "No. If you really want to, I won't stop you."

Stephanie turned to look at her sharply, her eyes widening with surprise. "You mean that."

Drina shrugged. "Why stop you now? If you're determined to do it, you'd just come back and do it at a later date."

"Right." Stephanie frowned and glanced back to the house. "But trying to have any kind of contact with them would be superselfish, wouldn't it?"

Stephanie said grimly, "They'd have to be taken into protective custody to keep them safe from Leo-nius in case he got wind of them. My brothers and sisters would lose all their friends, and my parents would lose their jobs and friends, and everyone would lose our aunts and uncles and cousins. No more family picnics, or trips up north. Their whole lives would be disrupted and wrecked like mine was. And it would be my fault."

Drina glanced to the house. They looked like a big, busy but happy family from here, like millions of other families in the world, chattering and smiling over their breakfast. She couldn't blame Stephanie for wanting to stay a part of that. But even being here was endangering that very normalcy. Stephanie and Dani had been kidnapped up north, six or seven hours from Windsor. Lucian didn't think Leonius knew where Stephanie and Dani's family lived. But even if he'd sought out that information, he hadn't shown up to bother them, probably because he knew the family believed the two females dead and knew nothing. But her coming here could change things if he found out about it.

If he didn't already know, Drina thought, suddenly worried that she and Harper might have led the man here from the gas station. She had been so distracted by worries for Stephanie, she hadn't considered that possibility.

"We should go," Stephanie said suddenly, worry now in her voice too, and Drina knew she'd plucked her thoughts from her mind.

She slipped her arm around the girl's shoulders and turned her to walk back to Harper, saying, "Don't worry. We'll call Lucian before we leave town and have him send a couple of men over. They'll watch for trouble and get your family out of here if there's any sign of Leonius."

"What if he's here now and does something before they get here?" Stephanie asked, suddenly stopping.

Drina frowned and glanced back toward the house, torn.

"What's wrong?" Harper asked, moving to join them.

"Leonius may have followed us from Port Henry," Drina pointed out unhappily.

Harper shook his head. "I was watching for anyone following us. We weren't."

Drina stared at him blankly, both embarrassed and angry at herself for not thinking of it. She was supposed to be the professional here.

"Thank you," she breathed on a sigh. "I should have thought to watch for it myself."

Harper smiled crookedly. "I told you I'm good with details."

"Yes, but I'm the rogue hunter here," she pointed out with vexation, as he caught her free hand and tugged to urge them to move again. "I should have—"

"Hey," he interrupted, squeezing her fingers gently. "You were worried about Stephanie."

"So were you," she pointed out dryly, as they approached the end of the alley.

"Yeah, but you haven't slept in more than forty-eight hours. I have," he countered.

"Has it been that long?" Drina asked with a frown.

"I'm afraid so," Harper said.

"Actually it's forty-seven hours and ten minutes right now," Stephanie murmured. "We got up at eight the day before yesterday and you sat up on the stool all night while Harper and I were healing from the fire."

"Right," Drina murmured with a shake of the head, and then they'd spent the day playing cards, looking for Stephanie, and then driving down here to search for her. Harper and Stephanie hadn't slept in almost twenty-four hours. Stephanie could sleep in the backseat on the way back, but Harper . . . She glanced to him, and asked, "Are you okay for driving?"

"I think so. Besides, we don't have blood. We have to get back," he pointed out quietly.

The reminder made her glance to Stephanie, and she frowned when she noticed her pallor. Unless they wanted to find emergency donors, they had to get back.

"I can't feed on people the normal way," Stephanie pointed out grimly, as they reached Harper's car. "And I am so not cutting up some poor person to feed. Let's just go back. I'll survive two hours."

"Sounds like a plan," Harper said, as they reached the car.

It took them several minutes, but they found a pay phone at a corner store. While Stephanie and Harper stocked up on junk food for the trip home, Drina called Teddy. The police chief was relieved to hear they'd found Stephanie and promised his first call, even before he started calling in the search party, would be to Lucian to have him send someone to Windsor to keep an eye on the McGills for the next little while just in case. He then asked what their ETA was and assured her he'd be waiting up to see they got back okay.

Drina had expected Stephanie to sleep for the journey home, but she didn't. Drina was determined to keep up a lively chatter to help Harper fend off sleepiness, and Stephanie joined the effort. It made the sudden silence that hit the car when they passed

the Port Henry limits sign that much more noticeable.

It was nine thirty on the nose when they arrived
at Teddy's. Both SUVs and Teddy's car were in the
driveway. Drina had to smile when Harper parked
behind Anders's SUV, blocking it in.

"Nice," Stephanie said from the backseat.

"What?" Harper asked innocently, and Drina
chuckled softly as they all got out of the car.

Mirabeau had the front door open before they
reached the porch. She peered over them with amusement and shook her head. "You all look exhausted."

Drina smiled wryly. "Probably because we are."

Nodding, she stepped to the side to let them enter,
squeezing Stephanie's arm as she passed.

"I smell food," Stephanie said, sniffing the air as
she paused in the front hall.

"We made breakfast. It should be ready in a few
minutes," Mirabeau said with a grin as she followed
Drina and Harper into the house.

"We?" Stephanie asked, eyeing the woman dubiously as she kicked off the overlarge shoes Teddy
had loaned her when she'd left with Anders.

"Well, all I did was toast the toast and butter it,"
Mirabeau admitted with a grin. "But it's a start."

"It's more than I know how to do," Drina said
dryly as she removed her borrowed boots.

"Lucky you, then, that I'm a chef." Harper kissed her
on the forehead as he reached past her for a hanger.

"Lucky both of us that we landed with life mates
who could cook," Mirabeau said with amusement,
and then tilted her head, and said, "Hmm. The

nanos couldn't have known—" She shook her head. "Nah."

"Where's Anders?" Drina asked as she took the bomber from Stephanie and hung it in the closet.

"Here."

She turned to see him standing in the doorway to the dining room, and slipped her arm protectively around Stephanie even as Harper slid his arm around her.

"Relax," Anders said dryly. "We're eating and sleeping, then we'll talk."

Drina heard Stephanie's relieved sigh and squeezed her shoulders, but her eyes went to Mirabeau in question.

"He said he was going to take Stephanie to Toronto as soon as you guys got back," Mirabeau said grimly. "But Teddy piped up and said he suspected Anders would have a mutiny if he tried it. But it didn't matter anyway, because if Anders tried to drive out of here when he hasn't slept in over twenty-four hours, Teddy'd have to arrest him for dangerous driving and—as he put it—throw his immortal arse in the clink for twenty-four hours."

Drina smiled, thinking she really liked the police chief of Port Henry.

"So," Mirabeau said with a grin, "Anders backed off and agreed to wait until everyone has eaten and slept before heading back to Toronto."

Drina sensed the tension in Stephanie and clasped her shoulders knowingly as she assured her, "You won't be going back alone. I'll beat the crap out of Anders if I have to, but I'm coming with you."

"*Can* you beat the crap out of him?" Stephanie asked dubiously.

"Hey, she used to be a gladiator," Harper told the girl encouragingly. "Besides, I'd help beat the crap out of him. But we won't need to. I'll call my office after we've eaten and arrange for my helicopter to pick us up tonight after we've slept. That way Anders can't refuse us. In fact, he'll be lucky if we let him come with us."

"Thanks," Stephanie said huskily, but her expression was troubled as she slipped out from under Dani's arm and made her way into the dining room.

"She's worried about turning no-fanger and being put down," Harper murmured, watching Stephanie walk away.

"We're all worried about that," Mirabeau said on a sigh, and then shook her head with frustration. "It isn't fair. She's a good kid. There has to be something we can do to help her."

Drina leaned against Harper, her gaze slipping through the door to the dining room and the kitchen beyond, where Stephanie was retrieving a bag of blood from a cooler on the kitchen counter and asking Tiny if she could help him with anything. "I've been thinking about that."

"So have I," Mirabeau admitted. "We need to find older edentates and see if any of them had to deal with this and how they did." She paused to frown, and then added, "But that can take a while, and I don't know how long Stef can handle being bombarded with thoughts and energy."

Drina nodded. She'd considered the same thing

and the same problem. "We have a little time before we leave. We'll just keep thinking, maybe have a brainstorming session after we eat."

"Good idea," Mirabeau said.

"Speaking of eating," Harper murmured. "Just the sight of that bag of blood Stephanie's puncturing with straws is making my fangs ache. I need blood."

"Me too," Drina admitted on a sigh, allowing him to urge her out of the entry.

Harper hung up Teddy's phone with a weary sigh and stood up to stretch in front of the desk in the dining room. He'd been making calls for the last hour while Tiny and the women brainstormed in the living room with Stephanie over ways to help her. He knew that Drina had included the girl in an effort to reassure her and give her some sense of hope, but when he entered the room, he found Stephanie curled up on the couch sound asleep and the others gathered in chairs at the other end of the living room talking quietly.

"Any luck?" he asked quietly as he settled on the arm of Drina's recliner and rubbed her back.

"We had a couple of good ideas, I think," Drina said, tipping her head up to smile at him crookedly. "But we're all so exhausted . . ." She shrugged, and then said, "You were on the phone a long time. Was there a problem arranging for the helicopter?"

Harper shook his head. "It's coming for us at midnight. That gives us . . ." He automatically glanced down at his wrist, but recalling that his watch had been another victim of the fire, glanced around the room for a clock. He spotted the digital time readout on the DVR beside Teddy's television. It was 10:58. "Thirteen hours to sleep, take turns at the shower, and get ready. We should also be able to fit in another brainstorming session before it arrives."

"Good thinking," Tiny rumbled, catching Mirabeau's hand and standing up. "We'll be more clear-headed then."

"Yeah," Mirabeau sighed, slipping her arm around Tiny, and then glancing to Drina and Harper with a grimace. "Are you two going to be all right in the recliners? I feel bad that we get the bed."

"Don't," Drina said, a wry smile curving her lips. "I'm so exhausted I could sleep on a bed of nails."

"We'll be fine," Harper assured them. Teddy had decided the sleeping arrangements; Tiny and Mirabeau got the spare bedroom, Stephanie, Drina, and he got the living room, and Anders was presently sharing Teddy's bed. Or possibly sacked out on Teddy's bedroom floor, Harper thought with amusement as he recalled Anders's expression when Teddy had made the announcement. He hadn't looked terribly pleased, but it was Teddy's house, so his rules.

No one was fooled. The police chief had made Anders share his room so he could keep an eye on him and ensure he didn't try to slip away with Stephanie while the rest of the house slept. Drina's and Harper's sleeping in the living room with Stephanie was the second safeguard against that as well as the possibility of another attack by Leonius.

Harper sincerely hoped there wouldn't be another

attack. He was exhausted. They all were. If they could just make it through the next thirteen hours without Leonius trying something, they would get Stephanie away from here and at least that risk. Then they'd only have to worry about helping her handle her new gifts and convincing Lucian to give her the time to do so.

"Well, good night then," Mirabeau murmured, as Tiny turned her toward the door and urged her from the room.

"Good night," Drina and Harper whispered together.

He watched them out of the room, and then bent to press his lips to Drina's forehead. At least that was the intention, but she lifted her head to say something just as he did, and his lips landed on her mouth. Exhausted as he was, his body immediately responded to the contact, and Harper found himself thrusting his tongue eagerly into her mouth to taste the passion bursting to life between them.

When she moaned and arched her back in response, thrusting her breasts upward, he couldn't resist reaching for them. They both groaned at the excitement that bounced between them as he palmed her breasts, but Harper forced himself to release her and break the kiss.

"Christ," he whispered, leaning his forehead against hers. "I'm so tired I can't see straight, and I still want to rip your clothes off and sink myself into you."

Drina gave a little sigh, and then pulled back to glance toward Stephanie. Her smile was wry when she turned back, her voice a mere whisper as she said, "Sleep."

He nodded and started to rise, but she caught his hand, and said, "Thank you."

"For what?" he asked with surprise.

"For coming with us to Toronto. When you asked at the house if I'd stay here if Lucian decided to replace me, I wanted to say yes, but Stephanie—"

"I know," Harper assured her quietly. "It took me a minute to reason it out, but we're life mates. We'll be together. We just have to work out the particulars of where and so on."

She smiled, and he caressed her cheek gently, and then pushed himself wearily to his feet. Drina shifted her chair into a reclining position as he walked to his own. He got in the second chair, shifted it into the reclining position, and then reached across the end table between them for her hand. She smiled at him gently and squeezed his fingers, and they both drifted off to sleep.

It was something cold and hard pressing against his forehead that woke him sometime later. Harper frowned and blinked his eyes open. His head was turned to the side, and the first thing he saw was Drina in the next chair, her eyes open and narrowed in concentration on something beyond him. Bending his neck to the side, he turned slowly to see what had been at his forehead and stilled when he saw the woman standing over him, pointing a gun at his head.

Seventeen

Harper stared at the slender mortal female with short, dark hair and a pinched, angry face. She was trembling, no doubt trying to fight the control Drina had taken of her.

"Sue?" he said finally, his voice as blank as his thoughts as he stared at Susan Harper. He hadn't seen the woman since Jenny's death, and his brain was having a little trouble accepting that Jenny's sister would be here at all, let alone pointing a weapon at him.

"Why can't I pull the trigger?" she growled, sounding furious. "I'm trying to, but my finger won't move."

Harper glanced to Drina.

"I woke up as she entered the room," Drina said quietly. "At first, I was half-asleep and thought it must be Leonius, but then I realized she was a woman and mortal and she wasn't going for Stephanie but heading for you. I waited to see what she was up to, but when she pointed the gun at you . . ."

Harper nodded, not needing her to tell him that she had taken control of the woman enough to prevent her harming anyone but leaving her free to think and speak. He shifted his gaze back to Sue; his eyes slid from her face to the gun and back, before he asked with bewilderment, "Why?"

"Because you killed Jenny," she said bitterly.

Harper sagged in his chair, his old friend guilt gliding through him like a ghost . . . Jenny's ghost. If he'd been the one controlling Sue at that moment, his control would have slipped, and he'd no doubt have a hole in his head. Fortunately, Drina didn't slip at this news, and after taking a moment to regather himself, he cleared his throat, and said quietly, "I never meant for that to happen, Susan. You must know that. I wanted to spend my life with Jenny. She was my life mate. I'd sooner kill myself than my life mate."

"She wasn't your life mate," Susan snapped with disgust. "Jenny didn't even like you. She only put up with you so you'd turn her. She bought into all your promises of young and beautiful and healthy forever . . . but you killed her."

Harper winced as those words whipped him. He didn't know which hurt him most: the suggestion that Jenny had only been using him or the reminder that she was dead because of him. Susan's saying that she hadn't even liked him fit with what Teddy had said the night he and Drina had flown back from Toronto in the helicopter, and he supposed it was possible.

They'd only known each other a week or so before she'd agreed to the turn. And while he was immortal and had accepted her as his life mate the moment he couldn't read her, she was mortal. Mortals didn't understand the importance of being a life mate, didn't automatically recognize the gift of it. She may have just gone along with it to let him turn her. But he was sure that she would have eventually recognized that he was the only one she could find peace with and passion.

Harper frowned as he recalled that he hadn't experienced that passion with Jenny. He'd been putting it down to the fact that she'd kept him at arm's length, and still believed that. If she'd even allowed him to kiss her, they both would have been overwhelmed by it, he was sure. Just as he and Drina were constantly bedeviled by it.

Finally, he said solemnly, "She was my life mate, Susan. I couldn't read her."

Susan snorted. "Jenny figured that was the brain tumor."

Harper stilled, his heart seeming to stop in his chest at the words. It was Drina who growled, "Brain tumor?"

Eyes locked on Harper, Susan flashed an unpleasant smile that suggested she was enjoying his shock and dismay. "She was having headaches, and her vision would blur at times. She was also having trouble concentrating, and her memory was suffering. It turned out she had a tumor. They'd started chemo to try to shrink it before they operated, but then Jenny met you and decided she didn't need any more treatment at all. She'd just let you turn her and live forever."

"Harper?" Drina said quietly. "A brain tumor could prevent you reading her."

"She was my life mate, Dree," he said quietly. "I was eating. My appetites had been reawakened."

"We can always eat," she pointed out gently. "We just get tired of it and stop because it's a bother, not because we can't." She paused a moment to let that sink in, then asked, "Did the food taste as good then as it does now?"

Harper automatically opened his mouth to say yes, but caught himself and really thought about it. In truth, he realized, it hadn't. It had been okay, some of it tasty even, but he'd only eaten when the others had, and hadn't found himself stuffing himself until his stomach ached, or constantly wanting it as he did now.

"And you didn't have the shared dreams," she pointed out quietly.

Harper nodded silently, thinking that it wasn't just the lack of shared dreams but the lack of passion. He'd been eager to experience it with Jenny, but not eager enough to try to change her mind when she'd insisted they wait until after the turn. Harper had just let it go, thinking everything would be fine after he turned her. He certainly hadn't been obsessed with it as he had been since Drina had arrived here in Port Henry, his mind constantly undressing her and doing things to her that left him half-erect when she wasn't even in the damned room.

By the time Harper had actually kissed Drina

outside that restaurant in Toronto, he'd already un-dressed and made love to her in his mind a hundred times. During their shopping expedition, he'd fanta-sized about her in every pair of pretty panties and bras she'd bought, and the black dress had been no better.

Harper had assured himself that it was just the appetites Jenny had reawakened, that they were making themselves known again now that some of his depression was easing, but those damned boots had kept him under a cold shower for nearly an hour as he'd got ready for their trip to the city, and it hadn't eased any in Toronto. As she'd spoken of Egypt, he'd imagined her dressed up like Cleopatra and mentally stripped away her clothes and laid her on a bed of pillows to sink his body into hers. As she'd told him about her time as a gladiator, his fan-tasy had switched to ravishing her in the middle of an arena with the crowds cheering him on.

It had been the same with each revelation of her life. In his mind, Harper had made love to Drina as a concubine, a duchess, a pirate, and a madam all before he'd even touched her. But even that hadn't prepared him for what happened when he'd finally kissed her there outside the restaurant. The passion that had exploded over him had been overwhelm-ing, and he was quite sure that if the waiter hadn't happened along, he'd have made love to her right there pinned up against the wall.

Harper hadn't experienced anything like that with Jenny. He hadn't imagined her naked or dressed or anything. He'd mostly thought about how happy they would be once she was turned, and they were able to enjoy the shared pleasure and peace a life mate offered.

"Harper?" Drina said quietly.

"She wasn't my life mate," he acknowledged quietly.

When she released a small sigh, he glanced over curiously, surprised to note that she looked relieved, happy even. Harper took a moment to wonder if she had been jealous of Jenny but didn't have to think hard. He could still recall his rage at the idea of her going downstairs to give the doorman "the night of his life." He hadn't reacted much better to the idea of Marguerite finding her another life mate. Still, he smiled crookedly, and asked, "Were you jealous of Jenny?"

"Of course," she said simply, not taking her eyes or concentration off Susan. "I don't share well, even with ghosts."

Harper smiled faintly and reached over to squeeze her hand. He knew it wasn't well-done of him, but he actually liked that she'd been jealous.

Drina glanced his way long enough to note his expression and wrinkled her nose at him. "But now I don't have to be jealous of the selfish little mortal."

"Don't call Jenny selfish," Susan snapped, fury replacing her glee of a moment ago.

"Why not?" Drina asked coldly, her full concentration on the woman once again. "It's what she was. She didn't care for Harper at all. She was using him. And she stole his one turn for her own selfish purposes."

"She wasn't selfish; she wanted to live," Susan snapped. "And she didn't steal anything, he turned her willingly. And look where it got her anyway!" She was furious, almost foaming at the mouth as she spat the words. "That wonderful turning killed her. *He* killed her."

"She killed herself," Drina said grimly. "Her heart, her whole body would have been weakened by the chemo. If she'd told him about the cancer, Harper would never have turned her until she'd had the chance to heal and build up strength. She killed herself by keeping it a secret. But then she couldn't tell him, could she?" Drina added dryly. "He would have realized she might not be his life mate then. He would have been more cautious and had others try to read her."

"She wanted to live," Susan cried.

"And in so doing didn't care that she was condemning Harper to a living death with no chance of ever turning a true life mate when he encountered her," Drina said heavily.

"Oh, right, he's really been suffering!" Susan gave a bitter laugh, and then her expression sombered and she turned her gaze back to Harper. "You really seemed to care when Jenny died. I thought you were suffering like me, so I tried not to blame you." Her gaze shifted to Drina, and her lips twisted bitterly. "But then this slut showed up, and Jenny suddenly meant nothing. I couldn't believe it when Genie called and told me how the two of you were humping in the schoolyard. She was sure you'd have screwed her right there in the snow in front of everyone if Teddy hadn't come along to stop you." Her mouth tightened. "I didn't believe her at first, so I was going to come over and see what was going on, but then I saw you through the back window as I walked up to the house, the two of you going at it in the pantry like a couple of horny teenagers, groping each other through your clothes and . . ." She paused, her mouth twisting with disgust and grief.

"I thought I saw someone in the yard," Drina muttered with a frown.

Harper raised an eyebrow. He knew what Susan was talking about. The day Stephanie had given them ten minutes alone while she prepared for their trip to London. He'd drawn Drina into the pantry and—

"How could you forget Jenny so quickly?" Susan asked plaintively.

He shifted uncomfortably, not sure how to answer that. Just days ago he'd felt guilty for letting go of his grief over Jenny so soon, but that was when he'd still thought her a life mate. All of that had changed, however, and his mind was swirling with confusion between what he'd always thought and what was true. But Sue didn't really want an answer anyway, and continued.

"I hated you for that. Jenny died, and it was your fault, and you were just moving on, humping on this—this ho—like she was some kind of bitch in heat. I followed you when you left a few minutes later. I trailed the three of you all the way to London and you were all laughing and having a good time as you walked into the mall. You had your arm around Bat-bitch here and kept kissing her and squeezing her."

"Bat-bitch?" Drina asked with disbelief, and then her eyes narrowed. "You are the one who tampered with the car brakes."

Susan lifted her chin defiantly. "I knew an accident wouldn't kill any of you. I just wanted you to suffer. But it didn't even slow you down. The next night you two were up in the porch, going at it against the windows for anyone and everyone to see."

"You threw the Molotov cocktail into the porch," Drina said wearily, and then arched an eyebrow. "And the one at the gas station I presume?"

"By then I wanted you dead," Susan said, staring at Harper and not bothering to glance Drina's way, even as she added, "And slutty vamp there too. Jenny was dead and the two of you were—" She paused and took a breath, rage burning in her eyes, as she said, "I knew the Molotov cocktail probably wouldn't kill you when I threw it at the porch. But then when I saw your car at the house the next night and crept in to see what was going on and caught her going down on you in the upper hall . . ."

Harper's eyes widened incredulously. He was amazed that she'd managed to get into the house and up the stairs without their realizing it. The house was old, the stairs creaky. They should have heard something. Of course, they'd been a bit distracted at the time, he acknowledged with a grimace, thinking it was a good Goddamned thing that Leonius hadn't been behind this. The man could have slaughtered them that night before they'd realized he was there.

"I wanted you both dead then," Susan finished dully. "You shouldn't live and be happy when Jenny is dead. I went home and fixed up another bottle. I was going to come back and set the house on fire, but I was afraid you'd just get out and heal like you'd done the last time, so I waited. I heard you saying you would go to the gas station, and I knew that was perfect. If it exploded . . . well, you couldn't survive that. So I followed you there, but she got out and went inside. I almost threw it anyway, but by then I wanted her to suffer too."

"So you waited until I came out," Drina said, sounding impatient now. "Only he caught it, and you fled. So when you heard the search had been called off, you came here to watch the house, and when everyone went to bed, you came in intending to blow his brains out and presumably mine too. All because your stupid, selfish sister decided to steal Harper's one turn and basically killed herself."

"She wasn't stupid. And she was dying, she was desperate," Susan said at once.

"She wasn't dying yet," Drina said coldly. "It was a benign tumor. They were trying to shrink it and then planned to remove it, but she thought it would be more fun to be a vampire. Young and pretty forever, banging any guy she wanted and then getting them to give her whatever she wanted by controlling them. Don't bother denying it, I'm in your head. I can read your thoughts," Drina added coldly.

"That was just wild thinking. She wouldn't have done that," Susan muttered.

"The Jenny I knew would have," Teddy said dryly,

making his presence known, and Harper glanced over to see him in the doorway, with Anders, Tiny, and Mirabeau crowded behind him. The police chief shrugged, and explained, "I'm an old man, don't sleep well, and have to get up ten times a night to take a leak. I was in the bathroom when I saw Susan creeping around the backyard headed for the door. I woke Anders, and we came down to see what she was up to. Decided not to interfere, though, till we knew what was what."

When Harper's gaze slid to Tiny and Mirabeau, it was Mirabeau who spoke.

"We weren't asleep yet," she said with a shrug, but the color that crept up her cheeks gave him a good idea of what had been keeping them awake. That bedeviling new-life-mate horniness, he thought wryly, as she continued, "We heard someone going downstairs and thought Anders was trying to pull a fast one, so came to investigate."

Anders rolled his eyes at the words but slipped past Teddy and into the room to take the gun from Susan's hand, saying, "So, no Leonius this time."

"Does that mean I don't have to go to Toronto?" Stephanie asked quietly. She had apparently been awake to hear what was going on as well. Harper watched her sit up on the couch, and then turned to Anders, along with everyone else, waiting to hear what he had to say.

"Well, answer the girl. There's nothing worse than not knowing," Teddy said grimly when Anders didn't respond right away. He then turned and marched out of the room.

"No," Anders said simply.

Stephanie frowned, "No, I don't have to go? Or no, it doesn't mean I don't have to go?"

"Lucian wants you in Toronto," Anders answered.

"It's all right, Stephanie," Drina said quietly, and Harper noticed she'd relaxed now that Anders had Susan by the arm. She was no longer bothering to control the woman. "I'm sure it will just be temporary. Once Elvi's place is fixed up, we'll come back."

Harper hoped she was right but knew they'd all do everything they could to ensure that was the case. Stephanie had gained herself four champions during her short stay in Port Henry. Five if you counted Teddy, he thought, as the mortal returned to the room with a cordless phone pressed to his ear.

"Yeah, I need you down here at my place. You need to take Susan Harper into custody," he said into the phone as he handed Anders a pair of cuffs. "I'll explain when you get here." Teddy hit the button to end the call, and then raised an eyebrow at Anders. "What are you waiting for? Cuff her. She's under arrest."

"Teddy," Susan said with dismay. "You can't arrest me."

Teddy arched his eyebrows as he peered at the girl. "Four counts of attempted murder is serious business, Susan. I certainly am arresting you."

"But he killed Jenny," she wailed. "And he's a vampire. Not even human. He's a monster."

"Jenny's death was an accident, one it's sounding like she brought on herself," he said, and then added sternly, "As for his being a monster, Harper never intended her to die, and it wasn't his fault since she didn't tell him about the tumor and chemo. You, on the other hand, have been deliberately cutting brakes and firebombing Elvi's house and apparently the gas station. If I were you, I'd rethink who the monster is here."

"You can't arrest her," Anders said quietly.

"What the hell do you mean?" Teddy asked with amazement. "Of course I can. The woman's a menace. She needs to be locked up, probably in the hospital, but the courts will decide that."

"You can't charge her with trying to kill Harper," Drina said quietly.

"They're right," Harper said, when Teddy opened his mouth to protest. "How are you going to explain that we didn't die from any of the attacks? And what happens when she starts squawking about vampires and Jenny's dying during the turn?"

Teddy's troubled gaze slid to Susan. "Well, what the hell are we supposed to do with her then? We can't just let her loose. She'll just try again."

There was silence for a minute, and then Anders quickly cuffed Susan and urged her across the room. "You can lock her up, but I suspect Lucian will want her in Toronto as well."

"Teddy," Susan cried, jerking around and looking at him pleadingly.

He frowned, but sighed, and asked, "What will Lucian do?"

Anders shrugged. "Depends."

"On what?" Teddy asked at once.

"Does she have family here?"

"She and Jenny were all that was left. Grand-parents were all gone by the time they were out of grade school. The mother died while they were in high school, and the father had a heart attack a couple years back." He paused, and then added, "I think they have an aunt and a couple of cousins in London, but they weren't close as far as I know."

"Then he'll probably have her memory wiped and relocate her to the other end of Canada or some-where down in the States," Mirabeau said quietly. "Give her a job with someone who can keep an eye on her and a new home. The works."

"Memory wiped? Like she won't know who she is?" Teddy asked with a frown.

"No." It was Drina who answered this time. "They'll wipe her memories of Harper and vam-pires in general, alter her memories of Jenny's death so she believes she died from the tumor alone, and probably put it in her head that Port Henry is full of bad, sad memories for her, and she doesn't want to return." Her mouth tightened, and she added, "They'll probably veil her sense of loss over Jenny too so she can move on."

Teddy grunted at this and shook his head. "So she tries to kill Harper, nearly kills you and Stephanie along with him, and gets into the immortal version of the Federal Witness Protection Program?"

"That's about it," Mirabeau said wryly, and shrugged. "She isn't wholly in her right mind, Teddy. Jenny was all she had. She's grieving."

Drina made an impatient sound, and Harper squeezed her fingers gently, knowing she wasn't too pleased by this outcome. Not that Teddy looked as if he thought it was a fair deal either.

"And she calls you guys the monsters," Teddy muttered, shaking his head. He scrubbed one hand through his gray hair, then sighed and stepped back out into the entry when they heard the crunch of snow under tires. Glancing back into the room, he gestured Anders forward. "My deputy's here. He'll take her down and lock her up until Lucian can send someone for her."

"Teddy?" Susan said unhappily, as Anders walked her to the man, "please don't let them—"

"I don't want to hear it, Susan. I'm tired and heartsick. You did this to yourself," Teddy said sternly. "And you're getting a hell of a good deal. If it were up to me, you'd be locked up for what you've done. You tried to kill the man, caused no end of pain to all three of them, damned near burnt down Elvi's house . . . and you could have killed that semi driver or someone else with that brakes stunt too. Just thank your lucky stars they aren't demanding your head on a platter."

Shaking his head, Teddy turned to the door to watch his deputy approach the house, muttering, "I thought I lived in Goddamned Mayberry with a bunch of Aunt Beas and Andies. Who knew Port Henry had so many homicidal nutcases running around? I think it's time I retired," he added wearily as he opened the door.

They were all silent as Teddy turned the woman over to his deputy. The moment she was out of his hands, Anders slipped his cell phone from his pocket and started punching numbers. Calling Lucian Argeneau, Harper supposed.

"Well, that takes care of that." Teddy closed and locked the front door, then turned back to stand in the doorway to the living room to survey his guests with a sigh. He grimaced as he noted Anders talking quietly into his phone, then glanced to the others, and said, "I'm hoping this means we're off high alert and are back to thinking that this Leonius fellow is still in the States?"

"It looks that way," Drina said, sounding a little more cheerful than she had at the prospect of Susan's lack of punishment for what she'd done.

"Right." Teddy turned away. "Then I'm to bed. I'm too damned old for this nonsense."

"Sleep well," Harper murmured, a sentiment echoed by the others. They all smiled wryly when the man snorted at the very possibility.

"He means it about retiring," Stephanie said sadly. "He's very depressed about what's happened in Port Henry the last couple of years."

"He just needs some sleep," Harper assured her, and hoped it was true. He liked the man. Teddy Brunswick did his best for the people in this town, mortal and immortal alike. Unfortunately, the man was nearing retirement. Unless he turned out to be a life mate for someone, they would lose him in another year or so. Harper frowned at the realization and thought perhaps he should suggest Drina talk to her aunt Marguerite about setting that special skill of hers for sniffing out life mates onto Teddy. She usually found mates for immortals, but she might be able to find an immortal for him. It would certainly be handy if Teddy became one of them.

"Lucian's sending someone for the woman," Anders announced, putting his phone away. "I'm going back to bed."

"So are we," Mirabeau said on a sigh. "Good night, guys."

Harper murmured good night, and then glanced from Stephanie to Drina. The two females were peering at each other, Drina eyeing the girl with worry, Stephanie peering back, her expression a portrait of misery.

"I don't want to be a no-fanger," the teenager said suddenly.

Harper winced, guessing the girl had read that worry from one of them despite their best efforts to keep the thought from their minds.

"We won't let you," Drina said quietly. "We'll find a way to help you."

Stephanie nodded but didn't look as if she believed it as she lay back down and turned over to face the back of the couch.

When Drina sighed unhappily and settled back in her chair, Harper released a little sigh of his own. He wanted to tell her everything would be all right, but he wasn't yet sure his plan would work, so simply gave her hand another squeeze and closed his eyes to sleep as well.

Eighteen

'I don't think I like helicopters.'

Drina smiled faintly at Stephanie's words as Harper urged them both out of the elevator and into his apartment. In truth, she hadn't been too thrilled with the helicopter this time either. It was extremely windy tonight, and the ride had been a little bumpy. But they were here now, safe and sound and much more swiftly than it would have been by car.

"I guess you may as well call Lucian and let him know we're here, Anders," Harper said as he shrugged out of, and hung up, his coat.

"No need."

Those two words brought everyone to a halt. Frowning, Harper moved to the end of the entry and peered into his living room. Drina could tell by the way his eyebrows rose that he was surprised, and not necessarily pleased, at who he found there.

Lucian Argeneau. Drina would recognize her uncle's voice anywhere.

"How did you get in?" Harper asked, sounding annoyed.

Drina hung up her coat, kicked off her boots, and moved to join Harper as Lucian answered, "Your doorman is mortal."

It wasn't much of an answer, but pretty much said it all. Lucian had controlled the man to let him in, Drina deduced, eyeing him where he sat looking relaxed and comfortable on Harper's sofa. It was a con, of course; Lucian wasn't at all relaxed. He was reading Harper. She'd bet her life on it, Drina thought, and then stiffened when his gaze suddenly shifted to her, and she felt the telltale ruffling as he now rifled through her thoughts as well.

Drina glared at him for it but didn't try to block him. When his gaze slid past her and narrowed, she knew before turning that Stephanie had finished removing her own outer gear and moved up to join them. Drina spared the girl a reassuring smile and slid her arm around her, then glanced to Anders as he joined them.

"Yes, I can," Stephanie said suddenly, and Drina glanced to her sharply, then peered warily at her uncle. One eyebrow was raised on his hard face, but otherwise, he looked as emotionless as ever. Standing, he walked toward them, and Drina stiffened, but he merely moved past to the closet to retrieve a long, leather coat.

"Anders, you're with me," Lucian announced as he drew it on.

The man immediately joined him at the closet, and Drina scowled. "That's it? You dragged us all the way to Toronto, and now you're just going to leave?"

Lucian shrugged. "Between your brainstorming and the arrangements Harper has made, you have everything under control."

Drina's eyes widened. She wasn't at all sure she had anything under control, and she didn't have a clue what he was talking about when he said "arrangements Harper has made."

"So we return to Port Henry?" Harper asked.

"After the repairs and renovations you commissioned are done," Lucian said.

Drina glanced to Harper with surprise, and he explained, "I made some calls last night after arranging for the helicopter to pick us up."

"Stay here till then," Lucian ordered. "Keep Stephanie inside unless you can find a way to disguise her."

Drina nodded solemnly, knowing that Leonius was still a worry. While the man was supposedly in the States, that could change, and Toronto was one of the places he'd look for the girl.

"I'll see what I can find out from the few older edentates, and tell Bastien to help you any way he can with whatever drugs he thinks might be useful," Lucian announced.

Drina glanced worriedly to Stephanie. That idea had come up after the girl had fallen asleep. It was Tiny who had suggested that perhaps there was some sort of drug that might help block the thoughts of others for her until she learned to do it herself. It wasn't a first choice, but a last resort to help her hold on to her sanity until she was able to deal with the thoughts, energy, and electricity herself.

"I want regular reports," Lucian barked, drawing Drina's attention again as he pressed the button for the elevator. He then glanced back. "And I want the truth. Help her if you can, but if you can't, I need to know about it."

Drina nodded reluctantly, and his eyes narrowed on her.

"This is a temporary gig, Alexandrina. Elvi's already raised and lost a daughter. She and Victor were happy when I asked them to be in charge of Stephanie, and I won't take it away from them now. They make final decisions until it's safe to put the sisters together again." He didn't wait to see how she reacted to that, but turned and led Anders onto the elevator. "I'll have blood deliveries set up for you while you're here."

Drina let out a slow breath as the elevator doors closed, and then glanced to Stephanie and Harper. "Well, that went better than I expected."

"Yes," Harper said dryly.

Drina chuckled at his expression and glanced to Stephanie. "How are you doing?"

Stephanie forced a smile. "Good. Tired though. I didn't sleep much last night."

"Well, there are three guest rooms in this apartment," Harper said at once. "All of them have their own attached bath. Go take a look, pick which one you prefer, and have a nap, then we'll figure out how to disguise you so we can see some plays and stuff while we're in the city."

"Plays?" Stephanie peered at him with interest.

"Yeah, I hear there are a couple good ones in Toronto right now," he said easily. "And you'll need a break from all the work Drina and I are going to make you do to try to learn to block thoughts."

She nodded and started to turn away, then quickly whirled back and hugged Drina, mumbling, "Thank you for wanting to help me, and for my room at Elvi's," she added as she then hugged Harper.

Before either of them could respond or even hug her back, she was off rushing across the living room and away up the hall toward the bedrooms.

"Her room at Elvi's?" Drina asked with confusion.

Harper smiled faintly and turned to slip his arms around her. "When I called about repairing the fire and smoke damage to Elvi's house, I also arranged to have insulation, a wall of brick, and several different kinds of soundproofing and whatnot put in Stephanie's room. I'm hoping that will help block thoughts and give her a quiet place to get away when it gets too much for her."

"Oh." Drina sighed and leaned against him. "You're a clever man."

"I like to think so," he said lightly, rubbing his hands up and down her back. "I'm thinking I might do it to whatever room she chooses here too."

Drina pulled back to peer at him with surprise. "But we're only going to be here until the house is repaired."

Harper shrugged. "I can afford it. Besides, that

way she'll be comfortable if we can bring her back to Toronto for visits. Elvi and Victor may be in charge when they return, but we can be the doting auntie and uncle figures who drag her off to the city for plays and shopping on occasion and give them a break."

Drina nodded solemnly. "You're going to be a good father."

"I sincerely hope so," Harper murmured, bending to kiss the tip of her nose. He then straightened, and asked, "I presume that means you do want children?"

"Yes," she admitted. "Do you?"

"Definitely," he assured her. Letting his hands slide to her waist, Harper lifted her up. When Drina instinctively wrapped her legs around his waist, he began to carry her through the living room toward the hall Stephanie had disappeared down. "And where would you like to raise those children?"

"With you," she said simply.

He smiled and paused at the start of the hall to kiss her, but then continued on, asking, "And where would that be? Where do you want to live, Drina? Your home and family are in Spain."

"And your home and family are here in Canada," she pointed out.

"Actually, my birth family are in Germany," he said wryly, "but you're right, Elvi and Victor and the others have become my family, and they're here. As is Stephanie."

"You consider me family?"

Harper paused, and Drina glanced around to see

that they were halfway up the hall and in front of an open bedroom door. Stephanie stood in the middle of the room, her wide eyes on them.

"We'd like to consider you family if that's all right with you?" Drina said solemnly.

"Oh, yeah!" She grinned. "Everyone needs family, and you two are pretty cool. Kind of annoying with your new-life-mate horndoginess, but still cool."

The words startled a laugh from Drina, and she said, "So you wouldn't mind if we settled in Port Henry or somewhere nearby and stayed a part of your life?"

"I'd like that," she assured them quietly.

"So would I," Harper said, and glanced to Drina. "You're sure? Your family is in Spain."

"You're my life mate, Harper. And I love you. You are my family," she said solemnly. "And so is Stephanie. My home is here now."

His eyes widened, and he seemed to hold his breath for a moment as if savoring what she'd said. That breath came out as if he'd been punched when Stephanie said, "Well? Aren't you going to tell her you love her too, Harper? I know that you do."

He smiled wryly, and then turned to the girl to say, "I'll tell her. Now go get some sleep. We're going to nap too."

"Oh yeah." Stephanie rolled her eyes as she moved to the door. "I bet you'll get *so* much sleep."

Drina wrinkled her nose. "Maybe we should cut your hair. That might help disguise you."

"No way!" Stephanie said at once. "Actually, I'm thinking a goth look might be a cool change. Black hair, black lipstick, maybe some purple or pink streaks like Mirabeau. Oh, and some chains and nose rings. I could really rock the goth look," she assured them with a wicked grin as she closed the door.

Drina groaned as Harper started moving again. "She's going to be trouble, that one."

"No doubt," he said with amusement. "But you can handle her."

"I can, can I?" she asked wryly, as he carried her into his room and kicked the door closed.

"Dree, darling, you've handled pirates and prostitutes. You can handle one little teenager. And together *we* can handle Stephanie and ten more," he assured her, moving to the bed and kneeling on the edge to lower her to it.

"We . . . I like that," she murmured, as her back hit the bed, and he came down on top of her. And then her eyes widened, and she squawked, "Ten?"

"One at a time," Harper assured her, pulling her upright with him so that he could remove her T-shirt. "Every hundred years or so as law insists."

He had removed her T-shirt and bra as he spoke and now pushed her back on the bed and shifted down between her ankles to tug her joggers and panties off.

"So you're going to have me barefoot and pregnant in the kitchen every hundred years, are you?" Drina asked with amusement, as he tossed the last of her clothes aside and turned back to survey what he'd revealed.

"Oh no," Harper assured her. "Barefoot and pregnant in every room *but* the kitchen. I am the cook in this household."

"Hmmm." She raised one foot and caught the hem of his T-shirt with her toes and began to lift it up his chest. "I don't know. I enjoyed what we did in the kitchen the last time we were here."

"Well, I am willing to make exceptions," Harper assured her, helping her to remove his T-shirt, and then pausing as she lowered her foot to his lap and hooked her toes in the waist of his joggers to begin tugging at them. She couldn't remove them with him sitting, but enjoyed the way he grew under her foot as she rubbed against him with the effort.

"Did I mention you have talented feet?" he asked, his voice a growl.

Drina grinned. "I have many talents."

"I don't doubt that for a minute," he assured her, catching her foot and lifting it to his lips to press a kiss to her toes. Harper set her foot down to one side so that he was between her ankles, and then shifted to his hands and knees to climb forward.

"Not going to take your pants off?" she asked, arching an eyebrow when he settled on top of her.

Harper kissed her until they were both breathless. He then broke the kiss and shifted lower to nuzzle her breasts, murmuring, "If I take them off, I'll want to plunge myself into you, and I'm determined to make slow love to you this time."

"Good luck with that," Drina teased, and then gasped as his mouth closed over a nipple.

Harper swirled his tongue across the nub as he suckled, and then let it slip from his mouth and raised his head to ask, "Do you really love me?"

Drina nodded solemnly. "With all my heart," she assured him.

He smiled, and finally said it. "I love you too."

Drina slid her arms around him as he pressed up to kiss her again. When his tongue plunged into her mouth, she moaned and wrapped her legs around him again, pressing her heels into his behind to press him against her. She shifted her pelvis at the same time so that they ground together, his hardness against her soft moist center. Harper groaned and broke their kiss.

"Next time we'll go slow," he muttered, pushing his joggers down just enough for his erection to break free.

"Next time," Drina agreed, and then gasped and clawed at his back as he filled her. They had a long life of next times ahead and she planned to enjoy every one.

For an early Christmas present,
turn the page for a sneak peek

AT LYNSAY SANDS's
next delectable vampire romance
Available November 2011

Katricia took her time closing bedroom doors, peering curiously into each room as she went. It was partially out of curiosity and partially to give Teddy some breathing room. She didn't need to read his mind to know that he wasn't comfortable with her. She supposed she'd come on too strong too fast, but hadn't been able to help herself. The very fact that he might be her life mate made her want to test it. She wasn't hungry yet, but then the only food around was in cans and boxes. There was nothing really to tempt her palate. Which meant the easiest way to know for sure was to kiss Teddy and see if she experienced the shared pleasure she'd heard so much about.

Unfortunately, it was looking like that might be a hard objective to achieve. Teddy didn't appear to be comfortable with what he thought was their age difference. That seemed obvious to her from the way he'd quickly removed his hat and scarf and then turned, as if presenting some monstrosity to her.

This was going to take some patience, which had never been Katricia's strong suit. She was already struggling with the urge to simply walk out into the kitchen and jump the man's bones. The only thing stopping her was the worry that she might give the poor guy a heart attack or something. That would be just her luck—kill her life mate with a heart attack before she could woo and turn him.

Grimacing at the thought, Katricia continued checking out the rooms. She found the one with Teddy's suitcase and smiled faintly, thinking it was the room she would have picked too. It was the last on the left with the window overlooking the driveway, where he could easily look out to see who was approaching should anyone come up the driveway.

It was a good defensive position and his cop instincts were showing in the choice, she thought with a smile, before pulling the door closed and moving back up the hall. Her eyes widened slightly when she found Teddy kneeling by the fireplace, situating a couple of pots at the edge of the fire.

"What are you doing?" she asked curiously, moving up behind him to peer over his shoulder, but inching back a bit when she sensed him stiffening.

"Experimenting," he said gruffly, straightening and stepping around her to get back into the kitchen. "Boiling water to make drip coffee and heating chicken soup. It's not the usual breakfast fare, I know, but beggars can't be choosers."

"Clever," Katricia murmured, watching from the fireplace as he walked into the kitchen and began to measure coffee into a filter.

"Hardly clever," Teddy said with amusement, setting his coffee fixings aside and rifling through the box. "More like desperate. I'm useless without my java."

"Java?" Katricia asked, warming her hands at the fire.

"Coffee," he explained, and then said, "Since you're over there, keep an eye on the soup for me, will you?"

"Sure," Katricia said, watching him cross to the table to put on his hat and scarf.

"I'm going to go see if I can get my truck door open and the engine started so I can charge my phone," he explained as he moved to the door. "If I can get the phone hooked up, I can call Marguerite and see if we can't get the power back on."

"Marguerite?"

Teddy paused to glance her way in surprise. Probably because she'd barked the word in her surprise, she thought, and grimaced to herself. Clearing her throat, she asked more calmly, "Who's Marguerite?"

"Marguerite Argeneau, a friend. She arranged for me to rent this cottage. I want to call and find out who I should report the power problem to," he said slowly, still eyeing her a little oddly. But then he shook his head and turned to walk out into the vestibule to put on his boots. He pulled the door closed behind him and Katricia stared at it, biting her lip.

She had a cell phone. It was in her pocket and had been since she awoke, and yet she hadn't once thought of using it . . . not even to check on her blood delivery. That more than anything told her just how upset she'd been since finding she couldn't read Teddy.

Muttering under her breath, she pulled out the phone, but then paused and simply stood there listening until Teddy finished donning his boots and stomped out of the cottage.

Katricia then turned to give the soup a quick stir before moving into the kitchen to peer out the window. Spotting Teddy by the door of his pickup fiddling with the lock, she quickly pulled up contacts on her phone and found her aunt's listing. Marguerite answered on the second ring, her voice cheerful and happy as she said, "Hello Tricia, dear, how is your vacation going?"

"I can't read Teddy," Katricia blurted, not bothering with niceties.

"Oh, how lovely!" Marguerite didn't sound at all surprised. "I hoped the two of you would meet. Isn't he a handsome man?"

"Yes," Katricia breathed. Teddy Brunswick was the most beautiful man she'd ever met. Of course she might be biased since she couldn't read him and suspected he was her life mate. It tended to color things. Still, he *was* handsome.

"He's so dignified-looking and such a gentleman. I've seen pictures of him when he was younger and I promise you he'll be even more gorgeous after he's turned. He—"

"Does he know about us?" Katricia interrupted, zeroing in on what was most important to her. If he knew about them, she could just tell him she couldn't read him, then jump his bones and find out for sure whether he was her life mate or not.

"Yes, he does, dear. He's the police chief in Port Henry, a nice little town where your Uncle Victor now lives with his Elvi. Many people know about us there. You can let him know what you are. He won't be horrified."

"How much does he know exactly?" Katricia asked. "I mean, does he know about life mates and such?"

Marguerite hesitated briefly, and Katricia was sure she was about to say no, but instead, her aunt said, "Well . . . yes, he does know about that, dear. However, it might be a good idea if you don't blurt out that you can't read him until he's gotten a chance to get to know you a little better."

"What?" Katricia asked with alarm and then almost whined, "But why?"

Marguerite chuckled softly, "I know it's tempting to just tell him that he's your life mate and so on right away, but—"

"Is he?" Katricia interrupted eagerly.

"Is he what? Your life mate?" Marguerite asked with surprise. "I thought you said you couldn't read him?"

"Well, I can't, but sometimes mortals can't be read because— "

"Teddy is very readable," Marguerite interrupted soothingly. "In fact, you're the first immortal I've heard of who can't read him. Even Elvi and Mabel are beginning to be able to read him, and they're still quite new to this business."

"Oh," Katricia breathed and bit her lip. "But then why shouldn't I tell him—"

"He's mortal, dear," Marguerite interjected gently. "It might be a little much for him to handle so soon. Maybe just let him get to know you a little better first. You don't want him jumping in his truck and heading back to Port Henry in a panic."

"He can't," Katricia assured her, and then quickly told her about the tree blocking the road and the power outage.

"Oh dear," Marguerite breathed when she finished. "I'll call Lucian and have him send some men to clear the road and—"

"Oh, no, don't do that," Katricia said at once, and then explained, "If the road's cleared he might leave. Besides, right now I'm staying at his cottage and sharing Decker's food with him. If you clear the road—"

"There won't be any need for you to both be at his cottage," Marguerite finished for her with understanding, and then paused briefly before asking, "So you have heat and food?"

"Yes."

"I suppose there's no real urgency to clear the road and get the power back on then," Marguerite murmured. "But call at once if the situation changes and you need things fixed quickly."

"I will."

"I'll call Bastien about the blood delivery though," Marguerite went on. "They can bring it in by snow-mobile. Perhaps they can even arrange for a snow-mobile to be brought for the two of you to use. That way you can still share the cottage but also leave to get provisions if you need them, or even just get out for a meal so you don't get cabin fever."

"That would be nice," Katricia said, a smile curving her lips as she imagined Teddy sitting behind her on a snowmobile, his arms wrapped around her as they roared off into town for groceries or dinner. Or even herself on the back holding onto him as he drove them back. In her experience, men tended to prefer to drive and she was willing to share . . . especially if it meant getting to ride with her arms around him and her chest pressed to his back and—

Dear God, I'm pathetic, Katricia thought with a shake of the head. "Are you sure I can't just tell him? He might be all right with it if he knew."

"He might," Marguerite agreed uncertainly. "I just think it's better to err on the side of caution. This life-mate business is such a delicate thing. I'm just suggesting you maybe wait a day or two. Right now you're a stranger to him, dear."

"Yeah," she agreed on a sigh, her gaze moving to Teddy out by the truck.

"I'll suggest Bastien have the blood courier bring food too," Marguerite said suddenly. "And more blankets and— It might take a while to get everything together, Katricia. Are you okay for blood if it doesn't show until tomorrow morning or later?"

"Yeah, I'm good," Katricia said on a sigh. "I can go two or three days without if I have to. Twenty-four hours is nothing."

"All right then, leave it to me. I'll take care of everything."